First published i
Jemme
31 F
Grea
Ay
Buck

Paperback version worldwide 2022
Jemmett Affection

Cover design by Aspire Book Covers.

Acknowledgements

This book would be unreadable without the impeccable diligence of
Rebecca Carter, who corrected a million grammatical errors.
Karen Slade, for her astute observations, amendments and preventing
us from using some ridiculous words.
And, Sylva Fae, for her constant support, help, advice and beta reading skills.

We thank you all.

Eight Million Children go missing worldwide
every year.
One percent of them are never found.

This book is dedicated to all the lost children of
the world,
their parents, grandparents and extended
families,
who will never give up the search.

In Memory of
Christine Ovett
Our days without you, are never without you.

Contents

The Fridge Magnet

1

The snow kept falling

They'd made an effort this year, the high street looked magical, a hybrid, somewhere between downtown Reno and *A Christmas Carol*.

The snow had settled three inches thick on everything it had touched, and still it was falling. Tyre ruts like crystal tram lines indicated where cars had rolled along at a snail's pace, inching their way home, driven by taut-armed drivers concentrating on not losing control of their icing-topped vehicles.

Footprints on the pavements, made by invisible passers-by, meandered, crossed and melded with others, only to be refilled by the tiny spiralling doilies floating silently to earth on a mission to blanket Britain under a glistening frozen eiderdown.

Despite an arctic blast, I stood at the open window of my second-storey office, in just my shirt sleeves, humbled by the scene, and smiling as if I'd just invented Amazon. For it had taken twenty years to get to this position, twenty years of foil and failure, but tonight, even though I might be jumping the gun a little, it seemed like the gods were on my side.

To put you in the picture, it was an age-old primal drive that had me so pleased with myself, a calm excitement and a justification I suppose. After all these years, I had to be right one day. I just needed to be patient.

The compulsion, needless to say, was money, or the prospect of it to be precise. A bet that I had placed year on year with our friendly local bookmaker at a very respectable 1000/1 odds; it would snow on Christmas day. Sid the bookie, two doors up, was happy to take my £100 flutter every January, self-assured that I was banking on a very rare event indeed; we'd only had four white Christmas' in the last fifty years.

I wouldn't consider myself a gambling addict. The only other event that I take a chance on is the Grand National, and there I have a mad traditional system, where I pick the three horses with the highest odds and place £200 on each of them to win. A foolish thing to do I hear you cry, but with odds sometimes in the region of 100/1, it's potentially a big payday if it ever comes off.

One might say that, tonight, I was counting the old chickens before they've hatched, for it was only December 23rd, Christmas eve, eve, but the met office had been uncommonly right this week about the events leading up to this flurry and were predicting that over the next few days we were going to get the biggest snow dump, that we have seen in decades. The east coast of America was in the midst of a mini ice age, and the tempest was heading this way across the pond.

I closed the window and turned to my desk. A tumbler of extremely expensive ten-year-old malt whisky had my name on it, and I felt justified in partaking of the amber throat tickler, not as an early celebration for liberating Sid's cash, but as a well-deserved bonus for securing an out-of-court divorce settlement for a very content client of mine, saving him more than £300,000. A bottle of whisky was the least he could do.

My thoughts turned to Sid again. If the wily old devil offered me a deal today, would I take it? As a professional bookmaker, he would have offset the bet, to be sure, but he was still about to hand over a huge sum of money.

The tumbler had just graced my lips when the reception doorbell rang downstairs.

"Sid, you're so predictable," I uttered with a little shake of my head.

I creaked my way across loose floorboards, down the corridors of my Grade II listed Tudor building, and descended the stairs. All the while pondering whether to go easy on the old crook, or prolong the agony, wait a couple of days, then scoop the whole jackpot. I decided, even if he offered me a whacking ninety grand right now, I'd still say no.

The only illumination down in reception was the lamp on Mary's desk; it warmed the room with a soft golden glow akin to firelight and was bright enough to allow me to navigate through the room without cracking a knee on something solid.

Mary had been with the firm since its inception. She was receptionist, secretary and technical marvel all rolled into one, and a very dear friend. She'd gone home at 5:30 p.m. leaving just me in the building, contemplating life and our next case.

To my surprise, through the glazed front door, I could see that it wasn't slippery Sid at all, but a rather attractive, elegant young lady, quilted against the cold like an opulent Cossack, hat, fur coat and scarf, lightly dusted with the unabating white lustre, still falling from the heavens.

Resting my untouched malt on the reception desk, I smiled kindly as I approached her. Maybe she was lost, or having car trouble. Either way, I'd be happy to help.

The opening of the door brought with it a fluster of snow, an icy squall and a choir of piped carol's coming from a string of loudspeakers strewn up the high street. Once again, the portent of Christmas overwhelmed me.

"Dave Skipper?"

The fact that it was me she was after settled my snow globe.

"Yes, my dear, what can I do for you?"

"My name is Sophie Baker. A good friend of yours has recommended that I come and see you. I... Can I come in? I know you're probably closed, but..."

Her soft brown eyes had rendered me immobile, but her words brought me to attention.

"Yes, yes, of course. How rude of me. I'm never totally closed."

I stepped back so she could enter. She smelt of Parma violets as she passed. It was heady but not too overpowering. I closed the door and led the way up to my office, the temperature change for her evident as she started to disrobe as soon as we got inside. She pulled off her fluffy cream hat, letting her brunette locks unfurl and bounce around her fur-clad shoulders.

"Do you like the snow?" she inquired with wide eyes.

"I do today," I replied, pursing my lips with an assured smile.

"It's warm in here, Mr Skipper. Do you mind?"

As she began unbuttoning her coat, a startling thought flashed across my mind that she might actually be a stripper-gram and that my divorced client had gone a little too far with his appreciation. Our fee and the whisky had been payment enough.

To my relief, and I admit, slight regret, she was fully clothed underneath. I helped her with the coat, a heavy thing, and hung it up on an old fashioned coat stand in the corner of the room.

"Please take a seat." I indicated a large old brown leather Chesterfield opposite my desk, then went around and sat in an office recliner.

"Now, how may I help?"

It was at this point I noticed that she was wearing a long pleated skirt, the kind you would associate with an older woman, and a pair of Ugg boots, just the sort of thing for this type of weather. I was familiar with the brand; I'd bought a pair for Elizabeth this week and didn't get much change out of £200.

Sophie sat upright, with her legs together and her hands resting in her lap, the epitome of prim and proper. She began.

"Today, I had a meeting with your associate Stanley Wright; he wasn't able to help me, but he highly recommended you. I'm sorry that I have shown up without an appointment, but when my train from Bournemouth to London stopped here at Kings Ridge, I was afraid of a missed opportunity and was compelled to get off."

Stan and I had worked together back in the late seventies and had earned a colossal amount of money in the fraud department of an American insurance company. But it turned out that we were both destined to work for ourselves in the Private Investigation business.

Stan's wife, Iris, was from the Black Country and was reluctant to move down south, so when Stan started up his firm in the market town of Chaphurst, twenty miles north of Birmingham, we went our separate ways.

We've remained tight over the years and helped one another out on cases from time to time. The last I saw of Stan was about four months ago. He told me then that he and Iris were retiring to Spain: arthritis was getting to them both, and they needed to be in warmer climes. Already owning a holiday villa in Catalan, they decided to end their days in the sunshine. I couldn't blame them. None of their three kids wanted to inherit the business, and they'd all moved away. It was about time Stan and Iris got a little self-indulgent.

Stan told me then that he wouldn't be taking on any long-term cases; he'd already sent several clients my way, so it was perfectly acceptable for another one to turn up unannounced. But, all the cases Stan had sent to me would pale into insignificance compared to the one about to be laid on my table.

I'd say that 80 percent of the world's population over the age of 20 would have heard of this case and her family name. I just hadn't connected the dots yet.

"Seventeen years ago, my twin sister Molly…"

Then it hit me, a blood-draining shudder that gave me goosebumps. Molly Baker, *the* Molly Baker, the one-year-old baby who vanished while on holiday with her family in Portugal, whose disappearance became the largest and most costly investigation since policing began, and the most media-covered abduction in history, which turned every household into armchair detectives.

I didn't know what to do. This case had gone cold years ago. Everyone involved had given up, the files had been shelved, and the media circus had packed away its big top.

I stopped her mid-flow. "I know who you are, Miss Baker. I'm just wondering why me, why now? I mean, hasn't every avenue of inquiry been covered over the disappearance of your sister? What could I possibly do that the British and Portuguese police haven't already done, let alone all of the other private investigators your family has hired?"

Sophie stared at me, her mind obviously in overdrive. I realised then who she reminded me of, her namesake, a youthful Sophia Lauren, beautiful.

"Would you like a cup of tea Miss Baker?"

"No, thank you, I had a lovely cup of tea on the train."

It seemed uncommon in this age of coffee-swilling youngsters, that a teenager would appreciate a 'nice cup of tea'; it had a bearing on her upbringing I suppose.

"I'll come straight to the point if I may, Mr Skipper?"

I closed my eyes and inclined my head slightly sideways.

"A week ago I turned eighteen, and my parents gave me what I wanted for my birthday. This may sound odd, Mr Skipper, but I'm not like most eighteen-year-old girls. I've been living in the shadow of my sister for all my life, and it has denied me a normal childhood."

I listened as she played on my heart strings.

"My parents, older brother and I have always maintained that Molly is still alive, and that is my dilemma. We are probably the only ones on the planet who still do. A little over six years ago, the investigation was shelved. The police won't say so officially, but that is the case. At present there is £682,500 left in the fund set up to help find her. It's just sitting in the bank accruing interest. My parents are willing to remortgage the family home, which would raise in the region of £200,000, and I have £90,000 in trust, left to me by my grandparents. Now that I am eighteen, I can have access to that money. All together Mr Skipper, that's a tad under a million pounds available to find my sister in one last unequivocal attempt."

Sophie took a breath like she was about to go underwater for a long time.

"My birthday present gifted to me from my family is to take charge of the case. The first job is to hire a private investigator; Mr Wright couldn't help, so my quest has led me to you. You are highly regarded, Mr Skipper. Mr Wright says you are an investigator who thinks outside of the box, a man he said, with 'grit'."

I smiled and humphed. "He's been watching too many Western movies."

"He's like my dad then. He watches Westerns and war films all the time. It's the one thing my parents don't have in common."

"Bit of a man's thing, I think."

"I feel a little embarrassed, Mr Skipper, coming to you as the second choice."

"It's something you had no control over, Miss Baker."

Affection spread across her face. "I suppose you are right..." She stopped short and turned her upper body towards the doorway. "I'm sorry, Mr Skipper, I didn't realise we had company."

I didn't either. Slithering Sid had slipped up the stairs unnoticed and was eavesdropping under the doorframe.

"What's that white stuff on your head, Sid?" I joked.

Sid attempted a rueful smile, but couldn't quite muster the strength for one. "It's a huge hole in my bank account unless you want to do a deal tonight!"

He was the epitome of disappointed, downturned mouth and tired eyes. His grey cashmere overcoat with its collar up around his neck was dripping snowmelt onto my carpet.

"Come in, mate. I'm starting to feel sorry for you."

Sid ventured inside fully aware he was interrupting something but didn't appear bothered. He ambled over to my Georgian oak tallboy, pulled out a large business cheque book and opened it on top of the chest of drawers.

"How much?" he said clicking down the top of a silver Parker pen.

A little presumptuous, I thought, but formalities first.

Not wishing to divulge any more information than was necessary, I simply introduced my guest as Sophie; the bookie didn't need to know any more.

Sid smiled thinly at Miss Baker. "Sorry to infringe on your meeting, my dear. Important business. It shouldn't take long."

14

"That's quite alright." She replied, remaining in a statuesque repose on the couch.

I joined him beside his open cheque book, an event I'd fantasized over for a couple of decades, but now it was here, it didn't seem that important. I'd always philosophised that it wasn't the winning that mattered, but the pursuit of doing so, and besides, there was still a slim chance that the snow would ease off and dissipate before the big man in red did his rounds.

There's no such thing as a poor bookmaker of course. However, because Sid was one of a very few independent operators, this payout was going to hurt him.

"I think it's down to you to make me an offer, Sid, and see where we go from there, mate." It was game on.

Sid sensed an opportunity. "Fifty grand." He snapped.

"What, half? Sid, this is a dead cert here, ol' mate. What we are doing tonight is easing the misery. You gotta do better than that."

Knowing I had him over a barrel, he conceded big time, damage limitation.

He sighed. "Eighty."

"Done," I said, thinking, that was too easy.

While Sid scribbled, I poured out two glasses of malt. We clinked crystal and wished each other a Merry Christmas. A dram of Macallan rare cask had never tasted so sweet.

After Sid had left, like the ghost of Christmas present, I explained to Sophie what had just taken place. She gathered her thoughts.

"Considering that you back outsiders, Mr Skipper, might you be willing to take a gamble on me?"

I was being offered the most prestigious unsolved case in history. The temptation of all that inside information certainly got my juices flowing, and of course it would pay handsomely, not to mention the notoriety for actually discovering the truth. But if the world's police and a ton of resources had all turned up a blank, what chance did a small-time PI and two staff have, with no international experience, no foot soldiers on the ground and no clue as to where to start? At one time you couldn't turn on a TV or radio station without hearing something about the disappearance of Molly Baker, but now that was distant, a fading article destined for the archives.

When the case was on everyone's lips, the whole world had an opinion. I'd kept my thoughts to myself. I never wanted to be drawn into any conclusions or debate. I reserved an open mind. But one piece of reason had always stayed with me: whoever took that little girl from her bed that fateful night must have seen her at least once before the diabolical act, and for whatever despicable reason, had chosen her for abduction.

I understood that the Bakers were only on holiday for seven days and that Molly went missing on the sixth night, so there must have been a very small window of opportunity in which to take her. My PI mind went into gear. Where might she have been selected, somewhere the police hadn't yet covered? If I was to take this case on, that's where I'd start.

"Miss Baker, if I were to turn you down, what would be your next move?"

"That's easy, Mr Skipper. I'd ask you to recommend someone else."

"I thought you'd say that. To be honest, the only person I'd recommend is the bloke that sent you to me… Look, is there anything you can tell me, a glimmer of hope to convince me I wouldn't be wasting my time and your money?"

She looked forlorn; I got the feeling I was this family's last throw of the dice. If I let her walk out of this office with a million quid, she'd have no problem hiring another private detective agency. The worry was, would she get value for her money? She would from me, but were we in a no-win situation?

Sid had downed his whisky in one rapid movement, triumphant in saving himself 20 grand. I'd just sipped at mine and was staring at the remainder languishing at the bottom of a tumbler on my desk, its golden tannin qualities toying with my tastebuds.

Sophie shattered the silence. "Mr Skipper, up until I was about four years old, I used to dream of my sister playing in front of an extremely large house. The dreams were vivid, ultra-clear. Molly was always happy and playing in a garden. These visions or dreams, or whatever you'd like to call them, felt real to me. They were like I'd actually had a window to her existence, like I'd witnessed her playing in that garden. The smell of the grass, the sunshine on my skin, I'd literally been there with her. It still feels like a true experience. I believe it's a twin thing. She was alive then, I know it, and although I haven't had those visions for years, I know she's still alive today."

Her statement rang a chord with me. "My secretary Mary is a twin; in fact, she's an identical twin. They are so alike, even after 20 years I can't tell them apart. She has often said that they can feel one another's anxiety and pain, so I don't find what you have told me to be strange at all. Did you pass this information on to the police?"

Sophie offered a lamentable smile. "Yes, but a four-year-old's dreams fell on deaf ears."

"And you've never had this vision since?"

"Well, not until recently, not the dream as such, but a prompt that brought it all back. Have you ever seen a TV programme called *Versailles*?"

"Can't say I have."

"It's a drama based on the Sun King, Louis XIV."

"Okay, haven't seen it."

"I watched it for the first time about two months ago and seeing the palace of Versailles reminded me of the building I dreamt that Molly used to play in front. I mean, nowhere as big a Versailles but something palatial for sure."

"Have you ever drawn any pictures of the dreams you used to have?"

"No, I'm not that adept with drawing, Mr Skipper."

We stared at each other across the room. I still wasn't convinced. What we had here was desperation and conviction, nothing more.

At length, I said, "Miss Baker, my office is closed for the next two weeks. During that time I wish to carry out a feasibility study on whether there is enough evidence to open up a new enquiry. From that, I can give you an honest opinion. I'll do this for free, in my own spare time. But I'd like access to all of the evidence your family has had at its disposal. If, and I must stress, if, it seems that we can press forward, then I'd like your assurance that we keep this under wraps. Not a word from anyone, to the media or the police, that a new investigation is underway. We don't hold many cards, Miss Baker, and any whiff of a new line of enquiry will tighten the ship of anybody holding your sister."

"Absolutely, of course…"

"Six or seven years have passed. They may be getting sloppy. We'd want to capitalise on that."

For the first time tonight, she appeared her true age, when a tinge of hope softened her face.

"I reiterate, Miss Baker, only your parents and your brother need to know."

"And Aunt Aida," revealed Sophie.

"Aunt who?" I said rather curtly.

"Oh, my great, great, Aunt Aida, she's ninety-seven and lives on her own in Golders Green. I'm staying with her tonight, and she's going to want to know all about it."

She may be 97, but it's another possible leak, I thought. Sophie went on to tell me more about Aunt Aida; she was a remarkable woman by anyone's standards. Working secretly at Bletchley Park during World War II, and then in government institutions until retirement. She apparently still completes the *Times* crossword and sinks a glass of whisky every day, my kind of woman. She has always encouraged the family not to give up hope and supports the idea of Sophie taking the reins. Telling her great, great niece that finding the right person to lead this investigation would be the key to finding Molly. I wonder what the astute old lady would think of me.

"Your Aunt Aida sounds like someone who can keep a secret. I think that will be okay. Maybe I'll get to meet her one day."

"I think she'd like you, Mr Skipper. From what I've seen, you have integrity and a touch of verve."

I was flattered; a young lady giving me compliments was like the kiss of a cool breeze on a sweltering summer's day.

My pride bolstered, I said, "I am a resourceful sort of chap, Miss Baker. Perhaps imagination is what is needed to solve this case."

"What are our chances, Mr Skipper?"

At this point, I thought, zero. But you should never say never. I decided to give her some cheer, falsely perhaps.

"About the same odds as Sid gave me for it to snow on Christmas Day, and look how that turned out."

That brought a smile to her face.

"Miss Baker, in my experience, a criminal always leaves a trace of evidence, no matter how minute or insignificant it might seem. And finding those incriminating little bits of nothing is what I enjoy doing most of all, and if you are enjoying your work, well, it's not really a job at all, is it?"

I glanced at my watch; it was approaching 7:00 p.m.

"How are you getting to the train station, Miss Baker?"

"Oh, I'll get a cab."

"Snow's pilling up. It might be a stretch. I'll call my usual cab firm."

It was going to be an hour wait, so instead, I called Sophie an Uber. They were there in five minutes. Kings Ridge train station is only a third of a mile away from my office. It is quaint, Victorian and beautifully restored. I reminded Sophie once again of the importance of keeping everything close to our chests. She promised she would.

As she crunched on virgin snow to the curb, she turned and said, "Thank you once again for considering me, Mr Skipper."

"Please," I said, "call me Dave."

She smiled and her face lit up brighter than the high street, which in turn highlighted the snow that was still falling.

2

Reason

I'm a stickler for good timekeeping. I'm anxious when I'm late and agitated when I'm left waiting. So when I walked through my front door two hours overdue, Elizabeth was surprised by my calm demeanour.

Before either of us could utter a word, a swarm of various sized ankle-biters hurtled my way down the hall, frothier than a well-shaken bottle of Krug. "Grandad!" they squealed in unison.

All six of them tugged at various bits of my clothing, enticing me towards our conservatory and a deep pile of shiny, patterned shapes lodging under a heavily burdened Norwegian Spruce.

Elizabeth rolled her eyes skyward, coinciding with an upward nod.

"Sorry, love," I mouthed above the din. She wouldn't have been able to hear me even if I'd shouted.

There'd been a debate and consultation amongst the parents, and a conclusion had been reached. All the grandchildren were getting the same thing this year, the latest in tablet technology.

Being a dinosaur with modern gadgetry, I'd enlisted the help of my assistant, Paul, in choosing the right model, and like any thoughtful, hands-on grandparent, sent him out to buy them.

Our traditional pre-Christmas family gathering was always a warm delight, and it made sense with such an expanding family to have everybody over to ours, to get the gift-giving out of the way, without having to traipse around the country going from house to house. Christ knows how Santa does it.

I had secured all six guest rooms at our local pub, The Oak. It was only a two-minute walk away, so my kids could all let their hair down without the annoyance of having to have designated drivers, which is such a sterile assignment.

The grandchildren all slunk off to quiet corners, heads buried in blue screen wonderment, the parents helping out the smaller ones, my wife and I looking on humbled by the unity. We were mightily proud of all our children had achieved so far in life; each of them had decent jobs and fair incomes. Our only regret was that we didn't get to see them as often as we'd like, but with their busy lifestyles, it's something we've had to accept. However, talking to my son Jamie's girlfriend, it appeared that a wedding might be on the imminent horizon, and that would be the perfect excuse for a big family bash.

Sam, my eldest daughter, was the only one who had followed me into the business of fighting the bad guys. As far back as I can remember, she wanted to join the police force. From Hendon College, she has worked her way up to being a much-respected Commander in the Metropolitan police, one of the youngest in the country, and based at New Scotland Yard. It still tickles me to hear lower-ranking officers call her ma'am, and seeing her being interviewed on the TV on occasion is all too surreal.

My daughter doesn't suffer fools gladly. She is as honest as the day is long, and if I posed to her the question of why the Molly Baker case has never been resolved, she would keep it professional and give me no flannel. What I needed to do tonight was get her on her own. The next face-to-face opportunity might be a long time coming.

Nobody knew the reason for me being late home, not even Elizabeth. I'd address that tomorrow, but Sam was about to find out right now. When my wife asked Sam to check on the mince pies in the oven, I saw my window, gave her a minute, then followed her into the kitchen.

"If they taste as good as they smell, then your mum's done it again."

She was bent over, midway through pulling out a baking tray with a reindeer emblazoned tea-towel.

"I reckon you must have antennae attached to you somewhere, letting you know when food's coming out of the oven."

"It's called a nose, Samantha."

Her face pinched tight. "Samantha, eh? You must have your serious head on, Dad. What's up?" Her glasses had temporarily steamed up; they cleared while she was waiting for a response, fists on hips.

"I need some advice on a dilemma I'm facing, well actually it's information I need more than anything…"

"Is it work-related? You know I can't divulge anything ongoing."

"…It, it's nothing you're working on, love. As far as the police are concerned, this is a cold case, a very large and very public one."

Now she was intrigued. I went on to tell her of the meeting I had earlier with Sophie and the quandary I now faced, finishing with me asking if she could give me a copper's take on why Molly Baker's case had never been resolved.

She looked miffed. "So your quandary is pivoted by a four-year-old's dream, is it? That's hardly what we'd call hard evidence in the incident room, Dad."

"No, no, not just that. There's the twin thing. You know how it is with Mary. There's also my instinct and a need for justice, The Bakers need closure, Sam. This has gone on way too long."

She took a long resigned breath. This was old ground and it had been travelled over time and time again. We sat at the kitchen table, Sam pinching the stem of a large goblet of rosé wine.

"As you know, I haven't personally been involved with any of this investigation, so I'm not privy to all of the evidence. But as I'm in the force, the information does go around, things get shared, and I've heard stuff. So this is just my own personal opinion. Seventeen years on, Dad, and we're nowhere nearer finding out what happened to that little girl than the day she went missing…"

I didn't want to hear that.

"…The cooperation between the Portuguese and the British police has always been strained, tenuous at times, and now broken down altogether. From the outset opportunities were missed, evidence contaminated. You know how important the first few hours can be in an investigation. It's vital you act straight away, and the Portuguese were so lackadaisical in their approach. If it wasn't so serious, it would have been farcical…"

I listened and nodded.

"…Then there's the funding for the case. It ran out seven years ago, and apart from a liaison officer who waits to hear from the Portuguese, no one else is involved."

"Right," I said deep in thought.

Sam carried on. "The most brutal part of all this, of course, is the black cloud of suspicion hanging over George and Jill Baker. They've been cleared obviously, or rather, there exists no evidence at all that they had anything to do with their daughter's disappearance, but if those accusations hadn't so vehemently been contested over, both publicly and judiciously, then I think a more focussed attempt could have been made towards finding that baby."

I blurted out a question that I immediately regretted. The one that had been on everyone's lips a decade ago. "Have *you* ever thought that the parents had something to do with it?"

Because of her position, it was unfair of me to put my daughter on the spot like that. To lose a child, there can be no greater pain, but to then be accused of having something to do with their demise, had to be devastating. It would take a mighty amount of self-control not to lash out at any of your accusers. I have the upmost admiration for the Bakers over the way they have conducted themselves the past seventeen years. They have remained steadfast, stoic, and composed under enormous pressure.

"My gut feeling, Dad, is no. I don't believe they did. But I know about as much of the case as you do. I read the papers as well."

She sipped at her wine.

"This liaison officer, do you know him?"

"What Alfie? Yeah. We're old friends, known him ages. Alfie Fields, he's a DI. For the last seven years his total involvement with the case has been to have meetings with the Bakers four or five times a year, to give them a progress report, which he finds embarrassing because apart from a few insignificant or ridiculous sightings of Molly, there is nothing whatsoever to report. He also meets up with his Portuguese counterpart a couple of times a year. That's it."

"So he's had access to all the evidence?"

"I believe so."

I pondered that thought as Elizabeth came in to retrieve the mince pies. She gave us a quizzical look. "Come on, you two, you're missing all the fun."

"Be there in a minute, pet." I assured her with a squint. I turned back to Sam. "Do you think he'd talk to me, this Alfie Fields?"

"I'll set up a meeting if you like. I'm sure he'll be more than pleased to see you."

"How do you mean?"

"Oh, I'd better explain. Two months ago Alfie had a very serious skiing accident in France, holidaying with his two boys. That's where I got to know him. His boys are the same ages as mine. We met eight years ago on the piste. I'd recognised him from the Yard. Not only did we work in the same building, but live about a ten-minute drive away from each other. It's been really handy for the boys. They're good mates. But I digress. What I meant was, he's been laid up with his legs in plaster for the past eight weeks, and he's pulling his hair out, so a chat with someone other than via a Zoom call might be quite refreshing, especially you being my dad."

"Blimey, he must be climbing the walls."

"Not with those legs." She smiled and dived into her wine glass once more. "Alfie feels like he's been given a bit of a short straw being assigned to this case, Dad. The opinion on the force is that it will never get solved. Of course, no one will ever say that outright, but that's the fact of the matter, and Alfie has to front it. He's been given a detective's worst nightmare, no starting point, it'll take a…"

Sam paused and we locked eyes.

"…I was going to say miracle, Dad, but that's not very professional of me is it? We deal in facts and hard evidence. That's how we solve crime in this country."

"Yes, and confession and eye witness accounts."

"That too, as well as catching the buggers bloody red-handed. I'll tell you something that Alfie said to me one day at a colleague's funeral, something that summed up his frustration. He described this case like a headline he'd seen on one of the red-tops: *Martians abducted Molly Baker!* They may as well have, Dad. There's not one shred of evidence to kick off this investigation. After thousands of man-hours and a million pound spent, it seems like she has just vanished into thin air, so the Martian theory is as good as any. We believe that both police forces have done all they can and left no stone unturned." She sighed and looked around the room. "I reckon even your twelve mates working together couldn't solve this one."

She was referring to the pictures that littered my study walls, my twelve favourite fictional detectives. With so many crime busters influencing my kids as they grew up, it wasn't any wonder that one of them would join the police force.

She toyed with me. "If you were to pick one to help you with the Baker case, who would it be?"

My lips curled. They all had a different approach. Poirot, Foyle, Morse, Kojak, Columbo… "I think I'll need them all, Sam."

She nodded in cynical agreement.

My twelve-year-old granddaughter Saffie burst into the kitchen. "Mum, nan said you've both got to come into the conservatory now. Bring the Champagne and glasses because Melissa and me are going to give nan and granddad their Christmas presents."

Melissa belonged to my youngest daughter, Kathy; she and Saffie were roughly the same age.

"…And nan said that Melissa and me are allowed to have a glass of Champagne with orange juice."

She was about to leg it when her mum told her off for not saying please.

"I don't think she'll be following me into the police force, Dad, twelve going on twenty; give me boys any day of the week."

I chuckled. "You two weren't too much trouble."

"Things have moved on, Dad. We didn't have half the pressures kids have today. I'm pleased I grew up in the eighties."

Maybe we lucked out with our children, but I'd like to think that they were just from good stock.

Elizabeth and I have had some extraordinary Christmas presents from our children in the past. Year on year we have always been delighted with our gifts. Collectively they've bought us weekend breaks, trips abroad, thrilling experiences. We've never been disappointed. One year we even had an overnight trip to Venice on the Orient Express, which of course brought out the Poirot in me.

"Listen," I said, "before we start, and seeing that we have Champagne in our hands, we've already got something to celebrate that I haven't mentioned yet."

They all wondered what the hell I was talking about.

"You know that bet I have every year with Sid Slater?"

The penny was dropping.

I pulled out the cheque from my shirt pocket.

"Well the so and so has admitted defeat and paid me off early... Eighty grand, boys and girls. Thank you very much!"

Whoops and gasps abounded. "Get in!" shouted Jamie.

The spume was definitely flowing now.

"How about a big family holiday next year?"

The cheers went up. The kids had no idea what was going on, yet they were just as excited as the rest of us. We settled down for the big gift-giving event.

I had been trying to guess what they would conjure up this year. I was way off.

We sat down on the sofa, expectant yet reserved, like the time we waited at the hospital for Melissa to arrive. She handed Elizabeth her envelope first. My wife smile-

28

shrugged at me excitedly. When two gold-edged concert tickets ascended out of the white vellum, I knew exactly who they were for. Front row seats at the Palau Sant Jordi, Barcelona, to see our favourite artist, Rod Stewart. We both adored him; our only disagreement being which was his best track. Seeing him sing live was on our bucket list and something we just hadn't got around to yet. Elizabeth was open-mouthed. I sat there grinning, pleased as Punch, then Saffron handed me an envelope.

Mine was a little bulkier, containing a suite reservation at the Hotel Catalonia in the heart of Barcelona and flight tickets to and from Spain. I was overwhelmed.

Kathy's husband, Pete, piped up, "Happy Christmas…" It was obvious we were thrilled with the presents; we were both beaming. "…There's just a little problem though, Dave. Because the Spanish celebrate more after Christmas than on the big day, we had trouble flying you into Barca' in time for the concert, so you're going into Gerona, where we've booked a limousine to take you to Barcelona. It's only an hour away."

"No problem at all, Pete. This is an amazing present."

"Yeah, but it's a seven a.m. flight out of Luton, Dad," said Kathy, "which'll mean a very early start for you two."

"Don't worry though," continued Pete. "We've booked Tim the Taxi to pick you up."

"Bet that pleased him," I ribbed.

"It took some persuading," smirked Kathy.

"Your flights back are much more congenial though, 3 p.m. out of Barca', first-class, British Airways," confirmed Pete. "Sorry it's a bit of a juggle. It's the best we could do."

I stood up. "Don't be silly. This is perfect." I outstretched my arms. "Come 'ere. Group hug."

The entire family came in for a huddle.

The Oak has an impressive breakfast menu, and by the looks of things, my lot had put the kitchen staff through their paces. The adults were walking back to my place like they were eight months pregnant.

They were coming over for a last goodbye before heading off on their individual ways. The snow was deep in parts, on the paths, and in gardens, but the main road had been gritted and was passable even if a light flurry was still drifting in the wind.

A snowball thudded into the glass on the front bay window, a misaimed shot meant for a gaggle of screaming girls running for cover. Simple entertainment, I thought. It's always the best, thinking back to the fun I used to have playing outside. There'll be a snowman built on the lawn before they leave.

Both my sons-in-law had four-wheeled-drives, but Jamie didn't. I offered him my Range Rover, but he said he'd be all right. He would follow the others out to the main road, and then it would be plain sailing home. I reluctantly let it pass.

Sam beckoned me into the kitchen, where she made a phone call to Alfie Fields, giving him a brief explanation. He was happy to see me, but due to hospital appointments and some physiotherapy sessions, the earliest he could do was New Year's Eve. I nodded that it would be fine; 10 a.m. it was then.

Sam was the last to leave. She kissed me on the cheek and said, "Do you still believe that things happen for a reason, Dad?"

I pondered it for a second. "It seems to Sam, a lot of the time."

She hugged me. "Let's hope so, eh."

Arthur Truman had been pulling my pints in the Oak for twenty-five years. He was an old-school publican, or

30

Inn Keeper, as we liked to call him, and as jolly as he was red-faced. Christmas day was the only day of the year that the Oak closed, apart from, and traditionally, one hour, starting at midday, for all his regulars to get in a livener before lunch, first drink on the house.

I ambled in at ten minutes past, amply dusted in icing sugar that advertised my windfall distinctively. My drinking buddies all knew the score and cheers erupted as I crossed the threshold. A pint of Traveller's choice bitter waited on the bar in anticipation, like the big red finishing button of an endurance game show. I was going to savour this pint.

After downing half a glass and belching my approval, I produced two fifty-pound notes and shouted like the Milkybar Kid, "The drinks are on me!"

That tight grip on my shoulder from behind told me one thing, my mate Antonio Serrano had arrived. Spaniards tend to do this, and it always makes me jump.

"Feliz Navidad!" shouted the Iberian. "Feliz Navidad everyone!"

"A pint of Estrella, please, Arthur," I ordered for my friend. Thirty years on British soil and he still can't stand our beer.

"Who was that elegant young lady I saw you with the other day, you old charmer?"

Antonio had his back to the bar and a mischievous grimace.

He must have clocked Sophie getting into the Uber.

"You can wipe that smile off ya face, old friend. It was purely platonic."

"A nice platony all the same."

I ignored his lecherous remark. "That young lady has left me with a difficult dilemma. As it happens, you being a solicitor might be able to offer me some clarity on the matter."

"On Christmas day, my friend. Remember that is quadruple time."

"Don't be so stupid. Come on, let's take a pew."

The Oak had two bay windows that looked out onto picturesque views of the common and the churchyard opposite, and today's was particularly special, glinting, Christmas card perfect, deep and crisp and even, yellow lights in the church windows and black branches making cracks on the porpoise grey sky.

We sat in wonderment watching the snow continue to fall.

"It's ironic, Dave, how something so beautiful can cause so much disruption."

"Thankfully, Antonio, there's not much it can disrupt between here and my house."

My friend hooded his eyes submissively.

"So who is she then?"

"Sophie Baker." The name rang a bell, but I could see in his face he hadn't made the connection.

"Molly Baker's twin sister."

"Molly Baker! The baby who went missing?"

"The very same."

I went on to tell him what had transpired two days ago, my conversation with Sam, and of the forthcoming meeting with DI Fields. Reiterating what Sophie had said to me before getting into the cab, "You are the last throw of the dice." Those words were bouncing around inside my head like an inertia-less squash ball.

It was like Antonio had just witnessed the other side. He stared straight through me, paralysed by my words. I thought for a moment that he was having a stroke.

"What's wrong, mate? What's up?"

He stared down at the table, then out of the window for a while before eventually facing me ashen skinned and teary eyed.

He spoke gravely, "The last time somebody spoke those words to me, two people lost their lives."

Well, that took the cheer right out of Christmas.

If he didn't look so ruined, I would have taken his statement with a pinch of salt. Clearly, something devastating had upset him at some point, and he had locked it away until I came along rattling the keys.

"Go on," I said.

"I haven't spoken of this to anybody, Dave, not even Caterina. Client confidentiality and all that, but I gotta let out; it's tearing me up inside."

"It won't go beyond this table, mate."

Antonio nodded solemnly. He drew a sharp intake of breath like he'd had an electric shock, then puffed it slowly through his rubbery lips

"July 18th, a Monday and one of the hottest days of the year. I was in my office and as is the tradition in my country when it is roasting outside, I had closed all the windows and drawn the curtains, as you know it keeps it cooler inside."

I nodded in agreement.

"I had an appointment at 2 p.m. with a lady called Beverly Forster and her daughter Carol. They'd asked if Beverly's parents could attend also, so it was quite crowded in the dim light of my small office."

"You only have two chairs in there, mate. Where did they sit, on the floor?"

"They stood mostly. Sally took the chair. I was impressed right from the beginning when Beverly handed me an envelope containing my full fee in cash. No one ever pays upfront, Dave, and that gesture gave me an angle on their integrity. They had a thick file containing concise and accurate documentation, with a timeline that detailed their case. I would read that later, but first I asked

Carol, who seemed to be the spokesperson, to give me an explanation as to why they were there."

Antonio paused, screwed up his face, and chewed his bottom lip, obviously re-living that afternoon. I could only wonder where this was leading.

"Carol told me in a clear and most understandable manner how four years ago their nightmare began. An anonymous phone call to social services led to her two children, Oliver and Alison, being taken away from her. They were two and three years old at the time, and the social workers came and whisked them away from school without Carol's knowledge."

"They can do that?"

"Oh yes, if they suspect that children are at risk of being harmed, then they have the power to intervene, forcibly if necessary."

"And were they? at risk?"

"Well I don't believe from Carol, no, but social services had been involved in the past. The children's father was an absent alcoholic, there had been a number of fights between the parents, and the police had been called many times. Carol's way of protecting her children had red-flagged her to Child Protection. Anyway, the anonymous phone caller accused Carol of beating her kids, and that was enough to send in a snatch squad. Of course, the Forsters were devastated and jumped through all the hoops to get their children back, and things seemed to be going their way when one year later the father was tragically killed in a horrific forklift accident at work. He was drunk again and was making, how do you say, doughnuts with the tyres on the warehouse floor, with the forks fully extended and the truck on full lock. The thing turned over squashing him between the cage and the concrete as he tried to roll away; it almost cut him clean in half!"

34

"Bloody hell!"

"That's not the worst of it, my friend... I could tell from the way Carol was welling up that despite their differences, she still had a lot of love for this man, and now he'd been taken away from her as well. It was tragic, but still, it gets worse. Even though Carol had done everything the courts had asked of her, doctors reports, psychological assessment, three months in a unit in Bedford to examine her parenting and domestic skills, got a job, redecorated her house, even with all the support her parents and grandparents gave her in abundance, after four years, four years. Dave, it became clear that her children were being put up for adoption by the family court."

"What, even after she had turned herself around?"

"It didn't make the slightest bit of difference. She showed me several examples of how social services, barristers, health professionals, and representatives from other organisations are prepared to stand up in court and lie to get a result. There's an entire invisible industry, a self-perpetuating circle surrounding child-snatching in this country. Once the children have been taken into care, there's no way the parents are going to get them back. It's a huge money-making scam that costs the taxpayer millions. Carol used a term that I have heard bandied about before, 'you go into court with both hands tied behind your back'. Within a short space of time, I was in no doubt; a great injustice had been done to this family."

"And this is going on in England today?"

"Absolutely, it's criminal, and if you try and rock the boat, you just get stonewalled and pushed from pillar to post."

I was astounded; this didn't sit well with me at all. "No wonder you're upset. Did you take on the case?"

"That's upsetting, yes, but I haven't come to the travesty yet, Dave. I felt duty-bound to take on their plight, but I had to be honest with them. If we were to take social services to court for perjury, the hurdles we faced were insurmountable. With the number of people involved, all putting up a resistance, it would take at least three years to get before a judge. Another problem would be the cost. Legal aid was out of the question, and we were looking at probably half a million pounds in fees, again, given the amount of people involved."

I blew through my lips. "That much, are you sure?"

"Barristers are very expensive, my friend. Ask the Chancellor. We also had to consider this; if by chance we actually got to court and won the case, the outcome for those who played a part in this illegal adoption would amount to a light slap on the wrist, a sideways move, and no change to the despicable practice. Governmental bodies, especially social services look after their own, Dave."

"But they'd get the kids back, right?"

"Not necessarily, no. All that time and effort, and money, if it could be raised, might just prove to be futile. And this is what I really didn't want to reveal to the Forsters: even if we won a case against social services and proved that they committed a crime in retaining the children, no judge on the planet would remove children from a family that they had bonded to over a period of seven years. They were only babies when they were first taken away and probably do not remember their natural mother. Now, this is criminal. I respect the laws in this country, Dave, or else I wouldn't be in this business, but sometimes the law gets it wrong, and this is one of those times."

Antonio was confusing me. "So you didn't take the case on?"

"I couldn't, Dave. It was a no-win situation, and I could almost taste their disappointment when they got ready to leave. They'd gone over the allotted time of our meeting by twenty minutes, and even though they were blatantly devastated by my decision, Joe Forster put his hand in his pocket to offer me more money for my time. I couldn't take it, of course. How could I? That act just raised their esteem in my eyes. When Beverly shook my hand, she held it a little longer than expected and spoke those words, 'You were the last throw of the dice.' That phrase has haunted me ever since. All I had to give her in return was an apology."

We sat in silence for a few moments, Antonio staring at the patchy varnish on the oak table, and me staring at him, wondering why he was so destroyed by the case. Okay, it was absolutely awful for the Forsters; I can't imagine the pain of having your children taken away, and the loss of your partner, especially under those horrific circumstances. But why was it affecting my friend so badly?

"Wait, did you say there were two deaths?"

Antonio raised his maudlin head to meet my eyes. "Indeed, I did, Dave." He took another sorrowful inhale and began again. "After they left my office, I never expected to see or hear from them again. The case was a sad one, but I had much work to do. On that Thursday about 4 p.m., Jackie buzzed through that there were two detectives in reception wanting to have a word with me. I had no idea what it could have been about and asked Jackie to send them up. They introduced themselves, asked me to confirm my identity, and then asked if I had a meeting with the Forsters on Monday. My suspicions aroused, I told them I did and then they asked me what the meeting was about. I couldn't tell them, of course, protocol, you know. It was then that they told me the reason for their visit. The older of the two detectives, DI Reg Hall, did most of the talking. At 9 a.m. that day a suspected suicide had been called into the station and a squad car had been sent to investigate. The deceased's name was Carol Forster. Her grandparents, Joe and Sally, discovered the body hanging from the loft hatch."

That horrible sinking black dread washed through me, sending blood to my feet and reducing my stature in the chair. Antonio was blaming himself, he continued.

"There were three sealed envelopes on the kitchen table, one each for Carol's children, her mother and grandparents. Beverly's letter contained references to the meeting we had on that Monday, so the police naturally wanted to talk to me. At that point, I could see no reason for withholding any information at all and went on to tell them everything that transpired in my office. It was clear to me immediately why Carol had taken her own life: she couldn't bear another waking hour without the prospect of having her children back. Her desolation must have been overwhelming. The police said they would be in touch regarding the inquest, and they left. I was physically sick, Dave; I was responsible for Carol's death…"

Water was welling up in my friend's eyes. This pre-Christmas little drinky-poo was turning more dreadful by the minute.

"Now hold on a minute, mate. You can't possibly be at fault here. They came to you with an irresolvable situation. All you did was tell 'em the truth. It's the system that's let 'em down; social services are to blame for Carol Forster's death, not you."

He looked at me with dead chocolate button eyes. "That's not all, my friend."

Christ, I thought, there's more?

"At 8:30 the following Monday, I arrived at my office to find the same two detectives waiting for me outside. DI Hall informed me that Beverly Forster had been found dead at her home on Saturday afternoon. Two suicide notes were in the house, one for her grandchildren and one for Joe and Sally. I was again mentioned in the letter to her mum and dad, and again I was told I would be required at the inquest."

I was about to console my friend when a couple of hands placed two glasses of malt whisky between us on the table.

"There you go, you old buggers. Merry Christmas!"

It was 'Will the Plant', so-called due to his plant hire business. Antonio averted his gaze, shielding his bloodshot eyes. I gave Will a wink as if to say, cheers, mate, but not now. Will took the hint and sensitively retreated to the other end of the pub. The gesture couldn't have been better timed; we both needed a stiff one right there and then. Antonio's went down in one easy slide; he was actually shaking as his hand came down.

"You alright, mate?"

"Yes, Dave. Just recalling the nightmare."

We stared out at the glistening snowscape, beautifying the common with wintery decadence. I shivered.

"If I could turn the clocks back, Dave, it would be to that meeting in my office. I could have offered pro bono, taken the case on for free, given them some hope. I could have saved Carol and Beverly's lives, if I knew what I know now. I would have fought tooth and nail to try and get those children back."

"You mustn't blame yourself, Antonio. These women were betrayed by bureaucracy. Your involvement was unfortunate but quite innocuous. We'd all like to go back in time now and again, change some things maybe, but we can't. We've just got to deal with what we've got and make the best of it."

My rhetoric was having little effect.

"Her head came off!"

"What?"

Antonio appeared frozen, a mannequin devoid of sensory perception.

"During the inquest, I heard the grizzly details and I wish I hadn't gone."

"Whose head came off?"

"Joe and Sally had gone to Carol's house to bring her a chicken casserole and keep her company. Carol's car was on the drive, but she wasn't answering her front door. Joe went around the back to retrieve the spare key from the garden shed. As he passed the kitchen window, he saw three envelopes on the table with a yellow rose placed on each. He knew instinctively right then that Carol had taken her own life. As soon as he opened the front door, he could see his granddaughter at the top of the stairs, hanging by her neck from the gaping loft hatch. In the hope that she may still be alive, Joe ran up the stairs, climbed the chair she'd used to step off of, grabbed her by the waist, and took her whole weight. She'd used a high tensile sea fishing line to make a noose, her dead partner was an Angler, I believe, and had tied that to a length of two by four timber, which she had strewn across the loft opening. Joe tried in vain to dislodge the wood, but it was impossible whilst trying to hold up his granddaughter's body. Sally was paralysed at the foot of the stairs, still holding the casserole, and couldn't assist; frozen with fright. Whilst struggling, with the weight of the two of them, the spindly chair gave way, forcing Joe to the landing, still holding on to Carol. The tension on the fishing line severed right through Carol's neck, sending the torso halfway down the stairs emptying blood like a haemoglobin flood down the carpeted treads, and her head to bounce to the ground, landing at Sally's feet with a sickening thud."

"Oh my God."

"Sally fainted. Fell backward out of the door and smashed her head on the concrete step. It put her into a coma for five days."

I couldn't take in what I was hearing; it was like a scene from a slasher movie.

"Is Sally alright now?"

"She's distraught obviously, but they are coping."

"Crikey, what happened to Beverly?" I almost daren't ask.

"Joe was steadfast giving evidence, a rock; it was unbelievable how he didn't break down. He'd spent time in the army, saw action in the Suez crisis I think, during the 50s, but the way he appeared that day in his Khaki shirt, trousers, and ravaged body, it looked more like he'd spent time in a Japanese prisoner of war camp. He told the enquiry that he'd gone to pick up his daughter so that they could support each other and go visit his wife in hospital. He found Beverly lying on the settee surrounded by family photos. She'd taken a considerable amount of sleeping pills and washed them down with a bottle of vodka. This obviously wasn't a cry for help, Dave. She too could no longer live in this cruel world, even with the knowledge she would leave behind devastated parents, destroyed by grief."

Tears tracked down Antonio's cheeks, momentarily clung to his chin, then splashed down onto the oak.

"I could have done more, Dave. I could have done more," he sobbed.

Reaching across with a reassuring hand, I gripped his shoulder.

"You did the only thing open to you at the time, mate. You're a professional. You knew they were never gonna get their kids back. You mustn't reproach yourself for what has happened; you're a decent bloke... Look it's hideous what Joe and Sally have had to endure, but it's not your fault. Now come on, perk up, it's supposed to be Christmas."

A white hankie appeared and blotted his face.

"Yes, I'm sorry, Dave. I didn't mean to lay this on you." He took another shuddering intake of breath, before relaxing back into his chair. The bell rang for last orders. We'd been there an hour and only had two drinks. I would have to make up for it this afternoon at home.

Before we got up to leave, he said one more thing to me. "I believe that you should always do something rather than nothing at all, Dave. Don't be like me and carry a heavy regret. Take the Baker case, Dave; take it on."

Bidding 'season's greetings' to Arthur and the 15 or so reprobates still clinging to their beer mugs, my solicitor and I ventured out into the Arctic-like landscape. There were no tyre ruts on the tarmac, only footprints and they were rapidly being filled by the relentless white stuff floating to earth.

We hugged each other, a manly hug involving pats on the back. He said, "You're a lucky man, Dave."

"Eh?" I said.

"Samantha told me about your Christmas gift two days ago in the pub. I am envious. Can I come too?"

I smiled. "Only two tickets, mate, and I don't think Elizabeth would be impressed if I left her at home."

"Buen viaje," he said, shaking my hand. It meant, have a good trip; he'd said it many times in the past. I thanked him. We turned and both trudged our separate ways back home like a couple of malnourished bears out of hibernation.

Antonio had struck a chord with me, with each crunchy footstep I made in virgin snow; I couldn't help feeling sorry for the poor Forsters and the utter misery they had to endure. I couldn't imagine how the grandparents were coping, especially over Christmas. It was a wretched thought.

There was no way to help Joe and Sally Forster, but I could help the Bakers, at least give them hope. The trouble was, they'd had seventeen years of false hope. Could I do any better?

There was never a shortage of traditional yuletide cheer in our house. I entered to the timeless classic of Frank Sinatra's 'Have yourself a merry little Christmas' wafting out of Elizabeth's old tape player. She saw no reason to update the thing and bin her collection of cassettes. My wife is very much a waste not, want not type of person, and in this throwaway world we've created, we need to cling on to more of that behaviour. The smell of a roast turkey dinner, homemade chestnut stuffing, mince pies, and Christmas pudding, hit me like a delicious freight train, I was more than ready for it.

"Perfect timing, love," she said as I stepped into the kitchen. "Can you get the turkey out and rest it on the charger please?"

"Your wish is my command, petal."

I placed my coat on a hook, washed my hands, and did as I was told. The turkey crown was done to perfection, succulent and juicy, but with crispy brown skin. I nearly collapsed with delight.

The charger was soon accompanied by bowls of roast spuds, Brussels sprouts, Parsnips, carrots, and far too many pigs in blankets for the two of us to consume, completed by Yorkshire puddings, the stuffing, and thick homemade gravy, it was a feast to be reckoned with.

"Did you put the wine in the fridge, dear?" I asked.

She pre-empted me, knowing that I like my red slightly chilled.

"Of course."

She was looking at me bemused.

"What's wrong?" I said.

"What's wrong with you? You'd normally have eaten half a dozen pigs in blankets by now. Have you been picking at the pub?"

"Arthur laid on some nibbles, but I didn't touch a thing. Antonio and I sat by the window and had a beer. Oh, and Willy bought us a malt each. That's it."

You don't live with one another for forty years without knowing that something is amiss. I knew that only a full explanation would douse the inquisitive fire catching in Elizabeth's mind. So, I broke confidence with Antonio and over dinner gave her an abridged version of the Forster story, leaving out the grim details for fear of ruining our superb meal.

When I'd finished, she matter of factly said, "Sally Forster isn't dead, no more than Molly Baker."

I didn't need to question my wife's remark and for very good reason. She has what some people refer to as 'The Gift'. Like all the women in her family before her, she could hear the voices of the dead. Not all of them at once. That would be ridiculously confusing, but now and again, she'd get a line from the grave to pass on to somebody specific. A messenger, she likes to call herself.

This can also be a curse, of course, because it can happen at any inopportune moment. Trust me, it has. Thankfully none of my girls have inherited the ability, but Elizabeth's talent has proved to be helpful on more than one occasion. Finding people that you are assured are not dead is a complete game-changer, and knowing that Molly Baker was still with us bolstered my resolution.

Everybody is entitled to their own opinion, certainly, but for us, knowing that there is somewhere else we go when our bodies are spent, gives us great comfort.

When we had cleared the table, we retired to the living room with our Christmas pudding, mince pies, and cream to listen to the Queen's speech on the telly. It was ten to three, and as I ate, my mind drifted to the conversation I'd had with Sophie Baker and the promise of doing a feasibility study over these two weeks. My gut feeling now was to stuff the feasibility study and just go for it...

"A penny for them?" interrupted my wife.

We had already discussed the Baker case the day before and had decided that it was best to sleep on it before I made any decisions.

"It's gonna take more than a few pennies, my dear."

She knew what was occupying my mind.

"Whatever you decide, Dave, I'll be behind you one hundred percent, you know that, but let me just say this; you've had two professionals telling you this week that taking this case on would be the right thing to do, one of them being our Sam, a highly respected police officer with some inside knowledge, and I'm sure the rest of the family would give you their full support. I honestly believe in my heart, Dave, that you are Molly Baker's best chance of being found. Do what you always do, love: give this case your all for one year, because I know that when your back's against the wall and you're under pressure, you're at your best."

Elizabeth was right, making this case time-sensitive would stir me into action. She topped up our drinks, and we clinked glasses. "To the year ahead," she said, and then leaned in and kissed me. We took a sip and settled down to watch the Queen.

Comfortably perched at the end of the sofa, Elizabeth nestled with her latest novel and an ample glass of Bailey's Irish cream. She would lose herself amongst the pages for a couple of hours, whilst I sunk into my favourite armchair and savoured the spell of a seasoned apple log fire burning in the hearth, and slowly devoured a twenty-year-old malt, eventually succumbing to the alcohol and the hypnotic effects of the flames, by nodding off.

However, my nap was short-lived. Gently drawn into consciousness by four mellow chimes of our Grandmother clock in the hall, I roused myself from the confines of the chair, stretched my protesting bones, and then headed to the kitchen to make coffee.

Elizabeth didn't want one, so I just made a mug of strong black stuff for me and sat at the table with my notebook and a short pencil. Now I had decided to take on the Baker case, the cogs were starting to be set in motion. The things Sam had said to me were on repeat in my mind. I wrote them down; a copper's take on why Molly has never been found. The money to continue this case for a year, that wouldn't be a problem. Working with the Portuguese police, that can be resolved. Eliminating the Bakers as suspects for good, a tough one, but essential.

Once I have spoken to Alfie Fields on New Year's Eve, I should have a clearer picture of the investigation to date, and of where to begin. With an old case like this, I am bound to upset a few people who are trying to forget and move on, open up old wounds, travel over-well trodden ground. I'm not going to be popular.

A germ in my little grey cells kept reoccurring; whoever took that baby must have seen her at least once before the night she was abducted. Find that place, and I have a starting point.

3

Pushchairs

Tim the Taxi's Mercedes tyres crunched over frozen snow, the sound akin to a succession of spoons breaking into a never-ending Viennetta ice cream. The ground temperature outside was way below zero, and another flurry of the white stuff was descending delicately like goose down expelled from a heavenly pillow fight.

It was a rather pleasant sound, giving you the kind of satisfaction you get from rolling pastry, crushing garlic or shelling peas, a sort of soothing reward for your toil. The car was levelling out the jagged ruts that had been sculpted outside our house in the road by diehard motorists trusting their luck.

Elizabeth and I had been up since 2:30 a.m. giving ourselves plenty of time to wash, dress and have a little breakfast. Our body clocks hadn't agreed to it yet, but we were awake and on our way to the airport.

Tim was always punctual, he'd been driving us about for decades. Yet for all the familiarity, he still insisted on calling my wife Mrs Skipper. He was a gentleman and a diamond. He caught my eye in the rearview mirror. "The main roads seem clear this morning, Dave."

"That's reassuring, Tim." I leant forward and laid my Range Rover keys on the passenger seat. "Just in case we get another snow dump, you can use the Range to come and get us when we get back."

"Don't tell me you've put another bet on?"

I chuckled. "I may have."

I could see Tim grinning with judicious admiration.

He got us to Luton with plenty of time to spare, which suited me just fine. Elizabeth, however, could have done with another hour in bed. She was still weary.

We checked in; the flight was scheduled on time, so we decided to peruse the moderate shopping area out of interest more than anything. We weren't planning on a purchase; we were just killing a few hours. After a while, we went upstairs to the departures area and had a coffee at Costa Pretty Penny, before waiting by the windows for our plane to come in. It was still gloomy outside. Dawn had just broken, but I could see the aeroplane lights, taxiing, taking off and landing, and it wasn't too long before our 737 pulled into the gate to offload its cargo of passengers from somewhere warmer, no doubt. Boy, were they gonna get a start when that north-easterly chill smacked them in the face. There are no cosy jet bridges at Luton to step onto; it's down the steps and onto the concrete, before trudging to the terminal, whatever the weather.

I'm always amazed by how quickly the ground crew can turn around an aircraft. Within half an hour it had been cleaned, re-stocked and re-fuelled, ready to take on the next batch of eager travellers.

We waited for the call to board. Travelling with Budget airlines tends to have more down than upsides, but our kids had paid a little extra for us to be given priority boarding, so we were up and out of our seats first and down the stairs, to be held at the front of the queue by the automatic glass doors. These opened and closed intermittently several times, triggered by the slightest movement from us keen fliers, itching to get going, causing a blast of freezing snow-moted air to assault us unfortunates at the head of the queue.

I was wondering what we were waiting for, when I noticed some exiting passengers with small children had been forced to the rear of the aircraft, supervised by a ground crew member dressed head-to-toe in Hi-Vis yellow waterproofs, to retrieve their kids' pushchairs and strollers. Obviously, they were needed for stowing the little ones before baggage reclaim.

It occurred to me that this scenario must happen in foreign airports. Faro in particular back in 2003 was just like Luton, no jet bridges. I remembered a mate who goes on golfing holidays regularly to Portugal complaining that it was always a bit of a schlep across the hot tarmac.

So if the Bakers had taken their twins' pushchairs with them, they would have had to do the same, because two one-year-olds would have definitely needed a pushchair to take them through arrivals. You couldn't carry bags and three struggling kids through the airport. This meant, the first people to see the Bakers in Portugal had to be the baggage handlers offloading the plane. Interesting. I wondered if the police had interviewed everyone at the airport, or even considered it.

The doors trundled open again, but this time stayed ajar whilst the lemon-clad people director ushered us towards the plane. Happy to be back in the warm again, we found our seats in the emergency exit row (more legroom) and rapidly discarded our coats, stowing them with our carry-on bags in the lockers above.

The 737 has 174 seats. I bagged the window seat, Elizabeth sat in the middle and a good-looking Spanish chap in his late thirties took the aisle. My wife had made sure to retrieve her bag of barley sugars from her coat pocket before sitting down. It was routine and somewhat nostalgic for her to suck on boiled sweets during a flight. She suffered more than most from her ears popping, which I can understand is annoying, but it really didn't affect me much until we descended.

She offered a barley sugar to her fellow traveller, explaining the advantage of the sweet. I'm sure he probably knew anyway and took one graciously. His English was good, and they conversed for much of the trip, allowing me to practice one of my favourite past times of shutting my eyes and going for a mind wander.

The Spanish chap reminded me that I had to set up a meeting with an old friend, Olavo Rebelo. I was hoping that he was willing to take a year off from a job he was dedicated to, as an intensive care nurse. Since the death of his partner, five years ago, he has thrown himself into his work 24-7; I think it helps him with the grieving process, and it was going to take some convincing to prize him away. Also, I was battling myself for wanting to deprive the N.H.S of one of their finest, but Olavo was imperative to the team I had in mind. He was fluent in five languages, apart from English; he spoke Spanish, Portuguese, German and Italian. He was also a whiz with a computer and a person I could trust emphatically. I wanted him on my team, but for the sake of harmony, it would expressly have to be his decision.

Our daughter Sam had told me that during the first year of Molly Baker's disappearance, more than two hundred British and Portuguese police officers had worked on the case. I was intending on tackling the job with just six people.

Mary and Paul were a given. We had a system that worked beautifully. Add to that Olavo. We just needed two more, preferably serving British and Portuguese coppers, to open doors and gain access to certain material.

I also needed to start thinking about acquiring a base of operation in Portugal. My train of thought was interrupted by warmth blooming on my face. We had left the murk shrouding the UK, shaken off the gloom. Heading south-east, we were over France, in brighter skies, and the illustrious dawn was blinding my watery open eyes through the portside window. The view beneath us, a verdant rural landscape with meandering silver veins that glinted now and then, refracting light like liquid diamonds, pleased me intently.

Elizabeth and her neighbour had gone quiet, her nose was deep into the paperback novel she'd bought in WH Smith; it was time to make some notes.

Even though I should put all work aside and just enjoy this special once-in-a-lifetime trip, the old cogs just wouldn't stop churning, I took out my notebook and a stubby pencil from my inside jacket pocket and began to scribble.

Baggage handler, I wrote, followed by a question mark. It was the only thing I had to go on at this point in time.

The ground crew would have been the first contact the Bakers had with Portuguese locals, up close to the kids, an exchange of words perhaps. If there was a predator amongst them, they might be seasoned professionals and looking for certain criteria. If one of the twins fitted the bill, the perpetrator might want to follow them, but how? They were at work.

A lady on the other side of the aircraft stood up and reached for the overhead locker. I watched her pull out a light blue fleece; she must have been chilly. Her actions revealed a small black Samsonite case wedged in tightly, with destination labels dangling from the handle. Gold dust, I thought. Talk about advertising where you are going to be staying. A label like that will have your name on it and the resort you are booked in to. Anyone in the travel business would be well savvy to all the resorts, and if they didn't, it would be easy to find out.

I didn't have the foggiest notion of what the Bakers did after they stepped off the plane back in 2003, but I was going to use my imagination, and it's surprising just what you can fathom from a surmised scenario.

I made another note: pushchairs. Followed by, did the flight labels have return journey information on them as well? If so, a potential abductor would know how long the family were staying in the country.

Armed with the resort information, a perp' at their leisure could easily case the joint, find out about its facilities, swimming pools, babysitting arrangements, kids clubs, etc. They could hang out in the bars, restaurants, by the pool maybe and soon get an idea of the family's habits. If they were local, or local looking, they could almost certainly blend in, pose as workers perhaps.

My mind was racing. I pictured the Bakers, hot and tired, laden with carry-on luggage, duty-free booze, struggling kids, and having to walk to the back of the plane to collect their buggies. The last thing they would be thinking of would be to take note of the baggage handlers. Why would they? And if they were saddled with drink, an abductor might see this to his advantage; British couple, like a drink, drunk every night, heavy sleepers perhaps?

But surely the airport runs security checks on all its employees? Any perverts with previous aren't gonna get jobs working with the public, are they? Maybe it's a different situation on the continent; I made another note to check.

Someone working at the airport would probably live in the vicinity, but also close enough to be in easy driving distance to where the Bakers were staying in Viana do Fao, yet still, be under the radar. The perp' almost certainly had transport.

The Bakers were travelling with two other couples, also with young children, I believe. If they all had to collect their buggies from the rear of the aeroplane, then there were multiple labels to read and plenty of time to glean all of the details.

The abductors only had a window of a week to make their move, if this wasn't a botched burglary, which I'm leaning away from, or a chance snatching by an opportunist, then the longer they had to plan, the better for them. Somebody picking Molly right at the start of their holiday had the advantage.

My thoughts were interrupted by a stewardess wielding a drinks trolley. "Beverage, sir?"

"Oh, um, do you have any brandy?" A little tonsil warmer would be just the ticket right now.

"I have Napoleon, straight?"

"Is there another way, my dear?"

She smiled, handed me a miniature and a plastic tumbler, then whacked me with the price. "£6.50, sir."

Internally I swore, but I held my reserve. "I think my wife would like something as well."

Elizabeth opted for a cup of tea, for which a further £1.50 was added to the bill. I made another mark in my notebook; bring hip flask next time.

Back to the investigation. I tried to picture the Bakers movements from their home in Dorset. They drove themselves to Gatwick airport and left their car in the long-stay. Did all the usual: check-in, baggage drop, the perusal of the shops, wait in the departure lounge, board the plane. I discounted immediately anybody at the airport who wasn't travelling on that same flight. Too much of a stretch to find them from somewhere else in the world in one week.

Might someone on the plane have singled the girls out as a target? Quite possibly. Even if they weren't travelling to the same resort, an offhand friendly question to either George or Jill as to where they were staying wouldn't have seemed amiss to a bunch of fervent holidaymakers. The potential here for a suspect was at least 168 random strangers. I wondered if they had all been vetted. Would a perp' on the same flight have taken a risk? Doubtful.

The Bakers arrive at Faro, go through the airport, pick up their hire car and drive to the holiday resort. Hundreds of potential suspects here, but unless they were followed, only the baggage handlers, the car hire staff and their friends knew their destination, and as far as we are to believe, all of these people have been questioned and cleared.

That leaves the possibility that they were tailed. By who: another tourist? a perv' hanging around the airport car parks, a taxi driver?

Taxi drivers would be waiting in line; they would all know each other unless there was someone new on the block. If a cab suddenly peeled off without a fare, following a hire car, it would raise a few eyebrows, especially if it was an unknown cabbie. The police would have gotten word of that for sure.

I assumed because I hadn't had the time to look into it yet, that the holiday complex at Viana do Fao had a full set of amenities to suit family holidays, and having three very young children, I doubt whether the Bakers left the resort much at all. Presuming the entire workforce there had been interviewed and vindicated results in a strong suspicion that any abductors must have come from the outside.

A lone wolf, spying on the family, planning, waiting for a break, if they are not known to staff, they are going to be suspicious, questioned maybe. No, it doesn't seem plausible that there was some unknown hanging about.

Did the perp' see the Bakers outside of the complex? Maybe they went to the supermarket, or the beach, a chemist, a doctor perhaps. The possibilities were endless, but I had little idea of the family's movements whilst in

Portugal at this point. I really needed to have a conversation with George or Jill.

If we'd had to make a crash landing, sitting next to the emergency exit, we'd be the first ones out. But for some reason, when our plane did land, it seemed like the whole plane emptied before we got the chance. We tramped into the arrivals hall looking for salvation. Our rep', suited in black and holding our nameplate to his chest, couldn't have mistaken us. We were the last ones out.

"Ah, Señor Skiipper." His pronunciation gave my surname an extra vowel in the middle. "I am Jesus, from Platinum Transfers. buenos días, Señor y Señora. If you would follow me, your limousine is waiting."

Jesus took our bags and placed them on a trolley, then got on his mobile phone, speaking Spanish in hushed tones as we walked towards the exit.

A pristine, sparkling, black stretch limo' awaited us in the pick-up area just outside the terminal, its chauffeur, also dressed in black, including hat, was out and opening the rear doors for us to bundle in. A few onlookers were trying to determine whether we were celebrities or not. We certainly felt like it, right there and then.

"This is Santiago," said Jesus, "he is your driver for today." Santiago nodded curtly. "I will accompany you to Barcelona also; Santiago's English is not too good."

Both of the Spaniards got into the front. A soundproof glass window divided us.

This was no party limousine. It was top spec. The kids had splashed out. It even had a mini-bar in the back.

"Fancy a drink, love?" I said opening the discreet little black door.

"Ooh, what do they have?"

"Some miniatures, beer, pop, water and OJ."

"I'll have orange juice then."

"Ice?"

"Blimey, they have everything in there."

"Yeah, nearly." I found my wife's reaction amusing. I think she was a little bit overwhelmed by the luxury.

I cracked the lid off a tiny bottle of Jameson and lined the bottom of a tumbler with the amber liquid; it would be gone in two gulps. I needed a livener before I made a phone call to the Bakers. But prior to that, I explained to Elizabeth some of what had been going through my mind on the plane. I didn't want to spoil our trip with work, but I needed a few answers pronto, or I wouldn't be able to sleep. She said she didn't mind, so I retrieved my mobile phone. Elizabeth reassured me with a hand on my knee that everything was fine.

I rang the Bakers' home number.

"Hello." The female voice was short and brusque. It halted me.

"Ah, hello, is that Jill? It's Dave Skipper. I apologise for phoning so early, but do you mind if I ask either you or George a couple of questions?"

Her tone morphed into something more cordial.

"Oh, hello Mr Skipper. We speak at last. No, no, that's quite alright. We're early risers. What is it you wanted to know?"

She was quite chipper now, excited in fact.

"I'm sorry to call you like this. We really should be meeting face to face, but I'm away in Spain for the weekend with my wife, and my machine of a brain hasn't turned off. There's so much of your story that I just don't know about yet. I feel I need a bit of background to feed the monster."

"We can leave it until you're back if you like…."

"No, no, it's fine. It won't take long."

"Oh, okay."

"Back in 2003 at the start of your holiday, could you tell me your exact movements between getting off the plane and reaching the resort on the Costa do Andrea?"

There was silence on the other end. I thought that maybe we'd been cut off.

"Hello, Jill?"

"Sorry, Mr Skipper, I was just trying to take myself back to that day. I've blocked so much out…."

"That's alright; of course, please take your time."

"Well the first thing we did, and I remember this quite clearly because Molly, Sophie and Nile were all miserable and crying. When one starts, they all kick off…."

"I remember it well; we've bought up three of our own."

"Well you know then how hard it is … We had to carry the kids to the back of the plane in that sweltering heat, to where the luggage was being taken off, and collect the twins' buggy. After strapping them in, which was a struggle, we then followed the herd across the tarmac to arrivals, waited a while by the baggage carousels, collected our suitcases and then went and picked up the hire car from the Thrifty people. Well George dealt with that, while I waited in the airport. It was a lot cooler inside and I could deal with the kids, get them a drink. They were all burning up."

"And after that?"

"We drove straight to Viana. The car didn't need fuel; it had a full tank, and we weren't planning on visiting a supermarket until after we'd got settled in. One of us could do that on our own."

"You didn't speak to anyone in all that time?"

"Well apart from our friends, George spoke to the car hire people of course, and the reception staff at the resort, but nobody else."

"Okay, I won't keep you much longer, but just briefly how many times did you all leave the complex, and where did you go?"

She must have been over this a million times, so it was probably fully ingrained in the memory.

"We went to Lidl three times, on the Tuesday, Wednesday and Friday. On Friday George went by himself. Saturday, we drove to Monte Clérigo, to spend the day with George's uncle and aunt; they've lived in Portugal for more than twenty years. We had a lovely day, didn't get back to the apartment until 8 a.m."

"I see. Did you speak to anyone in Lidl? Meet any other Brits? Tell anyone where you were staying?"

"No, just the cashiers, and then just about the money."

"Right, and you didn't stop anywhere else, a service station perhaps?"

"Ah, we did stop at a service station, because Nile had spilt a drink all over himself, but we didn't go in, just pulled up on one side of the forecourt and used the toilet to sort Nile out. We were only there a few minutes."

"And you didn't venture outside the holiday complex at all apart from those four times?"

"Yes, on the Sunday, we went down to the beach, but it was a complete waste of time. We paid out for two sunbeds, then the weather totally changed. It turned cloudy and the wind got up terribly. The cheeky sun-bed man had a right royal payday. We were forced to fork out for a couple windbreakers as well, and we were only there for two hours max."

"Did you use a car park?"

"Yes, another waste of money. George paid for all day."

"Speak to anyone there?"

"No, it was a machine."

"Okay, Jill, I won't take up any more of your time, until I've gone over the case files, I've got plenty to get on with…."

"It's no bother, Mr Skipper. Anything I can do to help."

"Dave, please call me Dave."

"Oh, okay, Dave."

I had to be selective in my choice of words for signing off. I couldn't wish her a Happy New Year. It didn't seem appropriate with what they were going through. So I simply said thank you, and that I was looking forward to meeting them in person a week on Saturday.

"Informative?" Elizabeth's tone was playful. She knew that if I'd gained some bits of the puzzle, my mind would be quelled enough to enjoy the weekend. She kept her hand on my knee, but turned her gaze to the landscape rushing by; it was somewhat different from Buckinghamshire.

Notebook in hand once more, I jotted down the things I had just learned.

The small amount of shielded time the Bakers spent on the beach was a good thing. It narrowed their visibility to prying eyes.

They could have been spied at the car park. CCTV is probably employed there, and the police would have gone over that.

The supermarket, that's a minefield; anyone could have followed them back to the complex from there. I hoped Lidl also had CCTV footage which had been examined.

Botched burglary went through my mind again; that headline had been raised many times in the media. Petty thieves, in my experience, are by nature quite lazy individuals, who will hastily grab something of value that they can flog on rapidly, usually to feed a habit or clear a debt. Trying to sell a one-year-old baby, unless you were involved in such markets, would not be an easy thing to do. No, I'm not going to entertain that idea.

Elizabeth glanced at my notes; I'd underlined Peeping Tom by the pool?

"I don't think that's really viable, Dave."

"Oh, why's that?"

"Well with what I can remember from all of the news coverage, the swimming pool the Bakers used was heavily screened from the road. You'd have to go inside the complex to see who was using it and so have to have a legitimate reason for being there. And everyone's been questioned, haven't they?"

"Good point, although I'll need to have my feet on the ground at Viana to be one-hundred percent sure."

I knew I was pushing it. This was supposed to be a mini holiday for the two of us, our Christmas present, a special treat, not a working trip. But I had to make just one more phone call, to help get the ball rolling in my absence.

"Sorry, love, I gotta call Alfie Fields. I promise it'll be the last one."

"That's alright. You do what you gotta do, Dave … Until we get to Barcelona that is."

That was me told; I gingerly tapped out the detective's number.

"Alfie, It's Dave Skipper…."

"Hello, Dave, this is unexpected. What's up?"

I gave him a heavily abridged version of where we were heading today and what I had discovered this morning. "…There's a couple of things you could do for me, mate, before we meet at the weekend."

"Go on."

"As I said before, I don't want to cause any waves just yet, so if you can use your utmost discretion, would it be possible for you to get me a detailed list of all baggage handlers that worked at Faro airport the month Molly Baker disappeared?"

"Baggage handlers? You know, Dave, I've only been assigned to this case for the last six years, but I can't recall any investigation into airport staff, ever."

"It's just an idea, Alfie, but maybe it's one that's been overlooked … If anyone asks what you are doing, perhaps you can say it's just out of self-interest."

"I'm a serving police officer, Dave. If anyone asks what I'm up to, I'll have to come clean. This will have to be official at some point."

"Let's hope no one asks then eh?"

The other thing I asked Alfie was did he know somebody in Portugal that he could trust emphatically. He only knew one person in Portugal, his counterpart Faustino Vela, and he believed that he could trust him.

Like Alfie, Faustino was just a front for the ongoing investigation; neither of them was doing much at all towards discovering what actually happened to Molly Baker. No police force likes to admit they have failed, so keeping the case simmering on the stove gave the public the impression they were still trying.

Alfie seemed to think that his counterpart would be extremely up for re-opening the investigation; he was deeply ashamed that such a thing could happen in his country and then be simply brushed under the carpet.

I put my phone away, sat back and relaxed. Now we could enjoy the weekend.

Bare-branched deciduous trees, the occasional pine and winter-soaked grass verges flashed by the tinted windows. Galvanised steel barriers and sandy coloured soil bordered the tarmac; it wasn't all that different from the M40 after all, one stretch of motorway, much like many others around the globe.

All of a sudden I became aware of Jesus and Santiago having a heated row in the front seats, gesticulating dramatically as Mediterraneans often do.

Elizabeth and I looked on in stunned amazement. This wasn't company etiquette surely.

Jesus came on the intercom. "I'm sorry, Mr and Mrs Skiipper, we are forced to make a short pit stop at the service station ahead. We are running low on fuel."

The mic' clicked off, and the pair of Spaniards went back to waving their arms about. We looked at each other and burst out laughing. Here we were being driven in complete luxury with Laurel and Hardy at the wheel.

The car sailed up the off-ramp and rolled onto the pumps of a Galp filling station somewhere south of Gerona. It was handy actually because I needed a pee.

When I came out of the loo, Jesus had gone inside the shop to pay, while Santiago was still filling her up. I strolled over to the perimeter, where some trucks had parked, to stretch my back and admire the view. From here, there was an uninterrupted panorama of the snow-capped Pyrenees Mountains. Wisps of smoke from wood-burning stoves in distant farmhouses smudged the foothills, the smell of pine sap and fragrant burning logs on the air, stamped a uniqueness upon this place.

Jesus joined me. "Wonderful isn't it, señor?"

"Hmm?" I said dreamily.

"The smell of Catalonia, it's more intense in the wintertime."

"Inspirational, old boy. One could paint a picture, if only one could paint."

I had confused the chap. He apologised again for the sideshow and for having to make this unscheduled stop. I told him not to worry a single jot. If we hadn't stopped, I wouldn't have witnessed this awe-inspiring view.

He gave a continental shrug, and we returned to the car.

As soon as we pulled up outside the hotel, Santiago was out and opening our doors before the concierge could get a look in. I extracted a couple 50 euro notes from my wallet and gave one each to our driver and escort. It had been a first-class service, despite the pit stop, and we'd also had a chuckle along the way. They were as pleased as Punch, we shook hands and they were off.

A bell boy grabbed our cases and beckoned for us to follow in his wake. We did so in awe. The Hotel Catalonia was splendid, a huge block of a building situated on the Plaça d'Espanya, that from a distance looks like a modern, precision cut, sandstone, checkerboard castle, with its offset turret and remarkable massive glass clock face, at midway point of the front facade.

We entered via the stainless steel revolving doors, and into the expansive foyer, which was brightly lit and sleek, with huge gold pillars, an abundance of armchairs and couches, and some colourful spherical work.

The receptionist spoke impeccable English. We checked in and took the elevator up to the eighth floor and our luxurious suite on the terrace, right beside the stunning rooftop pool. Shame it was only ten degrees Celsius outside; otherwise, I might have been tempted to take a dip, but the view from up here was spectacular, overlooking the entire city, the hills to the north and Castell de Montjuïc down south, guarding the ports.

Our suite was stylized in a 1960s vibe, spindle-legged furniture, lots of ovals and curves, laminate walnut flooring and panelling. Two main rooms: an en suite bedroom with a lounge area in front of a log effect gas fire and a giant TV on the wall, and another lounge/dining room, with a second TV and a moderate minibar.

The king-size bed was enormous; we could smuggle our entire family in it and be missing for weeks. A good night's sleep was surely guaranteed.

After unpacking our few meagre items, we went out exploring. First, we strolled through Parc de Joan Miró, along the water channel to its 22-metre-high Dona i Ocell (Woman and Bird) sculpture. Despite it being multi-coloured, it still appeared rather phallic to me. We then doubled back past the hotel and down an avenue to the Font màgica de Montjuïc, a magic fountain spouting illuminated jets of water high up into the air, accompanied by the Lord of the Rings movie soundtrack. It was some display.

Looming above this, accessed by many flights of steps, was the Palau Nacional, an impressive art museum built in an ancient Italian style. It would take many days to walk around the interior of this building to do it justice; we neither had the time nor the inclination.

We passed the four columns of Catalan and headed east along many streets until we reached the harbour by the Columbus monument, a kind of Nelsons Column look-a-like, complete with four lions. This was the beginning of the street we had hoped to explore in earnest, La Rambla, a vibrant, intoxicating, widely-paved thoroughfare arrayed with superb restaurants, kiosks, stunning architecture and market stalls selling everything from pets to pottery, and famous for its living statues, performers who remain inhumanly still for hours on end, imagined as angels, ghouls, soldiers, clowns and historic icons. Some actually appear to defy gravity in sitting positions without any means of support. There was even a guy made up like the Hindu elephant god Ganesha, who was floating cross-legged in mid-air. It was an amazing illusion.

The pavement had a rippled pattern in the concrete slabs, like waves, depicting the fact that this was once a watercourse. The trees that lined both sides of the wide avenue were naturally bare at this time of year, dark fingers beseeching the baby blue sky. But they had been strung with white bulbs, which were going to look amazing at night.

Elizabeth and I were hungry now, and we were assaulted on every front by the exotic smells of street food being conjured up on the many stalls we passed. A whiff of pine smoke caught our attention, bringing me back to the vista by the gas station on the E15. We followed our noses to an open-fronted restaurant that was heaving.

Tables and chairs spilled out onto the street, umbrellaed by Calor gas heaters. It was obviously very popular. There was just one meal on offer, unique to Catalonia, Pollo a l'ast, Rotisserie chicken marinated with herbs, spices and lemon juice, over a roaring log fire, served with just roast potatoes. The aroma was incredible; we had to sit down at once. Luckily, a couple was just leaving, so we eagerly slumped into their warm seats.

A waiter appeared out of nowhere and rapidly cleared the table. Instinctively he knew we were British and told us in good English that he would be right back.

He was, bringing with him a basket of bread and a carafe of water. He asked us what we wanted to drink. We opted for a bottle of house red. There was no need to order the food; it was a done deal. That's what we were there for, and everyone got the same. What we didn't realise was that you also got tapas as a starter, and four small dishes were brought out for us to nosh on while we waited for the main event. Green olives, little balls of fried cheese, some curls of thinly sliced cured Jamón, and some fried cod croquettes. Each dish was heavenly, especially the ham. It was superb, so I ordered another plate, noticing for the first time that inside the restaurant, hanging from its ceiling, there must have been a hundred legs of ham dangling above people's heads, each with its own little white conical umbrella stabbed into the underside, to catch the drips of fat. It was an unforgettable image, a unique experience.

Without a doubt, the chicken remains one of the best meats I've ever tasted. It was incredible, a whole chicken between us, the flavour indescribable, juicy, tender, crispy-skinned. We ate it with our hands and felt like mediaeval nobility. The potatoes were so moreish, cooked in fat, crunchy on the outside; they melted in your mouth.

For dessert, the waiter recommended the Crema Catalana, a lighter version of a crème brûlée and delicious.

All this for 60 euro; it seemed impossible. We'd be leaving a 20 euro tip.

As we sat there fully sated and people watching, feeling wonderful, my mobile phone piped into life, spoiling the moment. It was Alfie Fields. It had only been around six hours since I had spoken to him, and I wondered what had occurred to make him ring back so quickly.

"Hi, Dave. Alfie here."

"Hello, mate. What did you find?"

"I called Faustino as soon as I came off the phone to you. He's come back with some interesting facts and figures…."

"Oh, yes?"

"In April 2003 there were 68 baggage handlers on the payroll at Faro airport. He's emailed me the details, names, addresses, wage slips, start and finish dates. He's also done a security check on all of them. Nothing came up, but we expected that. They wouldn't have been employed with a criminal record."

"Did he keep it all discreet?"

"Apparently so. No one raised an eyebrow. He's also emailed me a list of baggage handlers employed at the airport between January 2001 and 2006. There seems to be a high turnover in that department."

"The boy's done well. What did he think of us re-opening the investigation?"

"Yes. Dave, his exact words were, 'It's the only right thing to do'."

I asked Alfie to thank Faustino. Maybe we'd get to meet one day and have a drink. I said I'd see *him* on the 31st.

It took all of our resolve to get up from that table and leave the little haven behind. We could have sat there all night, watching the world go by, but it was a long walk back to the hotel, and we knew we would both be knackered by the time we returned. It had been a very enlightening day, and I had lots to think about.

We had a couple of hours to kill before leaving for Rod's concert that evening. I had booked a cab to pick us up at 8 p.m. We both needed a shower and to get changed, but Elizabeth wanted 40 winks before all that.

Her head hit the bed, and she was out like a light. I pulled a blanket over her, then went and sat in an armchair by the window, looking straight down Avenguda de la Reina Maria Christina and the magic fountain.

I wasn't in the habit of comparing myself with Winston Churchill or Margaret Thatcher, but like those two icons of state, I only needed four to six hours sleep per night to keep me going. I'd sleep much, much later. For now, I would sit here and contemplate what I had learned in the five days since Sophie Baker walked into my office.

The scenario that Molly was a chance find on the night of her abduction seemed highly unlikely, possible, but a long shot. I put that idea way back in the cupboard.

If somebody didn't follow the Bakers out to Portugal, again highly improbable, then the children had to have been selected in that country, either at the airport, the holiday complex, at the supermarket, or on the beach, and that was also a bit thin.

I referred back to my notebook. The abductors most likely had transport. There were possibly two or more people involved, maybe one a female with experience of looking after babies. Besides it would look more natural to any observers if a couple had a baby with them, rather than just a man, say. They were likely local or Mediterranean in appearance, so they would blend in. There had to be a base of operation. Perhaps they lived close by. I needed a map to do some reckoning. I would purchase one tomorrow.

Reasons to abduct a child: maybe a couple or a single mother perhaps were bereft of a baby and were desperate to replace her. Even so, you would have to be viciously callous, or deranged to want to put another mother through that despicable anguish.

If this is the case, a couple who foolishly took Molly without considering the consequences, then they couldn't have expected the recoil, the unprecedented international outcry, revulsion and the ongoing manhunt. They would find themselves outlawed, paranoid, constantly looking over their shoulders, in hiding, living a lie and suspicious to everyone and of everyone. Not an ideal way to be living and a major dilemma, they couldn't return the child, not without the shame and a hefty prison sentence, let alone further bereavement.

This would have been a very volatile situation for Molly to be in, one that could have put her life in danger.

If this sort of situation was the case, then the abductor's house would have to be remote, away from village life, away from people that knew them well enough to know they didn't have a child of their own or had lost one. And if they worked in the vicinity, it wouldn't be too far away, say within twenty-five miles to make it comfortable to travel to and from work. So this profile would have a couple who weren't wealthy, lived in an isolated homestead in a rural setting, at least one of them had a job, they would have a car of some sort, and be somewhere between the ages of twenty and forty.

That narrows it down a bit, I thought caustically.

Another scenario may be that the baby was stolen to order. Several possibilities sprang to mind: an abductor working for money, taking children for organised criminals to sell on, for grooming, or for sex. The thought of that made me ill. Or, and this is probably the best situation, if you can call it that, for a wealthier couple who have lost a child to bring up as their own.

Again, the perp' would have had to have spied the family some time previous to the abduction, observed their movements, and then acted when the chance prevailed. As with the first instance, it was highly likely to be undertaken by a couple of people, one to act as a lookout, the other to enter the apartment, both to make the escape appear natural. Because nobody has come forward yet, to my knowledge, who saw the crime actually taking place that night.

The third and worst-case scenario, which I could barely bring myself to contemplate, was that of a perverted child killer. But I had to face it, even if my wife and Sophie are convinced that Molly is still alive. Sickening though it was, I would have to harden myself to examine that avenue.

Experience has taught me that an evil monster like this would strike quickly, take a victim to somewhere secluded, sexually gratify themselves either during or after the act of murder, and then dispose of the body and all evidence, sometimes never to be found again. They are by no means *all* clever enough to achieve such anonymity; a trail of evidence is nearly always left behind, but now and again such criminals totally evade capture.

I very much needed the case files, to be able to narrow my field of investigation. Right now, I was just pissing in the wind, and I'd only packed a couple of pairs of trousers.

Palau Sant Jordi was a part of the Olympic ring; opened in 1990, it had a capacity of more than 17,000 seats. Brilliantly lit on the outside, it looked like a huge hovering flying saucer, with its black Pantadome roof and pale walls. The taxi dropped us by the causeway to the entrance, and we followed the flock into the building via a corner entrance.

Once Elizabeth and I had shown our tickets and checked our coats, we were ushered to our position, the best seats in the house, right in front of the stage.

The room was cavernous, its dome completely exposed, with light gantries above and to the front of us, surrounding the stage, which wasn't too high off the ground. We were going to be real close to our man.

The hall lights were still on at this moment. The room was almost full, and the buzz was electric. I turned to Elizabeth. "Excited?" I said shoulders tense.

She nodded rapidly with a huge smile on her face.

The lights dimmed, a hush descended, and beams of purple and red spotlights fingered down onto the stage. A giant screen flicked into life on each side of the apron depicting supposed live footage of a white limo pulling up to the artists' entrance at the rear of the building. Dry ice rolled onto the stage fogging our view as Rod stepped out of the back of the limo in a crisp, neon blue suit and grinning like a Las Vegas chicken dinner winner. Out of sight, the band had taken up position on stage, and over the speakers, the jingle jangle of two guitars picked up the intro to one of Rod's oldest hits, '*You wear it well*'. The bass guitar joined in, followed by the rich organ chords that played the round over, as Rod could be seen coming through the doors and corridors backstage, past the crew and coils of wires and spare equipment, until he entered side stage to a roar from the audience that drowned out the band. He'd picked up a silver mic stand along the way, twirling it adroitly in time to the music. As soon as he hit centre stage, the drummer hit two beats on the snare drum, in time with Rod's opening line, "I had nothing to do on this hot afternoon…." The show had begun.

It was a joyous evening. Rod went through most of his hits. My favourites, the early stuff like *Cindy Incidentally*, *Stay With Me* and *Maggie May*, had the crowd dancing in the aisles. It's a shame he didn't play *Reason To Believe*, but he only had an hour and forty minutes to cram it all in. We were treated to songs from all his eras, thankfully Elizabeth's favourite included, *You're in My Heart*, during which he looked our way and winked at my wife. He finished with an absolute classic which had the entire audience singing, *Sailing*, and we were still singing it in the cab back to the hotel.

After a delightful continental breakfast of eggs, cold meats, cheese and coffee, brought up to our room, I showered, put on fresh clothes and took a wander down to the lobby shop, where I purchased a 1:500,000 scale map of Portugal. I meandered back to our room, spread it out onto the dining room table, and studied it for an hour, while Elizabeth got herself ready for the trip home.

Right now, I saw three possibilities. Either I was looking for a lone wolf who acted on an opportunity, murdered Molly and disposed of her body. In which case, with no witnesses, evidence, informers or a confession, I had close to zero chance of finding them.

Or it was a professional international gang, who selected the baby for a specific requirement and seized her in a covert operation. That investigation would need considerable police cooperation, perhaps with Interpol, to look at the movements of known gangs in the area on the dates in question. But I reckoned the gang would still need a safe house somewhere not too far away, to maybe make an exchange.

My third scenario, the one that gave me the greatest hope, was for a desperate local couple who needed a replacement child. That could mean that Molly was alive and well, and still in the Algarve.

The abductors must have spotted the Baker girls somewhere between Faro airport and the resort at Viana do Fao. Travelling west from the airport, the populated areas are almost exclusively between the coast and the A22, a three-mile wide strip above which there is only sporadic civilization dotted amongst the rugged hilly interior of the country. Logic told me that a remote farmhouse up here would make a perfect hideout, away from suspicious prying eyes.

So, unless they had travelled in from abroad, scouting for suitable targets, somewhere along that 80 mile stretch above the A22 was likely to be the abode of the abductor. In those hills. Which was a lot of ground to cover.

I sat at the airport bar in Barcelona, nursing a cold pint of Guinness and some okay tapas, watching a football match on a TV with incomprehensible commentary, whilst waiting for Elizabeth to do some duty-free shopping. Her list included a bottle of Johnnie Walker Black Label for me and a bottle of Bacardi for Tim.

Elizabeth would probably get herself some perfume, she normally did, but I was surprised when she arrived back with an iPad instead. "About time I had one," she informed me.

I supposed she was right; computers and I had an adverse effect on one another.

Our flight left the runway at 3 p.m. British Airways first class, and the seats were so much more comfortable. Just two abreast in each row on either side, big comfy leather numbers, with plenty of legroom. I was transfixed looking out of the window as we roared along the tarmac until lifting speed. I enjoy the take-off more than I do the landing, it seems safer to me, to be leaving the ground rather than hurtling towards it. Spain bid us adios as the sandy soil and green verges continued to diminish. The deep blue Med was visible for a while, but soon we were up above the clouds, bathed in the rose light of a sinking sun, creating pink candyfloss from the blanket of Altocumulus below.

A flight attendant handed me a glass of bubbly. It's not my usual indulgence, but being treated like a dignitary for a rare change eased me into the part for a couple hours. I took Elizabeth's hand and smiled at her. We touched glasses. "To a wonderful weekend," I said, before knocking back the Champers in one.

We finally arrived back to our snowbound home around 7 p.m. both ravenous, and within fifteen minutes we were tucking into one of the finest meals known to man, beans-on-toast with a mug of tea, or as we liked to call it, a thousand men on a raft, with the sun coming up.

Later, as Elizabeth settled in her usual spot on the sofa, getting to grips with her new toy, a glass of Baileys in one hand, I nestled into my armchair by the open fire, to stare into the flames once more and lose myself in thought.

Some time passed before Elizabeth asked what I was cogitating over.

"I have five people in mind for the perfect team to attack this case, love. Paul, Mary, Olavo, Alfie, and Faustino, and I'm just wondering if they'll all agree to get on board."

There was a contemplative pause before my perceptive wife replied.

"They will."

"What makes you so sure?"

"It's the right thing to do."

4

The team

The stack of Christmas cards, balanced precariously atop one another on my study desk, resembled folds of crisp white ice cream, destined to slide off and melt into a milky sweet mess unless I devoured them quickly. They came home with me from the office for Elizabeth to peruse. Seeing that half of them were also addressed to her, it was not only the correct thing to do, but a tradition we observed after all the festivities were over. I liked to share the well-wishes with my wife.

The seasonal greetings came from neighbouring businesses in Kings Ridge and former clients, the ones I'd helped to an agreeable outcome, that is.

One card rose above the rest. It had arrived just in time for Christmas, hand-delivered by Jim Maxwell himself, and accompanied by three wooden crates of wine, a mixture of red, white and Rosé, all from the same 'Terroir', the Côte D'Or, Burgundy, and splendid it all happened to be. But it was the contents of the card that stood out, suddenly fortuitous and as a happy reminder, because I had shelved the sender's generous past offer, as a thank you for a job well done. It was an invitation for my staff and myself to stay at any one of his holiday homes, of which he had three: a beach house in Barbados, an apartment in St Tropez and a villa on the Algarve.

Jim rented out his holiday homes when he wasn't using them. Each property had its own website, and I was staring at the Portuguese villa's page on my Mac Book now. It was splendid, with eight ensuite bedrooms, four reception rooms, a shaded veranda, a fully stocked cellar, and a rooftop sun terrace. It had a large pool, sat in 50 acres of a manicured, walled garden with electronic gates, as private as you like, and on top of this, it was only fifteen minutes away from Viana do Fao, perfect for investigation headquarters, if only he'd rent it to me for a year.

I got involved with Jim Maxwell last March, via a firm of solicitors down in Dover, Cartwright and Newport. We had carried out work for them on previous occasions, and our relationship was amicable.

I met Martin Newport in his office on a Friday morning; he wanted me to carry out a background check on one Sarah Lange, the maiden name of Mrs Maxwell. After knowing each other for just a year, they married nine months ago. Martin handed me a folder with the info he'd acquired already, including two photographs. She was a pretty girl, blonde, and 31 years old; her husband was in his 50s.

Jim Maxwell. His name dawned on me sitting there that day. Every motorist would have known his name. It was emblazoned on the sides of hundreds of freight lorries, which steam up and down the motorways of Great Britain all day and night. You can't go on a road journey without seeing one of his transports; the man was a legend, and a very wealthy individual.

Martin revealed more of the circumstances leading up to this enquiry. Jim's first wife had died suddenly 25 years ago, leaving him to raise three young children singlehandedly, as well as building his fledgeling business. He worked tirelessly and the haulage/vehicle leasing company is now a multi-million-pound enterprise. His three children, Amy, Ben and Dylan, are all directors of the company, so when their dad announced his engagement to his relatively new girlfriend, nobody was

76

worried. The firm's assets were all tied up. However, Jim had a personal fortune estimated to be around the 250,000,000 mark, yet despite the pleading from his offspring, he shied away from their advice of a prenuptial agreement.

Cracks started to appear in the marriage in as little as one month, and within two they were living apart. An out-of-court settlement for eight million was reached, which satisfied both parties, and was to be completed in April. But Martin, chewing his bottom lip, signalled to me there was more to come.

Amy had been in to see Martin the previous day and had requested the investigation. She was adamant that all was not as it seemed with Sarah Lange. Woman's intuition, she labelled it, and Martin had concurred. They wanted closure, hence my employment.

There was always the possibility that this was nothing more than a whirlwind romance gone awry after the magic had happened, and that an eight million pound settlement was a fair and reasonable amount to shell out to someone who had high hopes of a long and comfortable life ahead of them. But with the marriage only lasting a month, I had my doubts. I asked Martin if Sarah was entitled to such a large sum of money after only a short period of wedlock. He told me that technically she wasn't, only a fifty percent share of the wealth they had accumulated while they were married, which was nowhere near eight million. Apparently, Jim was in love, and he felt the payment appropriate. The rest of the world, apart from Sarah, took a different view.

I had Sarah's last known address, in a village just outside of Dover. Martin also gave me Amy's mobile number. I called her immediately after I had left Cartwright and Newport. She didn't have much to add, only that her dad and Sarah had met at a hotel spa weekend, and she believed that Sarah had once lived in Chelsea.

I relayed all the information I had back to my office, and by the time I arrived, some three hours later, Paul and Mary had made a good deal of progress. Sarah Lange was on the criminal database. She'd served a two-year stretch at Askham Grange, a women's open prison in Yorkshire, for perjury. She was now co-habiting with a Linda Robinson, an ex-warden, with whom she'd started a relationship whilst inside.

A three-pronged investigation was initiated.

On the following Monday, Paul took a jaunt over to Kent to do some surveillance. Mary phoned the HR department of the prison, whilst I made enquiries at the spa hotel where Jim and Sarah had first met, an exclusive, lavish stately manor in Boughton Lees, Kent.

Paul arrived at Sarah's house early, hoping to follow her at a distance. After a few fruitless hours of watching from his car, he got out and did a slow walk-by the unkempt property. It was lifeless, dark and static; obviously, no one had stayed here the previous night.

Paul knocked at a neighbour's house, pretending to be a work colleague wondering of her whereabouts. The neighbour, a stay-at-home mum with three little ones causing havoc behind her, was quite forthcoming. Sarah and Linda had lived next door for three years. A week ago they'd jetted off to an apartment they owned in Marbella with half-a-dozen designer suitcases between them. "All right for some!" she had said.

Mary's inquiries also bore fruit. Linda Robinson had been struck off for gross misconduct. Apparently having a sexual relationship with an inmate under your care is a serious breach of civil service rules, and classified as misconduct in a public office. She received an eight-month jail sentence, unfortunately for her, served at a different prison to Sarah's.

I phoned the hotel and managed to get through to the spa manager on the ruse that I was Detective Skipper, which vocationally I was, just not with any police force. I told her I was looking into the disappearance of one of their customers, Sarah Lange, and wondered if she had been in to use the facilities recently. The manager didn't need to look at her books. Miss Lange had been a regular a few years back, and well known to all the staff. They called her Kanye, apparently, the rapper had released a single at one time called 'Gold digger'. I needed no other information.

Paul and I grabbed the next available flight to Malaga, booked a couple of rooms at a hotel in Fuengirola, and hired a car for the duration of our visit.

We had no idea where the couple were staying, so decided to split up and peruse the bars hoping for a positive id. Paul found them liberally soused in the Amare Beach Club and followed them home after kicking out time.

We made an impromptu visit the following morning to their apartment on a quaint, narrow, paved street called Calle San Cristóbal. All of the buildings had white painted walls, black wrought-iron barred windows and balconies. Gloriously, the block paved walkways were crowded with a myriad of urns, pots and planters, displaying an abundance of flora. The recently watered plants added to a tranquil cool atmosphere and the close proximity of the buildings provided a welcoming shade. Contrast to the greeting we got from Miss Lange. She was furious that we'd tracked her down and were then standing on her doorstep accusing her of duplicity.

She was obviously hanging from last night's binge, and hardly in the mood for an interrogation. In her mind the settlement was a done deal, hence the vacation. Jim Maxwell was happy to hand over the money, and it was legally what she deserved.

But when I presented her with the evidence we had gathered and brought to light that her actions were described in law as obtaining a pecuniary advantage by deception, a criminal act, for which, given her past record, she would definitely receive a custodial sentence, she changed her tune, asking me if Jim had decided to press charges. I told her that it wasn't Jim but his family, at which point she got nasty again.

I gave her an ultimatum. If she walked away from the settlement and out of Jim Maxwell's life for good, she would receive a one-off payment of 50 grand, for her expenses, and the Maxwells wouldn't pursue criminal action.

For that, I was told to "fuck off," and had the door slammed in my face.

I slipped my card under the door of her apartment and we left her to stew in her own vitriolic juices.

That afternoon, Sarah called my mobile phone and acerbically accepted the offer. Obviously, she and Miss Robinson had had a chat about their prospects and decided that another spell in the clink wasn't very appealing.

Cartwright and Newport sorted out the arrangements, and the Maxwell people were left very happy with the new situation. So much so that Jim gave my company a £15,000 bonus, which I split three ways, and the promise of a holiday home of our choice any time we wanted it. Now would be the perfect time to cash in on that offer, but would he rent it to me for twelve months?

Only one way to find out, I made a direct call to his personal number. He was happy to hear from me but cautious about my request. After some deliberation he agreed. He wasn't planning on using it for a while himself, and as far as he knew they had no bookings in the place so far this year. He wasn't even going to charge me any rent, but I insisted. After all, the place had expenses, utility bills, a gardener and a housekeeper. I couldn't expect Jim to shell out for those as well. The costs would come out of Molly's fund.

Understandably, Jim wanted to know why I needed the villa for such a long time. The truth would have to wait until the investigation was over. For now, although I hated to give him a cock and bull story, I invented a fictitious holiday company that was looking for property to buy in the Algarve and needed a base of operation in situ, and Jim's Villa was absolutely ideal for our endeavours, a gift from the gods perhaps.

****

Mary Wilkins had worked for me for more than 20 years. Although it didn't start out that way, she was a tenant of mine, renting a small office space for her novice accountancy business, next to mine. But within two months, she was doing more work for me than she was for herself. Not only as a bookkeeper but receptionist, secretary and mini super-sleuth. She was a marvel: astute, academic and amiable, a triple 'A' all-rounder. She was also a very dear friend.

I'll never forget the day our friendship seeded. It was a Friday afternoon and I wanted to catch the 4:30 p.m. post. Mary had been with me for a while and had got used to my ritual pacing up and down the office dictating letters and her filling in the blanks. I had an annoying habit, without realising, of saying et cetera, et cetera, after starting a sentence, which she would competently finish off.

Amidst my second letter of the afternoon, I noticed a smirk across her face. Something I had said was amusing her, but she was too polite to share what was tickling her, and when I said, "Did I make a faux pas?" she smiled, said no, and got on with typing out the letters, as the deadline was looming.

After work on a Friday, I always used to nip into the Swan pub opposite, for an end-of-the-week sherbet before driving home. I'd just taken my first sip when Mary walked into the saloon and came and plonked herself next to me.

"I've got a confession to make," she blurted.

I couldn't think for the life of me as to where this was going.

"Have you ever seen the film *The King and I*? It's a musical."

"Musicals don't appeal to me, Mary, or Elizabeth either in fact."

"Well the main character in *The King and I* is played by Yul Brynner. He's the King of Siam, the old name for Thailand. You know who Yul Brynner is?"

"Of course, he's in the *Magnificent Seven*, the best Western ever made."

I knew where this was going now; people have often said that I bore a resemblance to the actor, especially when I've caught the sun, and seeing that my great-grandfather was from Vladivostok, the place of Yul's birth, maybe it's not surprising.

"Well, you look a bit like him."

"That has been said, Mary."

"And you've never seen *The King and I*?"

"No."

Mary toyed with her phone for a bit, then brought up a film clip of the said movie in which the king, dressed not unlike Sinbad, was pacing a room dictating a letter to

82

Deborah Kerr and ending his lines with, et cetera, et cetera, just like me. No wonder Mary found it funny; it was as if I'd based a part of my persona on Yul's performance. It made us both laugh. From that moment on, I knew we were going to be great mates.

****

Mary, as part of my team for the Baker investigation, was imperative, her assets were invaluable. Having a female perspective in past cases proved time and again to be a huge advantage, and her intuition was sometimes spooky. We also needed to continue with the day-to-day running of the Dave Skipper detective agency. Mary can do this blindfolded with one hand tied behind her back, and definitely via a luxury villa in southern Portugal. The office in Kings Ridge would have to be mothballed for the time being, internet and phone calls only.

The obstacles standing in the way of me poaching her for the duration were all too obvious, her husband and her children. But, when I thought about it, they weren't too insurmountable. Both of her daughters had fledged the family nest. They had careers and partners, and neither had children, so there wasn't that grandchild bond holding her back. And her husband, Nick, was such a keen fisherman. He seemed to be more married to a riverbank than his wife. He'd possibly relish more time to himself.

I hadn't seen Mary since Christmas Eve; she had no idea about the Baker case, so I arranged a meeting with her and Nick at their house on Saturday morning at 11:30.

She was curious of course but kept her questioning in reserve until I had laid out my plans.

The first thing I had to iterate was that everything I was about to reveal was confidential, and could not be disclosed to anyone outside these walls for fear of ruining the whole operation. I was gravely serious. They totally agreed.

I then went on to outline the events so far and my intentions on how to conduct the investigation, including putting together my dream team for a year-long stay in Portugal.

When I had concluded, Mary and Nick said nothing, just stared at me, their minds going ten to the dozen.

I softened the blow. "Every four weeks, I'll make it mandatory that all of my staff can have a long weekend off, to either go home or have their families come and stay at the villa, all expenses paid. I can't expect all of you to be away from each other for such a long period of time."

Mary was pensive; she didn't even look at her husband. "Of course I'll go, Dave, no question."

"What are your thoughts on Mary spending a year away, Nick?"

"Mary who?" he joked.

His wife tutted and smacked him on the shoulder with a backhander. "See what I have to put up with, Dave?"

She spoke for him, "Nick won't mind all. He'll be more than happy to sit by a lake fiddling with his tackle…" I'm certain there was no euphemism intended, so I only laughed internally. "…And I'll be more than relieved to be spared another of his One that got away stories."

Nick protruded his bottom lip and nodded at me solemnly.

"If anyone should ask where Mary is over the next twelve months, tell them that we have started up a holiday company in the Algarve, and we are out there prospecting for new apartments. That'll throw people off the scent for the time being."

Nick nodded again, his head full of questions.

"You think you gotta chance of finding her then, Dave?"

"Somebody in the wide world knows what happened to Molly Baker, Nick. We've just gotta winkle 'em out, mate. Portugal is the only place to start, and we gotta have boots on the ground turning over every stone. It's gonna take time, but I have every confidence in the people I have in mind for this investigation, most of all Mary; she is essential."

"I'm very happy for Mary to assist you on this particular case, Dave. What the Bakers have gone through is horrendous. I wouldn't wish it on my worst enemy, and if you can bring their nightmare to some kind of conclusion, whatever that might be, then I'm all for it. It's a righteous crusade you're taking on, and I'm proud for Mary to be a part of it."

Mary sidled up to him and gave him a hug.

"I mean, how have the Bakers kept sane after all these years of not knowing what happened to their child? I…" Nick went within himself and shook his head.

"I know, mate. It must take a lot of faith and self-control. I'd 'ave cracked years ago."

I left Nick and Mary's house safe in the knowledge that I'd secured my first team member. It was perhaps easier than I had imagined. Paul was going to be even easier; he took on mandates without question and he loved to travel.

My right-hand man had done 18 years in the British army, 13 of which he'd been attached to the Special Air Service, a fact not widely known in Kings Ridge. I actually found out quite by accident, at his house one time after several years in my employ. I asked to use the loo, but went into his study by mistake. On the wall was a framed scroll of commendation from his commanding officer, awarded to him for an action. Paul seemed almost embarrassed that I'd learnt his secret and asked that I keep it between ourselves, which I have. His select sets of skills have been extremely beneficial to the company in the past. His ability to gather information undetected is surreal. He has an almost robotic eye for detail and is highly versed in all things IT-related. He is also extremely cool under pressure. Unassuming, clinically neat and tidy, and positive, always positive.

Paul's private life is spent renovating his 17th century thatched cottage or riding his Harley Davidson motorbike. He has a girlfriend, an American called Cody, but I didn't know her that well. I had only met her on a few occasions. She is cabin crew for Virgin Atlantic, so is often away on long haul duties. She stays over when she is here, but never for long periods. From what I gather, she is intelligent, level headed, and free-spirited, so I doubted that Paul will have a problem as far as Cody is concerned.

His cottage lies at the end of a leafy single-track cul-de-sac, bordered by fields to the front and woodland to the rear. Its white walls are complemented with climbing roses and clematis, with neat stone paths and immaculate planted herbaceous beds. The words quaint and cosy are an understatement.

Paul was surprised to see me unannounced on a Saturday afternoon but welcomed me into his warm, amber glowing abode. The wood-burning stove took me instantly back to Catalonia.

After I apologised for cold calling on him, I went on to give him the sit/rep. He listened intently, his pale blue eyes not once averting from my own, his chin resting on the thumb of his raised fist. He waited for me to finish before speaking.

"When do we leave?" was all he needed to say on the matter. He was loyal to the core.

We then discussed the cases we had open at the moment and determined we could have them all sewn up by the end of February. It was a go; I had my core team members, the best possible start.

Before I left, I asked Paul if he had any pre-formed thoughts on Molly Baker's abductors. He contemplated his answer carefully. "I think that they are probably resourceful, audacious and smart. To have got away with this for so long, I doubt if they are opportunists. They may well be professionals, or invisible."

'Invisible', now that could prove to be tricky.

The shame and embarrassment weighed on me like a sixty kilo Bergen; I could barely climb out of the car. My good friend Olavo only lived at the opposite end of the high street to my office, yet I hadn't been to visit him in almost a year.

Olavo occupied a slender terraced cottage in attractive mews which only had residential parking. So I was forced to park in the high street and walk the length of the cobbled pavement to reach his house.

Somehow he'd seen me coming and opened his post-box-red front door to greet me, his stout silhouette haloed with yellow lamplight.

"A bit late with your Christmas present, Santa," he quipped.

"Olavo, mate, I'm sorry it's been so long. I feel so inadequate."

"You're here now, Dave." He shook my hand. "Come on in."

He used to hug me and kiss me on the cheek, but since his partner, Neil had succumbed to cancer three years ago, the flamboyance had departed from my convivial friend.

At one time you couldn't move in their living room without wrecking the Christmas decorations. It used to be more camp than a department store grotto, but now apart from a half dozen season's greetings cards trespassing on the mantlepiece, it could have been any time of the year.

From the kitchen, whilst making us both a coffee, Olavo enquired about the health of Elizabeth and my children. I assured him that all was good. When he trudged back into the living room holding two steaming mugs, he looked worn out, baggy faced and despondent.

"You look, knackered, mate. Had a long shift?"

My friend was a triage nurse in the A & E department of Stoke Mandeville hospital.

"Twelve-hour shift turned into a fifteen. I'm dead on my feet, but it's okay. I have tomorrow off, thank God. Back to work Monday morning." He sighed and slurped his coffee.

"Look, I don't want to keep you long. You need to hit the hay, my friend."

"Oh sleep can wait. What is it that's so important to make you march down here on a Saturday night after such a long absence? An inquiring mind wants to know."

I narrowed my eyes and crinkled my brow.

"How would you like to take a year off work?"

Olavo appeared to have been tranquilised. He was totally committed to his job and since Neil had died, he had ploughed all of his time into his calling, hardly taking a day off. It was his way of dealing with the grief, so the idea of not being at the hospital for 12 months must have seemed like he was being asked to swap his body with someone in Cambodia.

"What?" he uttered confused.

I gave him a highly abridged version of events so far and ended with the fact that I needed someone who I wholeheartedly trusted to be our interpreter on the ground, and a paramedic should we need one. It had just also occurred to me that Olavo was an excellent cook; his credentials were becoming more apparent.

Olavo got to his feet. "I must have a cigarette."

He went out the rear patio door and stood on the slippery decking in the cold. An orange ember glowed in the dark like an imminent meteorite, arcing to-and-fro, from his face to a 45-degree position a forearm's length away from his hip. I joined him.

"What do you think, are you up for it?"

"I think there are better-qualified people than me out there, Dave. I can't imagine the job entails just translating."

We had to insist on honesty at all times, or else this operation would collapse from within.

"You would, for the most part, be working alongside a Metropolitan police officer from Scotland Yard, almost entirely as a translator."

"You'll be giving me a gun and a fucking badge next!"

That was the first time since Neil had passed away that I'd heard Olavo joke about something.

"You can have a bulletproof vest if it makes you decide to join us."

"I need some time, Dave. The NHS is screaming out for nurses right now; my bosses aren't going to be too happy if I drop them in it."

I respected his integrity and dedication, and I agreed with him. I would be taking a highly skilled member of the nursing profession from the front line. It was time for a different approach.

"If you don't mind me asking, Olavo, how much do you take home a month from Stoke?"

He exhaled a fathomless amount of spent smoke into the chilled air. It plumed grey and ghostly like the venting of a steam whistle.

Without turning my way he said, "A tad above forty-seven hundred."

I did a quick calculation. "So about fifty-six grand a year?"

"Yeah, no matter how many hours I put in, the salary remains the same."

"What if I were to give you sixty grand to be my interpreter for a year, and give a further thirty to Stoke to help with their recruitment drive?"

"That's a lot of money, Dave. Where's all that coming from?"

"The pot mate, the Bakers have a reasonable fund, although, it's not bottomless."

"You don't have to give the NHS trust any money, Dave. If I were to take a year's leave, they would suspend my pay packet."

"Yeah sure, but I'd want to. It'd ease my conscience."

There was a silence. We'd reached a junction. I was starting to shiver out there on the algae smothered decking.

"I'll talk to my superiors on Monday, see how they feel, and if it's okay, how much notice they will need. I bet they'd want at least a month, maybe more given the time of year."

"That's fine." The tide was turning.

Olavo extinguished his cigarette into a terracotta plant pot half-filled with sand and a dozen other butts. Then we thankfully returned to the warm.

He made us another coffee, and we talked some more about the case. Olavo was from the north of Portugal but was well acquainted with the Algarve; he'd done his training at Faro hospital.

He spoke of the embarrassment he felt after his country had so atrociously let down the Baker family, for their heartache, and for the persecution they had endured from his fellow countrymen and the world's press. In his eyes, they were totally innocent and had suffered beyond belief. If he could help to alleviate any of that and return some pride back to Portugal, then he was willing to do that. But it all depended on whether he could get the time off work with a blessing.

I walked out of there feeling hopeful, yet devious. I'd paired Olavo up with Alfie fields, and I hadn't even secured Alfie's employment yet.

Mention Surrey, and you immediately think of wealth. Leafy pristine villages in the Surrey Hills, where bankers and city traders reside, or large, prestigious, private estates, with houses that sit at the very pinnacle of the UK's property market, Kudos in green surroundings, never more than an hour from London's West End.

DI Fields was accommodated in one such abode, on Oak Moor Park, a stone's throw from Walton-on-Thames. As I drove past the white picket entrance gates to the estate, I thought to my self, how does a copper on Alfie Fields' salary get to afford a place in here? They must start around five million quid.

My Sat/Nav brought me right up to the brick pillared, black wrought iron gates which barred my entrance to Carpenters Rest, a modern take on a Georgian style, yellow stock bricks and a black slate roof, cornicing, a central apex topped with coping stones, and arched, lead roofed dormer windows. It was two stories high, seven white sash windows wide, and had a triple garage on the right-hand side that was as big as my whole house. What a beautiful place. He must have pulled off some Blags to afford this gaff, I joked to myself.

The gates opened electronically, effortlessly, my presence detected from within.

I drove onto the gravel, admiring the craftsmanship in the oak-panelled garage doors; they'd been a labour of love for sure.

Alfie appeared from the opposite end of the building, hobbling adeptly on crutches like a tri-legged automaton, his raised plaster cast skimming stones just inches from the ground.

By the time I'd parked my Range, he'd made it to me.

"Found us alright?" he said as I exited the climate-controlled atmosphere, into the cold crisp air.

"Not a hitch," I assured him

"This is my parent's house, Dave; I'll explain all when we get inside the warm."

He spun and took off at a nifty pace.

A glass-roofed pagoda sheltered a flagstone path down the length of the house and then took an acute left angle along the edge of an expansive, highly maintained stretch of lawn, with immaculate stripes, towards a granny annexe shrouded in mature shrubs that obscured it from view at the front of the property.

"Your dad did well for himself then, Alfie?" I remarked as we entered the single bedroom abode.

"He was a chippy, high-end, worked on some very exclusive pads; he built this place himself, just before he retired."

Alfie led us into the kitchen/diner, where I was greeted with the smell of freshly percolated coffee.

"Fully prepared I see."

"It's always coffee o'clock in my house, Dave. Want one?"

"Spot on."

I glanced around whilst Alfie tinkered with the crockery. The interior was cosy in an old-fashioned sort of way, but not the kind of taste I would have expected for a man in his 40s: patterned velour furniture, paisley carpets and heavy drapes.

"The annexe was added five years ago for my grandparents; unfortunately they only got to enjoy it for three, so when my marriage broke down last year, rather than sell our family home, my parents invited me to stay here, rent-free. It works out well. My kids are only fifteen minutes away, and I can look after this place when mum and dad are away, which is a lot; they have a villa in Spain."

"Oh, whereabouts?"

"Actually it's on Menorca."

"Oh lovely, I've never been."

"You should, it's a beautiful island, quieter than the more popular Balearics, better for family holidays."

"I'll bear it in mind."

"Shall we?" Alfie indicated that we relax in the living room. His laptop was open on the coffee table, alongside a couple of beige document wallets. The top one was marked in red felt tip pen 'Baggage handlers May 1st 2002 to May 15th 2004'.

Alfie clambered onto the couch, whist I surrendered to a rather pleasant armchair.

"I see that you have the baggage handlers file there, Alfie. What are your thoughts on the ground crew being potential spotters?"

"It's a good idea, Dave, one that hasn't been overly explored. As far as I'm aware, nobody has any solid evidence pointing towards a perpetrator whatsoever. This means everyone in Viana do Fao the day Molly disappeared is a suspect."

"But have any of the baggage handlers ever been considered a suspect?"

"I don't believe so."

I screwed up my face and pondered the information.

"I've gotta ask this, Alfie, before we proceed any further, just to see if we're on the same page. Do you believe that the Bakers had anything to do with their daughter's disappearance? Not your professional stance, but your own personal view."

His reaction was clear and crisp. "No way, no way!"

"Hundred percent?"

He gathered his thoughts before answering.

"I've worked closely with this family for many years now. I'm suspicious by nature. It's one of the reasons I'm a copper. I know when someone is lying, or trying to hide something. It becomes intuitive. There's nothing there, Dave, not a sliver. They've always remained open, forthcoming and honest. Considering the grief they've had to endure, it's a miracle they are still together as a family. God knows mine isn't, but they are strong, Dave, and definitely not guilty."

That's what I wanted to hear. Alfie continued.

"Mind you if I were new to the case, fresh out of training, I wouldn't be so sure."

"How do you mean?"

"There's a hole in the Bakers' story, one that is yet to be explained and therefore it casts doubt."

"What hole?"

"The missing 12 miles, or The Magic Miles, as the press dubbed them."

This was unfamiliar to me. I asked him to explain.

"The Bakers had a hire car for six days; its mileage is written down on the hire agreement when they took it out. The trips they made in the car have been meticulously examined many times, but the odometer when surrendered to the police, had 12 more miles on it than can be accounted for. The Bakers can't explain it, so therefore it remains suspicious."

I studied the patterns on the carpet. Something wasn't right, not just with the carpet.

"You're referring to it as missing miles?"

"Yes."

"But surely, it should be kilometres, it's a Portuguese car, right?"

"Yeah, but what's the difference, it's just our way of speaking, miles is what we are used to."

"There's a massive difference, mate. Look…" I got my phone out and swiped to the calculator: 12 kilometres equalled only 7.45 miles. "If the original report was in Portuguese, then they would have written kilometres. The British police thinking in miles makes it seem more difficult to write off. Seven and a-bit miles is much better for the Bakers to explain. Do you wanna try and find those missing miles?"

"I absolutely do, Dave. Where do we start?"

"I'll just call my wife and tell her I'm gonna be late getting back."

Elizabeth was not the slightest bit troubled; our traditional New-Years-Eve slap-up Indian meal could wait until the evening.

When I came off the phone, Alfie was shaking his head.

"What's up?" I said.

"All these years, Dave, we've been thinking in miles, it's been a bone of contention. Now you've come along and within half an hour made us all look like idiots. I feel so stupid."

"It's not your fault, mate. That report was done well before you took on the job. It's just a translation problem, something that I'm going to entirely correct."

"I still feel like a dip-shit!"

"Put it behind ya, mate. We're moving on. I don't suppose you have a dozen whiteboards kicking about, do you?"

Alfie grunted a laugh. "I've got a couple marker pens of different colours in my briefcase if that helps…. But hold on a minute, I've got an idea. Follow me to the garage."

Remnants of snow were doggedly still clinging to the verges, reluctant to leave, like inconsiderate party guests. We entered the cavernous garage through a side door that needed a persuasive shoulder to budge it.

"Hasn't been open in a while, Dave, a bit stiff, like my legs."

There were three cars side by side, under wraps within. Alfie told me they were a 1967 E-type Jaguar Roadster, his grandparents 1989 Rover Vitesse, which had only 12,000 miles on the clock, and a 1966 Ford Anglia van, his dad's first-ever work vehicle. I was tempted to pull the covers off, but we had a lot of work to do.

We passed a wide wooden staircase leading to the loft above, which I was told held a full-size snooker table, then carried on to the rear of the garage and a sectioned off carpenter's workshop. Against the back wall was a stack of six heavy white doors with over large handles.

"They were in the annexe, but I took them out when I moved in. It made the place so much bigger. Will they do?"

"Spot on mate." I was a perpetual user of the whiteboard.

We spent time taking the handles off the doors and then lined them up side by side against the wall.

Whilst I rustled up us both another well-earned mug of coffee, Alfie set to work printing off all the information he had on the hire car and its detailed, heavily scrutinised journeys. We also had a plethora of photographs to work with, pictures from every angle of the Renault Megane, and of every place they had visited.

Apart from the journey from the airport to the apartment, they had been to Lidl three times, once to the beach, and once to George's uncle's at Monte Clérigo.

We decided to break down each occasion, right up to when it was loaded onto the transporter to take it away for forensic investigation.

I wrote on the head of the first door in bold black letters 'Hire Company & airport'. On the second I wrote 'Airport to the apartment'. The next was for the three trips to Lidl. The fourth one was for the beach trip, the fifth for Monte Clérigo, leaving the sixth empty for now.

For my entire working life as a private investigator, I have used hire cars for surveillance work, and the best ones to use are the budget companies. Their cars are low end, inconspicuous and above all cheap to rent. The downside being the companies themselves are usually situated at airports, so you either have to go get them or have them driven out to you, which of course adds to the cost.

Now, if you book a car online, the paperwork is done at the time of the booking, apart from the mileage, which is recorded on a form by the person who is handing you the keys after an inspection. They might well do the inspection in a holding lot and then drive the vehicle to you at arrivals or at their pick-up point on the airport grounds. So, in theory, the odometer has gained some digits already, depending on how far it has travelled.

We knew that the Bakers used Thrifty car hire 17 years ago. We wondered if the company were still there and how far their holding pen was from the airport. The man to answer this question was Faustino. Alfie called at once, he was happy to find out for us. Within the hour, our Portuguese cop had the information we needed. Thrifty was still in operation in the exact same spot, and the holding pen was 0.8 of a kilometre away.

That was our first find, and it felt good to mark it up on our whiteboard (door).

In the Bakers' statement, it clearly states they followed their friends Alan and Claire's car from the airport along the N125. Alan and Claire had been coming to the Algarve for 15 years and knew the roads like the backs of their hands, and even though the A22 motorway was quicker, their preferred route was more scenic.

Whilst Alfie fired up Google maps on his laptop, I had an idea. We could double-check this if Faustino was still game.

"Alfie, could you ring Faustino back and ask him what he is doing today. It would be really helpful if someone could actually drive the Bakers' routes and get an accurate reading of the kilometres travelled on each journey."

"I can ask Dave, but it is New-Years-Eve!"

Alfie cupped his phone after a brief conversation with our Portuguese liaison officer. "He says he's busy today, Dave."

"Offer him £200 for a few hours work."

"He's just un-busied himself."

"Tell him we'll email him the exact routes."

Alfie did this. Then, we zoomed in on Google maps to an index of 500m = 20mm, laid the screen flat, and starting at Faro airport, used a length of string to follow the contours of the roads that the Bakers' party took.

In actual fact, the N125 route was 2.2 kilometres longer than the A22, but here it was in front of us, according to their report, the Portuguese police had assumed the families had taken the motorway as most holidaymakers would; another piece of incompetence which had gone unnoticed for 17 years.

I had another thought. Did the hire car company note down the tenths of a kilometre when filling out the odometer reading? If not, there could be another possible 0.9 of a kilometre already on the clock before the Bakers took it on.

The workshop was starting to resemble an incident room. I'd pinned the two maps I'd brought with me to the walls, one of Portugal and one of the Algarve. We had photos and statements scattered about the room and the whiteboards were taking shape. I made a joke, "Who needs an operations base in Portugal when we have one here!"

Alfie smiled, but I could see that I'd frightened him half to death. His parents would love a team of strangers working out of their garage.

The largest gain we made that afternoon was with the supermarkets. There are two Lidl in Viana, the one the Bakers had passed driving in from the airport was the one they had frequented three times. They didn't realise there was one closer to the apartment block, because they simply hadn't seen it. Once again the police had assumed the nearest Lidl had been the one the Bakers had used, a simple but costly misinterpretation of events. We calculated the extra mileage used via Google maps and found another 6 kilometres. Faustino later confirmed this.

We'd slashed a total of 9 kilometres from the 'Magic Miles', maybe even 9.9k, but we needed more. We read on, looking for mistakes.

The trip to George's aunt and uncle's house, Villa Sarah, was said to be a distance of 34 kilometres door to door, a round trip of 68k. And that is correct if the measurement is taken at the post box at the head of their drive, but according to Faustino, the dirt track drive which meanders up to the villa through wild scrub, Olive, Fig and Almond trees, is 0.6k long, adding a further 1.2k. We almost had it. What else could we find?

The Bakers' statement read that they had stopped at a service station on the way back from Monte Clérigo. The last time I had used a motorway service station abroad was in Spain, and we had to cross over the road to get to it via an off-ramp and a bridge. We checked out the one in question on the map. Sure enough, it was on the opposite side of the road. George Baker would have had to make the same manoeuvre as we did in Spain. Zooming in until the on-screen measurement was 20mm = 20m, we calculated that this pit stop added a further 0.8k to their journey.

There was one more thing. On the beach trip, George said that he parked at the far end of the car park, to be close to the beach shop and the pushchair ramp. This measured 0.2k from the entrance, times that by two for the outbound journey and we had it, near enough, the missing miles (kilometres).

It was exciting; we'd cracked a vital part of the puzzle. Nothing to aid us with Molly's disappearance, of course, but a significant piece to help exonerate George and Jill. We toasted our success with another mug of java.

Today's exercise, albeit painstaking, proved that Alfie, Faustino and I could work together to great effect. I dearly wanted them to be on the team and wondered how they'd react. There was only one way to find out.

When Alfie returned with the coffee, I was reclined in a lovingly turned oak carver, right foot on left knee, with a satisfied smirk on my face.

"What's up?" he said.

"How do you fancy being a part of the team in Portugal, my friend?"

Alfie grinned. "I thought you'd never ask!"

I was glowing. "Great," I said. "Can you get the time off work?"

"I'm not exactly busy putting bad boys behind bars right now, Dave, and pretty certain that I could get a year's non-paid leave sorted out. I'll talk to my Super tomorrow. I'm sure it'll be fine, when are you thinking of starting?"

"Mid-Feb' at the moment, mate. I've got a base sorted out, and it's only 15 miles from Viana Do Fao."

"Perfect. Who do we have onboard already, or is it just you and me?"

I gave him the team sheet thus far; he was keen to meet them all.

"I'll pay you for your time, of course, Alfie."

"I don't need a lot of money, Dave. Just pay me what you think is fair. I'm quite prepared to work on this case gratis. It's well beyond time for a conclusion, whichever way it turns out, for the Bakers' and the whole world's ease."

I concurred as the room got a little chillier with the thought of how this might end. The garage held its breath whilst both our minds wandered off for a few moments.

"We need one other person to make the team complete, Alfie."

He snapped back into the present, "Oh, do you have someone in mind?"

"Your counterpart in Portugal. He's come through brilliantly today, and you've already told me he's a decent human being."

"Faustino? He's a top bloke, moral, fastidious and brimming with integrity. He's also desperate to bring an end to this case, although he'd like to find Molly. As with the whole of Portugal, he feels disgraced that a crime such as this could happen on his own turf."

"But would he work for me? Would his bosses allow that to happen, outsiders pulling the strings in their dominion?"

"The Judiciária never wanted the British police involved in the first place. It seemed like they thought it a bit of an insult to bring in foreign detectives to do something they were competent to tackle, but we all know how that turned out. Their Policia has very different methods of investigation to ours. It took pressure from our government on theirs, before they relented and let us in. So to answer your question, no they would not be happy having a private enterprise doing their job for them, and poaching Faustino, I'd say would be near on impossible."

"That's what I thought, but I have a cunning plan."

Alfie then quoted a line from the TV show *Black Adder goes Forth*. "Is it as cunning as a fox who's just been appointed professor of cunning at Oxford University?"

I chuckled. No wonder he and Sam got on so well. They had the same taste in comedy.

"Indeed, it is, sir," I replied.

My plan was to send Bento Sampaio, the Chief Superintendant of the Policia Judiciária a letter, putting him in a deep quandary. Some might call it blackmail. I didn't care. Having the Portuguese police working with us instead of against us was fundamental.

The first thing I needed to do was phone Olavo, to see if he could translate my letter a.s.a.p. He was out taking the air, but he said he'd do it when he got home. I emailed him the pre-written letter, and within an hour it came back to me translated.

In the meantime, Alfie had called Faustino back and asked for Bento's email address. Faustino gave it to us but was curious as to why we wanted it. Alfie said that we had a proposition for him, but said nothing more at this time.

It was sent. When Alfie read the English version, he grinned. "I'd love to see the Bakers' faces when they read this."

"You can, mate, next Saturday."

"Afraid I can't, Dave. It's my weekend with the boys. We'll have to reschedule if you want me along."

"Right, I'll see if I can shuffle things around. It's an important meet."

It was 7 p.m. and high time I got going. I made an offer to help clear things up in the garage, but Alfie would have none of it. His boys would enjoy helping him next week, and besides he wanted to log everything we'd discovered today on computer, while it was fresh.

We shook hands. "Progress, may it continue," I said.

"Sam told me you had a way of getting things done, Dave. I can see what she means."

"It's team-work, mate. The whole is greater than the sum of its parts, Aristotle. We're gonna need a top team to see this through, and I think we're nearly there. Just gotta get Faustino and Olavo on board."

I pulled onto my drive at 9:15 p.m. Fortuitously, my phone rang as I cranked up the handbrake. It was Alfie. Bento Sampaio had granted Faustino a special role, to assist us for one year exclusively on the Baker case, but with one stipulation, that he be kept informed on all activities within his jurisdiction, and be privy to any new information connected to the case. This was no problem for me. The letter had worked. We had Faustino.

I tried calling Olavo to thank him for the translation. He didn't answer, so I just left a message wishing him a Happy New Year.

Before my front door key had entered the lock, a beam of headlights from a rain-soaked vehicle illuminated the porch. I turned to see Abdul from our local curry house, stomping towards me with a steaming white plastic carrier bag in his hand, perfect timing, the grub had arrived on cue.

"Lovely, Abdul. Do I owe you anything?"

"No, it's alright. Mrs Skipper paid for it over the phone."

I delved into my trouser pocket and pulled out a fiver. "Er, have a drink on me."

"Yeah, one," he said cheekily, smiled and retreated to his car. "Happy New Year," he shouted back."

I reciprocated.

We never change our order. We know what we like, and have it time and again. Half a Tandoori chicken, four vegetable samosas, four plain poppadoms, with salad, pickles and dips, delicious, especially with a large glass of Chardonnay to wash it down.

Boring, some might say, but we are all creatures of habit, especially criminals I find. But they sometimes digress, and it's this deviation that I hope to exploit. They have made mistakes, and honest old fashioned detective work will rout them out.

Elizabeth interrupted my train of thought with a question.

"This team you've put together, Dave. Do you think they've got what it takes to crack this case?"

"I do," I said earnestly.

"What makes you so sure?"

"We're all paddling in the same pond, my dear."

****

The letter:

Bento Sampaio
Chief Superintendent
Policia Judiciária (South)
Portimão
Algarve
Portugal

31st December 2020

Dear Sir.

My name is Dave Skipper, owner of a private investigation agency for nearly forty years.

I have been assigned by the Baker family to investigate in its entirety, the disappearance of their daughter Molly, from the resort of Viana do Fao, Costa do Andrea, in April 2003.

My writing to you is for two reasons. One is to make you fully aware of a terrible oversight committed by the Policia Judicicária, which has not only completely devastated a whole family, but put them under suspicion, and the world spotlight, as possible suspects in the abduction of their own daughter for almost two decades.

The oversight regards the so-called 'Magic Miles'. As you recall, twelve extra miles on their rental car's odometer could not be accounted for.

My second reason is to obtain your support and your trust in my team and me over the forthcoming year.

Permit me to explain:

Today, I went to the home of Detective Inspector Alfie Fields to discuss the Molly Baker case. At this meeting, I was made aware for the first time of the twelve missing miles, an anomaly that has smeared prejudice on top of the Baker family since its revelation. I was soon to realise that the phrase was unfairly disproportionate to begin with, by being called miles, it should have been kilometres, a shorter distance by far, and therefore, by definition, easier to explain.

In our opinion, this was a translation problem that nobody had the will or enthusiasm to correct. It labelled the Bakers' as liars, manipulators and murderers, in the eyes of the public, the media and the police, and played a pivotal role in leaving this case unresolved.

It was also inadequate policing from your own department.

When you impounded the Bakers' Renault hire car, the reading on the odometer was 62,692 kilometres. The reading taken by the hire company when they handed it to the Bakers was 62,528. A sworn statement given by the Bakers to your officers contained a detailed breakdown of the journeys they had taken with the car during their stay, which they did so willingly.

Your detectives then calculated how many kilometres the combined journeys should have taken. A figure of 152K was assumed. Adding this to the starting odometer reading comes to 62,680, twelve kilometres short, missing kilometres that, until now, have never been explained.

We have found them.

Using straightforward detective methods, in less than eight hours, DI Fields, your officer Faustino Vela and I retraced the exact car journeys; Faustino Vela even used his own car, in his own time, to drive the routes.

We discovered the missing kilometres, and this is how we did it:

1. Thrifty car Hire brought the Renault Megane from their compound to arrivals for George Baker to drive away. That distance was 0.8k, but not recorded by your police officers. Faustino Vela drove the distance twice to make certain.

2. Thrifty do not register tenths of a kilometre when reading the odometer. There may have been up to a further 0.9k on the clock before the car was handed over.

3. It was assumed by your officers that the Bakers took the A22 motorway from Faro airport to their apartment at Viana do Fao. In fact, they took the more scenic route of the N125, a journey longer by 2.2k. This was an elementary error on your department's behalf, one that could have easily been rectified, had they bothered to ask.

4. The Bakers used a Lidl supermarket on three separate occasions, one that they had seen on their way from the airport. Your police presumed that they had in fact used another Lidl, a closer one, but unbeknownst to the Bakers, at the other end of Viana. The mistaken difference between the two supermarkets added another 6 kilometres to the missing twelve.

5. On Saturday, the Bakers visited George's relations in Monte Clérigo.
Using Google maps your department worked out that they had travelled 68k on the journey, there and back. But that calculation only took into account the road leading up to the villa's drive entrance, and not the drive itself. Faustino travelled the length of the drive also; a dirt track through orchards 0.6k long, which when doubled added a further 1.2k.

6. On the return journey from Monte Clérigo, the family had to make a pit stop at a service station. The forecourt was on the opposite side of the motorway, meaning that they had to exit their carriageway, cross over the motorway via a bridge and two roundabouts and

navigate to the service station. Including doing this in reverse, it added yet another 0.8k.

7. The last journey the Bakers made in the hire car was to the beach. Faustino travelled there and discovered that where George had parked was at the far end of the car park, close to a concrete access ramp for buggies, pushchairs etc.; this distance doubled with a one-way system for exiting traffic, further added an extra 0.6k.

As you can see, this is a total of 12.5k, the 'Magic Miles' accounted for. The catchphrase that has cast a black cloud over the Baker family for 17 years, pointed the finger of blame directly at them, and diluted efforts into finding the real culprits of this heinous crime.

It took three detectives less than a day to discover the actual facts using good policing methods, and detailed analysis, something that should have been employed years ago by the police department investigating this crime in 2003, your department.

I am not presenting this evidence to you as a way of showing off, or to shame your department, but simply to show you the results my team can achieve.

Given access to all of the files in this case, and the cooperation and assistance of the Policia Judiciária, I believe that we shall finally bring a conclusion to the Molly Baker disappearance.

You have my assurance that our investigation, when completed, will widely be known as a joint effort between Portuguese and British forces, but will stay undercover for the duration, for the best possible chance of success.

I have secured a private villa close to Viana do Fao for one year's tenancy, and my team of six will be staying there in the guise of a holiday company looking for property to buy.

I close by asking your permission to outsource Faustino Vela to us for the entire operation. He is in agreement with our plans, and I feel his experience, local knowledge and dedication to this cause is paramount to our prosperity.

Please let me know your decision within 24 hours.

Yours sincerely,

Dave Skipper

5

Golden nugget

Victorian architecture has always impressed me. The attention to detail – the ornate brick bonds, the reliefs and cornicing, and the use of contrasting brick colours to make patterns on the facades – was so excessive for regular housing, yet the craftsmanship in these Gothic designs has endured the test of time, and then some. If you are considering buying a Victorian property, you are investing in a statement, a solid building with resplendent character, a dwelling that needs to be lovingly preserved as its originally desired concept.

I stood beside my Range Rover, hands-on-hips, on the Bakers' gravel drive admiring the beauty of their three-storey red and cream bricked detached house. My breath made vapour plumes in the cold morning air.

It had taken me two and a half hours to drive to Branksome Wood, on the outskirts of Bournemouth, Dorset, and my spine was appreciating the full arch I was giving it to relieve the tension in knotted muscles.

The horseshoe drive had an island of mature tight-budded Rhododendrons at its centre and was generously wide enough to accommodate my big lump of a vehicle, six times over. A pad like this would probably carry a price ticket of around £600,000 in these parts, so the Bakers must have been on quite good incomes at some point to afford it.

The 7ft high wooden gates were wide-open and sported large signs on the outside warning, 'Beware of the dogs'. I presumed this was a deterrent to keep the paps and the nosy Parkers away, but I couldn't hear any barking, so if there were guard dogs, they weren't doing a very good job, or maybe they were obedient to a word.

My eyes were drawn to the inset porch: a semi-circular arch entrance, partially glazed with stained-glass panels, and decorative ceramic floor tiles. Standing in front of an overly wide red front door was Sophie Baker, beaming a radiant smile that helped to illuminate the dimly lit space.

"Mr Skipper!" Her words were light and playful. She sounded almost surprised to see me, even though I was fully expected.

"Dave, please," I implored her.

"Yes, of course. Sorry, Dave. You found us okay then?"

"Sat/Nav, brought me straight to your door." She smiled again, a smile that said of course.

In my line of work, we often come across some very unsavoury canine abettors. So naturally, I've become rather jaded towards the beasties.

"What kind of dogs do you have, Sophie?" I gingerly enquired.

She laughed. "We don't have any. We're not really doggy people. Those signs are just to keep the riffraff away. Some people think they have a right to come and harass us. The signs help, and well, it's not as bad as it used to be now. Come on in."

I was mightily relieved.

She led me into the hall and took my coat. The place was decorated to a high standard, hung with some quality paintings and interesting artefacts. A broad carpeted staircase ran up the left-hand side of a partition wall. I could see through to a bright kitchen at the rear and was invited into the sitting room on the right.

It's a surreal thing, meeting infamous people in the flesh, and it's obviously a status they never intended to acquire, yet, abhorrently, the Bakers had become celebrities by default. Which I can only imagine was debilitating at the very least. Who'd want what they had become?

George, Jill and Nile got up from their seats to greet me. It was an awkward moment. I wanted to appear as confident and professional without proclaiming that I might be this super-sleuth who'll definitely find their daughter, and alive. Yet at the same time, I didn't want to treat them as TV personalities, but I'd seen them on the telly so many times, it was hard not to be affected.

My preconceptions soon waned. They were warm and attentive people, calm, but ever so slightly expectant. Jill offered me a coffee, which I accepted and she nipped out to the kitchen to make me one.

George suggested a deeply cushioned armchair for me, whilst they took up the couch on the other side of a low mahogany coffee table.

"Alfie Fields sends his apologies; he couldn't make it today, family commitments."

"That's fine. We'll catch up with Alfie," said George.

"Well…" I began, "apart from it being appropriate and necessary to meet you all in the flesh, so to speak, it gives us a great opportunity to talk without any pressure. Informally, to look at where we're at, and discuss whether there is anything different you'd like me to do. Whether you have any more information that can be of use and to tell me what your expectations might be from my investigation."

Jill brought the coffee into the sitting room; it was perfect, just the way I had asked her to make it.

"We also need to talk money, an ugly word I know, but we have to be crystal clear, we can't do this without proper funding…"

George interrupted me.

112

"We have £850,000 at our disposal, Dave. If this is not enough, we will find whatever it takes."

The sincerity burned in his eyes.

I pulled out a file from my briefcase and laid it on the table in front of them. Extracting a page, I said, "This is a breakdown of expenses thus far and an estimate of what I foresee it might cost for the year-long investigation. Incorporating, renting the villa in Portugal, all of my staff's salaries, plus travel expenses, sustenance and a slush fund for any further payments, such as other professional bodies that may be brought in during the investigation. There is also my fee, of course, paid at the end of the investigation. The contracts for which I have here for you to sign."

I handed duplicate papers to both George and Jill and to Sophie who had assumed the executor role for the family.

"I'd like you to read and sign those today, before I leave."

They all nodded earnestly.

"So, where's the villa you have rented, Dave. Is it close to Vianna?"

"We have been extremely fortunate there, George. It belongs to another client of mine who has lent it to us for a fraction of its real cost. It's an ultra discrete property about a fifteen-minute drive north of Vianna, in a secluded area near Colinas Verdes. My team can operate out of there with impunity. It's not too far from the A22 either, so handy to get about the Algarve."

Sophie spoke next. "Who do we have on the team, Dave. Are they all experienced detectives?"

"There are six of us, all but one are professional investigators. The only one who isn't, is a dear friend of mine, Olavo. He's also a medic. He's Portuguese and will be our translator."

I hadn't secured Olavo yet, but I was pretty confident he'd be on board. I then went on to give them the full breakdown of the team. They were surprised but delighted that Alfie Fields would be joining us. They considered him with high regard and as a friend of the family.

"I know that it's early days still, Dave, but have you formed any ideas on what might have happened to Molly based on the evidence you have obtained so far?" asked Jill, the anguish was taut in her facial muscles.

"Yes, I have some ideas, but I don't want to reveal too much at this stage that might result in false hope or cause you any more angst, but I will say this, and I'm sorry to be so frank, but I don't believe Molly's abduction was a random spur of the moment chance. I believe that this was a planned operation carried out by an individual or a group of individuals who chose Molly for a reason and that she was identified sometime before the night of her disappearance, either at the airport, the supermarket or the resort."

"And why do you believe that?"

"Well, firstly, Jill, it's my experience that an opportunistic thief going around randomly trying door handles wouldn't have an outlet for a stolen child. It's too problematic to try to make any money from and hard to execute without making a noise or being seen. And I'm sorry again to be so blunt, but according to my research, child molesters who act on impulse are usually already within the situation, and then seize upon it, not chance upon it by accident. I'd say that is quite rare. With child abduction for sexual gratification, there is usually a pattern of obsession, observation, and opportunity, meaning a child would be picked out first, and then watched for some time before they are taken."

"So you think this was definitely sexually motivated?" asked George.

I had to really detach myself from my emotions here, and deliberate this clinically, after all this was a baby we were talking about.

"Not necessarily, George, no. Some children, especially very young ones such as Molly have been known to be abducted for organisations that provide children for bereaved families who have lost their own, or for couples who cannot have a child for whatever reason. There's a diabolical industry hiding in plain sight. But look, I'm just speculating here. We have no evidence whatsoever that Molly's disappearance is any of these things, but my team is experienced enough to find out."

The family were subdued for a while, then Sophie said, "This has dragged on for so long, and so many people have investigated, and re-investigated, and searched and looked and looked. I find it quite astonishing that there isn't a single piece of evidence that might point to what happened to my sister all those years ago. I mean people talk, don't they eventually? Isn't that how most crimes get solved, through someone spilling the beans, grassing up, 'fessing?"

I nodded in affirmation. "You're right, Sophie. Ordinarily, but your sister's case is quite unique. The whole world wants to know what happened to Molly Baker, yet no one's heard a thing."

I then tried to placate her with some knowledge and inspiration.

"We have an advantage on our side. My agency is not the police. We are not so tied down with bureaucracy. Sure, we have to work within the law, but we sometimes stretch those boundaries to the limit, and I have no one to answer to, so I make my own rules. Meaning that we sometimes employ methods that the police, especially the Portuguese police, would not accommodate, and these methods often yield results."

Nile spoke for the first time. "Do you rough people up?"

"Not if I can help it, but Paul is very handy if it came to an altercation."

It felt like they needed more.

"I can see from what I've read so far that some key factors have played a part in thwarting the investigation..." All four of them stared at me intently, on the edge of the sofa. "...The funding being stopped on three separate occasions, that's a no brainer."

"That won't happen this time," assured Sophie.

"I've no doubt in that, Sophie... The lack of communication between the British and Portuguese police departments was scandalous. It seems to me that both sides wanted the glory and neither wanted to cooperate fully with the other. It's been a travesty of justice. That will not happen again. We have secured full compliance from both police forces. In fact, we have a member of each force on the team." I beamed.

"So where do you intend to start from when you get there?"

"Molly's case has never had a golden nugget."

"What does that mean?" asked Jill, wrinkling her brow.

"It's a detective term. It means the smallest of clues which lead to a breakthrough; it's a starting point and the one thing that has me frustrated. But I've got some ideas, some things that the Policia Judiciaria didn't peruse, and let's face it, after just 48 hours of investigation, when 98 percent of their leads went cold, they seemed to lose interest in pursuing anyone else apart from your good selves."

"Those bloody twelve missing miles!" blurted Jill.

"Quite," I said, "Or rather we should say missing kilometres."

"Eh?" said George.

I had been longing to produce the next document from my briefcase. It was going to lift 17 years of black cloud from the Bakers' crushed shoulders.

"The British media invented the phrase Magic Miles, a misleading headline. The Portuguese hire car's odometer measures in kilometres, a shorter distance by far, and easier to explain."

I gave them a bullet point rundown of the mistakes the police had made during their calculation of the kilometres travelled in the hire car.

After they had read it, tears were running down Jill's cheeks and George looked shell shocked. The kids quickly grabbed my report and scanned through it.

"Are these facts?" George was astonished, his mind working overtime.

"Took Alfie, Faustino Vela and me just one afternoon to discover this calamity, and I'm disgusted that the finger of blame has been pointed at you for seventeen years for no valid reason at all. If I were you, I would be filing for compensation."

"One thing at a time, Dave. Let's find Molly first."

"Do you all believe that she is still alive?"

"We've never given up hope, Dave."

"That's good enough for me."

"I can't believe this," sobbed Jill. "All those years of being spat on by half the world, and now this." She held up the paper. "Vindication!"

George put an arm around his wife. "Unbelievable," he said, shaking his head.

I went on to tell them how I had used the findings to put leverage on Chief Superintendant Sampaio into granting us his police force's full assistance in the investigation, and lending us Faustino for a year. George was dumbfounded.

We carried on talking for an hour, in which time I secured the release of 300 boxes of written correspondence and evidence that the Bakers had compiled over the years. It had occupied their dining-room, and Jill was hugely relieved to be getting the room back. I would arrange a van to come and pick it up during the week.

George asked if it would be alright if they could come out to Portugal to thank the whole team in person for what we were doing. But given the clandestine protocol we were working under, I had to deny his request. If one reporter spotted them in Colinas Verdes, it would blow the lid on the whole thing, and our covert operation would be scuppered. They were disappointed but understood.

As I drove away from the Bakers' house, Jill's parting words repeated in my head. 'Today was a good day in looking for Molly'. It contented me to think I'd brought some hope to the family. To paraphrase Winston Churchill in some manner, today was the start of the beginning of the end of 17 years of living bereavement. I was hoping I could live up to my proclamations.

I was itching to get the ball rolling, but my agency had at least ten cases on the go right now, all of which had to be concluded before we left. Alfie had a string of hospital appointments to attend. Olavo was working a two-month notice, and Faustino would be going to California for three weeks in February, to visit his parents.

I pulled into a petrol station, filled up with diesel, paid at the pump, and then parked in a vacant bay next to the shop to study my diary. The sweet spot was Monday, March the 9th, our official start date for Operation... It didn't have a name yet, that will come when we're up and running.

To rubber stamp it, I called everyone there and then. Nobody quibbled; Mary said she'd get online and book the flights right now.

I then made a phone call to Brian Wells, owner of a removals company I'd recommended clients to over the years. He could store the evidence boxes in his unit until it was time to ship them out, along with all the office equipment we'd need to set up for an investigation room in the villa. Mary could make a list on Monday, which would include at least 25 whiteboards. I did like my whiteboards. We'd use the slush fund to buy all the gear, and then sell it off when we were done.

Brian informed me that he had a half-loaded lorry going down to Marbella, then on to the Algarve to bring a removal back, a week on Tuesday. But nothing more that way until May, so I booked it. My stuff would only take up half a load anyway, so I would get the transportation cheap. Brian could be at the villa by 8 a.m. on that Friday, so I would have to fly out myself on Thursday to meet him. I asked if his lads would spend the day helping me to set up the office. He said as long as I paid their wages, he'd be happy to take the day off and install himself in a beach bar.

I then just had to call Jim Maxwell, to make sure it was okay to get in early. This was also fine; he'd inform the housekeeper to expect me.

***

Striding across the concourse in the arrival's lounge at Faro airport felt like I was walking on water. My upside-down mirror image reflected from the camel-coloured polished tiles. I'd left the frozen murk of London way behind me and was now beckoned by sunlight screaming through the glass frontage, demanding I abandon my coat and slip on a pair of flip-flops. Just a few hours away, it was a world of difference; no wonder people winter holidayed here.

I hadn't even spoken to Faustino Vela personally, let alone met him before, so was reservedly excited to get acquainted with the newest member of my squad, and all too surprised to be greeted by a fully emblazoned police car parked at the kerb.

"Senhor Skipper?" Faustino was reclining against his vehicle in a charcoal suit, one bent arm hugging the roof, sallow-skinned, lean and sharp-featured, with a black soup strainer above his top lip.

When I responded in the affirmative, he tapped the roof of the car twice and bounded towards me enthusiastically with his hand outstretched to greet me.

"Senhor Skipper," he said again, "it is a pleasure to finally meet you."

"The pleasure is all mine, Faustino. Please call me Dave."

"Ah, Senhor Dave."

"Just Dave."

"Dave, did you have a nice flight?"

"Very pleasant, yes. It's good to be in the sunshine at last; it's been a particularly cold winter this year."

"You had snow?"

"Plenty, more than enough. It's really only just cleared."

"We don't have snow in Algarve, only in the Serra da Estrela mountain range in the north. It's not for me."

"Look at us talking about the weather; anyone would think we were a couple of Brits."

"Not me, Senhor. Portuguese through and through."

Faustino straightened himself, testing his shirt buttons. His pride was impeccable.

"Good to hear it, fella. You gonna show me around in this?" I inclined towards the cop car.

"What? Oh no. I've just borrowed this from the pool. Don't have to pay for parking when you are in one of these babies…" He flashed his pearly whites at me. "…We'll go back to the station and get mine. I'm off this afternoon. We can take our time, get you settled in."

I knew his work ethic was faultless, but my first impressions of meeting the man were that he spoke perfect English, which was so handy, and that he was way too nice to be a detective. But this could have its advantages, seeing that we two would be working as a pair; the good cop, bad cop situation just might crop up.

After exchanging cars at his police station in Portimão, we hit the N125 again. Faustino wanted to show me the route the Bakers took to Vianna, the Lidl they used and the holiday resort itself, especially the infamous apartment block.

I'd seen pictures and TV footage, of course, everybody had, but nothing compares to being there. This was just a whistle-stop tour, yet sitting in Faustino's Peugeot 3008 outside number 27, the Bakers' old apartment really brought it home to me. A baby was snatched from that little block of white concrete, taken for God only knows what purpose during the night, vanished into thin air, leaving not a clue as to her abductors or the method used. It was like Scotty had beamed her up, yet this was no friendly extraction. This was something insidious. I shuddered as visions of despicable acts poisoned my mind.

Back on the road again we headed east, then before we hit Lagos, we took a left turn and went north up the N120 through rural villages, farmland and patchy scrub, continually climbing in elevation. The landscape here became crumpled, small villa topped hills and scattered white hamlets. After we passed under the A22, the road

121

itself was literally cut into the side of a large forested mound to our left.

We took a right onto a single-track road that cut through a lush pasture, crossed a small river and continued up another red-soiled hill. When we reached the brow, the vista in the valley below was pretty spectacular and reminded me a bit of the Vale of Aylesbury. A little further on we reached our destination, Colinas Verdes, a small number of private villas on the side of the hill with breathtaking views.

Jim Maxwell's villa, Vista do Vale, bordered the estate. Its drive curved around the white-walled grounds to an entrance at the rear, which offered the best views. From here, you could see the misty Atlantic, an endless strip, counter blue to the sky.

I'm gonna be quite happy here, I thought to myself.

Faustino levelled with the keypad for the electronic gates, but before I could relay to him the security code, they opened by themselves. Carlos, the caretaker had been watching our approach and beat us to it.

The drive meandered up through terraced gardens, switching back on itself twice before we landed at the front entrance, accessed by three tiers of large terracotta-tiled steps. Carlos and his wife, Ramona, stood patiently on the concourse, hands clasped in front of them, subservient yet undoubtedly the authority around here.

Faustino spoke to them in Portuguese. They shook hands, then spoke to me in very poor English, saying they were very pleased to meet me. I returned the greeting and continued by saying that I was grateful we could understand one another. Carlos pivoted his right hand like a seesaw, owning up to his limited vocabulary.

I only had one small bag; Carlos took it from me and said he'd show us around. Ramona went back to weeding the rockery, kneeling on a foam-cushioned pad, under the shade of an adolescent Cedar tree.

The house, I was informed, occupied 750 square metres, a series of linked whitewashed rectangles, simple straight lines, with minimalist décor, but each ornament exquisite and definitely expensive. The floor, throughout, was laid with one-inch square white ceramic tiles. Some rooms had plush colourful rugs down; others were bare. The furniture was grand and sprawling with an abundance of couches and day beds.

Because it was built on a hill, there were steps to go up to some rooms, and obviously steps to go down to others. The living room was the largest in the house, and on the lowest level. It had a huge fireplace on one wall and double patio doors that looked out onto the gardens to the west. This is where the investigation room was going to go. We had a lot of furniture to remove from here, but Carlos ensured us that it would be no problem to relocate it to other parts of the house. The only thing that would be staying would be the bar. Well, what's an investigation room without a bar?

We carried on with the tour. The kitchen had an industrial-sized stainless-steel oven/gas hob unit, light ash, smoked glass cupboard doors, stainless worktops, a giant stainless-steel fridge and dishwasher, and a large central island. It was big enough for a team of chefs to work in comfortably.

Each bedroom had ensuite bathrooms, lavishly tiled with their own unique diamond pattern motif, and every window you looked out of had a resplendent view. There was a central courtyard, connecting four of the bedrooms, and a roof-top terrace that contained more couches and cushioned wicker furniture, raised planters and huge terracotta pots inhabited by fan palms.

We didn't venture down to the cellar, but I was assured it housed a decent stock of wine, a snooker room, a multi-gym, a steam room and a cinema. We were never going to be bored.

Outside, the patio wrapped around three sides of the building, a continuous stream of terracotta, cleverly screened off in parts by white walls, arches, planters and steps. An umbrella-shaded patio whispered alfresco dining, charmed by scented pine and eucalyptus trees. It had a large, round, white wooden table surrounded with very comfortable-looking white canvas-backed chairs and an enormous white cushioned bench seat up against a wall, which could easily seat ten people.

Around to the left through a dry desert planted area, and with undoubtedly the best view of them all, the pool. A 180-degree panoramic view, down into the valley below, and the sea beyond. Low clipped hedges, mixed with mature cypress and Scots pine trees, hemmed in the ten-metre pristine pool, and again a multitude of sun loungers, beds and parasols offered all the luxury of a millionaire's retreat, which of course it was, only my team were going to be squatting here for a year and probably feeling quite spoilt. But surely, this sort of working environment can only result in a happy workforce and producing better results.

We had a fully stocked fridge and larder for the weekend; it was all at our disposal, including the bars, of which there were several. Before Carlos and Ramona left us to it, he told Faustino that he'd be back at 8 a.m. with his two sons, to help rearrange the furniture; Faustino would be here also, so with the addition of Brian Wells' men, the task would not prove too strenuous.

Faustino and I cracked a couple of cold long necks and sat by the pool drenching in the atmosphere. I couldn't but help feel glorious, and a big grin spread across my round face.

"This is indeed a beautiful, beautiful house, Dave," said Faustino, sunglasses on, staring out to sea as the waning sun descended in the west.

"We are very fortunate, mate; Jim Maxwell has blessed us with a fantastic opportunity. The budget would never have spread to this."

"What are your plans after tomorrow, Dave? I am free for the whole weekend."

"Really? That's marvellous. Well hopefully we can finish building the flat-pack furniture and setting up all of the electronic equipment by the end of Saturday, then on Sunday, if it's all right, I'd like to drive every route that the Bakers took in their hire car. I know you've been over it before, but I'd like to get a feel for those places myself."

"I don't mind at all, Dave. It will be my pleasure."

My phone rang. It was Brian Wells confirming he was en route and on time. He would see us in the morning. I promised him breakfast when they arrived.

Faustino made good on his pledge and brought with him armfuls of fresh bakery delights: croissants, Danish pastries and warm Torrada bread. Ramona had started her day early and laid the alfresco dining table with adequate amounts of jam, marmalade, butter, orange juice, water, sugar, cups and plates, etc., and had the percolator going, and a kettle on for tea.

I'd had a wonderful night's sleep, had risen at 7 a.m., showered and dressed in a light pair of slacks and a short-sleeved shirt. Out on the patio, a delicate southerly breeze tickled my toes in their soft leather sandals as I totally relaxed in my chair under the shade of the giant parasols. The citrus scent of pine sap danced with fresh bread and

Arabica beans, making me feel magnificent, I drew an enormous breath. Kings Ridge never felt so far away.

When Brian's yellow pantechnicon came into view, we watched it snake up the valley road. The lorry hissed to a halt on the drive after performing an expert amount of point turns, to get its rear end up by the steps. The crew disembarked; Brian and two blokes, Terry and Shane, dawdled sleepily towards the house. I went out to greet them, and together with Carlos and his two boys, who'd turned up freakily at the same time, there were now nine of us for breakfast, which was heart-warming.

Brian took up my offer of a bed by the pool. I didn't see the point in tracking all the way down to the coast for a beer, then come back for his men. We had plenty of beer here. They could sleep here if he wished and start fresh in the morning. But Brian wanted to get going to Albufeira this afternoon before the night set in. They had a tight schedule. A few hours by the pool wouldn't hurt though.

So, after he'd helped his lads unload the truck, he mooched off to grab 40 winks in a sun-lounger, whilst Terry and Shane gave us a hand moving couches, sideboards and expensive trappings to the garage and dining room. The boxes of evidence also went into the dining-room. We needed clear floor space in the living room to erect the office furniture.

Our front here in Portugal was the fictitious holiday company, and I'd had a load of fake paraphernalia knocked up to enhance the charade. Boxes of flyers, pamphlets, tee-shirts, balloons and baseball caps, all bearing our brand, Perfect Portugal, along with headed paper, business cards, pens and banners. I was leaving nothing to chance. If anyone wondered what we were doing around here, then that's what they were going to see, a British holiday company looking for property. Mary had even gone to the lengths of making a believable voice recording on the answering machine, should we receive enquiring phone calls.

If the abductees were indeed local, we were going to do our utmost not to reveal that the investigation had found new legs.

As a parting gift, I gave the lads a tee-shirt, baseball cap and a hundred Euro note. In a small way they could help to spread the illusion.

It was past 7 p.m. when Faustino and I finally finished putting the office furniture together, and we were pretty burnt out. I didn't want to see another Allan key bolt or fiddly grub screw as long as I lived.

We'd assembled 25 white-boards on easels and lined them up end to end around the room, but there were too many, so the train snaked up into the hall as well. This was going to be a linear timeline of events, suspects and their circumstances when we discovered links; they would be brought together on one central Crazy Wall, which should give us a clearer picture of what we are dealing with.

I was clammy and tired, so nipped off to take a shower whilst Faustino rustled up some dinner. When I came out of the bedroom, I was assaulted by this amazing aroma wafting through the house, born from a bubbling skillet on the hob. Faustino was tossing a large salad in a bowl, pausing briefly to drizzle on some oil and vinegar. Cubed shaped chips were roasting in the oven, a loaf of fresh crusty bread on the island and a glass of cold Rosé wine waiting for me.

"Cor, what we having, mate? That smells amazing."

"A traditional Portuguese dish, Dave, as a welcome, Carne de Porco Alentejana, pork and clams."

"Wow, did you knock that up while I was in the shower?"

127

Faustino laughed. "No, my friend. Ramona has been hard at it since yesterday. You have to marinate the meat overnight to get it really permeated. She brought it over earlier and sneaked it into the fridge; I just had to warm it up on the stove."

When the dish was ready, Faustino chopped up some cilantro and sprinkled it on top. We ate out on the patio again, and it was wondrous, the best gastronomic sensation I had experienced in my life. As the clams open up, their juices drip onto the pork resulting in a sauce unlike any other, savoury from the pork with mineral traces from the clams. It was superb.

Whilst we devoured the meal, we considered our next three days. We'd spend the Saturday installing all of the electrical equipment, firing it up, downloading programmes, updates, etc., making sure every facet worked, and then we'd erect some posters, banners and a board at the end of the drive advertising the Perfect Portugal. On Sunday, we would take Faustino's car and travel the routes the Bakers did in their hire car. Then, on Monday, Faustino would take me back to the airport before 11 a.m. Faustino went home and I retired for the night a very happy bunny.

The next day before my Portuguese policeman arrived with the breakfast, I rose early and took a swim. I recommend it as one of the most revitalising things you can do first thing.

I dried myself, then went and retrieved a large folded map of Portugal and a smaller one of the Algarve.

It was clear in an instant that the majority of the population lived on the south coast of Portugal, with the Algarve boasting one of the longest shorelines in the world, which is perfect for tourism. The expansion of the villages and towns in this region is proof that they have

128

capitalised on this lucrative business over the past 70 years.

Apart from the very high-end villas, it would be difficult to purchase a property that wasn't overlooked or ridiculously close to a neighbour. Stemming from the beach all the way up to the A22, it's almost constant development, but beyond the motorway, civilisation is quite sporadic: small villages, remote farmhouses, forests and hills, plenty of lands yet to be exploited.

Putting myself in the shoes of an abductor, up here is where you would want to hide your victim, whatever your mandate, away from prying eyes, secluded. It gave me much to think about.

My thoughts were interrupted by a Peugeot 3008 rolling up to the house. Breakfast had arrived, a moreish selection of little egg tarts, lemon doughnuts and Rabanadas (Portuguese toast) with sugar and cinnamon. These were a delight, and high above my usual Cornflakes or Weetabix. Washed down with freshly percolated coffee, we were all set.

Vianna was fairly quiet. I guessed they just ticked over in the winter season, but there were some visitors, and from what I could hear, making good use of the pool. We didn't attempt to go inside the complex. Non-guests were not permitted, and the recreation area was cut off from the road by a high wall.

Of the three trips to Lidl, George Baker made the last one by himself, which allowed only two windows of opportunity there for a potential spotter to see Molly. We ventured inside and bought some snacks and drinks for the road. The staff here at the time had all been vetted and released without suspicion, but the abductor may well have been a customer, of which in the peak season there were hundreds.

We reached George's uncle's villa at the end of its drive and turned the vehicle around. The uncle, a man in his late 60s, came out of the house to ask us if we needed help. I didn't want to engage him at this moment in time, the fewer people that knew what we were up to the better, so Faustino spoke to him in Portuguese, telling him we had made a wrong turn. We left the wary gentleman behind, blinking in a cloud of trail dust.

At the service station on the N22 where the Bakers had made a pit stop, there could have been any number of suspects. Again, the staff had been vindicated, but how many people were using the forecourt was unknown. I didn't know at this point if any CCTV footage had been examined.

The beach was less likely to have been a place where Molly was selected. It was a rubbish day back then, and very few people were about, plus they were shielded by windbreakers. I ruled this location out, almost entirely.

Faustino dropped me back at Vista do Vale around 6:30 p.m. He had invited me to dinner with his sister and her family, but I declined, I wanted a quiet evening where I could think. I was fairly hungry though, so the prospect of another fabulous Portuguese meal almost did tempt me in, but I still said no. Surely there'd be something here in the larder I could cobble together.

Sure enough, our caretakers had brought in a fresh round loaf of crusty bread, and there were eggs and bacon in the fridge, but what I settled for, and located in the 'English food cupboard', was a tin of Heinz baked beans on two thick slices of toast, the food of the gods.

Sitting outside in utter darkness, save for the subdued light coming from the open kitchen door, I experienced a wilderness quiet, even the crickets had ceased work for the evening. The silence had fabric to it, wrapping me in a warm void. My tinnitus became apparent in this quiet, and

130

very slightly annoying. I listened to my own head compensate for the lack of exterior sound for some time when all of a sudden, voices, followed by laughter broke the stillness with stark brutality. Two car doors slammed, an engine eventually sparked into life after labouring with a flat battery, more voices, then the vehicle drove off, fading in the distance until complete tranquillity was once again restored.

The saboteurs of the stillness happened to be Carlos and Ramona. They lived in Jim Maxwell's farmhouse, about a half a mile away by road, but there was a path linking the two properties, which was less than half the distance, yet the noise seemed as though it were on the drive.

Sound travelled up here much further than if I had been surrounded by a dense population, which reinforced my opinion that an abducted baby would have to be secreted way above the N22, somewhere isolated in the interior, unless they had a soundproof room.

On the other hand, if our perpetrators whisked Molly out of the country on the hurry up, they might well have been a couple who posed as a family, and no one would have paid them much attention. If that had happened, she could be anywhere in the world now.

There were too many variables. We needed a golden nugget like Carlos' car needed a battery, or we were never going to get started. The clues were out there, we just had to find them.

****

The weekend my team arrived at Vista do Vale, was an incredibly hot one, even for the Algarve. At 23C, the temperature was well above the seasonal norm, and delightful for us Brits who were still shivering under shark skin skies. I was the pathfinder, rocking up on Friday to get everything organised for my team's influx, whilst Paul, Mary and Olavo jetted into Faro on Saturday morning.

I'd hired a six-seater Nissan X-Trail for the duration of our stay, just in case our entire group had to go on a mission together. It might happen, so I picked them up off the blistering pavements outside arrivals around 10:30 a.m. Faustino was collecting Alfie later that afternoon in his own car.

We also had the use of a Mercedes Smart car and two Piaggio scooters that came with the villa, so there was no shortage of vehicles for our needs.

My lot were suitably wowed by the villa, Carlos and Ramona gave them the compulsory welcome tour, with me gratified and dawdling behind. Mary remarked that she could get used to this. I reminded her that Jim Maxwell was a single man still, at which she smiled wickedly. Paul commented with usual minimalism by just saying, "Ideal." It was a perfect description.

Olavo, on the other hand, was gushing at the luxury. He was comfortable enough in his little mews cottage back at Kings Ridge and had a well-paid job, but he had come from the slums of Porto in northern Portugal and had worked the streets whilst still at school, to supplement his family's pittance of an income; It's only by luck that he never contracted HIV. So to Olavo, this kind of opulence was at the complete opposite end of a scale deemed unobtainable to him as a child, an alternate universe, where other people dwelled, yet here he was, dipped in a dream, like a toddler in a ballpark.

In the afternoon, once the introductions had been dealt with, I knocked the corks off a couple bottles of Moët and gave a little team talk.

"Obviously this is a fantastic residence, and we've been blessed to have the use of it for our long stay. The house rules stand to reason. Don't wreck the place. It'll cost us a fortune to restore and kick the arse out of our earnings. Also, we are all equal here, except me. I'm in charge." Everyone laughed. "You don't have to do any cleaning. Ramona will do all that, even the laundry, but I don't have to tell you to keep it reasonable. She doesn't have staff. It's just her and Carlos. You can do your own smalls, if you're more comfortable with that. All the facilities are in the laundry room downstairs."

I continued. "Cooking, Faustino and Olavo are both superb chefs and have offered to do the meals while we are here, but it wouldn't hurt if one of the rest of us opened a tin of beans now and again. Plus, we'll have to draw up some kind of rota for shopping trips; I know she loves shopping, but we can't leave it all to Mary."

She gave me one of those 'I'll smash your face in' looks.

"I'm only joking, my dear. There's no M&S here anyway."

"Bastard!" she said with a grin.

I resumed, chuckling. "Now, we've got a ton of work to do, but we'll take Sundays off unless something urgent crops up, which I'll try to cover myself and as I said before, once a month you can have your loved ones come and stay, or you can go home. Apart from that, we start on Monday, make the most of this terrific home. Here's to a very successful investigation." I raised my flute of sparkles to the azure sky. Everyone reciprocated, "Cheers!" We sounded down the valley.

After we consumed a belly-busting delicious meal of flame-grilled Cod, garlic roasted potatoes and a peach and feta salad, our conversation justifiably turned to the case.

133

Paul was itching to get going. "What's first on the agenda, Skip?"

"Well, since we have no suspects whatsoever, no leads, no motive, no physical evidence and no body, we are going to have to start from the very beginning, and go through everything there is with a fine-tooth comb. Which is going to be painstaking I know, but until we can develop a profile on the Perps, we are stuck looking at the paperwork. Since I was last here, Faustino has collected all of the Portuguese police evidence available and has been gathering information on some personnel that I feel have been rather overlooked, the ground crew at Faro airport would have been the first contact holidaymakers had with Portuguese people, and in my mind, rather unnoticed, background noise, a part of the airport, and therefore perfect spies, spotters or actual child snatchers."

"How many are we dealing with, Dave?" asked Mary.

"Sixty-eight. Faustino has collated info on each of them. We need to go through that, and then I feel we need to pay each of 'em a visit, get a vibe off 'em, see if their alibis ring true."

"What's the mode of operation, Skip?"

"We'll pair up, Paul, I think it's best if you and Mary stay here and make a start on the mountain of files. Fresh eyes are gonna pull up on things that have floundered. I want Olavo to get some ground experience, so he'll go with Alfie, whilst Faustino and I will go together and interview the ground crew in their homes. A lot of them are retired now, so it'll be easy. We'll go with the pretence that we are investigating art theft between the years 2002 and 2004, and have a simple twenty questions. Where they were living at the time, what car did they drive, did they see anything suspicious, etc."

"Do you think this will work?" asked Olavo.

134

"The questions aren't important, old friend. They're not designed to winkle out the guilty. The whole ruse is just to get a feel for the type of person sitting in front of us. That will tell seasoned investigators such as ourselves so much more than where they took their holidays the year Molly went missing. If, however, alarm bells start ringing, we'll then ask the proper questions."

***

Three and a half weeks went by without a sniff of a lead. Paul and Mary had gone through dozens of evidence boxes, statements, eyewitness reports, interview transcripts. Nothing stood out. The only things pinned to the crazy wall were a timeline, photographs of locations, various drawings of suspicious people in the vicinity that night, and portraits of the Baker family. No suspects.

Among us, we had interviewed 66 ex or current baggage handlers and drawn a complete blank. As Alfie put it, they were all just good old boys trying to earn an honest living. He was right. Some of the ground crew had spent their entire working lives at the airport. None of them fitted the profile of a child abductor.

I'd been up a while, coffee cup in hand staring at mug shots on the whiteboards. Nothing jumped out at me. Olavo and Alfie had just left for Faro to interview their last bagman, João Pestana, 35 years at the airport, worked his way up to management, three children, all boys, the eldest played professional football for S.C. Farense. Wife works at Faro Hospital, so Olavo will have a lot in common with her.

But we knew already it would be a wasted journey. They were a model family, no convictions, not a single brush with the law.

Mary trotted down into the living room looking like a model from a 1960s fashion magazine: Roman cropped black & white gingham trousers, a tight-fitting orange tank top and a flowery headband holding her auburn locks at bay.

"You alright for coffee, Dave?"

I looked into my half-full cup. "Yeah, fine mate. This lot's got me stumped."

"Two more to get through, right?" Her air was chipper, optimistic.

"That's right."

"Who you got today?"

"Lourenço Braga."

"Isn't he like eighty-seven years old or something?"

"Yup."

"Well, he'd have been seventy when Molly went missing. Surely he can't be a suspect?"

"You'd have thought not, but we've gotta follow this through, leave no stone unturned and all that. It's just that I was quietly confident that we'd find something here that the police had missed, a gut feeling."

"There's some Gaviscon in the medicine cupboard for that."

I chuckled. "Yeah, maybe I should have had a swig; it would have saved us all a lot of trouble."

There was a silence.

"We've been chasing ghosts, squandered our time. I felt so bloody sure…"

"Don't beat yourself up, Dave; it was an integral part of our investigation that we had to conduct. At the very least, we can now eliminate these people from our enquiry, which is a plus."

"That's a positive spin to put on it, Mary, but I still feel like I've fucked up."

Faustino and I shot off around 9 a.m. for an area north of Faro called Troto, a journey of around an hour, so we had ample time for our 10:30 appointment.

Lourenço was understood to be quite a character, a devoted airport man, married for 68 years, four children, 12 grandchildren and 23 great grandchildren. So obviously family-orientated, it was inconceivable to imagine that he would partake in the abduction of another man's child.

The Braga family had lived in this narrow little street for an eternity. The blinding white-walled houses all had large, ancient, wooden front doors and closed shutters, if it wasn't for the presence of potted geraniums, verbena and hydrangeas on sills, you would think that no one lived here at all, for there wasn't a living soul to be seen in the street anywhere.

The door was answered by a man in his 60s who introduced himself as Nuno Braga, Lourenço's son. He led us down a cool, darkened red-tiled passage, past a living room containing three excitable children and a spacious kitchen where two old nattering ladies were preparing vegetables on a large pine table. They barely acknowledged our existence as we filed past. Something smelled good on the hob.

We stepped out of the back door onto a pagoda's concrete slab with a subdued lazy atmosphere and a roof of grapes. Orange and lemon trees bordered the pagoda on two sides, their heavenly scented blossom seductively thickening the air. A mixed garden of herbs, flowers and vegetables occupied the rest of the walled space, making use of every inch, and most of it for the dinner table, sat at which was the man we had come to interview.

Lourenço rose steadfastly from his knackered old chair to greet us and put out a paw. We shook hands. I couldn't think of a more tranquil idyll to want to sit and have dinner in my later years. It was basic but utterly charming.

Our host asked us what we wanted to drink. I could see that he was slowly getting mellow on an earthenware jug of rosé wine. I know it was early, but I wasn't driving, and it just felt right. I joined him with the wine. Faustino opted for a milky coffee.

In less than two minutes another cold jug of rosé, a bowl of green olives and a board of cheeses, smoked ham and sliced sausage graced the table, followed by Faustino's coffee.

"Mmm, Petiscos," said my cop friend with enthusiasm.

"What's that?"

"You might call them tapas, Dave. Dive in, dive in."

I was fascinated by the three canary cages hanging from roof supports. Each had its door open, yet the birds stayed inside, occasionally bursting into song, which only added to the tranquillity established in this little bubble.

Lourenço told Faustino that he always kept the cage doors open during the day. His birds weren't prisoners, they were guests, but they were safer to be locked in their rooms at night. It spoke volumes about the man sitting across the table from us.

We used the same cover story to explain the purpose of our visit. Faustino showed Lourenço his badge and told him I was his counterpart from the British police. It worked every time. No one had ever asked to see my credentials.

In 70 years, Lourenço had never seen anything remotely suspicious to do with art smuggling but had noticed a trend in smaller and smaller suitcases. People travelled lighter these days, apart from the golfers. Their club bags grew in size every year and were cumbersome to haul around and stack.

Lourenço asked if he could show us something. Thinking it may be of interest, we keenly agreed, but when he waddled back from the house carrying an armful of photograph albums, we knew we had made a blunder.

Not to be impolite, and because we were in such pleasing circumstances, we agreed not to spoil an old man's trip down memory lane.

Seventy years of faded or out of focus snaps of his old work colleagues, dead and alive. He also had an autograph album for all the stars that had passed his way and had the kindness to stop and leave a moniker. Quite a few of them were Portuguese celebs that I'd never heard of, but he did have a lot of famous golfers and Jose Mourinho.

Though disenchanted by hundreds of photographs of people I didn't know, I was warmed by the dedication and love this man had for his workplace. Even though I couldn't understand what he was saying, I could see that he was proud to have been part of the well-oiled machine there, probably a rare ethic these days.

When we got towards the end of the final album, I was looking forward to Lourenço turning the last leaf, when a face stuck out from the crowd. He was wearing a Hi-Vis yellow jacket and stood next to the players from PSV Eindhoven, the Dutch football team. Lourenço, along with another of our 68 baggage handlers I recognized, were also in the photograph, which led me to assume the guy in the Hi-Vis was also a baggage handler, but he was one that I did not recall from our records. He could have been one of ours, but his features were obscured by a bushy beard, red baseball cap and mirror sunglasses.

I got Faustino to ask who this fellow was.

His nickname was Verruga, but Faustino couldn't think of the English translation, so explained it was the name of a long-nosed mouse that lives underground.

"Mole?" I proposed.

"Yes, yes, Mole."

"And was he a baggage handler?"

"Yes."

"And what's his real name?"

Lourenço knew him as Marc, but couldn't remember his surname; he was also known as Dutch.

This didn't sound like one of ours; I excused myself, got up walked away and made a phone call to Mary, asking her to check the database for any one of the baggage handlers we had on record being otherwise known as Verruga or Marc, or Dutch. She came back with a negative.

Whilst I was talking to Mary, Faustino kept up a conversation with Lourenço. I knew from his occasional glances my way that he had something. After five minutes of talking, Faustino turned to me gravely and pointed at the photograph saying, "This guy, we need to look at him."

My heartbeat quickened. I needed more info.

Like a vampire of private investigation, knowledge was my lifeblood.

Faustino explained to me firstly why the mystery man in the red baseball cap wasn't on our list of enquiries, even though he was Equip. de. Terra do Aerporto (a baggage handler), because Verruga was part of Forcca Terrestre, meaning ground crew, but of a different type. Anyone working on, or in an aircraft comes under the umbrella of the ground crew, be they cleaners or from catering. This Marc was exclusively in the hold, the undercarriage, stacking suitcases or passing them out onto the conveyer belt. It's classed as a different department. I think in England they are referred to as Ramp men.

"Oh, Jesus, we've only had half the information. Ask him how many ground crew in total might there have been on any one shift?"

The reply was there could have been as many as a hundred.

I was confused now. "So what makes you think that this guy is suspicious?"

"Because Lourenço told me that red cap only worked there for two years and that he left abruptly in June 2003 without a by-your-leave. Lourenço remembers this because he retired in October of that year and thought it was very odd that this man should simply vanish after getting such a good job. It was one of those positions you only got because you knew someone on the inside, you know jobs for the boys kind of thing. But Verruga was a foreigner, so how did he get the job? He kept to himself, liked working alone, but worked hard, drank expensive coffees."

As profiles go, red cap's was ringing alarm bells. I could ask Lourenço a dozen more questions, but I didn't want to impose on the old boy any longer. He may have just given us the start we needed.

We asked if we could borrow the two photographs Marc was pictured in and promised to bring them back within a couple of days. He was all too pleased to lend them to us.

We thanked him for his more than generous hospitality and left feeling rather anxious to find out more about this Verruga bloke and all the rest of the Ramp men at Faro airport in June 2003.

Lourenço was left wondering what all this had to do with art theft 17 years ago.

Faustino drove us to Faro airport, making a couple of calls on speakerphone as we went. Within 15 minutes we were at the administration building north of the terminal. I waited in the car whilst he went inside, returning some minutes later carrying a big fat file.

"It's not what you know, it's who you know," he flourished.

141

"Whatcha got there then?"

"Employment records of forty-two Ramp men who worked at the airport between January 2002 and 2004."

"You beauty," I said.

"We didn't have any of these."

He sat there and rifled through the file. All the documents were naturally in Portuguese, but each contained a photograph of the employee. In seconds he pulled out red cap's details.

"Bingo!" he said, "Is that how you say it?"

I smiled. "It is."

"His full name is Marc Freese. He's a Dutch citizen. He worked at the airport between 24th February 2001 and 5th June 2003. He left when he was twenty-seven, without giving notice. His address at the time was 63, Rua Ataide de Oliveira, Faro. We also have his bank details."

"Brilliant. We need to talk to everyone in that file, but especially Mr Freese. I don't know about a Mole, but I definitely smell a Rat."

Freese's last known address was managed by Casas da Lapa, a letting agency/estate agent in central Faro. Faustino wasted no time finding their address through his department back in Portimão. Using his badge, we breezed in to see the boss, Joaquim Lapa, a short, round-faced fellow, with spiky salt & pepper hair and black thick-rimmed glasses.

Remarkably, despite the lapse in time, Senhor Lapa had no problem remembering renting to Freese. In 40 years of business, it was the only apartment he'd ever leased that didn't need refurbishing after the tenant had left. In fact, Lapa believed Freese had never slept in the apartment once; he thought it to be just a mail drop, an expensive one at that. He had paid three years' rent in advance and didn't even bother to reclaim his deposit. He just phoned in and said he wouldn't need the place anymore, and that was the last Lapa had heard of him.

An Asian family was living there now, and four different tenants had occupied the apartment since Freese, so a forensic swoop would be useless.

Lapa smiled at us and said that he wished all of his tenants were like this one, which furrowed our foreheads.

Red cap was definitely up to something crooked. The next logical step was to contact the Dutch police. I knew that Alfie had liaised with them in the past on Molly's case. I phoned him in the street. His contact was Daniel Van de Koning. I knew the name. He was a very outspoken high ranking officer who had made the news on several occasions. Van de Koning was an exponent for legalising recreational drugs. His hypothesis was that criminal activity would be halved if the illegal drug trade was eliminated, freeing up police resources at the same time bringing in revenue for the government. His movement was gaining favour in Holland, which, as we all know, has long since been quite relaxed on the use of cannabis.

My personal opinion on the matter echoed my daughter Sam's: our laws were quite antiquated and something better needed to be put into place, but what? I was yet to be convinced either way.

I filled Alfie in with the details we had learned today. He was calmly excited that we'd finally got a possible lead after nearly four weeks of dead-ends and would call Daniel immediately to get everything they knew on Marc Freese.

Faustino meanwhile had taken the initiative and was calling headquarters securing the necessary authority to gain access to red cap's bank account. Copies of his statements would be emailed to us at Vista do Vale.

143

We were entering through the villa gates when Alfie called my mobile.

"I've just heard back from Daniel Van der Koning. Marc Freese died in a motorcycle accident in December 2000; we're dealing with an identity theft here at least."

"Alright, mate. We're back now. I'll see you in a sec'."

My team was buzzing; we gathered in the investigation room. The email had come through from police headquarters. Thank heavens for the air conditioning, because I had quite a sweat on now.

Red cap had 6,550 euro in his account. He had opened it in February 2001 and had regular monthly payments made into it from his employment at the airport. He'd only made three individual withdrawals of small amounts in that time and hadn't made any since September 2002.

Obviously, the guy wasn't relying on his wage packet to get by, so what was his real employment? Being a baggage handler was just a front for something more lucrative, but what? Was this our man? Or was he up to something completely irrelevant to our investigation? Right now, we had uncovered a dubious criminal up to some dishonest activity at the time Molly had disappeared. It was a no brainer; we needed to find him pronto.

"Senhor evasivo," remarked Faustino to Olavo.

"What's that?" I queried.

"Mr Elusive," translated Olavo, "sounds about right."

"Mr Elusive," I said aloud.

I had a quick think about what to do next. Walking to a whiteboard, I cleared it; the guys we had interviewed already were no longer of interest. Grabbing a marker pen, I talked out loud as I wrote down the facts we had, possibly linking this guy to Molly Baker's disappearance.

"He would most likely have been working the day the Bakers arrived in Portugal. His shift was Monday to Friday, 7:00 a.m. - 4:00 p.m."

My team were fully attentive.

"He would have had plenty of time to read the labels on the pushchairs out of sight in the hold and link them to the people as they came to collect them."

Faustino spoke, "You're assuming that he's a predator on the lookout for a potential victim?"

"Of course, if he's a pro', then he'll have a shopping list, but if he's a paedophile, then he's always alert; this is what feeds him."

A feeling of distaste floated through the room like a foul spirit ruining the air.

I continued, "He disappeared without a by-your- leave, two months after Molly went missing, in June 2003… He's walked away from his pseudonymous bank account, leaving a six grand float."

"I think we can assume he's totally abandoned the Freese guise now, Dave," advised Alfie.

"Most certainly, he's evolved, and probably more than once, if he's still at large. What else do we know?"

"He's a loner?" suggested Mary.

"As far as we know, Mary, according to Senhor Braga, Freese kept to himself, had typical sociopath traits, liked to work on his own, never made small talk."

"He rented the Faro apartment for three years and never slept there once," added Faustino.

"Yep, meaning that was a part of his cover, and he actually lived somewhere else under another name."

"The Dutch police believe Marc Freese's passport was stolen from Amsterdam in 2001, the same year our guy turns up in Portugal," revealed Alfie.

"Good, right." I wrote that down.

"He never took off his baseball cap and sunglasses."

"Right, Faustino. He was in disguise, which means he's either got history, or he looked quite different in his ulterior habitat. So, summing up, we've got to change tack here. I think we need to re-interview all of the baggage handlers again, as well as other ground crew we haven't yet spoken to, and find out anything they knew about their ex-colleague, and at the same time go for this guy, big time. Whoever he is, he doesn't look like the picture we have of him. The operation's new name is 'Mr Elusive'." I wrote it in large letters and underlined it.

Paul spoke for the first time in a while. "Mary and I have been cooped up in the villa since we arrived, Skip. Is there any chance we could get in some fieldwork to stop us going stir crazy?"

"It's like you've read my mind, mate. I want you and Mary to fly to Amsterdam on Monday. Liaise with Daniel Van de Koning, give him all we know. If Mr Elusive is Dutch, he may have a criminal record."

Mary was straight on it, "I'll book the flights right now," she said.

Paul nodded in agreement; he was a man of few words.

It felt like we had passed a milestone and, seeing that the team was splitting up for a short while, I proposed that Olavo and Faustino really push the boat out tonight and serve up a banquet, which was easy for me to decide, seeing that I wasn't doing the cooking.

And delight us they did. Out on the rooftop terrace, they brought up a starter of Caldo Verde, a delicious green soup containing potatoes, kale, onion, olive oil and chorizo sausage, followed by a seafood stew called Cataplana de Marisco, containing cod, king prawns and clams, which was amazing served alongside some unforgettable frango no churrasco, spatchcocked Piri Piri chicken, some homemade bread and some excellent wines nicked from the cellar. Then came a cheese board with half a dozen different cheeses including sheep's and goat's, finishing with a cinnamon-laced rice pudding. In the dark of the evening, with the flame from the little oil lamps dancing in a delicate breeze, I felt as if I would burst with contentment let alone all the food.

We talked until it was late, finding out more about each other, but also about the case. Whether we made more progress would depend on if we could discover Mr Elusive's true identity and where he had really been staying here in the Algarve. Travelling there five days a week, it couldn't have been too far away from the airport.

6
Douro Calvo

The red squirrel, *Sciurus vulgaris*, nothing vulgar about them at all. They're really cute, and so much more beautiful than the common greys we have got used to at home in England, and, although rare, the only species to be found here in Portugal.

They had captured my fascination since the day we had arrived, nimbly negotiating the trees around the villa, right up to the very spindly ends of the branches, demonstrating their own frames to be as light as a feather, yet they are formidably intrepid climbers, ferociously territorial and forever industrious.

Carlos considered them a nuisance, forever digging up his lawns to bury their treasure. He'd shoo them off with a rinse from his hose pipe if he caught them. But I found them delightfully entertaining.

I watched one as my team and I sat around the pool terrace making plans. We'd all enjoyed a lie-in this morning; Ramona had kindly prepared a light breakfast for us, and a tepid breeze was rolling up from the valley, calming my soul. All of a sudden, the crack of a flimsy pine branch shifted my attention to the low wall at the other end of the pool.

This rusty bundle of fur bounded daintily along the top of the wall, stopping momentarily to assess the situation before moving off again, its bushy tail providing perfect balance and symmetry. When the squirrel reached the end closest to us, where the wall ascended to form an arch, it stopped, rose onto its hind legs and posed for a photo, showing the fullness of its blond tummy, an opportunity we all indulged in with our mobile phones. Tufty, as I called it, must have thought itself a real celebrity.

Where the wall cornered the villa, it made a herculean leap onto my balcony and disappeared, quick as a flash, into my bedroom, much to the mirth of my friends.

I stood up intending to run upstairs to chase the bounder off before it could do any damage, but it reappeared almost instantaneously with a pecan nut bulging in its cheeks. It made the massive leap again and then scurried off at lightning speed the way it had come and then back up the tree, stopping once to check that it wasn't being followed.

"Cheeky monkey," I said, "I wondered who'd been nicking me nuts!"

Mary smiled. The rest of the team were too busy thumbing through their phones.

"I bet it was one of those little buggers who left DNA in Molly's bedroom." She casually remarked.

I had no idea what she was talking about. It showed in my face.

"The non-human DNA…" she prompted.

My expression puckered.

"You haven't read it, have you?"

"Read what?"

"I left a file on your desk yesterday for a second opinion, you know, something that stands out as being a bit odd."

"Go on."

"Paul and I were going through statements made by the thirty-eight people who had entered the Baker apartment on the night she went missing. Amongst the statements was a report from the forensic department to the police and a letter from the police dealing with the case at the time, back to forensics, both translated into English."

"Right," I slurred inquisitively.

"The letter said that they do not intend to pursue any lines of enquiry regarding the fifteen different types of non-human DNA found in Molly Baker's bedroom, explaining that in their opinion it was unlikely the abductor would have contaminated the scene with such material."

"Material?"

"Animal hairs."

My immediate thought was why not? Anyone could pick up animal hair from all manner of places and drop it at the scene. Why would the abductor be exempt, unless he was wearing a fresh hazmat suit when he entered the apartment?

I needed to read that report pronto, so I left the table to retrieve it.

Within a few minutes, I was back with the file. Having started to read its contents on the way down the stairs. I finished going through it at the table, whilst my crew sat around me in silent anticipation. I then closed my eyes, trying to picture the scenario on that frightful night.

Two things were obvious. If the abductor came through the window as the police would have us believe, then they would have definitely scraped their clothing on the way through, easily dislodging any loose hairs, and, I doubted if the assailant would have spent time lowering the side of the cot, taking the baby out and then put it back up again. They would have just leaned in and scooped Molly up, again, brushing her blankets with their clothes. So, disregarding the abductor as having left animal hair at the scene beggared belief and yet another example of incompetent policing from the Judiciaria which ruined the chances of finding her all those years ago.

There was something else as well. I couldn't imagine that all 38 people that entered that apartment within the first 24 hours of Molly going missing, actually went into her bedroom. Surely most would have just had a cursory look through the door.

Mary broke my train of thought.

"How are you doing, Dave?"

"Yeah, fine, Mary. You and Paul did the right thing pulling this up; this is explosive and possibly our best hope to date of linking the abductor to the scene. I tell you, I'm flabbergasted at the ineptitude of the Portuguese police on this case. How can they not have followed through with this? It's blatant evidence."

Alfie leaned in. "What are you thinking, Dave?"

"If just one animal hair can be tied to Mr Elusive, we have our man."

"Right," said Olavo, "and how are we going to do that?"

Mary had more to add, "Of the thirty-eight people that are said to have contaminated the Bakers' apartment that night, three of them were dog handlers, with their dogs, and they have definitely been ruled out, and their dog's hair identified. It's not part of the fifteen other DNA. Just a moment..."

She went inside and came back out carrying a couple of whiteboards and set them up in the shade close to our table. Written on the first was headed, Feasibility study of the non-human DNA bought in by the 'Contaminators', according to the Portuguese police.

There was a 'no pet policy' at the holiday complex.

All of the floors and splash-backs in the apartments were ceramic, making them easy and efficient to clean.

A 'deep clean' takes place in each apartment by professionals during each turnaround.

The cleaners change into their uniforms at work.

Nearly all holidaymakers buy new clothes for their trip or buy new clothes while they are abroad, or wash them during their stay, rendering them free from animal DNA.

It would be unlikely to pick up animal DNA from a hire car, taxi, coach or aeroplane.

There are no zoos or animal parks in the area to visit.

People on holiday do not tend to touch or stroke stray cats and dogs, or any other animals.

It is unlikely they would pick up animal DNA at a restaurant or supermarket.

The people who entered the Bakers' apartment that night were hotel staff including the receptionist, baby minders, the night manager, bar staff, chefs and waiters, other holidaymakers, the Bakers' friends, and cleaners, all highly unlikely to have brought in animal DNA.

"All bollocks, of course," she said. "Anyone of those people could have picked up animal hair from a multitude of places, including the ones stated by the police."

"Agreed," I said.

Alfie puffed out his suntanned cheeks. "So, that leaves us with a bit more good old-fashioned detective work to do."

"Mary and I can get back on it today," said Paul. "It's going to take a while, but we can telephone everyone on that list and find out if they had any pets or came into contact with any animals during that week leading up to Molly's disappearance."

"Do they all speak English?" asked Olavo.

"I believe all the staff can converse in English, yes," replied Mary.

I'm so grateful to have this lot on my team; I didn't envy doing any of that.

"In the meantime," I said, "it's a priority to establish exactly what those non-human DNA samples are, what

152

types of animals they come from, and see if we can link any of it to anyone on that list, just for the process of elimination."

Olavo spoke, "Faustino will be here soon, perhaps he can pull a few strings and obtain the original DNA samples from police files."

"Defo, and if he can, I know exactly the right person in England to examine them and give us the correct undisputable results."

"Defo?" laughed Mary.

"Alright, alright, I'm down with the kid's innit."

"I don't think even kids say that anymore."

I laughed to hide my embarrassment.

When Faustino arrived, we bought him up to speed. He said that the DNA almost certainly will be stored at a forensic laboratory attached to police headquarters in Lisbon, where his ex-partner Frederico was now the head of department. Obtaining them should not be a problem. He wandered poolside to make that phone call.

The plan was for Faustino and me to drive to Lisbon tomorrow, pick up the DNA, then get on a plane to London. We'd then drive to Milton Keynes, where a good friend of mine, Professor Jennifer Lake, headed her department. We would leave the samples with her, fly back home, and no doubt get the results back within a few days.

I was just about to make a call to Jennifer when Olavo interrupted me.

"I'll be going with Faustino on this one."

His tone was authoritarian, something I had never seen in him before. It stopped me in my tracks. I conceded. It was no biggy, even though I was looking forward to seeing my old friend Jennifer and taking a detour to visit Elizabeth on the way back. But sure, it was fine.

I made the call to Jennifer, giving her all the necessary information. Our professional relationship went back eons, and we had a lot of mutual respect for one another. She said that she would make it a priority case and perform the tests herself. I promised to bank transfer the fee directly, as soon as the results were in.

When I came off my phone, Faustino was walking back to me.

"We're all set, Dave. Frederico will hand over the samples to us tomorrow at 7 a.m. It will take us two hours to get to Lisboa, so we'd better make an early start."

Olavo spoke before I could, "Don't worry, I'll be ready." And with that, he slipped into the house without saying another word.

Up until then, Faustino thought that I was going with him. He looked puzzled, but then shrugged, as if to say oh well.

"You had better take the hire car so that you can have the option of flying back to Faro if you like," I said.

"Okay," he replied, leaving to find where his new travelling companion had gone off to.

It was handy having one of those hire cars that you could leave at any one of their outlets, essential in this line of work.

Paul spoke, "Thinking outside the box, Dave…"

"Yes?"

"…If we have a situation here where Mr Elusive was the abductor, and he had an animal, and that animal's hair was on him when he entered Molly's bedroom, and it fell off…"

"Yes?"

"…That animal wouldn't be alive now to do any match testing, unless it was a parrot or a tortoise, which it wouldn't be, of course, because we're talking hair here."

Paul's sense of irony shone through every once in a while.

"Good point, mate. I'll have to think about that. In the meantime, scrub up another whiteboard in case you get any new leads. Excuse the pun."

It was a long shot because the abductor could have brought an animal or its hair into Portugal with them from abroad, but if they happened to have bought an animal locally, for whatever reason, there was a chance that the details of that transaction might still be on record. We needed an exclusive list of all the pet shops, breeders, rescue centres, vets and animal sanctuaries in the Algarve, and once we have the species of animal we are looking for, we can start doing some cross-referencing.

Faustino came back outside with some insight.

"We have in Portugal a very strict programme of rabies vaccination for dogs. Records are kept. If Mr Elusive had a dog say, then he would have to have had it vaccinated, maybe a good place to look?"

"Yes, indeed. Thanks, mate."

He turned and went back to the kitchen to help Olavo with washing up the breakfast things, which was strange because we had an enormous dishwasher that would easily take care of that.

When he was out of earshot, I turned to the team and asked if they thought that Olavo was a bit too keen to go on a trip with Faustino?

Paul and Alfie agreed, but Mary just sat there with a radiant smile.

"I dunno," she said sarcastically, "three master crime busters in front of me, and none of you can detect the bleeding obvious."

All three of us stared back at her expressionless face.

"Olavo is what we used to say in the olden days … stepping out with Faustino."

"Faustino's gay!?"

"Yes, Alfie."

The British policeman was astonished that he hadn't realised.

Come to think about it, it did make sense. All the time they had spent together up until now, I thought it was just because they spoke the same language. When all this time they'd been singing from the same hymn sheet.

One thing was for sure, since losing his partner, Neil, five years ago, Olavo has been in a very sad place. Working with us, and meeting Faustino has definitely pulled him out of the doldrums.

I called everyone into the operation room to make an announcement. Paul and Mary were no longer going to Amsterdam on Monday; our focus right now was on connecting an animal to the abductor of Molly Baker. Operation Mr Elusive had changed its name to Operation Squirrel.

My Portuguese team members had set off before sunrise, the residue in their coffee cups in the kitchen sink the only evidence they'd been and gone.

I made a fresh cafetiere, poured myself one and wandered out to the pool for some early vitamin D.

Sinking into the over-exuberant white cushions on a lounger, legs up, still in awe at the breathtaking scenery dropping away down to the coast, I had an abstract thought. What if that non-human DNA turned out to be from elephants, lions, tigers, monkeys and zebras? And it just so happened that the circus was in town the week Molly went missing, and she is now a world-famous trapeze artist. I could think of worse outcomes, but then chased them away.

We should get the DNA results back from Jennifer by Monday evening, or Tuesday morning at the very latest. In the meantime, the four of us left here at the villa would collate all of the contact details for the 35 Contaminators, as they had become known.

Once we had positive identifications for all of the animal types involved, we could begin the process of elimination. This was going to take ages and may involve even more forensic testing, because if, for instance, Labrador hair was one of the 15 samples, and Mrs Ferreira had a Labrador back in the day, then we'd have to somehow try and obtain her old dog's hair and have it tested to see if it was the same Labrador. It was starting to feel like a nightmare.

One thing I could do today though was phone George and Jill Baker, as I did every Sunday, to update them on any progress. This was a perfect opportunity to get the ball rolling on the eliminations.

I came off the phone enlightened. On the trip up to George's aunt and uncle's villa, Nile had played with the couple's elderly Border Collie. Jill also recalled that they had a decrepit old Tortoiseshell cat that shed hair all over the place. Nile also had two pet Guinea pigs at home, so there were three possible matches.

Olavo and Faustino arrived back at base, 11 a.m. Monday. Faustino hadn't spent much time in England at all before, and not for a while. He'd forgotten how cold it was and couldn't get warm for their entire stay. He was mighty pleased to be back on home soil, even though the pair of them had obviously seen a good time. New love does wonders for one's élan vital.

I put them to work straight away, ringing the Portuguese Contaminators, with the pretence of us being a magazine, writing an article on the changing fashion of animal breeds over the past 25 years. The ones that had kept pets were all keen to get their names in the mag' and forthcoming with the types of animal they'd had back in the day.

There we were indulging in our set tasks, clicking at keyboards, staring at screens, and jotting down information. The room had an apprehensive vibrancy, the sort of atmosphere I imagined there to have been in a World War II operations bunker at fighter command. The tension was palpable, waiting for the Luftwaffe to skip across the channel.

At 8:00 p.m. it came, an email from Jennifer Lake.

Paul vaulted into action, whiteboard pen in hand, whilst Mary read out the email.

Hi, Dave and team, please find below abridged analysis data from the sample results gleaned from the original material left with me yesterday by Olavo and Faustino, labelled 15 non-human DNA hair samples.
I have rushed these through the system and given you a basic breakdown of the results, due to the urgency you have implied.
I will send a full analysis tomorrow, after I have had some sleep.
Good luck with the investigation. Hope to see you soon.
Regards,
Jennifer.

The list went so:

Samples 2/10, both are same dog, German Shepherd, four years old.
Sample 3, Rat (*Rattus rattus*) Rodent, male, nine months old.
Samples 12/9/14, same dog, female Cocker Spaniel, three years old.

158

Samples 1/6/8, German Shepherd, female, nine years old.
Sample 4, Cat, Tom, 16 years old.
Sample 15, Cat, Tom, four years old.
Samples 11/7, Male Border Collie, 16 years old.
Sample 5, Guinea Pig (*Cavia porcellus*) Rodent, one-year-old.

The disappointment was visibly cramping my face muscles. Three of these samples came from the police dogs, another two from the Bakers' visit to George's relations and the other three were not promising, a feral cat, a guinea pig and a rat, all easily explained. I had to conclude dejectedly, that this had all been a waste of our time and money.

Then Mary said, "Hold on a minute, there's only fourteen here."

"Eh?"

"There are only fourteen samples on this list."

"Are you sure?"

"Absolutely, I've counted them twice."

"She's missed one," said Alfie.

Unlike Jennifer, I thought. She was the ultimate professional.

There was another ping on Mary's laptop. She read the email out loud.

"Sorry, Dave, forgot to add sample thirteen, I'm a bit tired. J.
Sample 13, Rhodesian Ridgeback, male dog, four years old."

"Get in!" I shouted, leaving my chair.

My outburst gave everyone a start. Followed by a perplexed look etched across Faustino's chops. "Get in what?" he said.

"The goal, mate. It's an expression. This is it, my friends, the missing link, our abductor kept a guard dog!"

The Rhodesian Ridgeback, once known as the African Lion Hound, was developed in South Africa by Boer farmers. They are a large breed specifically designed for versatile hunting and home guardianship, and renowned for their heightened ferocity.

Whilst Paul got on his laptop and searched for local breeders of the dog, the rest of us doubled-checked the minutes of our phone conversations with the Contaminators.

I felt in my water that this would be a fruitless exercise, but we had to be thorough.

As I had expected, none of them had ever owned or come into contact with an African Lion Hound, well they are a bit of a specialist animal.

"Right," I said, "all focus should now be on finding that Rhodesian Ridgeback."

"I think I already have," said Paul, in his calm orderly manner.

Our pause was tangible.

"On the 27th of April 2001, a Michael de Jong purchased four dogs from an animal rescue near Loulé, above Faro, a four-year-old ridgeback, a two-year-old Pitbull terrier and two Jack Russell terriers, a two-year-old and a three-year-old."

"Nappers and snappers," said Alfie, "the drug dealer's animal of choice."

I raised my eyebrows at him.

Paul continued, "Seems like de Jong had them all vaccinated for rabies at the same time, with the in-house vet. However, after 2003, the vaccination records for those dogs cease to exist."

"What do we have on de Jong, any internet presence?" I asked.

"Quite a bit actually, for a time anyway. He seems to have built up a very successful and renowned tomato farm at a place called Douro Calvo, up in the forests near Monchique. Their speciality, according to Google was a unique variety of beef tomato, which was highly sought-after in the region. No photos, I'm afraid."

"Is the farm still operating?"

"Nope. Ceased trading in 2003."

"Interesting. Any info on who owns the land now?"

"Certainly is. It's a 400-year-old farmhouse, with six acres, up for lease-hold directly from the owners themselves, a large farming concern called Cardosa. Their headquarters are at the family villa, about twenty miles away from the farmhouse."

"I know these people," said Faustino. "They are a big brand in the Algarve, a major supplier of fruit and vegetables to the supermarkets. They have been in business for generations, a well-established and trusted company."

"Good, they should keep records of all their tenants. Paul, this de Jong, it's obviously a Dutch name. Can you send an email to Daniel Van de Koning, asking if he can dig anything up, on him?"

"Already on it, Skip."

"Do you reckon de Jong is Marc Freese?" asked Alfie.

"Well they both fell off the map in 2003," said Mary. "So the chances are more than likely."

"Agreed," I said, "and, if we're lucky, there may be a way to find out. If we visit that dog rescue centre tomorrow with a picture of Mr Elusive, perhaps there is still someone working there that'll remember him buying those dogs."

We decided that after the dog rescue centre, Olavo, Alfie, Faustino and I would pay the Cardosa family an unannounced visit. We didn't want to alert anyone in advance to our investigation.

For now, we were all ravenous, and desperately looking forward to the evening meal that Olavo was expertly fashioning in the kitchen: eggs, chips, ham and beans.

Until we could pick up a new Nissan X-Trail from the hire company, we used Faustino's Peugeot to travel to Loulé. We pulled up outside the long-winded named Centro de resgate de cães e santario de animals, just after 8 a.m. The reception building was a modern pristine white-walled oblong, with lots of smoked glass and stainless-steel railings.

Alfie opted to stay in the car and make a few phone calls whilst the rest of us ventured across the car park. A switchback ramp led us up to the front door, thoughtfully catering for wheelchair users and tired old dogs.

Inside, the air-conditioning had tamed the morning down to a very respectable degree, a perfect working environment.

This was supposed to be one of the oldest dog rescue centres in Portugal, and a wall of ancient photographs, mostly in black and white, catalogued its history.

Two ladies occupied the front desk, obviously related, with raven hair and obsidian eyes.

Faustino introduced himself to the eldest of the two ladies. She was Christina Lima, and the girl beside her was her daughter, Calie. He showed them his badge, making it official police business.

While he was explaining the reason for our visit, an older lady in a rear office was staring straight at me with a

162

pained expression. Her eyes never wandered from me as she unsteadily rose from her swivel chair, wobbled into reception and interrupted Faustino and Christina, by asking them a question. Christina then spoke to me in perfect English.

"My mother, Louna, would like to know where you are from."

"Kings Ridge, in Buckinghamshire," I replied precisely, wondering how they sussed I was English to begin with.

"She says you look remarkably like my late father, David."

That sent icicles up my spine.

"Well, that is a spooky coincidence, because my name is David."

Christina translated.

The grandmother gasped and needed to steady herself.

"Your mum wasn't holidaying in Margate in 1971 was she?" I joked.

"I don't think so, why?"

"Just a thought."

"If you are English, why is your skin so dark?"

I went on to tell her about my great-grandfather coming from Vladivostok, which is near enough Asia and that the genes have carried on through, plus, we've been living in the sunshine for three months.

Then something freaky happened, the grandmother launched into a spiel in unblemished English. It was puzzling as to why she had held back until now.

Even though twenty years had passed, she remembered the guy who bought all four dogs like it was yesterday. He said that he wanted them to protect his land from wild boar, which was eating his tomato crop. They were the kind of dogs that would do that sort of thing, excellent guard animals.

These four dogs had been in the rescue centre for quite some time because they were not the friendliest of animals, difficult to find homes for. But what had made Louna Lima remember this guy so vividly was that the dogs seemed to be afraid of him.

At this point, she had to ask her daughter to translate a Portuguese word. "He was so menacing," she said.

Faustino pulled up a picture of Marc Freese on his phone.

"That's him!" she said with vigour, then screwed her eyes up, pointed at me and said, "David, be careful with this man."

We were all thinking the same thing. What kind of bloke are we dealing with here?

After bidding the Limas goodbye, we headed back to the car, reservedly optimistic we'd actually got a hold of Mr Elusive's tail.

With Louna's warning still echoing in my head, we set off for the farmhouse; roughly an hour's drive northwest. En route, I filled Alfie in on what we had just learned; I then called Paul and did the same. My right-hand man had been busy too, and had a hatful of information to give me.

Daniel Van de Koning's call had been quite fruitful; we were still dealing with a pseudonym, Michael de Jong's passport had been stolen in 2000 and used for four years. The address Mr Elusive used under that name was at a rundown part of north Amsterdam which has since been demolished and re-developed. But he did use his new identity to buy a 5-year-old Hymer motorhome from a Mercedes dealership in Eindhoven, which he sold back to them three years later. Daniel was sending the details of the motorhome over to us now.

Mary had scoured the internet and got the lowdown on all she could about the tomato farm and its landlords. The farm was originally called A Fazenda Escondida (The Hidden Farm), which would soon become apparent as to why.

The Cardosa brand was a large concern; their family villa was close to their production plant in Poços Fluindo. They farmed hundreds of hectares of fertile land in the valleys above the Algarve.

Paul had hacked into the local cooperative's accounts system and found that the last tomatoes he had sold to them were on 28th June 2003. Before that he had been raking in 3,000 euro a week in high season, which begged the question: why was he working at Faro airport for 200 a week if it wasn't for ulterior motives? And how on earth did he have the time to do both? Was he a twin or did he have help?

Paul advised us to proceed with caution. Mr Elusive may have gone off the radar, but he still might be living in that house.

As we neared our destination, the trees thickened on both sides of the road, so densely packed together that no sunlight could penetrate through to the forest floor. This ancient plantation was a hundred feet high and creaking with the burden of its own boughs, impenetrable on foot, save for the pencil straight fire breaks that ran like beige tram lines into infinity, every half a kilometre.

After 5km, we came to a right turn and a signpost denoting Douro Calvo 18 Km. We took it and headed north. The only vehicles to pass us now were two articulated, refrigerated lorries emblazoned with the Cardosa brand. We were on the right track.

Every so often, small signs were staked into verges with either one of two warning messages written on them. I asked Olavo what they said. One was a fire hazard area sign and the other read, do not park on the verges.

Faustino added that hot car exhaust pipes are often the cause of forest fires in this area, igniting the dried grass.

There were plenty of lay-bys for motorists to pull into anyway, had they wanted to stop, and fortunately for us, there was one close to the entrance of The Hidden Farm, which was pretty secluded itself. Nature was claiming back the dirt single track, to the point where you couldn't get a car down it without first attacking it with a chainsaw. Obviously, nobody was using this entrance anymore, but that didn't mean there wasn't an alternate way in, or out. Three of us in the car knew the way criminal minds worked; there was always an escape route.

Faustino wasn't taking anything for granted; in his boot, he had stashed an array of weapons for the occasion inside a large green metal box.

He pulled out four bulletproof vests, a holstered revolver, which he handed to Alfie, a holstered stun gun, given to me, and a pump-action shotgun for himself.

We all donned the bulletproof vests, and the policemen loaded their weapons. Olavo appeared a bit left out in the tool department, but with him being a nurse without any gun handling experience whatsoever, it was for the best. He carried a shoulder-strapped first aid kit.

We'd talked about this part last night. Better to be safe than sorry. Given the number of facts we had gleaned so far, we could be walking into a drug den.

Faustino put a hand on Olavo and asked him to stay a hundred metres behind us until we could secure the area. It was a tender moment, one of protection. Cometh the hour, cometh the man, I thought.

We all switched off our phones and crossed the main road; it was so still and quiet here in the forest that our shoes on loose chippings crunched like a herd of cattle coming through.

We negotiated the track, more akin to an army assault course than a road. Branches and creepers had leached into the open space, taking advantage of the light bonanza, and many times we had to stop and clamber over a wandering limb.

Every noise and every movement of some unforeseen swift animal proved to be startling and made progress a real sluggish affair. My nerves were on tenterhooks, every sinew tense, expecting the worst to happen at any moment, and my shirt was soaked with perspiration as we gingerly surmounted the obstacle course, mindful that there may be security cameras hidden in the trees, and our quarry might be armed to the teeth and fully expecting us.

With us as the vanguard, Olavo had it easier trailing behind, keeping his distance, but every now and then Faustino would check back to see if he was okay.

The track seemed endless, but in fact, it was only half a kilometre long, and soon we could see the gable end of a very large, granite-block building. We crept on until eventually we were halted by high, rusty, wrought-iron gates, chained and padlocked. A sign was attached to the gates with garden wire, Faustino translated it: Private property, keep out.

Like we were going to.

From here the forest halted, a living sentry wall, under orders not to advance into the clearing, watchful, impassable, the perfect barrier behind which to hide a clandestine operation. But it was overtly obvious that nobody had used this land in quite a while. The polytunnels had disintegrated into mere fragments of grey plastic, flapping in the breeze, polypropylene flesh rotting on galvanised skeletons.

What was once a tidy acre plot of commercial activity was now an overgrown ramble of ground cover, small trees, brambles and tall grass, nature's own re-wilding.

Either side of the gate, ten metres apart, were two wooden dog kennels.

"DNA," I whispered to Faustino.

He nodded in agreement; there'd almost definitely be some strands of dog hair in there still, and we needed to get it analysed as soon as possible. Our Portuguese cop knew how I felt about the Judiciaria's forensic capabilities, and their historic incompetence, but the fact that I was giving his colleagues a second chance to prove themselves meant a great deal to him, for he was determined to regain some respect for his own force.

I held Faustino's shotgun, as he scaled the gate. He was followed by Alfie, then Olavo who had finally caught us up. I handed the 12-bore through the wrought-iron bars then struggled over myself. I hadn't done this much exercise in months. The excess weight I had gained living a lavish lifestyle this year was showing. My legs were on strike and my arms struggled to keep my balance atop the rusty gate.

Once down and embarrassingly out of breath, I suggested we all turn on our phones again. Faustino had to remind us all that we were technically trespassing, seeing that we didn't have a warrant or the owner's permission to be here, and that photographing as much we could without contaminating anything would be very useful to the investigation before a forensic team could be brought in.

When activated, all of our phones began pinging at once; it was like a pinball machine starting up. Amongst other messages, Paul had been trying to reach us all; he had an update on the schematics of the farmhouse and its barn.

The oldest part of the house dated back to 1614. Its irregular boulder construction had oak framed windows and doors, and a terracotta tiled roof. Both buildings had a wine cellar, but the house also had an attic room.

Many windows were smashed on the ground floor. This could have been vandalism or perhaps natural deterioration due to a lack of maintenance. It was hard to tell, but birds were using the house as a nesting site and grateful for the unrestricted flight paths.

I knew why Paul had sent this information through; he was thinking the same as me, this was an ideal marijuana farm. Set up in either the basements or the attic under LED lighting. Using the tomato business as a front and a source for materials, who would ever suspect a thing?

But the obvious question was, how did the bloke do all this on his own? He must have had accomplices or at least some staff, which implied a larger network, and also a greater risk. And how did Molly's disappearance fit into this? This snoop was raising more questions than answers so far.

I asked Alfie and Olavo to walk around the house and take pictures through the broken windows, this would save an incursion. Faustino and I ventured to the barn.

The huge barn doors had a small inset in one. I tried the handle. It was unlocked. We stepped into the gloom, partially illuminated by the open door itself, so needed our phone torches to light up the contents of the room.

Lined up neatly, were a white Peugeot Boxer van, a red Peugeot 205 and a small tractor with a trailer about the size of a ride on mower. Behind it was yet another trailer, and stacked everywhere were wooden crates, dozens of them.

Everything was covered in a chalky layer of dust, proving they hadn't been touched in many years.

Some of the crates had polystyrene inner trays within them, on the side of which was printed a large tomato on the vine, the name of the fruit 'de Jong's Rapture', A Fazenda Escondida, and Pruduto de Portugal.

This was no cowboy operation in its day. A lot of effort and expense had gone into making this appear like a genuine farm, and it was evident that Mr Elusive did in fact grow and wholesale plenty of big beef tomatoes. But what confirmed for me and Faustino that something else was also being produced here in the secluded glen was a big old vintage generator nestled discreetly in the dark at the back of the building.

It was frustrating not to be able to get up close to these vehicles, and indeed the generator, for a more intrusive look, but we daren't corrupt the scene. So instead, had to be content with photographs of the cars' number plates, the tractor and a distance shot of the generator, with a hope that Paul could glean something useful from them.

After retrieving a good deal of dog hair from both kennels and putting it in sealed evidence bags, we got out of there and headed back for the car. A police vehicle was waiting for us in the lay by; it had been prearranged to liaise with us in that spot so that Faustino could give the officers the samples. They sped off without question, back to the laboratories at Lisbon.

Our next port of call today was southeast, to Poços Fluindo and the Cardosa family. It was a good half hour journey. On the way I asked Alfie and Olavo if they thought the hidden farm could have also doubled up as a cannabis farm.

Olavo spoke first, "We could only see inside the rooms at ground level. I counted ten rooms, but only four had been renovated, and to a high standard, but not in keeping with the style of the building. They were too modern and not of my taste, tacky I suppose you'd call it. And yeah, probably the sort of decor a drug dealer would want to surround himself with, flashy."

"What rooms were done up, mate?"

"Oh, the kitchen-diner, the living room, a bedroom and a downstairs bathroom."

"Hmm, liveable then?"

"Oh definitely."

I then asked Alfie for his thoughts.

"Well, he had the right dogs for the job, the Yappers and Snappers are an ideal early warning system, with that, and the fact that he seems to have an abundant supply of money, it could point in that direction, or he just liked his privacy and sold a shitload of tomatoes."

"Hmm," I said again.

Faustino added his perspective.

"That generator is powerful enough to light up a football stadium. Yes, it's a good backup if the power goes down out there in the forest. But apart from the house, he might have had an irrigation system to uphold and maybe heating for the polytunnels in winter, but honestly, it's a perfect tool for running a separate system so that the utility companies aren't suspicious."

"What do you think, Dave?" asked Alfie.

"Just the fact that he has an alias and works at the airport five days a week for two hundred euros means he's up to no good, mate. Now all this with the hidden farm. There's much more going on here than we've been previously concentrating on. Without the forensics on the dog hairs coming back to us, I'd stake my reputation on de Jong being the bloke who took Molly, but for what purpose, we can only guess."

As we drove down to lower elevations, we left the tree line behind and settled into gently rolling hills and eventually flat farmland, kilometre after kilometre of agriculture along the valley floor, all manner of fruit and vegetables, most of it belonging to the Cardosa Corporation. It was plain to see why this area was known as Portugal's breadbasket.

A roadside billboard depicting the crops we were passing and a big red arrow told us we were heading in the right direction. Within a kilometre, we'd turned onto the Cardosa road. You know you've hit the big-time when the council name a road after you.

We came to a fork in the road. One sign pointed towards the packaging plant, the hub of the Cardosa Empire, another towards the family's villas. We took the latter and soon came upon the boss' house, a palatial C-shaped affair of two stories finished in a cream-coloured smooth render, with terracotta canal tiled roofs, three circular turrets, each with conical hats and a courtyard paved with granite setts. The entire property was steeped in dappled shade being surrounded by at least a hundred mature eucalyptus trees, which added to its appeal.

Faustino pulled up to the massive, pillared porch entrance and switched off the engine.

"It's probably better if Olavo and I go in to do the interview," he said. "I'll make it official. Olavo can be my sergeant."

I agreed. This was the parents' home, country people, and we thought it unlikely any of them would speak English.

A lady in her mid-40s answered the glass and gold front door. Faustino flashed his police badge, and they were invited in.

Alfie and I stayed in the car and reported back to base. Paul had received all of the photographs and got to work on them. Both Mary and Paul agreed with us. The farm was just a cover.

Half an hour later, just when I began to fidget in my seat, our Portuguese pair re-emerged from the depths of the cool looking interior and got into the car. They waved back to an elderly couple standing close together under the porch with the younger lady who had let the boys in, turning out to be their youngest daughter, Noémie.

Not a word was said as we negotiated the courtyard and back out onto the Cardosa road, then Faustino spoke in a low timbre.

"Prepare yourself for this one, Dave, Alfie..."

There was a brief silence.

"...Mr Elusive had a wife and a baby girl! the same age almost to the day as Noémie's child. She would often see them at the surgery in Douro Calvo. She said the Tomato Couple, as everyone knew them, seemed to keep to themselves. It wasn't a language problem, because the Dutch couple and Noémie could all speak English..."

I listened wide-eyed as Faustino spoke and drove. They had a baby!

"...Noémie is fairly certain that the wife, she couldn't recall her first name, went back to Holland to have the child in 2002 and then came back to Portugal sometime later to help with her husband's business, and apparently, what a good business it was. Duarte Cardosa, the father said that he had never personally met de Jong, but we were welcome to speak with his lawyer in Douro Calvo, who had met the man."

"Did you show the daughter a picture of Marc Freese?"

"Yes, she confirmed it was de Jong, but said that he always wore a flat cap and sunglasses."

I spoke out loud the question going through my head, "Why steal a one-year-old baby girl when you already have one?"

Faustino answered me with official reticence, "You are jumping the gun a little, my friend. We haven't established with all certainty yet, that de Jong definitely abducted Molly Baker."

"No, no, you're right." I backtracked. "But let's just hypothesise that he did. What would be the reasons for taking a child, given his profile?"

Olavo offered a valid explanation, "To replace one that you have lost?"

That scenario had been broached before and, unfortunately, it wasn't an uncommon crime. And if this was the case, there was a fair chance that Molly Baker was still alive and totally unaware of her true identity.

At the surgery in Douro Calvo, Olavo and Faustino went in again as their double act. Olavo's medical knowledge might prove helpful at this point. Fortunately, the doctor who used to see to the Dutch couple more than any of his colleagues was still practising at the clinic, and after a brief wait was able to give the boys ten minutes of his time.

The doctor was reluctant at first to give our policemen any information concerning one of his ex-patients, doctor-patient confidentiality and all that, but after Faustino explained the extreme seriousness of the case, and that it had been 20 years since his patient had last attended the practice, the doctor relented and pulled out her medical records.

The name Mrs Elusive was using back then was Yvette de Vries. According to her, their daughter was born in Amsterdam on April 22nd 2002. The records showed that between 17th October 2001 and 16th March 2003, both parents attended prenatal classes at the clinic and that Miss de Vries came to postnatal checkups with the baby girl, called Hannah. Apparently, she attended a total of 22 times, which Olavo thought was rather excessive.

"So they weren't married then," I stated.

"Not according to the clinic's records," said Faustino.

Olavo continued.

"The doctor felt at the time that he had no medical concerns with either the mother or the daughter. But did make a note that Miss de Vries seemed very distant from her child, no maternal affection, he put it, almost the way a farmer is with a newborn animal. He knew how hard she worked on the tomato farm, and he put it down that, stress and exhaustion."

"The way a farmer feels about a newborn animal? Like a commodity?" I questioned.

Olavo arched his eyebrows as if to say, "I don't know, maybe. It's a horrible thought."

If Olavo's suggestion is correct, might we be dealing with a suspicious death as well? More questions.

All four of us sat in the car outside the surgery, pensively mulling over all we had learned this morning.

I phoned Paul to see if he had an update from Holland on Miss de Vries.

There was no register of birth in the Netherlands in April 2002 of Hannah de Vries. Also, Daniel said that Yvette de Vries' passport was stolen in Amsterdam 20 years ago and cloned because it had been used at border control several times.

Another false identity. It felt like we were trying to net wisps of smoke. Mr and Mrs Elusive were certainly living up to their name, and very good at leading pursuers up blind alleys. Except for one mistake, perhaps. If we can match the Ridgeback's DNA to the Bakers' apartment, then at least we'll have the face of the man who took Molly. If we have a face, we can find the man.

Paul added that the two Peugeots found in the barn were both registered to Michael de Jong, so nothing advantageous for us there yet.

We decided to split up. Faustino and I would stay in Douro and go see de Jong's bank manager, his accountant, the estate agent and the Cardosa's solicitor; they were all here in town. Olavo and Alfie would take the car and visit the cooperative where de Jong sold his tomatoes, and to the builder's merchant where he bought materials for the house refurbishment, to see if they could gain any further information on the couple.

All of the retail units in this pretty little market town were in one place, around the periphery of the town square, on three sides of it anyway. The other side had been made into a car park and a play area for the kids. In the centre, an ornate bronze scalloped fountain sported something akin to an old brown fence post in its middle, spitting water. It was an odd thing.

Mulberry trees in planters made up a spine on either side of the fountain, and also lined the cobbled square, providing excellent shading for the pavements, some of which boasted tables and chairs for the bars and cafes.

It was all very quaint, like we had stepped back in time 50 years.

The bank, a plain white cube on one corner, had charcoal glass doors but no windows. We strolled in, grateful for the air-conditioned sanctuary.

We were offered water while we waited patiently on a black leather couch for the manager to see us. She was engaged with a customer when we arrived, but we only had to wait 15 minutes.

Senhora Pereira had only been with the bank for five years, so did not know de Jong. However, because it was official police business, she could pull up his account details and give us an overview.

All she could tell us was that Michael de Jong had left a substantial amount in his account when he stopped trading, 17 years ago, but that money had all but gone now due to withdrawals over the years. She would not, however, physically show us the statements themselves.

We would have to apply officially to head office in Faro to obtain copies

We thanked Senhora Pereira for her time and left the building.

"We gotta find out where that money's been drawn, mate. It'll give us a map of his movements over the past seventeen years," I said to my policeman.

"I'll call it in right now and get it moving."

He did so while we walked to the solicitor's office across the square. It was above the estate agents, which, we were to find out, was owned by the same people.

The glass door on street level had the firm's name blazoned in gold lettering, Advogados Tavares e Pinto. We rumbled up the stairs.

Senhor Pinto was somewhat expecting us, having been telephoned and filled in earlier by Duarte Cardosa.

The solicitor was quite forthcoming when we told him the nature of our investigation was to do with tax evasion, both here and in the UK. We had to tread carefully because we had no way of knowing if Pinto was still in contact with de Jong, or even if he was a part of the same bent operation.

Pinto, told us that he had dealt with the leasehold on the farm personally, but he'd only met de Jong on four separate occasions. The hidden farm had been on the market for years, but nobody was interested in it since it only had well water to drink, no electricity at the time, was so remote and the house needed a total renovation. When Michael de Jong enquired about the property online, they were elated, having been inclined to think they'd never get rid of it.

But before even viewing the land, de Jong stipulated that he'd only be interested if he could have a 15-year lease, be able to erect eight large polytunnels, have mains water run up to the house, be allowed to have an electric generator on-site and have permission to refurbish the farmhouse. The company agreed on all aspects, of course, so he met de Jong and his partner for the first time on 16th February 2001.

On the 18th of February, quite happy with his acquisition, de Jong signed the lease.

The next time Pinto saw him was a month later, when the solicitor visited the farm to see how they were settling in and if they had any problems. They had none, but Pinto noticed that they had not had their chimneys swept yet, so re-iterated that the contract stipulated they have the chimneys swept twice a year. De Jong told Pinto they had no intention of using the open fireplaces and asked if it would be alright if they boarded them up with a removable steel plate. Pinto agreed.

The last time they met was in June 2003 when de Jong came to the office and informed the solicitor he was quitting the farm and going back to Holland for family reasons. He put it in writing and said his accountant would deal with the lease and he would continue to pay the rent for the full term. This was all very unusual, but de Jong must have had his reasons for leaving so suddenly. Pinto took back the lease at the end of the term, and the Cardosas haven't decided what to do with the land since.

Faustino asked if Pinto still had the letter of abandonment. He said he did, and the police were welcome to it. It meant little to the company now, but if he could just take a photocopy of it first. Faustino said of course, but could he use a pair of surgical gloves that the policeman had with him, just in case de Jong's fingerprints were still on the paper.

Pinto screwed up his eyes at the suggestion but put the gloves on regardless.

Faustino also asked if it would be alright to put an undercover forensic team into the farm for four days.

178

The solicitor didn't have a problem with that, though it must have seemed like a strange request for a tax evasion investigation. He'd also have to ask permission from Duarte Cardosa first.

When we got out of there, I said to Faustino, "Well at least we know where the money in his bank account went."

"Quite possibly," said the cop.

The next stop, the accountant, was only a few doors down. You could see why Mr Elusive had picked all of these people; he'd obviously come to Douro for the day and found it very convenient, all his peas in one pod.

The accountant, Ramon Souza, was long in the tooth, and possibly way past retirement age. With his shoulder-length grey wiry hair and horseshoe moustache, he could have been a character in a spaghetti western. He too occupied an office above a shop, a shoe shop. The office was a small affair, just one room at the back of the building, with a desk, computer, nicotine-stained walls and around a million lever arch files on shelves, from floor to ceiling.

He was quite suspicious of our intentions at first, but when we mentioned that there might be a cash reward for finding Michael de Jong, his demeanour changed dramatically. He had no forwarding address for the man, just a list of instructions and access to his bank account.

"He trusted you with his money?" Faustino was amazed.

"I'm a very trustworthy man. Besides, have you met Michael de Jong?"

"No, I haven't," said the cop.

"Well let's just say this; you wouldn't want to piss him off."

We both stared at him blankly, as he continued.

"I was instructed to continue paying the rent on the lease until it was up, pay the rates, his business and personal tax, my fees and any bills that arose on the farm."

"And this has all finished now?"

"Yes."

"And you haven't had any contact at all with Mr de Jong?"

"Not in the slightest."

"And you don't know where he is now?"

"He said he was going back to Holland. That's all I know."

"Do you not find this arrangement strange at all?"

"Very! Especially because his business was doing so well. Just to cease trading like that was in my opinion foolish. His tomatoes were excellent, a unique flavour, people fell over backwards for them."

We thanked the accountant and left, saying we'd be in touch if anything arose from our investigations.

There was still some time to kill before the boys were due back. The Elusives must have used the shops here in Douro. I wondered if anyone remembered them.

Fortunately, all the essentials were here in the square. We'd go from shop to shop with the old heir hunters act and try to pick up some more gen.

It turned out that the Dutch couple had made quite an impression on the locals for two reasons, still remembered after all this time. Firstly, they were two of only five foreigners in the region. The others being a Scandinavian couple who kept goats and produced fantastic cheese which they sold at the market every week, and the other, an eccentric English painter who behaved more like a hermit than a resident.

The second reason was the famous tomatoes, unusual and delicious were the common descriptive phrases used.

The tobacconist/newsagent was ancient, but was as sharp as a sabre; he told us that Mrs Elusive would come in every two months and buy three car magazines.

The butcher had a bird's-eye view of the square. He remembered de Vries because she always bought the most expensive cuts of meat and a big bag of bones for her dogs.

Across the square from the butchers was the hairdressers. Faustino went in there alone because I really needed a pee. Thankfully there was a public convenience in the car park, which I was very relieved to see.

Faustino was inside the hairdresser's for quite a while. I sat by the fountain and waited, lullabied by the tinkling of the water. When he came out, he was bursting with useful information.

The owner, Tiago, was apparently flamboyantly camp and had insisted on Faustino having a coffee with him in the office. It was a quiet day, and both the other two stylists had nothing to do but twirl listlessly in their Gabbiano barber's chairs.

Mrs Elusive was a creature of habit, every two months she would come in, have her hair washed and have the same short, side-parting haircut whilst reading her motoring magazines. Tiago, who also owned the barber's next door, had only been the head stylist back then, and Mrs Elusive always made sure that it was him who cut her hair. He knew that she was married to the fantastic tomato guy and had a baby, but to him, she came across as gay, possibly bisexual, at a stretch.

Faustino finished the conversation by asking Antonio if he would be able to recognize Yvette de Vries from a photograph. We didn't have one, but might be able to get a hold of a copy of her old passport through Daniel Van de Koning. He said he would, definitely.

This plot was thickening quicker than an overindulged jug of Bisto, and as for the tomatoes, we had an inkling that there was more to them than just a tasty salad item. This was reiterated by Olavo and Alfie when they returned.

We grabbed a pavement parasol table outside one of the petiscos bars. We hadn't eaten all day, and I, for one, was famished.

We ordered a bottle of Rosé and a bottle of fizzy water, then, from the menu, we decided to get a dish each of petiscos, and then share everything. The fried pork belly with pickled vegetables caught my eye, whilst Faustino went for Littleneck clams steamed in Vinho Verde. Alfie ordered spicy sautéed shrimp with garlic and cilantro, and Olavo opted for Fresh figs with Ibérico ham and goat's cheese, possibly from the Scandinavians. It was a fair assumption. We crowned it all with a big basket of bread and had a delightful couple of hours, in which time I had called Mary, filled her in with what we had learned this afternoon and advised her and Paul to go ahead and eat without us tonight. We were having a working meal on the road.

Alfie and Olavo had gone into the cooperative with little confidence in extracting any information from the rugged individuals that worked there. Mistrustful eyes followed them as they sauntered into the office.

However, the manager turned out to be a round, jolly fellow in his 50s, whose shirt seemed two sizes too small, straining the buttons to capacity, and was more than willing to divulge any information the boys wanted on Michael de Jong. The manager, Joao Cunha, didn't like him much. De Jong was brash, abrupt and unfriendly, not the type you have a joke with. But his tomatoes, the Raptures, were incredible, huge beasts, perfectly ripe, juicy with a sweet exotic flavour.

Half of the hidden farm's produce was shipped abroad, and as with most of the organic crop, via airfreight daily out of Faro, mostly for top-end restaurants and hotels in large cities. What was left, and still of a very high standard, but maybe varying in size, they sold to local markets and traders, some of which went to the market in Douro Calvo held on Wednesdays and Saturdays. Apparently, de Jong's Rapture would sell out before 9 a.m. People couldn't get enough of them.

If we capture him, I thought to myself, Elusive's going to be remembered for more than just his moreish tomatoes.

The boys had further insight into Elusive's temperament, extracted from the builder's merchant who sold him the materials for his renovations, backed up with second-hand gossip, supposedly from the builder who did the work. According to them, Michael de Jong didn't suffer fools gladly, and he wasn't the sort of person you'd want to argue with, but money was not an issue as long as the job was done right and within the agreed time.

There was one shop left that we hadn't explored yet. It was getting late, but the shops here stayed open until 9 p.m. So we had time. I hadn't considered it to be very useful for us, but we shouldn't leave any stone unturned.

The haberdashery shop hadn't seen a lick of paint for a few generations and the masonry needed some attention. Alfie and Olavo remained at the table, people watching and enjoying the ambience of alfresco dining on a warm tranquil evening, whilst Faustino and I went in.

The moment we entered the cramped little shop, we were overcome with nostalgia. You don't see businesses like this anymore, stuffed to the gills with everything you'd need for dressmaking, upholstering and tailoring. Buttons, zips, threads, needles, lace and reams of fabric in every colour of the rainbow and some in-between. We could barely move down the aisle towards the glass display-case counter without bumping into something.

It was warm in there, a geriatric ceiling fan whirled away above our heads, making no difference to the ambient temperature at all, but catching cobwebs instead.

A lady in her sixties leant with both hands on the glass with a half-smile on her face, her lipstick it seemed had had a hard day.

Two very elderly ladies sat in wicker garden chairs at the back of the shop knitting with competitive fury. They didn't register our presence, even when the younger lady said, "Boa Noite." They just carried on clicking.

Faustino said good evening back and then launched into his Detective Inspector opening lines. The younger of the three was the owner of the shop. The two old girls were her aunts, sisters who used to own the shop, but had passed it down when the going got too tough around 15 years ago. They couldn't break the habit of a lifetime, though, and came in every day for a social.

When the de Jongs were mentioned, the old girls both stopped knitting in unison, put their hands in the air and said, "Fio de algodao," three times.

I hadn't a clue.

The owner, Senhora Castenheira, spoke to her aunts briefly, and then to Faustino, explaining what was happening back there.

After what seemed to be a lifetime, my cop interpreter eventually divulged the contents of their protracted conversation to me.

The old girls knew in an instant who we were referring to. The tomato lady came into the shop with her husband about 20 years ago and bought the most expensive sewing machine they had at the time. They also bought several other things including the entire stock of the strongest thread available.

184

Yvette de Vries would come into the shop regularly to buy the odd thing, but always clear them out of strong cotton, in a yellow colour. She would often look at the lace section, but never buy any. The last time they could recall seeing her, she was heavily pregnant.

It had been a bountiful day. We'd learnt a great deal, and we were still yet to interview the company which supplied the polytunnels, but that could wait until tomorrow.

Right now, we all just wanted to get back to base, have a cold lager and maybe a dip in the pool before bed.

Mary must have read our minds, because four bottles of ice-cold Estrella were condensing on the patio table when we ambled in, along with a strong whiff of one of Mary's specialities that she and Paul had tucked into tonight, spaghetti Bolognese.

We grabbed the beers and went into the operations room, pleased to see our colleagues, who were still at it, writing up the last of the information we had gathered today. Seventeen whiteboards crammed with stuff, a proportion of which had come from Daniel in Holland.

We congratulated ourselves with a toast. We had all done well today.

"You coming for a swim, Dave?" asked Alfie.

"Eh? Yeah, in a bit, mate. I just wanna have a squint at this lot a mo."

My eyes had fixated on board number 17, all the information on the Hymer motorhome bought and sold in Eindhoven by Michael de Jong.

Daniel had been thorough, even sending us pictures of the actual vehicle inside and out, plus a photo of the guy who bought it from the dealership after de Jong sold it back to them.

Paul broke my train of thought. "An email came from Daniel just before you got back, Skip. He says that he's hoping to get a forensic team on the Hymer within the next couple of days, because of the slight possibility there's still some DNA on board that might prove helpful."

"Good one."

The boys were coming back through the operations room in their bathing shorts when Faustino's phone chimed into life. He checked the screen. "Forensics," he said.

This was it? The positive ID to tell us that Michael de Jong had kidnapped Molly Baker or just a slap in the face.

Faustino listened, as calm as a sloth on diazepam, said, "Aha, obrigada," then ended the call.

It took just three words for elation to erupt. "It's a match!"

Arms flew into the air, cheers thundered off the ceramics and a stack of papers took flight and floated to the ground like giant confetti.

"Get in!" shouted Faustino, emulating my terminology.

Elusive's first mistake. At last, we had the face of Molly Baker's abductor, indisputable proof. If he's cocked up once, it may not be the last time.

The boys went off for their swim more verbal than they'd been all day. I sat in my office chair feeling smug with the result.

"What are your thoughts, Paul?" I said to my number one.

He was as sober as a judge.

"It occurs to me, Skip, that this de Jong was no amateur when it comes to growing fruit. It's written all over these boards, how superb his product was…"

"You're not wrong there."

"…So we must presume he had some sort of formal training in horticulture."

"Agreed, mate, but where to start? He could have trained anywhere in the world."

"True, but why don't we start in Holland, his own country. Maybe we can narrow it down a bit."

"Absolutely. Can you get on that tomorrow?"

"First thing."

I was drawn back to board 17, the Hymer board.

What was I missing?

The odometer readings didn't add up.

I got a pen and paper, and a calculator, and went through it.

Michael de Jong bought the 1996 Hymer D564 on 14th February 2001 from a Mercedes dealership in Eindhoven. It had 57,873 km on the clock.

We knew from his solicitor, Pinto, that de Jong travelled directly from Holland to Douro Calvo to see the farm, a distance of 2,338.9km. This was some effort, it took him two days, so he must have been driving for at least twelve hours a day.

It took him a couple more days to decide on the lease, and in that time according to Pinto, he stayed at a campsite in Albufeira, 55.1km away.

He then went back to Douro, to sign the lease on the 18th of February, another 55.1km.

From there, he went to Faro and bought both Peugeots on the same day. I assumed that Yvette de Vries went with him to buy the vehicles and that she followed de Jong back to the hidden farm with one and then both of them went back to Faro in one of the new motors having left the motorhome at the farm, adding a further 136.1km to the tally.

I presumed the Hymer stayed on the farm for two years, and that they lived in it while the renovations took place, because nobody ever saw them in the motorhome during their time at Douro Calvo, only ever in the Peugeot 205 or Boxer van.

When he sold it back to the dealership on 3rd July 2003, the odometer should have had a reading of 62,797.1km, but instead, it read 63,286.1km, a difference of 489km.

We were back to the missing miles syndrome again.

Obviously, he went somewhere else before returning to Eindhoven, somewhere at least 244km off route or perhaps it was a summation of several trips made over three days. Why, when and where?

We knew he frequented Amsterdam. That's where the passports were stolen and where he once had digs, but Amsterdam is only 122km from Eindhoven, so it couldn't have only been there. We needed more sightings of that Hymer in Europe back in 2003; it was another needle in a haystack to find.

My gut feeling now was that we'd almost exhausted the amount of information available here in Portugal. We needed to interview the rest of the ramp men at Faro airport, and the polytunnel people, and get the results back from a forensic swoop at the farm. But apart from that, I'd say that we were done here, maybe a week or so left in this luxurious villa which we'd all come to adore.

Our families were going to be disappointed; a lot of them had booked flights to visit us over the summer, but I'd made up my mind. We were going to uproot and move our operation to Holland. In my water, I knew that's where the Elusives had gone, maybe with Molly, maybe with both children. We had no idea where either of the girls were yet, but I'd bet my reputation they weren't in Portugal anymore.

The boys were still splashing and yahooing out in the pool. But I was too tired to join them now. Before hitting the hay, I wrote on an A4 sheet: 1. Phone Daniel first thing. Tell him de Jong's our man. Inform Interpol for a Europe-wide search for his face. Need to find out where he and Yvette de Vries are now. 2. Call the Bakers. Tell them the good news. 3. Find a new base near Amsterdam (Paul). 4. Bring Daniel and two of his officers in on the team if possible.

The après breakfast briefing was a mixed feelings affair. No one wanted to leave Vista do Vale. It felt like ours, although I bet Jim Maxwell was going to be elated to get his Algarve retreat back.

Faustino was unsure whether the chief superintendent would allow him to leave Portugal and work abroad. Maybe some sort of exchange could be arranged with a Dutch policeman. He would have to write up a report highlighting all the progress they had made so far in this case, especially now we had a definite prime suspect.

Neither Olavo nor Faustino wanted to have a long-distance relationship, so for the sake of romance at least, they both needed to go to Holland.

Alfie was on the fence; he'd grown accustomed to this lifestyle in the sun, yet feared the coming summer would prove to be a little too hot for his constitution, and the Netherlands being much more like the English climate might suit him better, and besides, he'd be closer to his boys.

As for Paul and Mary, they'd hardly done any fieldwork at all since they'd been here. Mary wasn't too bothered about being cooped up all day in an office environment. It's what she was used to, but Paul was quietly going mad as an office Walla. He'd much rather be doing the legwork than tapping a keyboard.

The language barrier had been the deciding factor in who got to go out and who got to stay behind. Seeing that

189

most of Holland used English as a second language meant that everyone could be used as a foot soldier.

Within an hour Paul had found us the perfect base of operations in Holland, a short-term lease in Haarlem, an affluent area on the Zuider Buiten Spaarne, northwest of Amsterdam. Set in a secluded area with ten acres of ground, this house had six bedrooms, nine bathrooms and a 15m indoor swimming pool, a self-contained flat above the garage and a gatehouse with live-in staff. At £6000 a week, it was expensive, but we had it in the budget so we booked it until December with an option to stay longer if we needed to.

Goodbye Operation Squirrel; hello operation Hymer.

7
Ballet shoes

I went for a walk through the villa gardens to clear the murk in my head and order my thoughts. It's amazing how much a stroll, away from technology and modern living, can be so grounding.

Connecting with the natural world, even if it's just for a brief moment in time, I find, is so clarifying.

Carlos greeted me from across the lawn with a lazy salute; the sprinklers he had set in motion were creating great misty arcs of undulating waves like fine liquid skipping ropes. The water droplets vaporised in the still morning air, shrouding the grounds with a temporary humidity that the sun would burn off in under an hour. But it felt fresh at that moment and smelt divine.

This case was throwing up so many questions for us, and very few answers. All we had in the way of solid evidence was the face of the man who took Molly Baker, the DNA of a dog he'd once owned, the place he used to live in, a place where he worked, the vehicles owned and a defunct bank account.

He was still out there, elusive, a ghost, so was his missus and so, we believed was Molly Baker.

The Cardosa family had given us permission to put a forensic team into the hidden farm. Faustino had come up with the idea of disguising the technicians and their police guard as builders, cordoning off the entrance with health and safety restricted area tape and signs, just in case unwanted eyes and ears were still about.

They were starting tomorrow. Alfie and Faustino would be joining them, and they predicted the sweep would take three or four days to complete.

Olavo was sorting out transport for the big move to Holland. I wanted to take all the office equipment and evidence boxes together, in one load, so we needed a small truck and at least an estate car to cater for all our belongings.

Faustino was yet to hear back from Bento Sampaio, as to whether he could actually come with us to the Netherlands, but given that this case was starting to yield results, I didn't see why he should be denied.

Daniel Van de Koning was delighted to be asked to join our team. He had been granted special status to work only on this case for the rest of the year by his superiors, along with two of his colleagues, Rhonda Groot and Barbara Stoepker, both detective sergeants. They were to convene with us at the new house next week.

Daniel had brought Interpol in on the loop. They had initiated an international clandestine Red Notice on de Jong's passport photograph. The modern facial recognition software could elicit his face from millions of CCTV footage worldwide, as long as the recordings have been saved for whatever purpose.

My immediate task today, along with Olavo, was to start the process of contacting and interviewing all the surviving ramp-men who worked with Elusive 17 years ago. Five still worked at Faro airport, seven had retired, two had taken different employment and four of them had sadly died. You never know, they might yet disclose a titbit of information that could nail this nasty piece of work we were looking for.

Olavo and I had also been charged with taking a trip north towards Lisbon, to interview the guys who sold and erected de Jong's polytunnels. We were going in two days.

I wandered back to the kitchen, filled a mug with coffee and then sashayed into the operations room to make a start.

Mary looked up from her screen. "I've been on to the Registros Civis, the Civil Register's website, Dave."

"Oh, yes?"

"No joy I'm afraid, only three children aged around twelve months were registered as having died in the Algarve during the four weeks before Molly going missing, and none of them bear any relation to Hannah de Vries."

"I didn't think we'd find anything there, but it was worth a look."

"Yes, so, either they went through another elaborate false identity change to bury the child, she's not dead, or she did die and they've buried her somewhere in secret."

"Thanks, Mary. That was a grim task I set you there."

"No problem. It's just numbers. What would you like me to look at next?"

"Well, we should scrutinize everything. Leave nothing to chance; I think Elusive departed Portugal years ago. For whatever reason made him abduct Molly, he was spooked enough to jack in a profitable little business, plus whatever illegal activity he was up on that farm, and leg it back to Holland, sharpish. But for prudence's sake, we should take a look for any other fruit and veg growers that started up in the region after June 2003, in case he just moved premises. Check for similarities in dog registrations during that time and see if we can get a list of foreign nationals that applied for residency in the Algarve in the last 17 years."

Mary puffed out her lips. "Will do, Skip." She twitched her head sideways at the tall order.

It was Paul's turn to update me.

"I've drawn up a list of agricultural colleges in the Netherlands, Dave. Surprisingly, there are only four. All relatively close to one another in central Holland. One is in Zaltblommel, there's one near Arnhem and two in Ede."

"Hmm, I thought there'd be more. Have you looked through the student records yet?"

"Just about to, gonna start in 1990. Elusive would probably be in his early twenties then."

"Cool."

Olavo piped up, "That's done then. I've done a deal on a Mercedes Sprinter and a Mercedes SUV for next Tuesday. We can pick 'em up from Faro airport."

"Marvellous, mate. That should do us. Now let's crack on with these ramp-men. Oh, Mary, these whiteboards?"

She looked up from her task in hand.

"Do you photograph them every time you wipe 'em clean?"

"Of course."

"Just checking."

The fourteen surviving ramp-men all told a similar story. Marc Freese, as they knew him, kept to himself. On the odd occasion he did work with someone, he would treat them to a Starbucks or a Costa Coffee. He openly admitted he found it irritating working close to somebody else and preferred to crack on by his lonesome. They all agreed, though, that he was a grafter.

The interesting thing that they all commented on, so it must have been a stark contrast to the old days, is that passengers were travelling lighter and lighter as time went on. Which led to more space available in the hold for transported goods with short shelf lives, such as fruit and flowers, especially organic tomatoes, which led us to believe that perhaps Elusive's priority reason for working

194

at the airport was to make sure his special tomatoes arrived safely at their destination.

Were they that special he was willing to take ten hours out of each day to nurse them on their way? It seemed a bit extreme.

All Paul could winkle out of the agricultural colleges' student records for the '90s was a list of 600 male and 200 female names, no official photographs, no social media back then, and no names that were used by Elusive so far. It was frustrating and of little use.

Mary was also drawing a blank, nothing resembling the Elusives being flagged up at all.

I told them both to scale down the inquiries for a couple of days; they could correlate the findings coming in from Faustino and Alfie while Olavo and I were away, over in Lisbon.

We took the new X Trail, which only had 1,000 km on the clock, and drove the two hours up to an industrial estate near Loures, north of Lisbon, smoothly, like a silk dress over shaved legs.

One of the directors of Bosque de Framboesa, Rodrigo Coval, a slim, neatly attired man in his early 40s, greeted us with a warm handshake. He had sold the polytunnels to Michael de Jong back in 2001 and had been on the team who erected the 160m long tunnels on the farm.

Rodrigo's English wasn't that great, so Olavo had to interpret much of our conversation. Mr and Mrs Elusive had made quite an impression on him, but not in a good way, arrogant, he called them.

He went on to explain what he meant. His business was in its infancy back then. The three owners were all hands-on, and they only had 25 staff. Now they employed over 200.

Being single at the time, and having no children, Rodrigo drew the short straw and had to make the long journey every day with ten others, for two solid weeks, nine hours a day assembling the tunnels. It was very hard graft.

Michael de Jong set the rules. He was nasty, void of empathy, assertive and dogmatic. He reminded Rodrigo of the German concentration camp officer played by Ralf Fiennes in *Schindler's List*, evil.

Obviously, he never shot any of them for kicks from his bedroom window, but his whole demeanour was one of 'do as I say, or else'.

The job was worth 130,000 euro to the company, with a bonus of a further 30,000 if they finished it within schedule. That's why the lads worked so hard and put up with his self-importance. They were on a share of the bonus.

It was a blessing he said, that de Jong was only there for a short period each afternoon when he came home from work. Otherwise, it would have been unbearable to have him strutting about all day, making demands.

I asked Rodrigo why the polytunnels were so expensive. That seemed like a lot of money to me.

He answered that it wasn't just for the tunnels; they also installed flooring, benches, lighting, an automated irrigation system, heating, humidifiers and extractors, all state-of-the-art equipment, containers, soil, fertiliser, everything they would need to grow tomatoes, except the plants. During the growing season, these tunnels were so good they could almost be left alone to run themselves.

That answered a few questions.

I asked him if he could add anything else about Michael de Jong or his missus.

He paused for a while, his brain visibly ticking over, before finally admitting that he actually felt intimidated in de Jong's company, cicatrizado he said, scared. This must have been quite embarrassing to admit to a couple of unfamiliar men.

The only admirable quality that the couple possessed was that they paid promptly. There seemed to be no shortage of funding for their project.

Rodrigo gave us a copy of the original invoice; it had a breakdown of all the work carried out, and a detailed inventory of all the materials used.

We thanked him for his time and left; the visit had given us some new insights.

I drove back to the villa whilst Olavo went through the invoice; he was intrigued as to why de Jong had bought so many rolls of industrial polythene. I suggested he call Rodrigo to ask if he knew the answer. All Rodrigo could say was that de Jong wanted it for some sort of propagation room for his seedlings and that he didn't query it further.

That may have been a perfectly legitimate reason for having all that polythene, but in my mind, it was for only one thing, an indoor greenhouse for growing cannabis. I'd bet my life on it. Hopefully, in a few days, after the forensic sweep of the farm, I'll still be drawing breath.

What didn't make sense, though, was that if these two criminals were growing a fantastic legitimate product that netted them a fair few quid, and it was fronting an even more profitable marijuana business, then why would they suddenly jack it all in and take flight back to Holland when they were doing so well?

Was it because they had kidnapped Molly, for whatever reason, and couldn't handle the pressure? Or are we missing something?

Olavo's theory that their own daughter had died somehow and they had replaced her with Molly and run off to start afresh somewhere was a reasonable one, but we had all come to the conclusion that neither of the Elusives expressed the persona of doting parents. On the contrary, their profile is of cold, calculated sociopaths, in it just for the money.

The next four days gave us clear, indisputable proof that the Elusives were not just baby snatchers, drug dealers and a formidable couple, but also we were convinced that both of them played a part in Molly's abduction.

The forensic team found amongst others, hair samples that matched DNA for Molly Baker, hundreds of samples of cannabis production at the farm, and several sets of fingerprints, two of them children, none of which were on any police databases.

A daunting realisation came over us all at once. Molly could be buried on that farm. Maybe even Hannah de Vries as well.

Bento Sampaio knew it too; this could be the awful conclusion to Molly's disappearance and this, in his mind, was a chance for his police force to regain the worldwide respect and praise it deserved.

That very day, he ordered an extension on the forensic search and a gagging order on the Cardosa family not to repeat to anyone what the police were doing on their land. The lid needed to be kept firmly on the situation, expressly with the media. Faustino was the one selected to serve the order. He did it with mixed feelings. These were decent people. He didn't want to be the heavy hand of the law, yet at the same time, he desperately wanted to crack the case for all parties concerned.

Duarte Cardosa was the epitome of virtuous integrity; his word was his honour. Anything he could do to help solve this tragedy that had blemished Portugal's reputation would be a source of pride for him.

The forensic team spent another week at the farm, so Alfie and Faustino were obliged to stay with them. They used ground-penetrating radar to look for disturbed substructures and dug pits in suspect areas. They had the floors up in the house, checked inside stud walls and even down the well. They found nothing, not a single human bone, a fragment of clothing, or a tooth. The girls weren't buried there.

So for us, we had the knowledge that Molly had been at the farm, alive at least for a while. It was a huge step in the right direction, which totally vindicated her parents from any crime and proved that she didn't just vanish into thin air.

Faustino had finally been given permission to join us in Holland. I was inclined to think that Bento Sampaio only let him come with us so that a Portuguese would be on the team if we should solve the case, giving kudos to his country.

Our last night in Vista do Vale together was a sombre affair. We were glad to have made giant leaps for the case here in Portugal, but sad to be leaving our home from home.

We fired up the pizza oven out on the patio, and Faustino made some of the most fantastic pizzas I've ever tasted, the dough an' all, from scratch, topped simply with his own tomato sauce, mozzarella, black olives, capers and basil. They were delicious and washed down with copious amounts of Peroni beer. We talked until late, going over all we had achieved so far.

The next day Faustino and Alfie had already left for the farm by the time the rest of us surfaced. Our bags had been packed the day before, and the office equipment was broken down and boxed.

I had the rental vehicles brought to us. They arrived at 9 a.m., and their drivers were whisked away in a third Mercedes.

By lunchtime, the four of us had loaded everything we were taking, and the living room, with the help of Carlos and Ramona, was put back to its previous state, in readiness for Jim to reoccupy the villa, had he wanted to. Ramona was going to get a team of cleaners in and get the whole place immaculate as soon as Alfie and Faustino had gone.

Our caretakers had laid on a goodbye spread out on the patio, apart from the operations room. This area had been our most frequented at the villa. We'd had a lot of laughs out here. This afternoon it felt more official.

The grub, as usual, was divine, and way too much for us to devour. We declined any alcohol though; we had a very long road trip ahead of us and wanted to get at least six hours of driving in before we rested for the night in the middle of Spain.

By the end of the second night, we had reached Poitiers in Western France and stayed in a cheap budget hotel. This just left an easy eight-hour journey the next day through Belgium and up into Holland.

We arrived in the outskirts of Haarlem on the 23rd of June, road-weary, but without incident and all in one piece.

The house we had rented, Grote Bomen, which meant Tall Trees, was quite stately in appearance and, indeed, surrounded by lofty woodland. We slowed towards the black painted iron, electronic front gates, which opened effortlessly as we neared, and were approached from the gatehouse by our housekeeper and gardener, Julia and Finn Vos. Both apparently were ex-diplomatic protection squad officers and were held in the highest regard. Daniel knew them personally.

According to the property's blurb, many dignitaries had stayed there in the past, so having a couple of well-trained former police officers as security gave me the full conviction of having the sanctuary we needed behind these boundary walls.

And what a beauty it was. The brick-built house dated back to 1917. It had red plain tile, hipped roofs with tall chimney stacks, apexes and dormer windows. All the painted woodwork was cream, the windows and doors being of a Georgian style.

The main house was half-hexagon shaped, with the pool house a flat-roofed extension to the rear.

The grounds were immaculate formal gardens to the front of the property, planted around a granite sett drive. An orchard was to the right-hand side, a large patio behind the swimming pool, two tennis courts and a nine-hole golf course. All of the rest of the land was left natural, most of it woodland.

Julia and Finn greeted us with a smile. They stood together with their hands behind their backs until we exited the vehicles, then they led with a handshake.

They were both fluent in English.

"Welcome, welcome," said Finn. "We are very pleased to have you all staying with us here at Grote Bomen. It is a lovely house."

"And," added Julia, "for such a lengthy booking, I feel we will all get to know one another very well."

They were charming, both in their late 50s, smartly attired and both above average height. Julia had blonde, wavy, shoulder-length hair, whilst Finn kept his greying locks to a very short crop.

Finn's smile was expansive. "If you'd like to drive your vehicles up to the house, we will show you around."

The house itself had an impressive 26 rooms in total. We walked past the centrepiece, an oblong pond in front of a pair of huge French doors with an arch above made of Georgian lights. This opened up fully to one of the sitting rooms.

Next to this was the main entrance, through which we found ourselves in a roomy hall, tiled with slate grey marble and doorways to the rear, left and right, leading to other parts of the house, and a balustrade staircase on the right-hand wall painted in a brilliant white to match the walls and ceiling.

All the other rooms at ground level had parquet flooring and a bounty of windows and doors which brought in swathes of light. There were two large sitting rooms, both equipped with two massive couches each, a piano and a walk-in fireplace. But the room that suited us most was one of the two dining rooms, a long, sparsely-decorated room with four lots of double French doors on two sides which opened onto the patio area at the rear, an ideal conference room, and in our case our next operations room.

The kitchen had light ash cabinets and black marble worktops, not as big as the kitchen at Vista do Vale, but adequate for our needs.

The bedrooms and bathrooms were quite conservative, formal and pristinely presented, almost like an old London hotel, bright, again with plenty of light. All the bedrooms were carpeted, and all were ensuite. I chose one at the end of the landing on the right-hand side, with a view of the orchard.

We all were especially impressed with the basement. It had been converted into a gaudy disco room, entered via a pink florescent spiral staircase which led down to chess board vinyl floor, 1950s style bar and booth seating, gantry lighting and a working jukebox. There was also the nose section of an old red Cadillac on the wall and a life-sized model of Marilyn Monroe in her famous pose of her white dress being lifted by an air vent in the pavement. An ideal place for a party, should we feel the need.

We then got shown the pool and sauna room and finally the tennis courts beyond the rear garden. The golf course could wait for another day. We were all hungry and tired, and we were yet to unload our luggage.

Julia and Finn helped us bring in our bags and take them to our rooms, then for a special welcoming, they were going to prepare our first meal in the house, Dutch specialities we were told.

I had a quick wash of my hands and face, and then joined the rest of my team in the small dining room. On the menu tonight we had starters of Kroket, like potato croquettes, but with shrimp and satay chicken inside, and Bitterballen, savoury meatballs covered in breadcrumbs and served with mustard. They were really tasty.

The main course was the Dutch equivalent of fish and chips, bite-size strips of white fish deep fried in batter called Kibbeling along with Patat, fat French fries with mayonnaise and satay sauces.

For dessert, we were treated to Poffertjes, small puffed up, icing sugar-dusted pancakes topped with maple syrup and whipped cream.

Nuevo cuisine, it was not, but definitely new to my palette.

We thanked our housekeepers for a very filling meal, of which they even did the dishes. Then we all hit the hay. Tomorrow was going to be hard work, and I for one needed some shut-eye.

On Tuesday, we moved the furniture out of the large dining room, storing it in the triple garage, and then unloaded the Sprinter. The hire company came and retrieved the van in the afternoon, leaving us with the SUV. I decided to keep this for a while, but I planned to fly home soon to see Elizabeth and collect my Range Rover. I missed being high off the ground when I travelled.

By the evening we had set up the operations room to our liking, whiteboards around the walls and computers plugged in.

Mary began to write up a situation board that took up four whiteboards, and a 'things to do' board, which at the moment was blank.

She clicked the lid back on her marker pen and said, "It's been bugging me, Dave…"

"What's that?"

"…All this strong cotton that Yvette de Vries bought from the haberdashery in Douro Calvo. What do you think she was making?"

"I doubt if it was just for mending clothes…," said Olavo, "…and she wouldn't have had time to make some, not if she was the only one tending her crops."

"Hmm," I pondered, "they were making something."

"Stitching the polythene together to make the indoor greenhouse?" suggested Paul.

I couldn't see it. "Nah, they'd use duct tape for that. Polythene wouldn't take a stitch. Flag it up, Mary; it has to play a part in all this."

We ordered a takeaway that night; we needed something familiar to get our teeth into. Chinese is Chinese no matter where you are in the world, apart from China that is.

Daniel and his two officers joined us on Wednesday morning. I'd spoken to him many times via Zoom, but never realised how tall he was, at least six foot three. The policewomen too were both six-footers and built like

204

athletes. What was it about Holland that made its inhabitants very tall?

It was like having most of Abba join us. Daniel had dirty blonde hair and a beard. I reckoned he was about 56. Rhonda was a blonde bombshell, a real head turner, and Barbara, a sultry curly brunette with a husky voice. Both women were mid-30s, and I could tell instantly that Paul was impressed, by his change in demeanour. Mary and Olavo found his persona shift quite amusing.

"I should expect a forensic report on the Hymer by Monday, Dave. Our team has gone over it with a fine-tooth comb," said Daniel.

I needed to see that motor home. "Who owns it now, Daniel?"

"A couple from Nijmegen, Olga and Bernard Meijer. They've had it since de Jong returned it, and kept it immaculate I hear."

That wasn't a good thing; it meant they had probably cleaned all the evidence off it years ago.

"I don't wish to appear arrogant and neither do I want to undermine the Politie, but would it be impertinent of me to ask if I could have a look at that Hymer personally?"

Daniel opened his arms and protruded his bottom lip. "It's not impertinent at all. I'd like to see the motorhome up close as well, get a feel for the vehicle our abductors used to kidnap Molly Baker. It may well be quite revealing."

That brought a smile to my face. Daniel called the Meijers straight away and arranged to visit them at their home tomorrow.

"Excellent," I said.

"It is no problem." He shrugged. "You English are too polite. You should relax a bit more."

He smiled, the women smirked, and I chuckled. He was right.

It was time to set everybody to work; the Dutch officers had full access to the national police database through their laptops, which would give us so much more information than we could have possibly had without them.

None of us envied the tasks ahead. It was laborious and painstaking, but these things had to be undertaken.

We needed to check hospitals, both private and national, surgeries and clinics, for information on female births a month prior and after the date of April 22nd 2002. If Hannah de Vries was born in Holland legally, then her real name will be on a list.

Also, I wanted to take a look at any fruit and veg growers that have started up in Holland since June 2003. Elusive may have moved shop to here.

And, although they have been checked before and vetted by the airports, re-examine the files on all ramp-men at Dutch airports, especially any employees who joined them after June 2003. You never know. Some vital evidence may have slipped through the net, and each connecting piece gave us a broader picture of what to look for.

I was trying to keep the team focussed and positive, and above all occupied, because right then we had very little to move us forward. The bottom line was, this slippery pair could be anywhere in the world right now.

"Oh, Dave," remembered Daniel suddenly, "I have set up a meeting with two agents from Interpol for this Friday. I hope this is convenient?"

"No problem, Daniel. They coming here?"

"Absolutely, 10 a.m."

"Super. See what they can bring to the table."

On Thursday, Daniel and I found ourselves under the cream-coloured iron arch of the Waalbrug, the Waal bridge at Nijmegen.

"The last bridge to be taken by allied troops during operation Market Garden," I said with rueful pride.

"You know your history, my friend."

"I've watched *A Bridge Too Far* many times. Great film."

"Ah yes, loads of film stars in that movie, and quite an accurate depiction of events, but what a debacle, Such a loss of life for so little gain."

"Yeah, but it did liberate a part of Holland, didn't it?"

"About 20 percent, but the allies didn't achieve their goal of ending the war by Christmas 1944, did they? And 500 Dutch civilians died needlessly as a result of the battles. The operation was badly planned, badly executed and suffered from bad weather and bad luck."

I could tell it was a sore point for Daniel, and like the allied army back then, I was onto a loser trying to remonstrate with him. So I shut up.

The Meijers lived in a suburb called Wijchen, in a four-bedroom detached brick house on an affluent street. The motorhome was parked beside the house on a block paved drive. She looked brand spanking new.

We parked in front of it, and Daniel rang the bell of the glossy black door. It was answered immediately, like they were waiting behind it for us to knock, by Olga and Bernard, a retired couple who spent their twilight years discovering hidden gems all over Europe in the Hymer, their pride and joy.

They invited us in for a coffee, which we gladly accepted, and talked for a brief while about their travels; they'd been as far as the Black Sea resort of Sinop in Turkey, and up to Tallinn in northern Estonia.

I fancied a bit of that myself.

"Do you mind if we take a look inside the Hymer?" I asked.

"By all means," replied Bernard, "be our guests."

"What is it that you are looking for?" asked Olga, innocently inquisitive.

Daniel responded with his Detective Inspector head-on. "All we can tell you at this point in time is that the motor home may have been used in some criminal activity before your ownership. Detective Skipper here is here working in conjunction with the British police on the matter."

I knew it would be a hopeless task because of how clean the machine was. Still, I hoped upon hope that somehow I could connect metaphysically for the first time in my life and draw some spiritual energy from the metal and plastic of events gone by. A replay of the evil past this motor home had witnessed.

Nothing, not a sausage.

We went back inside, frustrated.

I tried a couple of questions. "Is there anything at all you can tell us that you didn't tell the forensic team that was here last week?"

They both delved within themselves, but slowly shook their heads.

"In all this time, you've never found anything that might have come from the previous owners, fallen down the back of the sofa, under the bed, on top of the wardrobe, a button, toothpick, sweet wrapper, hair clip?"

They continued shaking their heads, bottom lips protruding.

Daniel took up the mantle, "Have you ever had to pull up the carpet, or remove a cupboard for anything?"

Blank looks.

I tried one more time, "When you first bought the home, did you notice any unusual smells or odours of any kind, any stains?"

208

All we received was bewilderment.

I turned and stared at the Hymer, trying to think of anything that old bus could tell me.

Bernard began conversing with Daniel in Dutch. I presumed it was just idle talk and a thank you, but when I turned back to face them, I could tell it was of greater importance. Olga spoke, Bernard spoke, and Daniel spoke again. It was all gobbledegook to me. But then Olga paused and put her hand on my arm.

"There is something," she said.

My pulse quickened and a warm, fuzzy feeling engulfed me.

"It was six or seven years ago. We had to replace the fridge. The engineer said that the motor had gone. Anyway, when he pulled the old fridge out, there was this magnet underneath. Bernard was outside at the time, giving the home a polish and the engineer came out and handed it to him. He put it in his carry box of cleaning equipment, and quite honestly we haven't thought about it at all since."

"A fridge magnet?"

"Yes, a little white one with pink ballet shoes on, a dear little thing."

I asked Bernard if he still had it. He said that he imagined so, he hadn't thrown it out. It would still be in his cleaning box, in the garage.

I went with him into a carpeted, brightly-lit workspace, with every mechanics tool you could think of hanging on one wall and a tall, red, Snap-on roll cabinet, probably full of gleaming spanners.

Bernard reached to a high shelf and brought down an opaque plastic carry tray rammed with car cleaning products and cloths. Once on the workbench, he rummaged through it and soon produced a flat, oblong ceramic, slightly smaller than a business card. He went to hand it to me, but I stopped him, before putting on some disposable gloves and opening a zip-lock sample bag.

He dropped the magnet into the bag with a curious look on his face.

Holding it up towards my face, I examined it through the plastic. It had a faded gold rim around the white bubbled surface of the pictured side, depicting a pair of crossed pink ballet shoes and the remnants of an inscription, long worn away or destroyed by the ammonia on Bernard's cleaning cloths.

It was a shame that I couldn't read the writing, but this sort of trinket would be catalogued somewhere, which meant we'd be able to identify where it came from.

I asked Bernard and Olga once more to confirm that the fridge magnet wasn't theirs. They said absolutely not.

Daniel strolled off down the drive towards the road, telephoning the first owners of the Hymer as he walked, to see if the magnet had ever belonged to them. It hadn't.

This may be insignificant but, as it stood, this was the only piece of physical material we had, that once belonged to the Elusives before Portugal, their second mistake.

As we took our leave, it appeared that Olga and Bernard were exchanging strong words.

Daniel smirked. "She is scolding him for not speaking up about the magnet sooner. Empty headed, she called him."

Back at base, I asked Paul to search the internet for a fridge magnet like the one we had acquired, and if not, could he find an expert in the field or a magnet collector who might be able to shine some light on what we had.

Then I went and sat at my desk and began sifting through my emails.

210

Ten minutes later, I glanced over my screen to see Paul chuckling to himself, which was a rare sight because he was normally so stoic. It was a pleasure to witness.

Everyone was now curious as to what had amused him so much, so he shared with us the source.

He had likely found a couple of fridge magnet enthusiasts, who had more knowledge on the subject than anyone on the planet.

Colin and Sheila Whiteleaf, from Eastbourne. To date, they had amassed a total of 23,872 fridge magnets, had written three books on the subject, and next year, they planned on opening the world's first supermarket trolley and basket museum.

The room fell into open-mouthed silence, then Rhonda spoke, "Who would go to that?"

Mary put on a nasal voice, "So what first attracted you to Colin, Sheila? Was it his magnetic personality?"

We all chuckled. Barbara was really laughing. All I could think of was watching paint dry.

Apparently, they also owned two crazy-golf courses and ran a tearoom on the seafront.

I got their phone number from Paul and quick-stepped my way to the kitchen. Trying to have a conversation with either of the Whiteleafs might prove difficult with this lot taking the piss in the background.

The banter followed me through the hall, "Get me two tickets for the museum, Dave." "Ask 'em if they do season tickets." "Do they cater for coach parties?"

The cheerful, bubbly voice on the other end of the phone belonged to Sheila. I explained who I was and that I needed to know the origin of a faded magnet that had come into my possession, which might be of significant help to an investigation.

"Is there writing on it?" she inquired.

"No, it has been rubbed off."

"Any pictures?"

"Yes, some pink ballet shoes."

"Ooh," she squealed, "I'd better pass you onto Colin. He does the ballet shoes."

Colin sounded just as enthusiastic.

"Is it a white badge?"

"Yes."

"Does it have a gold rim around it?"

"Yes." My hackles were on the up.

"Then I'll have to see it in person to give you a true evaluation of what you have there. I have more than two hundred different ballet shoe interpretations; it could be any one of them."

I made a snap decision there and then to travel to Eastbourne and present the magnet to them. I hadn't been home in more than six weeks and would dearly love to see Elizabeth, at the same time pick up my Range Rover and drive it back via the Euro tunnel.

I told Colin that I could be at their home this coming Tuesday around mid-day; he said he was looking forward to it. I believed he was.

When I got back to the Ops room, they were still ribbing me.

"Positive outcome, Dave?"

"Was he a basket case?"

"Did he steer you in the right direction, or was he off his trolley?"

"Fuck right off," I said with a smile.

Mary booked me a ticket for Saturday morning out of Schiphol airport. And when my daughter Sam heard I was coming home for a while, she offered to pick me up from Stansted, which was very convenient.

Friday was a big day. Alfie and Faustino joined us at Tall Trees.

Because they were well-known to the media for working on the case, they flew in separately, so as not to agitate speculation, and journeyed from the airport by different means. Olavo fetched his partner, whilst Alfie caught a cab.

Our British cop's eyes nearly popped out of his head when he caught sight of our new Dutch policewomen. He was especially taken with Rhonda, who rendered him temporarily mute when she shook his hand.

After they settled in, the boys briefed us on the forensic digs, ten pits in all, with no finds in any of them. There were fingerprints on the vehicles in the barn, and all over the house, but none of them matched police records. Many hair samples, but again, no DNA on record apart from Molly's.

The biggest find though, and the most surprising, was the basement under the barn; it was vast, beyond the boundaries of the exterior barn walls. It had been dug out years ago, shored up with stone walls and oak joists. This is where the cannabis had been grown, in a room within a room. The polythene structure and the raised beds were all still there, but nothing else.

The police estimated that de Jong had the space to grow at least 1,600 plants at any one time in there, each plant possibly producing half a kilo of marijuana, with a wholesale value of 800 euro per kilo. So, in theory, he could harvest 1,280,000 euro every three months. A staggering amount of revenue to just walk away from, which raised another question: how and when was he paid? It certainly didn't go into his bank account at Douro Calvo.

It also highlighted a point I had raised earlier. If they were growing so much weed, they must have had help. You would need a small army of so-called 'Trimmers', to process it all, and then a distribution network. So it stood to reason that there were other people out there who knew this operation existed.

With all this wealth being made, it must have been a pretty dramatic event that made the Elusives abandon the farm and go into hiding, and that something was related to them stealing Molly.

Daniel seemed to think that Elusive wasn't a part of a large drug cartel. The Politie's underground informants didn't know this man, but there was talk of a new super-strain of skunk on the streets, perhaps that was his. So, he must be his own boss, with his own people, somehow.

The meeting with the Interpol detectives was interesting. They'd been involved all along, in the background, and wanted an update on the situation and a transcript of all the evidence we had gathered to date.

There were two officers, Mattise Toussanit, a male French inspector, and a female Dutch sergeant, also very tall, called Yara Teuling.

We gave them what we had, but reiterated that the need for clandestine investigation was paramount to our success. We had come to believe that Elusive was very clever in concealing his tracks, meticulous in his preparation, covert in his activities, an expert in disguise and false identity, has built a web of subterfuge and is both ruthless and cunning. If he got wind that we were on his tail, we were certain he would disappear from the map forever, and we would then never find Molly Baker.

They agreed. There were protocols in place to keep their surveillance searches top-secret. Nothing would leak from the commission, guaranteed.

***

No father could be prouder of his children than I. They had all done exceptionally well for themselves. But my pride and joy was about to be eclipsed, because today I would be working alongside my daughter Sam, well, for a couple of hours at least, as the stand-in official liaison officer between the Metropolitan Police Force and the Portuguese Policia Judiciaria. And it felt marvellous. I was honoured.

George Rivers, an officer who had worked on the Baker case alongside Alfie since its beginning, met me at arrivals inside Stansted airport.

Sporting a sign bearing my name, and impeccably turned out in an expensive suit, George shook my hand, said he was pleased to meet me at last, and unburdened me from my holdall.

We walked the concourse of the white metal and glass building out to the pick-up area, where an unmarked police car was waiting for us in a designated police parking bay.

My daughter, in full Commander uniform, was perched authoritatively on the back seat, whilst another officer, Jim Hawes, who had also worked on the case, was up front at the wheel. I got in the back with my daughter and, despite the etiquette, kissed her on the cheek; I hadn't seen her in months.

Neither detective could disguise their mirth at my actions, nor could they hide their impertinence. I felt I had to say something, "She may be your commanding officer, lads, but she's still my little girl."

I think this embarrassed her even more.

"As you were, gentlemen," she softly decreed.

"Ma'am," they responded in unison.

Alfie usually reported back to the Met once a week, but because he had been so tied up with the forensic sweep at the hidden farm he had missed the last scheduled

215

telephone call. So I had volunteered to kill two birds with one stone and bring them up to date with recent events. Sam could then pass the information on to the top brass.

It went without saying that whatever I disclosed in the car would be confidential and could not be discussed outside of police boundaries. George and Jim were trusted and carried high-level clearance so I wasn't at all concerned.

It was a Saturday, yet both the M11 and the M25 were flowing at a snail's pace. It didn't matter; Sam's appointment with the Home Secretary wasn't until 2 p.m. so it gave us plenty of time to talk about the case.

I felt reasonably confident that Elusive would have ventured into the UK at some juncture to sell his products, so I asked Sam if it was possible to put some sort of surveillance on fruit and veg coming through border control. She said that she would look into it.

She inquired after our team's finances. I said that we were okay at present, the fund was holding out; as long as nothing extraordinary happened, it should last.

"Good," she said.

I got a sneaky suspicion from her tone that should we need more funds, then there were ways to raise them.

When we reached my house I offered Jim and George a cup of tea, but Sam said time was too short. She quickly put her head through the door to say hi to her mum and then left for London.

It was marvellous to be back home and in the arms of my wife. I was going to make the most of these next three days.

The new addition to the family was a delight, and superb company for Elizabeth, especially comforting at night. She'd named him Chase, and justly so because he would run you ragged around the house all day if you let

216

him. He was a black and white Springer Spaniel puppy and had no off-switch, but the softest coat I think I've ever felt on a dog.

It was reassuring to know that at least my wife had an early warning system should anyone come snooping around, and although we hadn't had the time to get well acquainted yet, I reckoned that this energetic little fellow and I were going to be great mates. Elizabeth broke a corner off her toast and marmalade and sneakily handed it to the puppy under the kitchen table. I pretended not to notice; it was Hoovered up quicker than the blink of an eye.

I was due to leave this morning and didn't want to go. We'd had a lovely weekend and my heart knew where it wanted to remain but, regrettably, I had to say farewell once again to my wife. As we sat there in our cozy little bubble, holding hands across the table, I promised Elizabeth that I would not leave it so long before I popped back for another visit.

She told me not to worry; she had plenty to occupy her time with, and a new man in her life. Hopefully she was referring to Chase.

This brought a smile to my face; my wife had a knack for saying the right things at the right time.

As I loaded my beige summer jacket with the essential notebook, pencils, phone, disposable gloves, evidence bags and peppermints, Elizabeth picked up the fridge magnet from the table and held it in her closed hand for a few seconds before handing it over to me.

Both my wife and her sister could correspond with people who had passed over. But their mother also had the power to hold a living person's possessions, a watch, a wallet, a ring, and tell that person what was going on in their life.

Elizabeth didn't have that capability, but for the few seconds she held that fridge magnet, I was hoping that she did.

"Did you feel something?" I asked her.

She just smiled serenely and said, "My only thought at this moment is, could you ask Colin or Sheila Whiteleaf why it is that supermarket trolleys always get stuck together?"

It's true, more often than not, you go to pull a trolley out from a line, and it won't budge, and you end up either slamming it on the ground to unlock it or moving on to the next line and grappling with one from there.

"I'll ask them."

My wife was no different to the rest of my team; she, too, found it incredible that someone would want to start up a trolley and basket museum. How could it possibly be of interest to enough people to warrant opening one? It bemused her.

With the dog under one arm, she followed me out to my Range Rover to wave me off. I wound down my window and she kissed me goodbye.

"You're going to have a good day today, my love," she promised.

Her words echoed in the car all the way to Eastbourne.

Arriving with at least an hour to kill before our arranged appointment, I took a walk along the seafront, partly out of curiosity to see what was going on in this crusty old resort, and partly just to gather my thoughts.

Stan Wright once said to me, "It doesn't matter how small or insignificant a lead may seem, if it's connected to the case, follow it up."

Basically, it may seem like I was clutching at straws, but this small magnet was the only lead we had right now.

218

I hadn't been to Eastbourne in years, and nothing much had changed. Still had the terraced row of marble-white Victorian hotels, the formal flower gardens, pristine sandy beaches with an overload of sodden wooden groynes, which I thought looked like a giant brown octopus keeping a possessive grip on the beach and, of course, the illustrious 19th-century pier.

But what was new was the Sovereign harbour on the east end of the beach, an attractive, trendy, place-to-be, rammed with expensive yachts and sailboats, a retail park, restaurants and high-end properties with prime sea views. On a hot day like today, one could almost be hobnobbing with the elite somewhere in the Mediterranean.

Time was pressing on. I walked back to the Range in the car park and set off to find Colin and Sheila's street.

What I found was two adjacent rows of perfect detached bungalows, manicured gardens, award-winning hanging baskets, and lawns like snooker-table baize. It was surreal yet impressive, like there was a mandate for maintaining a model street.

I think in reality they were all just keeping up with the Jones', and everyone was at it.

Finding number 37, I had to drive past it and down the road a bit to park, then walk back. The house was appropriately named The Magnet.

An elderly gent next door was mowing his baize with a vintage manual Qualcast, the type my granddad used to have.

He stopped mowing and asked if I had come to see Colin and Sheila.

"That's right," I replied.

"They are in; I saw them around the back earlier."

"Oh, thank you."

"Have you travelled far?" he continued.

"Buckinghamshire."

I felt his eyes follow me up the path towards the Whiteleaf's front door.

In the private investigator business, a nosy neighbour can be worth their weight in gold, sometimes; others could be just damnright nosy.

I pushed the button on the doorbell and was greeted with the pleasing melody of Greensleeves, one of Henry the VIII's more endearing legacies.

Within seconds, the door cracked open and before I could utter a word, the neighbour got in there first, "Morning, Colin. You have a visitor."

State the bleeding obvious, I thought.

"Morning, Ted. Lovely day."

"Isn't it?"

Was I really here?

"Dave Skipper?"

It was my turn. "Yes, that's right."

"Come on in."

I felt like saying who needs a burglar alarm with neighbours like that, but quelled my ache for sarcasm.

Colin walked ahead of me, sporting ginger cords and a dark green cardigan; I tagged him to have been in his late 50s, and he moved in a leisurely, assured manner, confident and careful. His house was spotless.

He led me through to the lounge and offered me a chair, a single-seat floral number which was part of a suite.

No sooner had I parked my butt when a lady walked in, wearing a sky-blue summer dress almost completely obscured by a cotton apron depicting big lemons on the branch.

I stood up, and Colin introduced his wife.

"Pleasure to meet you, Sheila. Tell me," I said turning on the charm offensive, "what are those lovely smells coming out of your kitchen?"

She took the bait. "Monday and Wednesday are our baking days for the tea room. I've just finished baking six Battenberg cakes. They do have a lovely smell, don't they?"

"I couldn't agree more, Sheila. My wife, Elizabeth, enjoys baking, but she's not too keen on making Battenbergs, which is a shame because they're my favourites."

"Well, Mr Skipper, you sit back down, and I'll get you a nice cup of tea and a slice of your favourite. Do you prefer tea, or would you like a coffee?"

"Oh, please call me Dave, and tea will be fine."

It was definitely a cup of tea moment.

Colin re-animated. "Well, Dave, let's have a look at this magnet of yours."

"Absolutely," I said, reaching into my jacket. "I'm afraid it's an ongoing investigation, Colin, so it has to remain in the bag."

"Not a problem," he said, reaching for the zip-locked polythene with intent eyes.

He had a quick glance at the front and then turned it over.

"It's a single magnet!" His eyes flicked at me. "…you didn't tell me it was a single magnet!"

"Sorry, I didn't realise there was any other type."

He strode purposefully out to the hall and opened a cupboard door, then retrieved something small from the pocket of a jacket hanging on a coat hook.

Returning to the lounge, he commenced examining the fridge magnet in a better light by the front window, using a jeweller's loupe.

"It's Dutch," he announced with authority.

It had been a strong possibility.

He stopped looking at it and turned his gaze to me.

"Do you have the box?" he snapped.

I was almost afraid to answer him. "Er, no, this is how it came."

His excitement was bubbling. He called Sheila in and handed her the evidence bag.

"Don't take it out of the bag, love."

She held it up to the light. Her eyes flicked to him, then back to the magnet.

In a copycat enactment of her husband, she reversed it and said, "It's a single magnet, Dutch, have you got the box?"

I thought I was in a room with two parrots.

"I'm afraid not," I lamented.

She handed it back to her husband.

"Shame about the condition and the lack of a box," she rued, and then returned to the kitchen.

I turned to Colin. "What we talking, Col'."

"Well, Dave, if this magnet had been in pristine condition and you also had the box, also in mint condition, then what you would have here would have been the Holy Grail of fridge magnets, so to speak."

"It's a rare one, then?"

Colin jutted his chin out and nodded.

"Let me explain," he said. "In 1981, ballet schools across five countries in Europe, Germany, France, Luxemburg, Belgium and the Netherlands…" He held up the bag, indicating its origin. "…Decided to give the tiny ballerinas a welcome souvenir on their very first day of school. *This* beautiful little fridge magnet presented in a pretty blue box."

The gears were turning in my head.

"The problem was, the first edition of these puppies only had the one magnet; they weren't very powerful and tended to fall off fridge doors when you closed them."

I was getting the picture.

"…And, being ceramic, and kitchen floors being usually made of hard material, they often shattered or at least chipped."

"Therefore, reducing the numbers?" I surmised.

"Exactly. So, in 1982, October I think it was, the manufacturers upped the ante and put two magnets on the back, rendering the first edition obsolete, but not so for us collectors."

Collin chuckled.

This was fantastic; it meant that I had a small period in time for when this magnet was dished out in a Dutch Ballet school for little girls. I had no idea how many ballet schools were active in Holland in 1981, but they must have kept registers for their students, and I was betting that Mrs Elusive was one of those young ballerinas.

Colin was still rabbiting, "…so you can see why the single magnet is so sought after by we collectors, especially for Sheila and I, we have one, but it is broken in half and doesn't have a box. Unlike our other four from Germany, France, Luxemburg and Belgium, which are all in mint condition."

"You have some in mint condition!?" I was more than interested now.

"Yes, I'll show them to you after you've had your tea."

"I have a question for you, Colin. How did you know my particular magnet was Dutch?"

"Oh, that's easy. Both Sheila and I are fluent in several languages. It's how we met 37 years ago. We both worked as translators for governmental departments. Can't say any more than that."

He tapped the side of his nose with his hush, hush first finger.

At that point, Sheila floated in with a tray full of china and cake.

"You're being spoilt," said Colin. "She's brought out the Royal Doulton."

"There you go, Dave."

She placed a flowery bone china cup and saucer down on a small table that Colin had pulled out from a nest, and poured me a cuppa, the old-fashioned way, from a teapot, using a strainer. I thanked her and took a bite of Battenberg. It was superb.

I had to ask the burning question that must cross everyone's mind when they hear about the museum. How on earth did it come about?

Colin got the ball rolling with a wide smile. "Ten years ago, my uncle Fred died and left us two crazy-golf courses, the land with the old scout hut on it and his detached cottage, both of which have preservation orders on."

"We didn't know what to do with it all at first," said Sheila, "but because the summer is so busy down here there's always a need for a tea room, so we got permission for a change of use for Fred's cottage and opened one up. Now it's busy all year round. Never a dull moment."

"And crazy-golf's always an attraction for holidaymakers, so we kept them going," continued Colin. "Then we decided to turn the scout hut into a museum, and got permission from the council to do just that."

I was still in the dark. "So, why a supermarket trolley and basket museum?"

"Ah, well, that was uncle Fred again. His wife, my auntie Winn, passed away about seven years before him, and he was lost without her, needed something to do."

Colin paused for a bit, like he was still grieving for their loss.

"It's quite sad really, Dave. My uncle and aunt were like second parents to me. We were very close."

Sheila took up the story, "When Fred and Winn used to go shopping together, unlike most people, they tended to mix it up a bit and go to different supermarkets each time. Well, for some reason, Fred was fascinated with the differences in all the shopping trolleys. It became an obsession for him. So when Winn died, he started buying used and broken trolleys; repairing them, and displaying them at the golf courses."

Colin came back into the conversation, "It was the talk of the town, people drove for miles to see the weird collection. The trolleys came from all over the world. They were a great source of amusement."

"Well, it's all tongue-in-cheek really, but they are now housed in the old scout hut, and people are quite prepared to pay money to see the collection," said Sheila.

I had a change of heart. It was quite an endearing story and evidently a unique attraction.

"My wife has asked me to pose a question to you," I said. "I hope you don't mind, but why is it that supermarket trolleys get stuck inside one another?"

"A common occurrence," said Colin, "different spec."

"Eh?"

"Even if they are all Sainsbury's trolleys or all Tesco's trolleys, they'll be made in different factories around the world, with slightly different spec. Ram a fractionally larger trolley into a smaller one, and it'll be tough to pull it out."

There answered one of the world's deepest mysteries. It was truly satisfying to be in the know.

"And how did the fridge magnet collection start?"

"Sheila can tell you this one, Dave."

"Well, it's a story that most people find hard to believe. Colin and I had only been going out with each other for four months when we both had to go to Brussels for a week. After work, we would go exploring and find somewhere to eat. On the second night, I went into this souvenir shop for a look around and saw this fridge magnet with a glass of Belgian beer on it…"

"I do love me Belgian beer, Dave."

"…So, I bought it for him, only to be presented a few moments later with a fridge magnet of my own from Colin, a miniature snow globe. It snowed when you shook it."

"What are the coincidences, Dave? We'd both bought each other the same thing."

I nodded with fake incredulity.

"Anyway," continued Sheila, "by the time we got back to the hotel, we'd bought each other five more magnets each. Then that was it, the infatuation began. We often tell people, that because of our work, we didn't have children, but magnets instead."

They both laughed at their homespun joke.

I just grinned.

Sheila got up to return to her baking. "I better let you two get on," she said.

I followed Colin out through the conservatory and into the back garden, which could have easily passed for the Chelsea flower show. How they managed to do all this was beyond me. I barely had the time to cut the grass back home twice a week.

The brick-built garage had been extended to three times its length, all the way to the end of the garden. Colin unlocked the side door. It opened with a suction hiss. We entered and bright lights came on automatically. Inside, it was carpeted, and lining both side walls were vintage Mahogany map maker's drawers, of about belly height.

"Close the door, please, Dave, temperature controlled."

I did as he wished; it was so impressive in there. I asked if it would be alright to take a couple of photos for posterity. He said, "Feel free."

A few chests down, on the right-hand side, we came to the 'B's'. Colin pulled a drawer out, halfway down the chest, revealing 50-plus fridge magnets, all with a connection to ballet.

"There you go, the same as yours, only broken."

Next to it were the four other similar magnets from the other countries. I daren't touch them; they looked too precious in their royal blue boxes. I bent forward to get a closer look at the Dutch one.

"What does it say, Col'?"

"En hoewel ze misschien klein is, is ze fel."

"And in English?"

"And though she may be little, she is fierce."

"Profound, mate. That's enough to empower anyone."

"That's why Sheila loved it."

Colin moved back towards the door and a tidy workbench. On it was a stack of three books. He picked up the middle one and thumbed through it rapidly, stopping on a familiar page.

"Ah, as I thought, the single magnets were only in production between February '81 to October '82, four thousand Dutch models produced."

He snapped the book shut.

"Right," I said, thinking about the task ahead.

"I don't wish to pry, Dave, but why is this fridge magnet so important to you?" he wondered with curious eyes.

"Well, I can't tell you too much, but my agency is looking for a missing person, and this little magnet may hold the key to their whereabouts."

"So the little ballerina is missing?"

"Sort of. She's connected to the other person we are trying to find. If I can find the ballerina, I might be able to find the other."

"Gotcha."

"I hope to say that one day."

Colin half-laughed and nodded upwards.

"So, I now need to locate all those little ballerinas, who would be in their 40s now, who attended ballet schools in Holland between 1981 and '82."

"Er, not quite, Dave. Those schools may have bought a bulk of those first edition magnets and issued them over four or five years. That's a much bigger playing field."

"Damn, that's good insight."

"Pleased to help."

"Tell me, Col', where can I buy a copy of that book of yours?"

"You don't need to, Dave. Just screenshot the relevant pages off the internet; you don't need the whole book."

"Yeah, yeah, Paul can do that, but do you mind if I take a picture of the page you were looking at?"

"Be my guest," he said.

We closed up the garage and went back inside the house.

"Did you enjoy our little collection?" said Sheila, presenting me with a cake tin.

"Very impressive, Sheila. What have we got here?"

"It's a whole Battenberg and a couple of sausage rolls for the journey."

"You didn't have to do that!"

"I know, but I did."

"Here," said Colin, "a couple of tickets for the museum, on the house."

I was feeling over-endowed now; they'd been far too generous.

"How much are the tickets normally?"

"Three pounds for adults; pensioners and children go half-price," he was proud to say. "A percentage of the takings go to the local hospice."

"I'll tell you what. Give me another sixteen tickets for my work colleagues. They'll be pleased as punch."

I took out three 20-pound notes from my wallet and told him to keep the change for the hospice.

Sheila was smiling sweetly. "I hope we have been of some use to you today, Dave?"

"I think the information you have both provided me with will be critical in finding our missing person. Thank you so much, once again, for everything."

"No problem. You have a safe journey now."

I shook their hands and turned to leave, promising to keep in touch. The neighbour, Ted, was still in his garden. I bet he was itching to know who I was. All three of them stood on the pavement and waved me off.

I came away from Eastbourne with a lot of respect for the Whiteleafs. They had dedicated their lives to the pursuit of happiness, not just for themselves, but for the thousands of others they'd helped over the years. Fair play to them. They were good eggs. I also had a decent grasp on a lead for the Elusives. My wife was right. Today was a good day.

It took me ten hours to get back to Tall Trees; it gave me time to recap.

We knew the magnet didn't belong to the original owners of the Hymer, and we knew that it didn't belong to Olga and Bernard Meijer, so it must have belonged to Mrs Elusive. The question was, did she earn it at ballet school, or was it something she picked up at a boot sale, or a charity shop? Or maybe she was just given it?

But a part of me thought that if she felt the need to keep it with her during their criminal activities abroad, then it must have meant a lot to her.

The priority for the team now was to find out how many ballet schools there were in Holland between 1979 and 1986 and to try and get hold of their registers. We needed names.

I had a while to wait in the Euro tunnel terminal at Folkestone, so I perused the shops and picked up a bottle of Johnnie Walker Black Label and two massive Toblerones, which had by now become a tradition with any of my lot passing through duty-free.

Once I got on my way, I called Mary and asked her to put the conversation on speakerphone so the whole team could hear.

I gave them the basics of what had transpired in Eastbourne, and then relayed my proposal for the way forward.

We should put everything on hold and concentrate on finding the recipient of that fridge magnet.

I suggested we form three teams, with a Dutch speaker in each. Locate and visit all of the ballet schools that were, and are still in existence, and try and find the records of the ones that are not.

Then, once we have a list of names for possible recipients of the single magnet type, we have to find where those women are now and try and interview them. It was going to be a mammoth task.

By the time I reached base, it was midnight, yet Paul was still up and waiting for me.

"How was your journey, Skip?"

"Tiring, mate. Shouldn't you be in bed?"

"Yeah, I just wanted to keep a light on for you."

"Did you make any inroads with the new task?"

"We did; There were 58 ballet schools registered in Holland during that period. Alas, there are only 27 still running. Apparently, a change in trend more towards acting and performance art occurred and, nowadays, all the kids are interested in is becoming famous on reality

230

TV, YouTube or Tik Tok. Yet it's good to know some little girls still want to be ballerinas."

"Good start, mate. We'll reconvene in the morning. I'm bushed."

"Also, Dave, Rhonda has sorted out your first port of call tomorrow."

"Oh yes?"

"Ballet Masters from two of the closed schools are still in possession of the old registers and can show them to you. Daniel's with you."

"Where we off to?"

"Oegstgest, near Leiden, and then on to Middelburg. It's a bit of a trek, probably take you all day."

"Cool. I'll see you in the morning, mate."

I was late to rise; I'd had a blissful sleep, for, in this quiet secluded sanctuary, there wasn't much to disturb you.

It was 9:30 a.m. before I finally dragged my arse into the kitchen for some tea and toast. I'd missed the breakfast gathering out on the patio. All the doors and windows were open, allowing a blissfully mild draught to flutter through the building.

Julia had been through and tidied everything away, so it was a pity to dirty some more crockery, but needs must.

I entered the operations room, cup and plate in hand, to a flurry of activity. Everybody was either on the phone or had their head in front of a computer screen. Then the banter started.

"Afternoon, Dave," called out Alfie.

"Alarm clock broken, is it?" taunted Mary.

"How was your basket museum?" bayed Barbara. "Could you handle it?"

Everyone was smirking.

"Morning to you lot as well." I grinned back. "You'll be pleased to know, I've bought you all two tickets each to go and see the exhibition. It's fascinating."

The smiles faded. They were unsure as to whether I was joking or not.

"Maybe we'll make it a firm's outing," I ribbed.

Blank faces stared at me; only Paul was amused.

I moved on. "What we got then, people?"

Mary put me in the picture. "All of the ballet schools still operating can have their registers accessed online. We are compiling a list of names from those right now, and searching for current locations of these women…"

"Right."

"…In a bit," she continued. "Faustino, Paul and Barbara are off to Amsterdam to visit five retired Ballet Masters who have retained the old school registers, and Rhonda, Alfie and Olavo are going north to Heerenveen, Leeuwarden, Dratchen, Groningen and Emmen to do the same."

"Cool beans. You staying here then?"

"Someone's got to cook the dinner."

"Too right," I quipped. It was a good job Mary and I shared the same sense of humour.

Daniel and I arrived back at base around 6 p.m. with a list of 18 names, little girls who were given the single magnets between '81 and '84. We were the last to get back. But in my opinion, we had the best of luck, because one of the principals we had visited still had three single magnets in their original boxes, and she had given me one.

I knew who this was going to end up with.

In total, the team had collected 468 names from the schools still up and running and from the visits to old masters today, and we still had twelve more people to visit tomorrow. Seven former principals were either dead or could not be traced.

Before leaving, Daniel announced that it was his birthday tomorrow, so we weren't to have breakfast because he was bringing in some croissants and pastries.

"Yay!" whooped Mary. "How old?"

"Mentally twenty-eight, physically, twice that." He smiled.

The Dutch contingent left. We had dinner out on the patio, graced by the warmth of the evening sun. We had a wonderful crispy lardon and boiled egg Frisée salad, along with a selection of cold meats, cheeses and fresh baguettes, after which, Mary, Paul and I wrote up the list of names onto our whiteboards, while the other lads cleared away the table and did the dishes before relaxing for the night.

When we had all the names we could possibly get, we would start the process of elimination. Some of these women could possibly have passed away already, some may have emigrated, and some may not want to talk to us at all. And asking the question, "Where were you between 2001 and 2003 simply wasn't sufficient; Mrs Elusive wasn't going to say, "Oh yeah, I was on the Algarve for three years." No, we needed to be a bit more ingenious.

"Simple!" said Mary. "We just have to cross-reference these women's names with anyone who gave birth to a baby girl in Holland in April 2002."

"Yes, that's assuming Elusive did actually give birth in Holland. We only have her testimony to the doctor in Douro for that. But it's absolutely the right thing to do, Mary. Can you make a start on that tomorrow?"

"Sure. One of the girls can help me."

"Brilliant."

I was up at 7 a.m. and headed straight for the pool, soon to be joined by Olavo, Faustino, Alfie and then Paul. These early morning dips had become routine and were so invigorating.

After a few laps, we congregated in the Jacuzzi for a chin-wag.

Faustino's team were heading east to Arnhem, Apeldoorn and Enschede. Paul was going to Utrecht, Amersfoort, Zwolle and Hoogeveen. Whilst I was off to Tilburg, Eindhoven and some other place.

It was going to be another slog, but at least we were getting to see the country.

Up in the living room, unbeknownst to me, the Dutch girls had arrived early and had decorated the walls with Happy Birthday banners, in Dutch, of course, balloons and streamers. The large table had been covered by a protector and a table cloth and had been laid out for a breakfast bonanza courtesy of Julia and Finn.

A small pile of gifts and cards occupied a corner, plates and cups were laid, and a couple of pots of coffee and tea were being brought over when we lads ambled in.

"Blimey, you lot have gone to town!" I blurted.

"Well, it is a special day," said Rhonda, "a big number."

With that, Daniel walked in laden with cake boxes.

"Surprise!" everyone shouted.

"Fijne verjaardag!" said the Dutch girls. I suspected it meant happy birthday.

"My God," said Daniel chuckling, "I did not expect all this."

I went up to him and put an arm around his shoulder. "Well, it is a special day, old boy. How special is it?"

He laughed. "I have turned sixty today."

"Sixty! You don't look a day over eighty! Here let me take those cakes off your hands."

"No, no," he insisted, "you sit down. It is my birthday and I will serve my friends. It is the way we do it here in Holland."

And so he did. He went around to all of us and put a pastry on each of our plates and served us all a drink.

The leg-pulling and banter were running thick. Daniel opened his presents. Barbara had bought him an orange T-shirt with 'Geen heuvels in Nederland om over heen te gaan' written on it, which translates to 'No hills in Holland to be over'.

Whilst Rhonda had got him a Homer Simpson tie.

Somehow, Mary had managed to go out and buy him a pair of gold Union Jack cufflinks, as a present from all of us. I don't know how she found the time, but it was a perfect gesture.

All the girls gave him a kiss on the cheek and we sang him a verse of Happy Birthday to you, followed by calls for the bumps, and "Speech!"

Daniel just said, "Thank you all so much for the gifts. It has been a wonderful surprise. Now back to work the lot of you. We have so much to do."

He was right; we all had miles to do today.

We filtered into the operations room, breakfast still in hand, and gathered our itineraries from our desks.

Daniel had entered the room but stood stock still, staring at the whiteboards we had written up the night before.

The hubbub in the room subsided and the atmosphere died.

The look on Daniel's face had us all wondering what the hell was up. Was he having a stroke?

Suddenly, a rapid exchange happened in Dutch with Rhonda and Barbara. They joined him in front of the boards, before both scurrying back to their computers and smashing away at the keys.

More Dutch was exchanged before I intervened, concerned.

"Can somebody please tell me what the bloody hell is going on?"

The girls stopped typing and nodded at Daniel, who then spoke very soberly.

"I think that we have just found your Mr and Mrs Elusive.

8
Volgalaar

"What? Who?" I said, deep ruts crinkling my brown shiny forehead.

Daniel's eyes were closed and his right hand was gripping his face like the 'Facehugger' stage of the Xenomorph in the *Alien* movie.

Bar the whirring of computer fans, the room had descended into a hush.

He pulled his hand away, slowly opened his eyes and chewed on his bottom lip.

Obviously, some abhorrent creatures had just revealed themselves on the whiteboards and were apparently intimately known to the Dutch constabulary.

He pointed a reluctant finger towards the board in question.

"Ruby Van Dijk," he mouthed with disdain, and then inhaled involuntarily. "No need to search any more ballet schools. This is the woman we were looking for."

She had to be a high-profile criminal and an unpalatable one, too, by the look on Daniel's face.

"How do you know, mate?" I asked.

Daniel sighed. "If everyone could stop what they are doing… This will take a while."

It was plain to see how uncomfortable Daniel was in revealing this information. I asked him if he was alright. He bobbed his head a couple of times in the affirmative.

"Could I get three clear whiteboards, please?"

Alfie and Olavo jumped into action and set up the clean boards in front of the others.

Daniel then took to writing on all three of them with a black marker.

"The true identity of the man who stole Molly Baker is Jaden Janssen, Mr Elusive…"

He wrote Janssen's name on the top left of the middle board and then wrote Ruby Van Dijk on the right.

"… These two despicable human beings are partners, in life and in crime."

On the left-hand board, top left, he wrote Simon and Marion Van Dijk. Underneath he wrote (grandparents). Top right he wrote, Diana Van Dijk, underneath (Molly Baker?).

On the right-hand board, he wrote down seven male names, with their nationalities in brackets underneath each: Luka Heinz (German), Brian Lang (English), Emanuel Martin (French), Miguel Garcia (Spanish), Ionut and Marius Rusu (Romanian) and Yaroslav Fedorov (Russian).

What was impressive to me; he was doing all this from memory.

Whilst this was going on, Rhonda and Barbara were printing out photographs of the people being written up and sticking them next to the relevant individuals.

They also pinned up two palatial houses, one they adhered under Simon and Marion Van Dijk and the other under Jaden Janssen.

"Don't we have a photograph of Diana Van Dijk?" I queried.

"Nothing," said Barbara. "She has been kept in a bubble; homeschooled, no social media, nothing."

Mary, who was standing beside me, picked up on the Van Dijk residence. "That's just how Sophie Baker described it in her dreams, big house, massive garden in front."

"I remember," I murmured.

238

"Where is this Van Dijk residence?" I asked Daniel.

"It's right here, on the edge of the National park, about ten kilometres away," he said nonchalantly.

"She's here, right here!" I spouted, totally blown away.

"She might be," he cautioned.

"What!? Let's go and get her, now!"

"You have to hear this first, my friend."

Daniel asked everyone to gather around.

Paul said he would join us in a minute; he was just working online with something that would prove beneficial, but he would be listening.

Daniel knew Paul's strengths on the computer and understood that it must be relevant, so continued without him.

"Jaden Janssen…" The words seemed bitter in Daniel's mouth.

"… was born on April 15th, 1976. He was found outside St Lucas Hospital, in Winschoten, Groningen, northeast Netherlands…"

"Plate lickers!" voiced Barbara with a wry smile.

"Eh?" I said.

"It's what we call the locals of Winschoten. Because they lick their plates clean after they have eaten."

"Ja," said Rhonda, "Tellerlikker's."

Both girls giggled at the derogatory term.

Daniel reluctantly agreed, then continued.

"The doctors named him after the porter who had found him. The baby was eventually adopted by a childless couple called Janssen. Apparently, Mrs Janssen could not conceive. Later, they adopted two more children, a girl and a boy."

"Jaden excelled at school and, according to his teachers, was mature beyond his years. At the age of thirteen, he started to work part-time for his father who owned a moderate chain of pharmacies throughout Holland."

"The boy's job, after school and at weekends, was to keep the fleet of delivery vans clean. It was good pocket money."

Daniel digressed for a moment. "The single admirable trait that Janssen possesses is his work ethic. He has a ferocious appetite for hard work.

"It was during this time at his father's company that he befriended the Rusu brothers." Daniel stabbed a finger at their pictures.

"Part of their employment was to collect, bag up and deliver to the pharmaceutical manufacturers returned or out-of-date medicines that customers had brought back to the chemists, so they could be destroyed safely and in an environmentally friendly manner."

"A good majority of these returned medicines have never even been opened. They are in date and still useable, but can not be re-distributed by law and company policy. Jaden Janssen saw this as perfectly good medicine going to waste and an easy opportunity on the black market to exploit the unwanted goods."

"And so began his criminal career. With the help of the Rusu brothers, he developed a lucrative business selling literally tons of medicine destined for the furnace, to third-world countries. They even had contracts with other pharmacies and hospitals, to collect their surplus medicines and destroy them."

I was bubbling with questions. "Didn't anyone notice the medicines weren't being destroyed?"

"Nope, he played this game for four years. He is very clever this, Janssen. The guys at the furnace were on the payroll. They just had to burn bags with substitute materials in. No one batted an eyelid."

240

Alfie spoke up, "And what about the money he was making whilst he was a teenager? Surely that raised some red flags?"

"As I said, Alfie, even at a very young age, he knew how to hide and invest money. By the time he was eighteen, he had a company buying and refurbishing dilapidated properties, then renting them out. It's one of the best ways to launder dirty money."

"And he wasn't on your radar then, Daniel?" asked Olavo.

"No, he hadn't been caught doing anything illegal, so he was an unknown entity at this point."

"Go on," I said, biting the bullet.

Our Dutch cop scrunched up his eyes, coughed, and carried on with the briefing.

"About this time, Janssen's father decided that he'd had enough of the business, and sold it on to a competitor. This killed his son's drug re-distribution business, a very lucrative one, we were led to believe. So Jaden needed to fill that void with some other income. This is when he first dipped his toes into the illegal drugs business, with the help of some underground contacts he had made."

"Of course, you need to be able to handle yourself in these circles and though Jaden is tough, vicious and lacking in any remorse, he needed insurance, so enter Yaroslav Fedorov, a Russian thug from Saratov, who was working security for clubs in the red-light district of Amsterdam. He is a callous psychopath who enjoys splitting open heads with a Morgenstern bat. His inclusion in the mob was to put the fear of God into anyone who crossed Janssen."

Faustino was curious. "Did he come to your attention at this point?"

"Still no, my friend. Janssen's distribution network was vast and protected. The only players the drug squad got to know about were at the end of a long chain. And as you know, we have a relaxed way of dealing with the low-end drugs trade here in Holland, so if it's not causing any trouble, we tend to let it be."

"And what about this Ruby Van Dijk. How does she come into it?" I asked.

"I'm coming to that, Dave…"

I could see this was all quite vexing for him to unfold.

"…For the next six years, Janssen's empire grew, along with his underworld reputation. It seemed that there was equilibrium within the criminal fraternity and no one was rocking the boat. Janssen had two nightclubs, one in Rotterdam and one in Amsterdam. It was the one here in town where he met Ruby Van Dijk, the only child of the billionaire shipping and container tycoon, Simon Van Dijk."

"I can see the attraction," satirized Mary.

"Well, he may not have known that at first, but it certainly cemented their relationship later. Let me tell you something…"

Daniel paused for a second before continuing.

"The best way I can describe Ruby Van Dijk is to give you an eternal adage, one of life's most contested questions. Evil, is it nature or nurture? I believe that Van Dijk was born with some kind of evil, which flourished when she got involved with Janssen. So, in her case, it is both."

"As we have been led to believe, from a very young age Miss Van Dijk was rebellious, abusive, selfish and narcissistic, a perfect partner for Jaden Janssen."

"After two years together, Van Dijk had become chaotic, destructive and out-of-control, giving her parents no choice but to disown her. During the ensuing two years, the couple were inseparable. The criminal fraternity dubbed them 'Bonnie and Clyde', but in the limelight, because she was so high profile, the press just tagged them as a wild child and her mysterious businessman boyfriend. It was only then that his profile came into the public domain."

"But the police still had nothing on him?" I asked.

"No, why should we have? He was just a crazy socialite's fella, living it up. He wasn't being flagged for anything illegal at all."

"Then at the beginning of 2000, they vanished off the face of the earth. They were nowhere, which did cause a little ripple in the press for a while, but then nothing for three years."

More than curious, I asked, "This has clearly been a top priority case for the Dutch police, and one that has evidently frustrated you for some time, Daniel, but what made you start investigating Jansen and Van Dijk in the first place if they weren't connected to any criminal activity?"

"It started with gangland vendettas. Whilst Janssen was out of the picture, his empire continued to thrive, but there were turf wars, and always, the Rusu brothers and Fedorov came out on top, leaving a trail of bodies in their wake."

"Were arrests made?" questioned Alfie.

"Suspects were naturally brought in for questioning, but nothing would stick. These people covered their tracks flawlessly; we haven't been able to connect anyone to the murders, especially Jaden Janssen, who was off the radar at the time anyway, even if he was still the Kingpin. The paper trail of his money, too, is all above board, or leads to dead ends; he is a master at veiling his activities."

I sat on the corner of my desk. "And when did he come back on the scene, 2003?"

"Exactly so. We'd done all this investigation into the couple, knew everything about them, yet they weren't here. Then, suddenly, they were back, flaunting

243

themselves around town, back in the papers, and not just for raising hell in nightclubs. Simon Van Dijk also owned a string of builder's merchants throughout Holland. He very publicly gave the lot to his daughter, who subsequently gave them to her partner, just like that, a multi-million euro business handed over like a packet of chips. Janssen has been expanding the business ever since. He now has depots in eight other European countries."

Faustino was perplexed. "I don't understand. I thought Van Dijk had cut off his daughter. Why would he give her a huge corporation like that on a whim?"

"We believe it's because of the granddaughter, a despicable deal, the child for the business."

"What!?" gasped Mary. "The Van Dijk's bought a grandchild!!?"

My blood went cold; surely this thing wasn't planned before they'd even left for Portugal?

"We don't believe it was the Van Dijk's idea. We think that they were delighted when Ruby fell pregnant, to be getting a grandchild, despite being gravely concerned about the child's upbringing by these two self-centred sociopaths. The information we have received tells us that it was Ruby's plan to grab at least some of her inheritance from her parents. She didn't want the baby, only the money she could bring. And I'm sure the Van Dijk's were more than happy to adopt the little girl and give her an extremely privileged childhood. They are actually very decent people."

"Only one flaw," said Olavo, "that baby probably wasn't Ruby's to give."

Barbara, who had gone back to her desk, returned with data on the child.

"I have the birth certificate of Diana Van Dijk, born in a private hospital in Córdoba, Spain, on the 1st of August 2002, mother Ruby Van Dijk, and father Jaden Janssen."

244

I sighed. "Surely, Daniel, with all this information, when we first contacted you about Marc Freese and later Michael de Jong, you could have connected him with Jaden Janssen?"

"I hold my hands up, David. I feel foolish not to have. It's been many years since we last investigated Janssen. We've had a lot of other crimes since then. Plus, the photo you have of Marc Freese as a ramp-man at Faro airport looks nothing like the Janssen I remember. Your photo is out of focus. He has a beard and is wearing sunglasses and a baseball cap, very unlike the sharp-dressed Janssen I know.

"I'm sorry, everyone. I thought we were dealing with somebody completely new to me, but now, the drug connection, the car magazines, it all makes perfect sense. He's 100 percent the same guy."

"Why the car magazines?" I asked.

"Ah, of course, you wouldn't know. Janssen's passion is classic cars. He has one of the world's finest car collections, kept in an underground facility beneath his house in Groningen."

Daniel laid a finger on the mansion beneath Janssen's picture on the whiteboard.

"He has around 300 cars under here, mint condition, highly sought after, kept in a temperature-controlled, oxygen low, moisture-free environment. It is electronically sealed and guarded."

"He's sounding more and more like a bond villain," I quipped.

"A tomato-growing Bond villain," added Alfie.

"Yeah," I contemplated.

The room fell silent again whilst we all processed what had just been unveiled. It was a heck of a lot of information.

Rhonda shattered the silence. "Coffee, anyone?"

Everyone took up her offer.

Daniel resumed his discourse.

"I need to tell you all something that will give you further insight into the sort of animal we are dealing with here."

We all sat down again.

"About five years' ago, Janssen's name did come up again. A call came into the office regarding a 38-year-old off-duty nurse, who had been kneecapped and beaten unconscious. Rhonda and I went to the University medical centre in Groningen, in the hope of interviewing her. What we found was her husband, their two teenage sons and her parents, all in complete shock, as you can imagine.

The nurse, Sabrina Zegar, I think her name was, was too badly injured to be interviewed, so we spent some hours talking to a number of her colleagues and other relatives who had turned up enquiring about her well-being.

Rhonda and I were in total agreement. This lady was well-respected and loved, and nobody could understand why in the world anybody would have wanted to hurt her.

I noticed that her husband hadn't said anything yet and was suspiciously keeping out of the way.

I asked a nurse if there was an empty room I could use and was shown a vacant examination room, where I took Alex, the husband, for a chat.

He broke down and told me it was his own fault. He had brought this upon his wife. He was completely distraught, but through the tears managed to tell me a tale I'll never forget.

Alex worked as an elevator engineer for a small contractor. His boss had recently picked up a new contract to service the elevators of a four-storey car park under a mansion in the country. I knew, then, exactly who owned that mansion.

He was to work under extremely strict conditions, which he found highly irregular. He had to leave his phone in the van, not look at the cars, definitely not touch the cars, not talk to anyone unless spoken to, wear a new uniform, use a hand sanitiser and wear a face mask at all times.

Alex was shaking so much at this point that I had to call in the nurse to calm him down. She gave him a glass of water and a Diazepam tablet, and after a few minutes, we resumed talking.

He said that on the ground floor, the owner kept his racing car collection, Formula One cars, etc. Amongst these was a Ford Escort MkII Mexico, with full rally spec, a car that had never been used in competition.

That car happened to be Alex and his dad's dream motor vehicle, and just seeing it brought fond memories flooding back of the time they spent putting together their own similar machine. But theirs was nothing compared to the beauty hugging the red-painted glossy floor before him.

He went back to his van on the pretence of getting another tool and slipped his phone inside his overalls. When he was back down on the ground floor, he looked around to make sure that nobody was about, then took 10 pictures of the Escort, to show his dad.

When he turned around, two huge security guys in suits were standing five metres behind him, hands crossed over their crotches. The biggest guy then approached Alex with a deadpan expression. He wrenched the phone from Alex's hand and deleted all the pictures, before giving him the phone back without saying a word, but debilitating Alex with his eyes.

The kid nearly pissed his pants. He finished his work, shaking like a leaf, and went back to his depot fully expecting to be fired. But, nothing was said, and nothing happened.

Alex was now crying. He asked me if I thought that his actions were the reason for his wife's injuries. I knew they were, but didn't tell him so. I just said that we had to look into all possibilities.

He then said that he didn't want us to pursue the enquiry any further. He would not press charges, because if the bastard who did this to his wife, an innocent caring person, was angered further, what else is he capable of?

I've told you this story today for a reason. Barbara, Rhonda and I can tell you many more of a similar vein, but we will spare you the horror. I just want you all to be aware of what we can expect if we go after Jaden Janssen and his syndicate. The repercussions will be violent, brutal and personal, not just on yourselves, but on your families and your friends."

This had gone way beyond any PI work we had done before; this had now become deadly serious. I needed time to think about our next move. I made the announcement that I was going for a stroll to mull things over and headed out towards the orchard.

Finding a sturdy wooden bench to plonk myself onto, I sat in the sunshine and watched songbirds plucking caterpillars from the apple trees, and bees coming and going from the flower beds laden with pollen.

I truly wanted to bring down my entire wrath upon Jaden Janssen, not just because he had kidnapped Molly Baker and put her family through hell, but for the piece of shit he was, the crimes he had committed, and all the lives he had ruined and probably taken.

But, putting my family and my team's families at risk was not a price I was willing to pay. Yet we needed to get Molly Baker back to her rightful family, which was my commitment from the start, without Janssen knowing we were ever involved. If we could do that, it would buy us time to formulate a plan to bring down his empire in its entirety. There was only one way to deal with a bullying tyrant, starve them of their power.

A wasp that had been munching on fallen fruit headed straight for my face. I moved quicker than I'd moved in years, first jerking my head out of its flight path and then springing to my feet and getting away from the bench, pronto.

I'm allergic to wasp stings; I can go into anaphylactic shock if the buggers get me.

A sting, yes, a sting operation is what we needed, fronted by someone untouchable, someone Janssen or his thugs couldn't harm.

I strode back to the house, past the tennis courts where Finn and Julia were having a game and getting a sweat on.

"Morning," I said, passing the wire.

Julia checked her watch. "Almost afternoon," she replied.

She was probably right. Time was flying by today.

"You play tennis often?" I enquired.

"It's Wimbledon," said Finn, "always gives us the bug."

"Well enjoy," I said, leaving them to it.

Almost 40 years in the private investigation business has taught me many things, the least of which is always think outside of the box.

I tried to picture what the moment would be like if Sophie and Molly were finally reunited, how nervous they would be, how excited, how apprehensive. Two identical strangers who know everything and nothing about one another. There'd be tears for sure.

Then it hit me. What if they met by accident in a very public place, a place where the world's press were on hand to capture the moment, the most famous missing child in the world found by chance by her own twin sister?

It would go viral instantly. Janssen and Van Dijk could do nothing about it. You can't punish fate, and Dave Skipper's detective agency need not be mentioned at all. Perfect anonymity.

Of course, to set this up, we would have to get both sides on board, have the twins meet beforehand in private, convince Diana Van Dijk's grandparents that this was the best thing for all concerned, and find a situation that would be ideal for the public miracle.

I had no idea how to approach the Van Dijks, or how they would react to giving up their grandchild, but I was confident that my team would come up with the answers.

Effervescing with ideas as I stepped back into the operations room, a space that now had the atmosphere of a pending apocalypse, I smiled with the enthusiasm of a 12-year-old lad and said, "Cheer up, I have a cunning plan."

The looks I received were of curious contempt; seconds ago they had all been considering their own fragility.

"It had better be miraculous," replied Olavo. "I'm rather fond of my kneecaps."

"Who is the one person in the world who wouldn't suffer any retribution whatsoever for exposing Molly Baker's kidnappers?"

Blank looks stared back at me.

"Molly Baker!"

After I revealed my strategy, the room went quiet again, apart from Paul, tinkering at his keyboard.

"This could work," said Daniel. "But before we can put any of it into play, we need to be 100 per cent certain that Diana Van Dijk is Molly Baker. She may well be Simon Van Dijk's actual granddaughter, and Molly Baker may

250

have met her demise many years ago. We need a sample of Diana's DNA, but knowing how closely guarded she is, that might prove impossible."

It was at this point that Paul came back into the game.

"I've been trying to ascertain whether the Van Dijks are in residence at the palace, or away at the moment. Their luxury yacht is in the Caribbean, hired out to a corporation for 50,000 euro a day. Their private jet is in a hanger at Schiphol airport, and grocery deliveries to the palace have increased 80 percent in the past few days, indicating that they probably are."

"Nice one, Paul," I declared.

He'd also been looking at the palace grounds on Google maps and asked us all to gather around his desk.

We formed a semi-circle.

He zoomed out.

"As you can see, there is only one road into the palace. The only other ways to get there are cross-country or by helicopter. The road is two kilometres long and all bar the first quarter belong to the estate, including all the land on either side. However, the first quarter of land belongs to a farm on the main road, and hugging the intersection is a small copse."

"Right." I elongated the word, wondering where he was going with this.

"It's the perfect observation spot to monitor who's coming and going from the estate."

"Agreed."

"So, every eighteen-year-old girl likes to get out of the house, right? Even a big old palace."

"Absolutely," affirmed Barbara.

"What if I go in under the cover of darkness and position myself in the copse, camouflaged, with a two-way radio, and the moment I spot our girl coming down the drive, I pass the info forward to teams waiting in vehicles somewhere on the road, who can then follow her and see if there is an opportunity to lift a sample of her DNA, or her DI AN A?" he quipped.

I chuckled; he does come out with them now and again.

"What if someone discovers you in the bushes?" asked Daniel.

"I'll tell them I'm a twitcher."

"What's a twitcher?" queried Rhonda.

"A bird watcher."

"Ah, a Volgalaar," she said, "a twitcher, hmm."

To that I said, "So, if we're all agreed, let's begin operation 'Volgalaar'."

Paul said he needed a few things for the stakeout; some camo' gear, binoculars, a camera, radio, and a packed lunch.

Daniel asked Rhonda to go shopping with Paul to get everything he needed. She'd been in the army for six years before joining the police and could smell a fellow military man a mile off.

"Come on, soldier," she said, happy with her assignment.

Paul would position himself tonight, even though it was a full moon. It wasn't ideal, but the hedgerow he would be hiding in was adequate cover.

The plan was to have four mobile surveillance vehicles and tag each other during the tail. Daniel would team up with Mary, Faustino with Barbara, and Rhonda would travel with me. Alfic, the only other motorcyclist amongst us apart from Paul, would ride a Yamaha 125 motorbike. Olavo would stay at home and hold the fort.

Finn and Julia were happy to lend us their vehicles for the day, a Volkswagen Polo and a Ford Focus, two vehicles that wouldn't stand out, and a small white Fiat van.

We briefed the housekeepers on today's mission. They were both fully accepting and totally discreet. Daniel attested to their integrity.

Given the amount of movement and the security issues due over the next few weeks, we thought it best that Finn and Julia should be in the know. They were exceptionally professional in their response.

Being a Saturday morning, we surmised that a young woman might want to go shopping, or maybe meet friends, get a coffee somewhere, hang out at a mall, and probably in Amsterdam.

But, apart from a lot of waiting around, nothing is certain in the surveillance business.

Paul had positioned himself perfectly during the night, and had even managed to nod off out in the open.

We had installed ourselves at various pull-ins along the arterial road and had now been waiting for four hours. I was itching to get going, bored and fidgety. Rhonda was asleep.

At 11:03 a.m. our walkie-talkie crackled into life.

"Black Mercedes 4x4 SUV, registration G-001-GB. Two male occupants in the front, one female occupant in the rear, rear windows heavily tinted, turned right, heading your way, Skip. I will send photos. Out."

Rhonda plucked up. "That sounds promising." She yawned.

"My thoughts exactly."

I thumbed the button on the side of the radio. "Roger that, Volgalaar, Eyes peeled. Out."

Rhonda switched on the Ford's ignition and sat there, eyes fixed on the rearview mirror. There was a modicum of traffic on the road, but that was good, it gave us cover.

"Here it comes," she said. It whooshed by at speed; she let four more vehicles pass us before pulling out after it.

I let the others know the vehicle had come our way and we were now in pursuit. As expected, it was heading towards the city via the A9. My crew would catch up with us and we would take it in turns to tail the Merc.

Skirting the city, they turned left onto the A10 and headed east. I signalled for Daniel to take over with the Polo, whilst we dropped back. They pulled off the ring road and headed north up the Europaboulevard, crossing the canal on the Scheldestraat and staying north.

It was Barbara and Faustino's turn. Daniel turned off and circled the block to come back behind us. The traffic was much heavier in town and easier to get closer to the Mercedes without it being suspicious, but Faustino still couldn't get a view inside the car because of the tinted windows. But, he assured us, there was definitely just the one female in the back.

Along the tree-lined Ferdinand Bolstraat, then left onto the Ceintuurbaan, crossing the canal again, then up the Van Baerlestraat. Another tree-bordered avenue of single lane carriageways with a tramway running through its centre. There seemed to be cafés everywhere, a sea of pavement tables jam-packed with tourists and locals enjoying what Dutch cafés are renowned for.

We passed a large open park to our right, then the Merc itself turned right.

"Ah, the Museumkwartier, very expensive real estate, Dave," Rhonda informed me.

The Mercedes slowed and indicated right, it had to stop and wait for black electronic gates to open, then it disappeared into underground parking. We all passed and I clocked the number of the house on a shiny brass plate, number 35.

We all parked up around the block. Within minutes, Rhonda had the name of the house owners, Dennis and Chantal Boogman. They had three children, Fabian, Raf and, more interestingly, an 18-year-old girl called Evi, who had on her list of favourite activities a passion for tennis.

We arranged ourselves at both ends of the street, with Alfie nearby, so that we could not miss their exit, should they make a move. We didn't have long to wait. They were off again within half an hour, followed at a distance by Alfie who had greater mobility in these tightly packed streets.

After five minutes, Rhonda said, "I bet you a cup of coffee they are heading for the Festina Lawn Tennis Club."

"Oh?"

"Yeah, exclusive, private, members only."

She wasn't wrong; we circumnavigated the Vondelpark and halted at the top of a dead-end narrow approach road. It was pedestrians-only through the park.

The Mercedes went all the way to the end, stopped, and two young ladies got out of the rear doors in full tennis whites. It was hard to tell them apart at a distance, they both had long dark hair tied back into ponytails.

I was dying to get out, to take a closer look at Diana; if she was anything like Sophie, I'd know in an instant. But we decided that Barbara and Rhonda should be the ones to follow them in and talk to the receptionist officially, on the pretence of checking security due to a spate of burglaries in the area last night, and asking if they could look around.

The ruse worked. They were admitted without question.

Ten minutes later, Daniel's phone rang. He put it on speaker so we could all hear. What we heard was music to our ears.

"I don't think we need to bother with DNA," voiced Barbara.

"Why is that?" Asked Daniel.

"Check the photos I am sending you."

She rang off and a text message pinged.

Daniel brought up the pictures of the girls playing tennis and zoomed in on the one facing the camera. Molly Baker was born an identical twin, and she'd stayed an identical twin. It was like Sophie was in there, swinging a racket.

All the blood was rushing to my head; my face was tingling with elation. Months of speculation, investigation, soul-searching, dread, false leads, cold trails and mind-numbing miles on the road, and we'd found her, alive and doing very well.

She was just around the corner, and although my entire being was screaming to go in and get her, I couldn't approach her yet; this had to be handled with extreme care or it could implode on itself. We still needed that DNA, certainly from a legal standpoint, but also, without it, Simon and Marion Van Dijk weren't going to take lightly the news that the granddaughter they'd nurtured, cherished and adored for the last 17 years, a girl who was earmarked to inherit a colossal business empire worth billions, was not, in fact, a blood relative.

The Van Dijks would definitely reach for a legal team, the best they could possibly get, so without proof positive, our plan simply wouldn't work and we'd all become targets of Jaden Janssen.

Our Dutch cops returned to the cars, saying it was impossible to collect hair samples from Diana inside the club, so we stuck around and waited for them to come out. Maybe they would go somewhere else, where it would be easier to snatch a strand or two.

The black SUV returned two hours later, and the girls got in the back. Daniel and Mary followed them to a plush street lined with very swanky shops.

The vehicle stopped outside a boutique hairdresser/nail bar. One of the security guys walked the girls to the door and then kept guard outside whilst they went in. The driver sat in the car on the other side of the street.

The seven of us met in an adjacent street and planned our next move.

In fifteen minutes, Barbara and Rhonda would go into the salon and enquire about booking an appointment for Barbara's forthcoming wedding, whilst at the same time checking to see what the girls were having done. If it were a haircut, we were in luck.

We *were* in luck, both of them were having a trim, 500 euro a pop, I was told.

This called for a specialist refuse diversion technique.

Rhonda and Barbara were going to wait in the service road behind the salon until it closed. Meanwhile, Daniel and I would go and pick up Paul whilst the rest of the team returned to Tall Trees.

When all of the staff had left the hairdressers, our Dutch cops would retrieve today's rubbish bags from the dumpster out the back. I suggested they lay some material like cardboard or plastic, or whatever they could find back there, on top of the rubbish already in the dumpster, so that today's would be easily identifiable.

Just before 5 p.m., two junior staff members brought five bin bags out the back door and nonchalantly tossed them into the commercial bin, chatting as they went and locking the door behind them.

Our girls wasted no time in collecting those bags and driving them straight to the National police lab at the University of Amsterdam, who had been pre-warned of their arrival and advised as to the urgency of the analysis.

Just one of the bags had today's clippings in it, the rest were discarded.

Rhonda forwarded the pictures of Diana Van Dijk they'd taken at the tennis club, to the lab technicians to help speed up the identification. Mary sent an email, with Molly Baker's DNA profile.

Daniel treated us all to a Chinese takeaway that night. It was a bit premature, but we felt undoubtedly like we'd cracked the case. Even without the lab results, we all knew it was her. It was a brilliant team effort, and I, for one, was ecstatic beyond civil communication.

"We found her, mate. We fucking found her." I had both hands clasping Paul's red face, and he couldn't stop smiling.

"You've had too much whiskey." Mary jovially reprimanded me.

"The day whiskey starts to affect my work, Mary, I'm gonna give up working," I slurred.

The celebrations went on until at least 9:30 p.m. when we were all too tired, or, in my case, too pissed, to stay awake any longer. The Dutch contingent went home, and the rest of us slouched off to bed.

By 9 a.m. Sunday morning the test results still hadn't come in. We were all up now and in various stages of having breakfast on the rear patio. Mine was black coffee and a couple of painkillers.

Mary had been the first to rise, and was in the operations room manning her computer. She came rushing through the French doors and shut down all conversation. "Got it!" She beamed. "One hundred percent match!"

"Yes!" I shouted, clenching a fist.

Olavo didn't look so joyous.

"What's up, old friend?" I queried.

"My theory seems to have borne out. I couldn't sleep last night, wondering what might have happened to the real Diana Van Dijk; it's going to be too tragic to bear. I can feel it."

Olavo raised the back of a hand to his mouth and turned away, tearful.

"Hey," said Faustino, comforting his partner with an arm around his shoulder, "we don't know that yet. There may be a simple explanation that we haven't discovered."

Olavo nodded and sucked in his full lips. "Time will tell," he said, widening his eyes, before getting up and taking his breakfast things to the kitchen.

"I fear the worst, my friend, I'm afraid," I told Faustino.

He gave me a resignied look.

When our Dutch teammates finally arrived, I bade everyone sit down in the ops room for a briefing on my proposed plan.

It was thus: Mary and I would get the next available flight to London, then drive a hire car directly to the Bakers' house in Bournemouth, where we would deliver the news they'd been longing for all these years, in person.

We'd then explain the dangers expected by revealing the agency's involvement in getting Molly back. And then ask them if they would be willing to participate in our ruse.

"And what is the strategy for the sting, Dave? Have you formulated the plan yet?" asked Daniel.

"Indeed I have, Inspector."

I pulled out my trusty notebook for reassurance.

"Sophie Baker will accidentally bump into her missing twin sister, Molly, waiting in line with her grandparents, at the entrance gates of the All England Lawn Tennis and

Croquet Club, Wimbledon, on Men's final day, next Sunday, the 12th."

Everyone's eyes darted around the room. I continued.

"It will be a monumental moment, shock, disbelief, instant recognition and plenty of tears. We'll have undercover police there to act as spectators, also in line for the final, to get the ball rolling and start taking pictures of the event, causing pandemonium and a media rush to get the exclusives. It'll go viral instantly. Imagine the headlines. The press will go crazy. What are the chances?"

Alfie piped up, "How are the grandparents gonna react to that, Dave? They won't have a Scooby what's going on."

"They'll be in on it too, Alf'. I'll get to that in a moment."

"Right."

Now everyone was screwing up their faces.

"Because of the chaos being created outside of Centre Court, Van Dijk's security guys will whisk the Bakers and the Van Dijks away to their hotel, where you, Alfie, will be called in to pick up the official investigation. You will then inform Daniel over here of your findings, who, together with a large team of police, will arrest Jaden Janssen and Ruby Van Dijk."

Daniel liked the idea of that.

"I suggest that all the teams be set up in advance and be waiting for the go from Alfie. And the arrests to be done within an hour of the 'miracle meeting', otherwise, those two scumbags will get wind of it and be on their toes post haste."

"I can arrange that," affirmed Daniel.

"Faustino, I'd like you to go back to Portugal with Olavo and secure the hidden farm with a team of officers. Once the people of Douro Calvo get to know of its relevance to Molly's disappearance, they'll be all over it, spoiling the crime scene. I have a gut feeling that farm still has some secrets to reveal."

Faustino nodded pensively.

"Don't let anyone get near that farm."

"Of course," he assured me.

Paul raised his hand at the back of the class. "What do you want me to do while you're away, Skip?"

"Hold the fort, mate. Take a break. Invite Cody over if you like. Mary and I will stay in England for a bit, see our families, before coming back to crack on with Janssen's demise."

He collapsed his smile like Robert De Niro and nodded in agreement. But I knew Paul; he would probably continue to look for cracks in Janssen's armour.

Daniel wanted to clarify my methods for getting the Van Dijks on our side.

"And what about Simon and Marion? How on earth are we ever going to approach and convince them that it'll be a good thing to give up their granddaughter, let alone take part in the operation? The revelation that she is not their own blood is going to shatter their world."

"Obviously this is going to be tremendously hard to get their heads around and accept. And there's gonna be a whirlpool of hysteria swamping their ability to make rational decisions. But I believe the best way to proceed is to just tell them the truth."

Daniel was nodding like a dashboard dog.

"I don't know the people, so I can't say how they will react, but if they are level-headed, which they seem to be, then, given time, they will understand that Molly needs to be reconnected with her natural family, and not just for legal reasons."

"But after everything they have done for her," said Rhonda. "They love her like she is their own."

"I know," I replied, "but she is not."

My team was quiet, all dealing with their inner thoughts. Daniel shattered our contemplation with a large expulsion of breath from puffed cheeks.

"I will make a call to the Van Dijks in a moment and arrange for a meeting at their earliest convenience tomorrow. The girl needs to be there also."

"Good. I suggest you go in force, but police only, Barbara, Rhonda, Alfie and Faustino. The rest of us need to stay out of the picture as much as we can."

The briefing over, I got out my mobile and strode out into the sunshine by the front pond. It was a tranquil spot to make a gentle call to the Bakers. Water tinkled from the fountain making concentric circles in the pool, as the ring tone cycled a few times.

Sophie Baker answered. I simply told her that I would be in England tomorrow, and it would be nice to pay them a visit mid-afternoon. She said that it would be fine; she'd make sure everyone was at home.

Before I ended the call, I asked her if she liked to play or watch tennis. She laughed and said no, but her mum loved it. Before they lost Molly, Apparently, Jill used to play quite regularly. She asked me why I was interested. I told her that I love to watch Wimbledon every year, and wondered if she had a favourite to win. She laughed again and said no, but it probably won't be a Brit.

Eventually, there was no need to get a hire car. Alfie had arranged for an unmarked police car to pick up Mary and me from Luton airport. Jack Wheeler, a copper who'd worked on the case with Alfie six years ago, was there to meet us in Arrivals.

He had a spanking new, dark grey Audi S3 waiting in a police bay outside. Ryan Roberts, another copper familiar with the case, was in the driver's seat.

The glorious smell of new leather wrapped its arms around us in the rear seats.

"This is very nice," I said to the lads, who seemed to me to be fresh out of high school.

"Interceptor stealth car, Dave," said Ryan, "0 to 60 in 5.4 seconds, goes like a rocket if we need it to."

"You've got a fun job, then?"

"Can be. We get to drive 'em like we've nicked 'em on occasion."

I chuckled, realising there was a very thin blue line between boy racers and police boy racers.

"Now, before you start the engine, Ryan, I want to brief you on why we are here. And seeing that you two have previously worked on the case, I think it's only fair to update you on our progress."

"Right," said Jack, his eyes forward.

"First off, apart from your chain of command, of course, it is imperative that the information I am about to reveal does not leave this car. Understood?"

"Absolutely," said Ryan, "We are both under strict orders to keep all intel' in house."

"Good," I said. "We've found Molly Baker."

I have never seen two heads swivel round on their necks so fast in my life.

Mary confirmed what I said with a wide-eyed smile and a nod.

Spending the next five minutes giving the two policemen an update on the situation was slightly therapeutic, a kind of dress rehearsal for the real thing in a couple of hours.

We talked more during the drive, especially about the proposed sting operation in which they would be taking part under Alfie's command. The lads thought it ingenious and were keen to get involved.

When we arrived at the Bakers' house, because this was going to get highly emotional, I asked Ryan and Jack to stay in the car. They agreed.

Sophie let us in. George and Jill were perched on the edge of the sofa, whilst Nile and his wife Kate, cradling their six-month-old baby boy, stood behind.

Sophie went and sat next to her mum, whilst Mary sat in an armchair. I was offered the other, but I told them I'd been a long time sitting down in the car and wanted to stand for a while.

The family had rightly suspected that we weren't here just for a social, and the air was thick with tense expectancy.

"Would you both like a drink?" asked Jill.

"No," I said, "we're okay for a moment."

I was feeling proper nervous now. I just wanted to get the good news out of the way. All these months of frustrating investigation, and I was having trouble revealing success.

I cleared my throat. "Jill, George, Sophie, Nile." I smiled. "We've found her."

Sophie's jaw dropped. George and Jill inhaled sharply, then broke down in tears, hugging each other like they might meld into one. Nile went pale, puffed out his cheeks, then held onto his wife for support.

I continued talking over the sobbing. "She's alive and well and living with an extremely wealthy couple in Holland, who have bought her up believing she is their natural granddaughter."

Mary had pre-empted the situation and retrieved the photos of Molly at the tennis club on her phone.

She offered it to them, and the Bakers huddled on the couch, thumbing through the pictures with blurred vision and sobs of delight.

Seventeen years of not knowing; 17 years of anguish, finger-pointing, accusation, cross-examination. Seventeen years of imagining the worst possible scenarios happening to their daughter, and 17 years of guilt suddenly lifted by a few simple words.

I couldn't believe it was happening either, and both Mary and I were crying too.

Sophie was the first to speak. She asked when she could see her sister.

I held my hand up. "This is where it gets complicated," I said, and then began to tell them what was happening in Holland at this precise moment.

"Alfie will be showing the Van Dijks pictures of you all and, hopefully, I will receive a phone call in a while letting us know how things are going."

"These people aren't the ones who abducted Molly?" asked George.

"Oh no. They have had no idea that Molly wasn't their granddaughter."

"And they have cared for her all these years?"

"Exceptionally well."

"Then they will not want to let her go," said Jill.

"I'm sure they will not want to, and it is a horrible situation for them now, but they have unwittingly broken the law, and Molly will be re-united with you whether they like it or not."

Nile broke his silence. "But she is eighteen now. She can do whatever she wants. What if she does not want to leave Holland?"

I sighed. There was always that.

"Look, let's just wait for the phone call from Alfie. Best not speculate at this point. I think we could all do with that cup of tea right now, yeah?"

"I'll make it," said Mary, who got up to go to the kitchen.

Jill looked at Mary in an attempt to tell her where everything was.

"I'll find it," reassured Mary.

George, who had calmed down somewhat, asked me directly "Who took Molly in the first place and why?"

I am sure he had a million questions, but that one naturally was the fundamental enigma that had plagued them for almost two decades.

I gave the family everything we had on Jaden Janssen and Ruby Van Dijk and the circumstances as to how we discovered their true identity.

They were astounded.

George spoke, "So, essentially, Molly was taken to replace a baby they had lost, just to assure this pair of an inheritance?"

"We believe so."

"And what happened to their own child?" asked Jill.

"We are still trying to discover that, Jill, but we fear the worst."

She looked pained.

The tea came in on a tray: teapot, milk jug, sugar bowl, empty cups, the lot. Everybody took a cup.

"So, what happens now?" said Nile.

"Well, I think you can gather from what you have learned that Jaden Janssen and his wicked partner are ruthless evil people, who will not hesitate, in fact, they'd probably take great pleasure, in harming anyone who crosses them. I mean seriously harming them. So with this in mind, we want to go to great lengths to protect our agency, my employees and our families…"

The Bakers listened intently.

"The investigation needs to be seen to be carried out and concluded by the police of three countries, and not publicly involve The Dave Skipper detective agency at all."

George appeared confused. "So, how is it going to be announced that Molly is found, and how are they going to say that they did it?"

I smiled again. "Have you seen the film *The Sting*?"

"Yes, many years ago. Paul Newman and Robert Redford, right? A great film."

"Well, we're gonna do one of them, but it will have to involve your family's complete cooperation."

I explained.

Without question, to a person, they were willing to play their part.

This was fantastic, all that I'd hoped for.

The most blood-chilling aspect was that when I showed them pictures of the Van Dijk palace, where Molly had been bought up, Sophie said that this was exactly the house she had been dreaming of when she was a little girl.

This bolstered my belief in ESP between twins.

The atmosphere was more relaxed now; George asked me what our next move was. I said that it all depended on what was going on over in Holland. I decided to call Daniel and find out.

It was a delightful sunny afternoon. The two coppers were outside leaning against their car, having a conversation.

Since they were known to the Baker family, I said that I was sure Jill wouldn't mind if they went in for a cup of tea or coffee. They were mightily grateful and disappeared into the house.

On the blower, Daniel answered almost immediately.

"Dave, I was just about to call you. How is it going your end?"

"Perfect, mate. All is well; they are up for the plan."

"Excellent."

"How's it with you?"

"The same. We can't believe it. I never met such an amiable person in all my days such as Simon Van Dijk. He is a rock."

"And his wife?"

"Not so much. Disbelieving at first, then devastated, then angry. Diana has calmed her down though."

"And how has Diana taken it?"

"It hit her like a ton of bricks. She's always known about the disappearance of Molly Baker, but never once thought it might be her, although she did have some recollection of having an imaginary sister when she was younger."

"Makes sense, I suppose. They did know each other for a year, and I think that twins are always connected, no matter how distant."

"You know, Dave, the odd thing is Marion showed us some family photos and in one, her great-grandmother, who was from Malta, bore a striking resemblance to Diana. So although she looks nothing like her supposed mum and dad, they always believed her looks skipped a couple of generations. How that came to be, I don't know."

"Hmm, that's weird."

"Oh, and another thing, the Spanish paperwork for Diana's birth certificate, that all looks highly dubious too. When we capture that piece of shit and his bitch, he'll have some explaining to do."

"So are the Van Dijks on board with the operation?"

"Fully. They want to see justice done. None of this is going to destroy the love they have for their granddaughter, and Diana feels the same, although she desperately wants to meet her real parents and sister and brother. They all feel that they can work something out between them."

"And how do the Van Dijks feel towards Ruby?"

"They cut ties with her years ago. They feel their actions have been justified, and think that she should receive all that is coming to her for the part she played in this travesty. Diabolical devil, I think Simon called her."

"Has Diana had any contact with Ruby and Janssen since she was adopted?"

"None at all. Those bastards handed her over like she was a bag of shopping as soon as they got the builder's merchants, which incidentally are worth in the region of 200 million euro now. It was just a deal to them, complete with contracts. They have no hold over Diana whatsoever, and cannot legally put claim to any of her inheritance from her grandparents."

"Result," I said.

It was clear to us all now that Molly was just a commodity to Janssen and Van Dijk, a means to make money; they'd have done the same even if she were their own child. Whatever happened to the real Diana was a tragedy waiting to be found, and it was obvious to me that Janssen worked at Faro airport for the sake of his drug-smuggling enterprise and that the Bakers just happened to be in the wrong place at the wrong time, presenting Janssen with a despicable opportunity.

"How do you feel we should proceed until next Sunday, Daniel?"

"Well, keep it all quiet for sure! But Simon has offered the use of his private jet to bring the Bakers over here for a secret reunion."

"Wow!" I had to think for a second. "It's probably too risky by air. The Bakers are so familiar. The press will follow them. I think it's better if we all travel by car and use the tunnel. If we leave soon, we can be with you tonight, around 9 p.m."

"I thought you were going to spend some time with your families over there?"

269

"Needs must, mate. This takes precedence. We can always come back later."

"For sure, for sure. There's just one other thing, Dave. Can Diana speak with Sophie via Skype before you leave?"

"No problem. I'll set it up, mate."

The twins were beside themselves with excitement. Apart from the accents and the hairstyles, it was difficult to tell them apart. For Sophie, 17 years of heartache was remedied in an instant, and for Molly, her imaginary sister had come to life. After the tears, there came laughter, delight and amazement, finding out they both liked exactly the same things. It was a joy to witness.

Mary booked us all passage on the Eurotunnel in two cars and then she went off with Nile and Kate to get their passports and overnight things, whilst Jill held onto baby Henry. Nile would catch up with us at Folkestone.

George wasn't feeling well enough to drive all that way. The news had left him rather drained, and so he asked me if I wouldn't mind taking the wheel. His choice of vehicle was perfect for me, a silver Land Rover Defender, plenty of room for the five of us.

On the way down to the coast, Sophie and Molly must have talked to each other the whole journey, discovering what each of them liked, which was just about the same in every regard. They were both vegetarian and their favourite dish was cauliflower cheese. They also both preferred guitar bands, most of whom I had never heard of.

Nile arrived just in time for our boarding, and Kate took back control of baby Henry. It was somewhat befitting to have a mother and baby with us, seeing that the last time Jill saw Molly, she was only a one-year-old. But, it also made the journey feel like a big old family going on a holiday of a lifetime, all expenses paid.

We rumbled to a halt on the granite sett drive just before 10 p.m. and marvelled at the enormity of the place. A cream-coloured stone Georgian oblong built in a Roman Greco style, complete with columns, alcoves, statues, and cornicing, lit up with powerful ground-level up-lighting.

The front entrance had an expansive swooping curved ramp that led up to the front door, outside of which stood Alfie, Daniel and Simon Van Dijk.

It was somehow an unreal vision, like visiting Caesars Palace, Las Vegas for the first time.

Everything was pristine, manicured, highly maintained, and extravagant. I thought I might dirty the place just by being there.

After a nervous, subdued greeting, we followed our host through a massive, opulent hall and into a room on the right sporting six red-patterned couches arranged in a square, on which sat the girl the world had been searching for, next to the grandmother who had no idea.

Molly was so familiar to me, I felt connected, yet being in her company for the first time was surreal, almost like she was a fabled legend. I could do nothing but watch the story unfold.

Jill buckled and almost fainted when she first caught sight of her daughter. George, shaking like a leaf, together with Daniel, helped her to her feet. Molly instinctively protective rushed to her mother's aid and together with Sophie and Nile they bonded in a heart-melting cuddle, which had me welling up and breathless.

Tears were streaming down Mary's face, too; she took my hand and held it with both of hers, then gave me a sympathetic smile.

Kate was crying, and so was Marion Van Dijk. It was such an affecting scene I think even the impartial Daniel had a tear in his eye.

Simon, on the other hand seemed far too composed to let emotion get the better of him. He stood there, hands clasped behind his back, rod straight, waiting for the impassioned outpouring to subside.

After what seemed like ten minutes, the huddle broke and everybody took a seat, the girls sticking together like they were attached once again by the umbilical cord, close to their mum, who couldn't take her eyes off her long-lost child.

Drinks were served. I took to a large scotch like a newt to a pond, and Mary took ownership of a cold bottle of Pinot Grigio. Then the food came out, tray after tray of finger buffet fare fit for a state visit.

The twenty or so staff waiting on us must have been on a reasonable bonus for staying on, or perhaps they lived in the house. I was curious, but it didn't seem appropriate to ask.

I was pleased, though, to see that Mrs Van Dijk had grown no airs and graces. I understood she was from a working-class background and was chatting away to Jill within minutes like they were old friends.

Laughter now rang out in this ostentatious room. It warmed me no end to realise that maybe things were going to turn out alright between this new extended family, and they could share Molly without any bitterness or resentment.

Unexpectedly, the twins approached me while I was chatting with Alfie.

Sophie said, "Molly, I'd like to introduce you to Dave Skipper. He's the man who took your case on when everybody else had given up. He's the man behind the team who found you, and he's my hero."

I blushed and got all fuzzy. "Oh, it was a joint effort I can assure you," I said reaching out to take Molly's hand.

"Bugger that," she said in her Dutch accent, and then planted a kiss on my cheek, followed by a bone-cracking hug.

I hadn't been kissed by a beautiful 18-year-old in quite some time, and it rendered me senseless, but I did appreciate the sentiment.

"Thank you, Dave," she whispered. "You have done something incredible."

I was humbled once more.

Daniel and Alfie had been over the planned sting operation, and the reasons behind it, with Simon earlier during the day. Our host now had a firm grasp on his family's role and the justification behind it, to buy us time in order to bring down Janssen's criminal empire and to keep our families safe from retribution by Janssen's thugs.

Simon was completely unaware that the building merchants' he had given his daughter all those years ago were now distribution hubs for Janssen's illegal drug trade in eight different countries. He felt partially responsible for the whole affair and would remain guilty for his unwitting participation 'til his dying day.

He now felt it was his duty to try and make amends for his sins and do everything within his power to help obliterate the terrible wounds he helped cause, and bring down his despicable son-in-law.

As for Molly, she was resolute in dropping her given name of Diana, a moniker that only benefitted those who strove to deceive the people she loved.

The Van Dijks would fly to London this Thursday and book into the Savoy Hotel, and then spend a few days sightseeing and getting ready for the big gambit next Sunday.

We were all welcome to stay here at the palace for as long as we wanted. After all, they did have 30 bedrooms.

The Bakers' took up that offer until Wednesday, but Mary and I wanted to go back to England to see our families, so Daniel dropped Alfie, Mary and me back at Tall Trees on the Monday, and we took my Range back through the tunnel.

Before we left, Simon and Marion asked us to go over the plan once they got back to the Savoy on the Sunday, after the miracle. I think they wanted to be assured that their family wasn't in any danger.

I told him that all five of them, Jill, Sophie, Molly and themselves, would be interviewed by Alfie and his team of officers, who would have been alerted to the incident at Wimbledon. Uniformed police would also be there to keep the press and public at bay.

Within the hour, all of them would be transported to Heathrow and flown back to Schiphol and then driven back to the palace, where they would be safe from harm and intrusion.

Alfie would inform the Dutch police, through official channels, of the situation, who would then order the arrest of Ruby and Jaden Janssen.

Daniel, Barbara and a team will go in and arrest Janssen at his office, whilst simultaneously Rhonda and another team will go and pick up Ruby at their mansion in Groningen.

They will be taken to separate police stations to be questioned and eventually charged.

Janssen will naturally contact his lawyer, Hank Gutteridge, a dubious, yet accomplished American defender of high-profile criminals who is often mocked in the press for being a Donald Trump look-a-like.

Whilst all this is going on, The Policia Judiciaria in Portugal will be informed by Interpol of the arrests, and Faustino and his officers will create a tight cordon around the farm in Douro Calvo, where Molly was first held.

At this moment in time, Interpol had all seven directors of Janssen's company under surveillance. We felt it was paramount to bring down his entire illicit organisation. Because as soon as they learnt the man holding the purse strings had been captured and charged with Molly's abduction, the cracks would appear in his house of cards, and those rats would start to abandon the enterprise.

George, Nile, Kate and Baby Henry, will be flown back to the palace within hours, and in the evening, Daniel, Faustino and Alfie will release live TV broadcasts to the press, after which the whole world will know of the Miraculous Meeting at Wimbledon of the long-lost twin sisters.

The Van Dijks were satisfied that the plan would keep everyone safe, as long as those two malfeasants could be kept behind bars.

If it all goes like clockwork, I would be satisfied knowing that my team's names and those of their families are kept out of the investigation. My only regret will be missing out on the looks on both Ruby Van Dijk's and Janssen's faces when they learn that Molly has been found and reunited with her true family. But that is only a small disappointment for all that has been gained.

I'd learnt through Interpol that Janssen's seven directors did not get on well with each other, and that only his presence and power has kept a bloodbath at bay. This was exquisite news for us. With Jaden and Ruby behind bars, perhaps they'll hack each other to bits and save us a lot of trouble.

Interpol estimated that 60 to 65 percent of Europe's cocaine imports were being distributed through his building merchants', but as yet the authorities had little idea of how it arrived. One theory was that came in with bulk materials, and was so large scale, it had been impossible to police.

Hopefully, with the villains behind bars, and chaos ensuing, tongues will begin to wag, and old scores will be settled.

***

On Monday 13th July, just after 4 p.m. Mary and I arrived back at Tall Trees. Daniel, Rhonda, Barbara and Paul were there; they'd been watching the news channels and following the internet all day. It was strange seeing our friends reading statements on the TV. Alfie looked decidedly uncomfortable with it.

The sting operation had run without a hitch and the two arseholes that created all this heartache and pain were now firmly behind bars, taken unawares and both extremely pissed off.

Normally, even when things weren't going in our favour, Barbara and Rhonda carried a laissez-faire attitude about them, but today, in contrast, they were more morose than I'd ever seen them.

Daniel handed us a folder each, containing Jaden Janssen's statement.

Paul, Mary and I went and sat at a table to read the contents, whilst Daniel poured himself and the girls a large whisky each and waited for us to finish reading.

It read thus:

In early April 2003, I arrived home at the farm, from work at Faro airport, just before 6 p.m.

I could see lots of blood on the ground and, at first, what looked like pieces of meat near my front door. But it soon became clear that they were in fact parts of my baby daughter, Diana. Her bloodstained clothes were ripped to pieces and scattered about the place.

Horrified, I rushed inside, assuming the worst, to find my partner, Ruby, sitting on the floor, shaking uncontrollably, staring into space and clinging to what was left of our daughter's body.

In total shock, I managed to find some brandy and encouraged her to take to sip. This calmed her a little, and in time she was able to tell me the dreadful tale of events that took place earlier that afternoon.

Ruby had been up since 5 a.m., picking tomatoes; she always took Diana with her.

She had been back to the house several times, to change Diana's nappy and to get something to eat, the last time being around 3 p.m. She told me she had sat down and opened a bottle of wine.

The next thing she knew, a group of wild boars had invaded the kitchen and pulled Diana's cot over and were dragging her outside. We think maybe the smell of milk had brought them in.

Ruby tried in vain to fight them off, but they were too strong and in a frenzy, fighting with each other to get at the baby. They ran off when Ruby started hitting them with a broom handle.

I knew that Ruby would face manslaughter charges; she had drunk too much wine and had irresponsibly left the doors wide open. But she had already paid the ultimate price by losing our baby girl, and nothing would bring Diana back.

So, I decided to destroy the evidence by building a fire to burn the body parts and her clothes, because if I buried her on the farm, wild animals would only dig her back up again.

We made a pact to not tell anybody what had happened, and try to put it all behind us. I even went to work the next day.

Ruby seemed to be handling it, and it wasn't until later in the month, when I saw the Bakers' twin girls on the runway of Faro airport, that it affected me.

I became very emotional, and when I came home, I told Ruby what I had seen.

A few days later, I woke at 6 a.m. to the sound of a baby crying. I thought at first I was dreaming, but soon realised it was actually in the house. So I got up and went downstairs only to find Ruby trying to comfort a baby in her arms.

It was then that I learned that Ruby had gone to the resort of Viana do Fao, and had stolen the sleeping Molly Baker from her bed whilst her parents were out.

I do not know, to this day, how Ruby knew where the Bakers were staying; she must have driven around the resorts looking for them.

Ruby would not listen to my remonstrations. I wanted to take the baby and leave it at a hospital entrance, but she would not have it. She wanted this baby. It was like an illness.

I could not keep up the pretence for long. The police were all over Portugal looking for the child, and there were film crews and journalists everywhere. The whole of Portugal was searching for Molly. So I made the decision, in June, that we should abandon everything and move back to Holland.

But when we did, another problem occurred; Ruby all of a sudden rejected the baby. She was having a nervous breakdown.

Marion, Ruby's mother, was besotted by her new granddaughter. She could see that Ruby was in no state to raise the child, so offered to legally adopt her.

It was a way out for me, and a way to protect my partner, the woman I loved. The baby was not ours, and I hadn't bonded with her.

I am ashamed of my part in this travesty and have had to live with my actions to this day. This is why I have given, and will continue to give, millions of euros to children's charities in Holland.

I am glad it is finally over. I can only apologise unreservedly to the Bakers for the misery I have caused, and I for one, am pleased they are now reunited with their daughter.

When we had finished reading, it was my turn to pour each of us a scotch.

"What a bastard," I said. "Pinning all the blame on her. What does she have to say?"

"She's not saying a thing. She just glares at us."

I asked Daniel if he had spoken to anyone yet. He knew exactly what I was referring to.

"Yes, a retired high court judge, a friend of mine. He based his opinion on that statement, his knowledge of the case and seven other facts."

"Which are?"

"One, if the trial is held in Holland. Two, Janssen continues to claim his innocence. Three, Ruby Van Dijk's supposed state of mind at the time of the abduction. Four, the privileged life Molly Baker has been afforded over the past seventeen years. Five, the suffering Van Dijk and Janssen have endured during and since the death of their own baby girl. Six, the amount of money both of them have given to charities over the years. And seven, public opinion. Like it or not, the world is looking in on this case, and it will play a part."

I scrunched up my face like something vile had landed on my tongue, knowing that this statement was a complete fabrication. "And what is the judge's opinion?"

"You're not going to like it."

"Go on."

"Seven years for each of them. However, he thinks that, on the right day, with a lenient judge, it may be as little as five years in an open prison, out with a tag on for good behaviour after only two and a half."

Everyone in the room knew how imperative it was to keep Janssen and Van Dijk behind bars for life, to guarantee the safety of all who put them there. It was critical.

Two and a half years would never do, Janssen would take it as just a hiccup in his evil grand scheme, and then start murdering us all, maybe even before he got out.

We were unknown to him right now but, eventually, our names would filter through to him as the people who truly put him away.

Daniel offered us a little comfort. "I think it very unlikely he will try dishing out any sort of revenge whilst he is awaiting trial, which will be months yet."

"Hmm," I said, not really feeling the consolation.

"You know what," I said at length, "although we've rented this place until December, we have fulfilled our contract with Sophie Baker. She's got her sister back and we've caught the perpetrators. We could all just walk away from this, and go into hiding."

My team was looking to me for answers; nobody wanted that, living in fear, looking over our shoulders for the rest of our lives.

"I, for one, feel responsible for everyone's safety, and I'm personally not gonna rest until I bring Janssen's house down, cripple him for good and make sure he stays in the slammer for the rest of his days. I'm not going to ask any of you to stay with me on this. The police, I know, will follow it through, but as for my crew, none of you are obliged to stay here in Holland."

Paul's and Mary's faces could smash concrete, they were so resolute.

"There is still almost half the money left in the case fund," I continued. "I need to talk to Sophie about what she wants done with it, so that may not be ours to spend, but I think that we can support ourselves if you choose to stay and carry on investigating."

"Dave, there really is no need for you to carry on investigating. The police can take it from here."

"I understand that, Daniel, but according to your friend the judge's opinion, based on the evidence we have so far, we might as well all shoot ourselves in the head right now."

Daniel rubbed his chin like the Desperate Dan he'd become.

"No," I said, "there's only one option left for me, carry on and find every shred of evidence there is to collapse house Janssen and his seven henchmen."

"Of the apocalypse?" quipped Mary.

"Not if I can help it."

I came off the phone with Sophie at the Van Dijk palace. They had all switched off their mobile phones, not just because they were traceable, but they had been barraged by journalists all wanting to get a story. George was going to make a televised statement, in time, asking for the media to respect their privacy and give them time to adjust to having their daughter back. He would give interviews eventually, but not for the time being. They were all too busy getting to know one another.

Sophie said that the money wasn't an issue; the Van Dijks had offered them an extraordinary amount in compensation, which they were thinking about. If I thought I needed the fund to carry on investigating, then I was welcome to it.

***

Olavo came back to the fold a couple of days later. He'd been a spare thumb in Portugal and needed to be doing something before he went stir crazy in Faustino's apartment.

I called a confab to get some ideas flowing; we needed to disprove everything written in that statement.

Olavo was first to speak, "About burning little Diana's body, there's no mention of where Janssen built a fire. We know that the fireplaces were all covered with steel plates, so he couldn't have done it inside the house."

We had a printout of the lease agreement between the Cardosa Family and Michael de Jung. One stipulation was that under no circumstances were the leaseholders to have outdoor fires whatsoever. This included barbecues, fire pits and stoves, even candles.

Indoor fires were allowed, but only between 1st November and 28th February, because this area was a complete tinderbox during the dry season.

But would any of that bother them, if they desperately wanted to destroy the evidence of a child's manslaughter? Maybe not.

Paul then offered something that was unfortunately gruesome, but insightful.

"It would have to be a pretty large fire to completely disintegrate a human body; you have to reach temperatures of around 1800 degrees Fahrenheit, and that would take a lot of wood in an open space."

"Good one, Paul."

"Also," he said, "the smoke and heat haze would be spotted from miles away. There is a fire watchtower three kilometres north of the Hidden Farm. I've checked. They would have sent fire crews down there immediately. I also checked the weather for the week in question; it was mostly clear blue skies all week."

282

Mary was making notes. She stopped and said, "That farm is surrounded by all that woodland. Surely it's the ideal place to bury a body? If you dug a hole deep enough, animals wouldn't dig it up, would they?"

"Depends on how hungry they are, I suppose," I replied.

Paul then said, "What happened to the dogs? There's no mention of the dogs."

Olavo flicked through our written records. "All four dogs were last vaccinated for rabies on the 26th April, 2003, at the vets in Loulé."

"Janssen said he found Diana's mutilated body in early April," said Paul, "so the dogs must have been on the farm at that point, and there's no way that wild pigs would have come anywhere near that house if those dogs were about."

"Especially that Rhodesian Ridgeback. If they aren't afraid of lions, they wouldn't run away from wild boar," I reasoned.

Olavo reminded us that there were really long steel chains connected to the kennels, allowing the big dogs to come right up to the front door of the house.

The Dutch contingent had said nothing so far, just sat there listening to our exchange.

"Right!" I snapped, making Rhonda jump. "I don't believe that Janssen burnt that little baby's body. She's somewhere else. And I don't know where the dogs went, but he definitely didn't take them back to the rescue centre, or else they would have told us when we interviewed them. I also don't believe they went back with them to Holland, because there has been no mention of dog hairs in that Hymer from forensics, and after two or three days of travelling with four dogs in that confined space, it would have been covered in dog hair."

Mary stuck a pin through the pregnant pause. "Can't we just ask Janssen again, what happened to the dogs, and where he built the fire? Maybe he'll trip up or contradict himself."

"Is that possible, Daniel, to re-interview him today?"

The Dutch cop bent his neck towards his shoulder and twitched. "If we can get Donald Trump there, I don't see a problem. Janssen's still in a holding cell at the station until they are brought before a judge in a couple of days."

He nodded at the girls, who rushed off to set it up.

"You'll need a couple of tough officers to quick-fire questions at him…"

Daniel screwed his eyes up at me. "We know how to interrogate prisoners, Dave, been doing it a while now," he said sarcastically.

"Yes, yes, sorry. I'm just a bit anxious. Do you mind if I draw up some questions?"

Daniel gave me his unbothered look, "Of course not."

Regarding the fire, I wrote, we will email a diagram of the farm's layout to the station. Janssen can point to the exact spot where he was supposed to have had the fire to cremate baby Diana.

He needs to tell us what materials were used to build the fire. How long did it burn for? Did he try to conceal the fire? What did he do with the ashes? And was there much smoke?

If any fire took place around that farmhouse, forensics will find the evidence, even after all this time. My guess is he'll say he can't remember.

Concerning the dogs, the officers should ask where were the four dogs on the day that Diana was attacked? Did they take the dogs back to Holland when they left? Did they sell or give the dogs away? If so, who to?

Mary typed up these questions and sent them off with an explanatory note, and the diagram of the farm, to the leading investigator at the station.

I wasn't pinning my hopes on any answers; we'd probably get a 'no comment' for every question from now on. Which would in itself be helpful, because it signalled their statement wasn't credible.

I thought our next best move should be to get sniffer dogs in the forest around the farm. My instincts told me that the baby girl wasn't cremated near the house at all, and that the wild boar story was complete nonsense. Maybe it was an accident, or perhaps something more sinister, but I believed she was buried somewhere out there.

After voicing my opinion, Paul reminded us all how vast an area the forest was, and that we would need thirty or forty dogs to make an effective search.

"You're right, mate, but if we look at an area of one kilometre square around the house and tape it off in grids the size of football pitches, then one dog could complete each grid before moving on to the next. We'd cover it in a short space of time, and eliminate an area."

"Where you gonna get that amount of dogs from?" asked Olavo.

"Ah," I said, "When you are as well connected as me, you know people who can."

Antonio, my solicitor, was pleased to hear from me, it had been a while. He of course had seen the famous Miracle Meeting at Wimbledon and was over the moon for me. I didn't have to tell him the need for my team's anonymity, but I did anyway. He replied that I could totally rely on his discretion.

Antonio was responsible for Elizabeth's puppy; he thought it a good idea. Seeing that this old dog was away so much, she needed a replacement. He thanked me for the twenty bottles of Rioja I'd bought him in exchange.

After bringing him up to date on where we were now with the investigation, I then told him of our predicament with the sniffer dogs.

Without dropping a beat, he said he knew exactly where to get them from and would get on the case this afternoon.

Both his and his wife's families were from in and around Seville, just a two-hour drive away from the farm, and because it's where they originate, I assumed that all the dogs would be Springer Spaniels.

I then dropped the bombshell that I needed thirty or forty dogs with their owners, tomorrow.

After a few choice words in Spanish, and him concluding with, "Manana doesn't mean Manana in Spain," he said he would see what he could do.

I told him that money was no object. He could go high if it would secure the dogs; just do whatever it takes.

Within an hour, Antonio had called back. He'd had to dangle a very large 500 euro carrot for each animal and its owner, but he had managed to get me 28 dogs to arrive at the farm tomorrow around 10 a.m.

It would have to do. I got on the phone with Faustino immediately and warned him that he was going to need a good few kilometres of white tape.

I told him I would fly down tomorrow, and meet him at the farm with cash for the dog handlers. We'd pay them by the day. He said he would arrange the refreshments, the toilets facilities, and provide a translator.

It had been two hours since we had heard from Daniel, but given that Hank Gutteridge had to be hauled in once more, we gave it a further half-hour before we attempted contact with our Dutch cop.

Twenty minutes later my mobile sprang into life. It was one of the officers doing the interrogation. As we suspected, all Janssen would say was, "No comment."

The intriguing thing was, though, the officer said that Janssen and Gutteridge didn't seem to be getting on so well.

Daniel said he probably knew what that was all about. Although Gutteridge was the criminal's first choice and a much sought after lawyer, he was also a devoted doggy person, and four dogs disappearing without explanation must be plaguing his conscience.

At 6 30, Daniel picked me up at Tall Trees and drove me to Schiphol airport. I was catching the 9:45 flight to Faro.

For several reasons, I wanted to be at the farm.

I felt that I owed it to Antonio, to thank the Spanish farmers personally for providing the dogs, and for acting so promptly. It was an amazing response.

As we arrived at the airport, the heavens fully opened up, threatening to absolutely drown me. All I had brought along was a light summer jacket.

Daniel came to the rescue; he leant into the rear of the car and pulled forth his Hi-viz police coat.

"There you go, mate," he said. "That'll keep you dry. Just don't forget the Johnnie Walker and the huge Toblerones on your way back."

9

Dilemma

'Ripped to bits', and 'Farmhouse of Horror', were just two of the headlines fixating my gaze on the newspaper stand in Departures at Schiphol airport.

"Geez, these people don't hang about," I whispered.

I knew it wouldn't take long for Janssen and his cohorts to put out a twisted version of events, engineering a sympathy vote from the public, but it had been less than 24 hours since his last interview and between them, Gutteridge and Janssen had been tirelessly in concocting this crock of shit.

At a glance, it seemed like every international rag was covering Janssen's arrest on its front page, the Redtops with typical sensational bias, and emotionally loaded impressions of events.

One of them had managed to find a photograph of a forlorn-looking Janssen and Ruby Van Dijk, with the headline 'Molly Baker taken to replace tragically mutilated tot'.

I felt sick that the populous were being deceived by this rubbish. I purchased a copy just to see what other garbage they had come up with. Know your enemy, I thought.

I removed Daniel's Hi-Vis coat, shook off the last remnants of rain onto the concourse floor, and then headed for a bar, where I ordered a single whisky to take the edge off my disgust. I then settled myself in a corner to read.

The paper had dedicated six pages to the finding of Molly Baker, two of which gave detailed and unbalanced empathy towards Van Dijk's mental state and the anguish that drove her to abduct Molly as a replacement for the

288

unbearable loss she and Janssen had suffered with the hideous dismemberment of their baby, Diana, by wild boar, before her very eyes, the PTSD of which still traumatises her to this day.

"What bollocks!" I said out loud.

A gent at a nearby table peered over the top of his spectacles at me.

If I hadn't been privy to the real facts instigated by these two scumbags, I too might have been drawn in by the paper's regurgitated drivel. But knowing what I know strengthened my belief that we are fed utter bullshit by the media, daily.

Janssen's companies have indeed supported many children's charities over the years, some in fact to the sum of millions of euro, but this funding was all just an elaborate ruse, and a tax write-off, to create a crash mat should the shit ever come down.

Quoting Van Dijk, the paper wrote that the money she and Janssen had given away was solely compensation for taking Molly Baker, a form of atonement for her wrongdoing and for the pain she had caused Molly's family. But, according to the paper, the donations only gave her minor retribution, and her self-loathing and contrition, demented her continually.

"You lying bitch!" I blurted.

The fella across the room this time gave me a disdainful stare.

I read on, hoping in the back of my mind that Faustino would be unearthing the crucial evidence on the farm, that we needed right now, to show what a crock of shite these two evil bastards had invented, the proof that would put them away for good.

There were photos of the Baker girls and their families together at the palace, heart-warming, sincere pictures, taken from the press interview a few days ago.

When asked about their future, Sophie replied that Molly was going to teach her how to play tennis. But regarding the people who had abducted her, all Molly would say at this point was 'no comment'.

There was also a picture of the Hidden Farm's entrance, cordoned off and guarded by police officers, but no mention of drugs being grown there, just tomatoes.

The first boarding call for my flight was announced over the tannoy system, so I folded the paper and tossed it onto the low wooden table in front of me. It would make a decent beer mat at least.

As I made my way to the boarding gate, I could see through the large plate glass windows that the rain was still coming down in sheets, and observing my plane was quite a distance from the gate, I took great comfort in pulling on Daniel's hefty Hi-Vis coat once more. Hooded up, it would certainly keep the weather out.

The flight was only half full, and I was glad to be seated one row back from my preferred position, the centre of the plane, next to the emergency exit.

Three young Dutch girls occupied the row in front of me. I tried my best to not shower them with rain as I took off my coat, folded it and placed it in the overhead locker, but I still managed to drip on one of them, who squirmed, pulled a funny face, but then laughed it off with her mates.

Then I stowed away my overnight bag. There was plenty of room up there and no one else seemed to be waiting to use the locker, so I prepared to shut the door when I noticed a long thread of florescent yellow cotton trailing from Daniel's coat.

Deciding to snap off the offending loose stitching, I wrapped it around two fingers a couple of times and gave it a forceful tug.

The sharp, searing pain it inflicted was eye-watering and caused me to almost swear out loud, but I remembered there were women and children about. The cotton didn't break and my fingers went purple.

I unwound the thread, fully expecting there to be lacerations and blood. Thankfully there were neither, just two throbbing digits.

Flicking my fingers and giving them a rub, I noticed a young Portuguese mum seated in the opposite row with a baby on her lap and her partner beside her. She smiled sympathetically and said, "Fio de algodao."

The words were familiar, but I couldn't recall their meaning. "Painful," I informed her still rubbing my fingers. I smiled back at her and sat down.

After buckling up, I peered out of the blurred acrylic oval at the murky morning, and the ground crew still loading the plane's cargo.

It was miserable out there. I felt their pain. The wind was buffeting them hard, rippling their Hi-Vis wrappings and rocking the plane every now and again, with brutal easterly blasts.

Even though it was now 8 a.m., the rainstorm made it appear dark outside. It was grim, and as the last of the golf bags and suitcases rolled up the conveyor belt towards the ramp-man inside the hold, I felt glad to be heading towards the sun once more.

As the cargo doors thudded shut, the plane began to reverse away from its standing position, and the air stewardesses began their pre-flight safety demonstrations, it hit me, a serendipitous moment, a chain of seemingly unrelated observations which came together to form a singular outstanding revelation.

The ramp-men, all decked out in Hi-Vis hooded jackets and trousers, every one of the ground crew in Hi-Vis gear, even our stewardesses in Hi-Vis vests. The yellow thread that nearly sliced through my fingers, the words in Portuguese uttered by the young mum across the aisle, I remembered where I had heard them before, in the haberdashery shop in Douro Calvo: 'cotton yarn'. Yvette De Vries bought loads of it!

Our stewardesses had removed their Hi-Vis vests, revealing the smart navy blue uniforms beneath, and were now putting on the florescent life jackets that were clandestinely bestowed under our seats, and instructing us on how to inflate them.

I'd seen this drill so many times that I knew it off by heart, so I had closed my eyes and sunk into my seat. But I could still see the stewardess in my mind's eye, putting a jacket on top of a jacket, which seemed to me to be a bulky and uncomfortable thing to endure. Then I flashed back to an old black and white comedy film I'd once seen, where a Spanish conman was trying to rip off tourists by selling them fake watches, that he had dangling on the inside of his suit jacket. He had a dozen or so attached to the lining, along with moody gold chains and necklaces.

The thing that struck me at the time of watching this film was, although this guy was a complete crook, he was very enterprising and resourceful. His contraband hidden in plain sight.

It belted me in an instant, exactly what Yvette de Vries did with all that cotton yarn she'd bought, and how Marc Freese transported his illicit cargo around the world, hidden in secret pockets scwn within ground-crew Hi-Vis jackets.

I pulled out my notebook and pencil from my jacket pocket and jotted some things down.

How much cocaine, cannabis and or cannabis oil could be concealed inside the lining of a jacket without it being suspicious, or indeed too bulky to wear whilst working a very manual job?

How much was cannabis oil worth anyway?

I knew two people who took the stuff regularly. One was a multiple sclerosis sufferer and the other had been fighting pancreatic cancer for years. They both had said on numerous occasions that the drug had helped them in very specific ways. So they'd know the cost of such a product. I would call one of them and find out.

Ironically, I had a rough idea of the street value of cocaine due to another friend whose habit has, unfortunately, put him in the ground. At the height of his addiction, he was paying £65 a gram. That was every day, sometimes more.

My mind was working overtime now, imagining the kind of pockets that Yvette de Vries was stitching together. They'd have to be tough and slim, so as not to appear too padded around a body. Then the wrapped packages of the same shape could be stowed within the lining.

I wondered how much one could carry, four or five kilos perhaps. I did a quick calculation. Five kilos of coke at £65 a gram, that's £325,000. Bloody hell, I thought, I'm in the wrong business!

If it was cannabis bud, at a street value of let's say £10 a gram, then five K of that would be £50,000, far less money involved and way bulkier, but still a lot of dosh.

I broadened my thinking. What if he was importing coke from South America, then distributing it throughout Europe, along with his weed crop?

This could be done in the same manner, a simple jacket swap within the cargo hold. No wonder he insisted on working alone. And the hold of a cargo plane carrying perishable goods would be chilled, so he'd get away with wearing a big jacket whilst he was inside, which he tended to do.

I reckoned I'd sussed it. This was the method Janssen's organisation used to transport the drugs around the world. There must be dozens of employees in major airports around the globe doing the old swaperoo. If I'm right, Interpol is going to want to keep this operation going for the time being, after I reveal the method of transportation, to catch the operators red-handed en mass.

I'd lost track of time, I was so engrossed with my thoughts. The drinks trolley, and the duty-free cart had gone by without notice, and my ears were beginning to pop, so I knew we must be descending.

The sun was now streaming in through windows, flooding the fuselage with welcome Iberian light. I closed my eyes again, and smiled at the thought of spending the night at Vista do Vale. Jim Maxwell said I could use it at any time if it was free and I was in the area. It was, and Carlos and Ramona had been informed of my imminent arrival.

An ear-piercing scream emanating from the front of the plane shattered my thoughts.

Snapped into consciousness, I unbuckled my seatbelt and stood up for a better view, as did many others, obscuring my sightline. But it soon became apparent as to what was causing the terror; smoke was drifting up through the floor panels and into economy class; somewhere, the plane was on fire.

The 'fasten your seatbelts' signs went into a frenzy, swiftly followed by oxygen masks dropping from the overhead lockers like limp tentacles, which is always a bad sign. The stewardesses were robotically making their way down the aisle, hopelessly trying to promote calm, and asking for us all to sit down and buckle up. It was having little effect on dampening the escalating hysteria.

Methodically trying to evaluate the situation, I looked across at the Portuguese couple, who had successfully

294

donned their oxygen masks and were in the proceeds of attaching one to their baby, a bubble of serenity in all this panic. I placed my mask over my face and drew the elastic tight. At least I could breathe okay in this steel tube pizza oven, hurtling through the air at 500 miles per hour.

The airline's policy would be to get the plane down as soon as possible. We were dropping fast, but the ground still looked a mighty way off.

The captain came over the audio system, reiterating the need for us to sit down fasten our seatbelts, put on the oxygen masks and to not use our mobile phones. Apparently we would be landing in five minutes. Time to cook a hard-boiled egg, I thought.

The smoke was definitely getting thicker and coming from more places on the floor. I reckoned that the flight crew must be de-pressurising the plane to decrease the amount of oxygen in the fuselage, that way keeping the fire under control.

A stewardess with a portable oxygen bottle and mask had come up to the girls in front of me and was instructing them on how to open the emergency door once we land. Clearly, they were going to struggle; they were all teenagers and stick thin.

I unbuckled and stood up, indicating to the flight attendant that I knew what to do, she gave me the thumb's up.

It was a possibility that the fuel was low on the aircraft, but I believed that the crew would jettison what reserves they had before touchdown. It still meant there would be sufficient fuel in the tanks to incinerate us all once we landed and the open doors let fresh air gush in, igniting the smouldering fire like a fuse to a bomb. But what option did we have? People would rush to get out of the plane as quickly as possible.

Over the vague noise of weeping and prayer, I made a decision to let my team know my thoughts on Janssen's smuggling racket, and to let my family know how much I loved them.

I only had a couple of pages left in my notebook, so wrote fast and really small, with smoke now stinging my eyes, making me weep. I signed the pages with my name and date of birth, then ripped them out and folded them into little squares, pulled my mask to one side and put one square in each cheek of my mouth, knowing that in the event of me being burnt alive, the papers, along with my teeth, would probably survive, it's one of the reasons you cover your face in the crash position.

We were getting really close to the ground now, and seemed to be travelling way too fast to make a decent landing. I looked at the Portuguese couple once more, who were holding hands and visibly shaking. I tried to assure them with hand gestures that it would be alright, that I was going to open the door when we landed, and then pointed to her high-heel shoes, indicating that she should kick them off. She did.

But in my head, I wasn't that self-assured; 63 years of scrapes and near-misses had come down to this. The reaper had finally caught up with me, and he was about to take a significant bonus haul in one almighty scythe stroke.

Over the runway, the ground rushed past in a blur. Surely we'd have a blowout if we hit the tarmac at this speed? I assumed the crash position, closed my eyes, and pictured Elizabeth, her face as serene as I'd ever seen it. A deep peace came over me and I relaxed, ready for oblivion.

The tyres screeched with the first touch-down. It jerked me back to the situation at hand. The plane lifted once more, and then hit the ground again. The brakes engaged, everyone lurched forward, and my face pressed into the seat in front. The pilot throttled in full reverse, and the whole plane shuddered as it slowly came to halt with blue flashing lights and mayhem all around us.

The fire crews wasted no time in dousing the aircraft in thick white foam.

Within seconds I was up and round in front of the Dutch girls, holding my breath, and with one swift action had the door open and swung up out of the way. The opposite exit door was opened simultaneously, and a beam of sunlight flooded in, highlighting the density of the smoke now billowing from the plane.

I took the papers out of my mouth and shouted, "This way," then stepped out onto the wing of the aircraft, where I promptly slipped on my arse, slid off the airfoil and onto an inflated plastic slide, then the deck. It was the worst foam party I'd ever been to.

Dazed, I ungainly righted myself from a bundle of Dutch girls who had followed swiftly behind me and, coughing and spluttering, was ushered in the direction of a gathering of airport staff and busses, and by an emergency worker shouting in Portuguese and English.

Hearing cries behind us, I turned to see the young couple and their baby struggling to negotiate the tarmac. The man was holding the baby, but she was having trouble walking with bare feet. So, seeing it was my fault she was shoeless, I went back and offered to give her a piggyback ride all the way to the waiting busses in double quick time. For this, I was very nearly worshipped.

Our bendy bus wasn't even a quarter full before the doors closed and it headed for the terminal. Other busses would collect the rest of the passengers.

We were given much-needed bottles of water, and then led to a very plush lounge, possibly reserved for important dignitaries and high flyers; it was the most luxurious airport lounge I'd ever witnessed, with a bar, big comfy armchairs, TV screens, all sorts.

Paramedics and airline officials were over us like flies, making sure we were okay and asking a myriad of questions, about our names, what we saw, and what belongings we had left on the plane.

We were assured that all our possessions would be delivered to us as soon as possible. I gave them the villa's address.

Security was watertight. We weren't going to be leaving here soon, but I needed to be gone and up to the farm in a hurry, so I wandered to a less frantic area and called Faustino. If anyone could use their influence over my predicament, it would be him.

He said he'd be there within an hour. It took an hour and a half.

Slicing through security like a shark fin through still water, Faustino had a quick chat with the official in charge, who eventually agreed to let me leave.

The place was swarming with the press; getting through that lot would be like wading through treacle and cause us unwanted attention, so Faustino got a security guard to lead us through some non-public access areas and out onto the pavement at Arrivals, where my Portuguese buddy had a car waiting.

"Are you okay to travel, Dave?"

"Yeah, sure, just feel a bit out of sorts, you know, a bit disembodied."

"A traumatic event like that can have some very dramatic side effects which might manifest later; it can really upset your nervous system."

He looked at me probingly.

"I'm fine, mate, honestly; it'll be something to tell the grandkids when I retire."

I was shaken, but the urge to get the evidence to put Janssen away was far greater.

On the way to the farm, Faustino informed me of the latest grisly discoveries.

The Spanish dogs, with their handlers, had arrived at 10 a.m. and set to work immediately. At precisely 11.58 a.m. a shallow grave was discovered 700m northwest of the farmhouse. It contained the intact remains of a baby, wrapped in a black bin liner, which has been exhumed and taken to the police forensic labs in Lisbon for a post-mortem.

In another area, 50m north of the first, they had found a second grave. This contained all four dogs, still wearing their collars and leads. It appeared that they had been bludgeoned to death because the skulls were caved in, but the two larger dogs may have still been alive when they were buried; there were signs of them trying to dig their way out.

I felt sick. "Jesus Christ, Faustino, this bloke is fucking evil. Who could do that sort of thing to his animals?"

"A psychopath, my friend, callous, unemotional and morally depraved. His traits fit the bill perfectly."

"Gutteridge is going to hate that."

"Who?"

"Gutteridge, Janssen's lawyer. He's a prominent member of the American Kennel Club."

Faustino paused. "It's a horrible thought, Dave, but the way those dogs died might work in our favour, cause a rift between client and representative."

"My thoughts exactly, mate. He should learn that fact sooner rather than later. I'll see to it."

I puffed the air out of my cheeks. "And the baby, obviously Diana?"

Faustino nodded sideways with regret. "We need an official identification, but, yes, almost certainly."

"What a crock of shit they've concocted for their defence. They must have had that conceived a long time ago. How on earth did they think they'd get away with it?"

"An egotistical narcissist's mind has an inflated sense of self-importance; he's probably incapable of conjecture and accepting fallibility."

"Or he thinks we're all idiots."

"Yeah, that too."

As we continued to climb higher into the interior, I revealed to Faustino my thoughts on Janssen's transportation methods. We both agreed that because Janssen no longer was involved in cannabis production, he'd probably switched to importing cocaine. Having a greater value and being less bulky, each transport would have a much greater yield.

"I think we should look towards Brazil as the principal point of export."

Faustino looked surprised. "Why? Cocaine is mostly produced in Columbia, Peru and Bolivia."

"Ah, it might be made in those countries, but it could be transported from anywhere in South America and the Caribbean."

"So why Brazil, in particular?"

"Just look at how many Brazilians are working for Janssen; they are all over his network. How many were employed at his mansion?"

Faustino nodded in agreement.

"Also, the vast number of chartered flights coming out of Brazil, they all carry fruit and veg stored in the chilled cargo bays. Those goods don't get searched until they are in the holding areas inside the airports, which gives our double-jacket wearing ramp-men ample opportunity to do the business."

Faustino was concerned. "My understanding of international drug smuggling is that it is usually very large shipments at a time…"

Exactly, no one is looking for small shipments, multiple times; they're bringing it in under the radar."

"Hmm." It was starting to make sense to my Portuguese friend. "We should let Interpol know immediately."

"Yep. Might I suggest they instigate having hidden cameras set up inside the holds of all aircraft leaving Brazil destined for Europe?"

Faustino rippled his lips with a puff of air. "That's gonna take some doing, my friend. Even if the airlines agreed under federal order. The cartels are so deep. They have their fingers in many pies. It'll be extremely difficult to keep the cameras a secret."

"So, it's gonna take time?"

"I'd say, even if it could be done at all. I can only make a suggestion to Interpol. They will have to agree and instigate if they feel it a probability."

We pulled over and swapped seats so that Faustino could call Mattise Toussanit and put forward my theory whilst I drove.

Toussanit was sceptical but would talk to his superiors.

All I could do at this point was hope for the best. I'd given my two pennies worth, but I really didn't have any proof of this at all, just my intuition.

The entrance to the hidden farm was thick with a media horde, held back by a metal barrier cordon, manned by half a dozen cops. Our arrival sparked a flurry of camera action as we entered the drive.

It was now accessible by car, the vegetation having been flattened by a multitude of vehicles that had passed this way since my first visit. It looked entirely different.

At the house I was introduced to Lorenco, the lead forensic investigator. His English was better than mine; he bought us up to date.

An autopsy had been carried out on the baby's remains at 1:00 p.m.; they were waiting for DNA results for positive identification, but had no reason to believe she was anyone else but Diana Van Dijk.

Lorenco was formal and softly spoken; you knew in an instant you'd get the facts with no frills. "Initial analysis showed there to be high concentrations of cannabis resin on the child's clothing, leading the coroner to think that cannabis ingestion may have been the cause of death, but it may well only be a guess. Unless a confession can be extracted from the accused, because there isn't much tissue left on the corpse to analyse."

I was aghast. "What, a child could die if it eats marijuana?"

"There have been cases of it, yes. Officially, the children died from myocarditis, an inflammation of the heart muscle, a condition which is often caused by a virus that reaches the heart muscle, but doctors believe it can also be brought on by a high dosage of cannabis."

"And Ruby Van Dijk has said in her statement that she always took Diana into the greenhouse with her. If she left the child alone whilst she tended the crop, Diana could have quite easily put something in her mouth. Babies will eat all sorts of nasty stuff. I've had first-hand experience of that, many times."

Lorenco elevated his brow, protruded his bottom lip and nodded. "Of course, but most babies aren't raised on cannabis farms."

The forensic team had taken more than a hundred pictures of the grave sites; I was invited to take a look at the pits before everybody left the scene. I didn't realise however that the dog's bodies were yet to be removed.

After the initial shock of seeing the animals in their shallow tomb, I couldn't get over how well preserved they were. The fur was for the most part intact, as were their leather collars, still attached to nylon leads. The dog's had been dumped and covered over like spent articles.

It was one of the saddest, most grizzly things I think I have ever seen, and visions of the poor dogs being led to this place of slaughter, probably thinking they were going walkies with the human they trusted most, only to be beaten to death in front of one another, made me rush to a tree and vomit.

Foul-tasting sick, with burnt plastic overtones. Obviously due to all that smoke ingestion on the plane. Luckily, I still had a swig of water left in the plastic bottle given to me at the airport, in my jacket pocket. I took a gulp and spat it out, it washed some of the taste away.

I made my apologies when I returned to the grave site and those wretched, dilapidated pelts, but no one seemed that perturbed, or in fact, surprised.

Faustino vented his disgust in Janssen to me. "I'm going to make sure that bastard gets five years a piece for each of these poor animals."

According to him, that was the maximum sentence handed down for animal cruelty in Portugal. I didn't know how Faustino would impose this statement, but that was his conviction right there and then.

Before leaving the farm, I met with the Spanish farmers who had kindly brought their dogs all the way to Portugal for the investigation.

Other than the two graves they'd unearthed, they'd also found a deer carcass, a dead fox and, by sheer chance, some black truffles, a valuable treasure, which they intended to keep. It made me smirk to think that there was a legal little gold mine here that Janssen knew nothing about.

Faustino paid each man in cash; they were all either friends or related to Antonio, and asked me to pass on their regards. He seemed to be well-respected in their part of Spain, and so he should be. He is a man of high esteem and stoical integrity.

I drove Faustino's Peugeot whilst he contacted base to let them know the search at the farm was being wrapped up. I'd missed the languid air of the Algarve; it brought a satisfied smile to my face, the kind of reassuring contentment you get by seeing a loved one after a long absence. The olive, lemon and orange groves en route to the villa were heavily laden with fruit now. It was glorious to be back, even just for one night, in our remote little sanctuary.

Carlos and Ramona greeted us on the front steps; it was heart-warming to see them once more. My bag and Daniel's jacket had preceded me, courtesy of the airline, which was impressive. I asked our hosts if it would be alright for us to have a beer by the pool. "Of course," they said. While we were staying at the villa, we should treat it like our home.

Within the hour, Carlos and Ramona returned bearing gifts, which I wasn't expecting at all. A roast chicken, a Russian and a Portuguese salad, and a freshly-baked baguette straight from the oven. I thought I had died and gone to heaven.

We asked them to join us, but they declined. They were going out for the evening. Faustino thanked them in Portuguese and reiterated the need to keep our visit top secret. They in return confirmed their complete discretion and wished us a pleasant stay and a safe journey home.

Such lovely people, I thought, making a promise to myself to bring my entire family here for a holiday when this was all over.

Faustino and I ate dinner together and chatted about many things. We spoke of his relationship with Olavo. Apparently, my friend was considering selling his house in England and moving back over here. Love, it seemed, was on the table.

We also spoke of the case, of course.

"What will happen to the farm and all of Janssen's assets? Is there the equivalent to our Proceeds of Crime Act, here in Europe?" I quizzed.

Faustino was austere with his reply. "Directive 2014/42/EU."

"Sounds a bit imperialistic."

"The European parliament has so many regulations, my friend. I think they find it more practical to number them."

"So what does 2014/42/EU decree?"

"Well, so I understand, there is a trade and cooperation agreement within the council of Europe, a TCA, that bears the description 'The freezing and confiscation of the proceeds of crime', which, just like Britain's POCA, will split a criminal's assets three ways, between the police forces, the prosecution services and the governments involved in catching and prosecuting those criminals. Up until now, year on year, it hasn't been too lucrative, with only about one or two percent of the proceeds retrieved."

I frowned. "Doesn't seem like it's working at all well."

"What can I say. Major league criminals are very intelligent people. Rarely are their assets in their own names, and they hire top lawyers to fight their cases. The police forces arrest and send many people to court, but when they get there, it's out of our hands."

"Corruption?"

Faustino shrugged. "In some cases maybe. More often than not, it's a lenient judicial system."

My Portuguese cop gave me cause for concern. Janssen was very smart and he had a high-profile lawyer, but surely, we had him bang to rights.

Faustino left, with a promise to pick me up in the morning and take me back to the airport. Strangely, my earlier dice with death hadn't put me off flying, but it had been one hell of a day, and extremely hot.

I decided, there was only one thing for it. I stood up and stepped out of my clothes, suddenly immeasurably alone under the stars and as nature had intended. With that reassurance, I let all my thoughts and conflicts drain to my feet, leave me and absorb into the concrete like invisible ink, then I strolled to the pool and dived in.

My hot body pieced the cool water like a Gannet darting a tempestuous sea, rinsing my smoke-tinged skin and vanquishing the pent-up trauma I had hoarded today in an instant.

It felt glorious just to cling to the margins in temperate solitude, my legs free from toil and weightlessly swaying in the mellow current propelled solely by the filter system.

I stayed in the pool for a good 15 minutes, letting my mind go blank and soaking up the blissful evening ambience.

When sleep threatened to consume me, I forced myself out of the water and into the changing hut where I knew there'd be some clothes conveniently folded on the shelf, for guests who had arrived without the appropriate apparel. I dressed in a pair of blue swimming shorts and a white t-shirt, then went back to my seat and my pile of crumpled togs, besides which languished a fold of paper, one that I had stuffed in my mouth on the plane. It brought back a flood of horror and a realisation of how close to death I had come this morning, and prompted me to call home immediately.

Elizabeth was surprised to hear from me at such a late hour. It was quite out of character, so she knew instinctively something was up. I relayed the day's events to mostly silence on the other end of the phone. She was just concerned that I was unharmed, which I assured her I was.

She understood the pressure this case had brought to bear on me and also the extent of danger everybody involved with the investigation and their families were in if Janssen and his crew ever got to hear of our existence.

But my wife was dogmatically resolute that Janssen and Van Dijk had to be put behind bars for an extremely long time for the things they had done, whatever the consequences. I loved that about Elizabeth. She always had my back.

I told her to be vigilant. I thought we had enough on that evil pair to put them away for life, but we still needed to net the rest of his organisation, so I would be asking our daughter, Sam, if it were possible to have some undercover officers keep an eye on our house for the time being.

We signed off, telling each other how much we loved one another. She told me not to worry about her. Chase would keep her safe. I chuckled. He was just a puppy.

Talking to Elizabeth made the world seem alright again. She had that way about her, a special gift.

Next, I called Sam. She said she would see what she could do. Budgets were tight at the Met, but she was owed a few favours. She would also inform the rest of the family and put them on guard.

There was only one thing left to do tonight, open the bottle of Rosé which had been silently screaming at me from an ice bucket on the table, and get suitably desensitised whilst I pondered the dilemma of how Interpol might entrap Janssen's henchmen.

They certainly weren't going to be found wearing Hi-Vis jackets, unloading contraband in the cargo hold of various aircraft around the world. This was going to take a massive amount of manpower and a huge surveillance operation over a long period. Unless we can get Janssen to rat on his own men; but why would he do that? Even if he and Van Dijk got time, he'd run his empire from the inside. He had vast amounts of money entwined in the business, and he was the emperor, so why would he throw it all away?

The statement Faustino made earlier in the day, about making sure Janssen would get the maximum sentence for each of the four dogs he'd slain was playing on my mind.

If Janssen received the maximum sentence for all of the crimes he is charged with, I wondered how much that would equate to.

Not having any notebook pages left to write on, I hurried into the villa to grab some A4 printer paper and a pen from the office, and then I returned to the poolside.

For the brutal killing of his four dogs, I wrote down 20 years. The manslaughter of Diana van Dijk, 30 years; the abduction and unlawful imprisonment of Molly Baker, 30 years; the growing and distribution of marijuana, 20 years; the importation and distribution of class-A drugs, 40 years; the knee-capping of the nurse Sabrina Zegar and the torment of her husband Alex, 15 years at least. Daniel had had a conversation with them only yesterday, and now that Janssen was behind bars, they were at last willing to give the police a full statement of their abuse. And, finally, 15 years for money laundering, tax evasion and fraud.

In total, it came to 170 years.

Obviously, no judge in Europe is going to dish out that sort of punishment, more likely some of the sentences would run concurrently, but I couldn't see them both getting anything less than 40 years apiece. Which would do nicely, but that wouldn't be Janssen's only problem.

Even if he got out early for good behaviour, he has broken the law in 16 different countries. When he comes out of prison in Holland, they may all want to prosecute him, especially Portugal.

I have great faith Interpol will do an excellent job in bringing down the Janssen drug-smuggling enterprise, but that could take months, maybe years, to execute, and we needed something more immediate to end that operation and bring in all of his generals before the word gets out that a team of private investigators from England were pivotal in his downfall.

No, I needed a new super plan to put forward to the Openbaar Ministerie, the Dutch public prosecution service, one which will force Janssen to grass up his colleagues and bring down his own cartel.

I'd sleep on it.

***

One week later I was underground, in a low-lit observation room, flanked by senior Dutch detectives, transfixed by the man on the other side of a two-way mirror in the interview room below police headquarters in Amsterdam.

Janssen couldn't know I was there, not even know of my existence, yet his eyes seemed to burn through the glass and immobilise me with contempt.

I was here as a guest. The OM was impressed by my proposal and had agreed to integrate it into their procedure. It may well shorten this whole process and benefit all. It was certainly worth a try.

Gutteridge was, as always, in attendance, as were two specialist officers, in case Janssen kicked off.

Daniel, who was now the lead investigator on the case, entered the room with Rhonda, each of them carrying several beige pocket wallets.

The arrogance of the man spiked immediately, chastising Daniel for being late. Daniel ignored him. The officers sat down at the table and, before they could say anything, Gutteridge stated that his client would not be answering any more questions because he has already pleaded guilty to the charges presented and has made full statements. He sat back with his arms folded and an imperious cock of the head.

Daniel drew a long breath. "Have you finished?"

Gutteridge arched his eyebrows.

Rhonda pressed the record button on the machine by her side, and the interview began.

Daniel went through the formalities of mentioning who was in the room, the time of day, etc., and then hit them with, "New evidence has come to light during our investigation, which will bring about further charges to both you, Mr Janssen, and Ruby Van Dijk."

Gutteridge looked perplexed. Janssen just sneered.

"What evidence?" said the Trump look-a-like sardonically.

With that, Rhonda pulled out six A4 photographs from a wallet and carefully placed them right side up in front of the accused and his lawyer.

They were forensic photographs of Diana Van Dijk, still in her grave.

Janssen was physically stunned.

Gutteridge shot a look towards his client.

Daniel spoke directly at Janssen, "During a thorough search of the grounds around A Fazenda Escondida, Monchique, Portugal, the Hidden Farm you leased under the name of Michael de Jung from the Cordosa family, and occupied between February 2001 and June 2003, a

310

grave site was unearthed containing the remains of a one-year-old female infant whose DNA has been analysed and matched to both you and Ruby Van Dijk, in essence, your daughter, Diana. Not torn to pieces by wild boar as you have previously claimed, but intact, and with decomposition expected for a body that has been in the ground for seventeen years."

Gutteridge sat back in his chair, flabbergasted.

Daniel continued, "Traces of highly concentrated cannabis resin were found on the child's clothing, and in the DNA of her hair, leading our forensic scientists to suspect that ingestion of marijuana leaf may have been the cause of death, by inducing a heart attack."

Janssen leaned into Gutteridge and whispered something inaudible.

"Is this how Diana died?" asked Rhonda. "A tragic accident that you covered up through fear of having your drug production site revealed? Was losing a child acceptable as collateral damage for your illegal activity, a reasonable hiccup in your illicit empire building?" Rhonda was turning on the pressure, "Or was it just the fear of losing Ruby's inheritance, Mr Janssen? Were you selfishly, greedily afraid?"

"No comment," spat Janssen.

I could see that Gutteridge wasn't as comfortable as he was earlier; he was shifting nervously in his plastic seat. Neither the defendant nor lawyer expected this evidence to surface. It blew Janssen's statement right out of the water.

Daniel then pulled out six more photographs from his file and laid those in front of the pair opposite.

Janssen closed his eyes.

"These photographs were taken at another grave site close to Diana's. As you can see, here are the remains of four dogs, four rescue dogs that you once owned, Mr Janssen. Am I right? Animals that you bought from Centro

311

de resgate de case e santario de animals, in Loulé, Portugal, in April 2001, yes?"

"No comment."

Daniel continued, "Animals that you fed and cared for, for two years, until one day you decided to bludgeon them to death. What was that a whim or were they just no longer of use to you?"

Gutteridge was staring at the photographs, utterly horrified; we all knew he'd have this reaction.

Rhonda took up the questioning, "Each of these poor souls suffered massive blunt instrument trauma to the head. The two terriers we think died instantly, but there is strong evidence to suggest that the two larger dogs were still alive when they went into that pit because they had made some attempt to dig their way out before they suffocated."

Janssen's icy grimace was like a weapon. If he wasn't cuffed to the table, I'm sure he would have erupted out of his seat and done some damage to either detective.

Gutteridge, agitated, asked Daniel to remove the photos, which he did. The lawyer then turned to his client and spoke in hushed, determined tones. It became obvious that an argument was taking place and that Janssen was threatening his brief, gesticulating aggressively the best he could in handcuffs.

Daniel intervened by extracting a stack of papers from a file and tidying them in front of himself. "We know about your cocaine distribution network, Mr Janssen. As of this moment, sixteen countries around the world are cooperating with Interpol in a giant surveillance operation to catch your guys red-handed. We don't know how you do it yet, but it's only a matter of time." He lied.

"So far, eight countries want to extradite you and Ruby Van Dijk to face multiple charges on their home soil. This can be arranged after you have served time here in Holland," pointed out Rhonda.

Daniel nodded. "As of today, a Council of Europe judge has granted a directive under the trade and cooperation agreement to freeze all of your assets, both private and business, until the case is concluded. That's everything, including your house and all of your bank accounts."

Janssen's lips curled on one side of his face like he knew something we didn't. Like this threat didn't bother him one ounce. Obviously, he had access to funds elsewhere and/or was carrying a trump card we knew nothing about.

Gutteridge had had enough; he shot to his feet, pushing back his chair in one action. He closed his briefcase and announced that he would no longer be representing Janssen, then he marched out the room like he was running from a bad smell.

Again Janssen snarled. His contempt for the situation was unbelievable.

Rhonda formally paused the interview recording, saying that it would continue as soon as new representation could be arranged for Mr Janssen. Then she and Daniel also left the room.

I wasn't sure whether I should stay where I was or leave as well. Janssen stretched out his legs, slumped backwards in his chair and closed his eyes as if he wanted to take a nap. I took it as yet more insolence, pretending that he couldn't care less.

A couple of slow minutes passed by before I got a call on my mobile from Daniel. He wanted me upstairs in his office. The senior officers escorted me all the way.

When I got there, Daniel was in a familiar position, perched on the corner of his desk. Rhonda was standing, hands clasped in front of her, clutching the beige pocket wallets from the interview.

"Hank Gutteridge was just in here," said Daniel.

"Oh, yes?"

"I asked him why he suddenly quit when he'd been Janssen's lawyer for years."

"And what did he say?"

"Many reasons. He didn't like the way he was threatened in there. He knows what Janssen is capable of and it scared the life out of him. Secondly, he's no dummy. He knows that there isn't a chance in hell of getting Janssen off this rap, and with all of his client's assets frozen, he knows there is no money in it for him and he doesn't do pro bono work. Gutteridge admitted that he'd been trying to get away from 'that piece of shit' for some time now, and this was the perfect opportunity, but I think the straw that broke the camel's back was the dogs, Dave. That was a great strategy; it really broke Gutteridge's heart."

Rhonda cut in, "Janssen is going to be feeling rather vulnerable right now. He's blown his most trusted council."

"Better get him a new brief then," I said, "any about?"

"There's always a duty solicitor milling around. I'll see who's free."

An hour ticked by before a fresh-faced 30-something bounced into the office with purpose.

Luuk Snijder was straight from court, where he had been defending a street musician who had been performing in the city for the third time without a licence.

The solicitor had managed to get the fellow off with just a 50 euro fine; successful mornings for both of them, a cheery outcome. No wonder he had a spring in his step. But Mr Snijder was about to be baptised by fire.

Daniel was familiar with Luuk. He said he was optimistic, forthright and brimming with moral integrity. Janssen was going to hate him.

After introductions in English, where I was given the pseudonym Mr Woods, a private detective who had helped in the investigation, Daniel gave Luuk a brief synopsis on the infamous defendant we had waiting for him down in the cells, what he had been charged with and the number of years he was facing in jail.

Snijder flicked through the paperwork with a demeanour of serious concern. This was something far greater than he'd ever experienced, yet, tight-lipped, he was duty-bound.

"Can I go see my client now?"

"Of course, we want you to," said Daniel. "But first, we want to go over a proposal we have devised, which will, if accepted, be beneficial to all parties."

"A deal, you want to make a deal?"

"Yes, but please hear me out. As things stand Janssen is looking to spend the rest of his life behind bars and lose everything that he owns, a massive fortune, and the love of his life, Ruby Van Dijk. But, if you can get him to turn on his six generals, and make statements on each of their involvements in his criminal empire over the past thirty years, then together with Interpol, we can scoop up the whole filthy network in one go and close down his global drug cartel."

"And what will Mr Janssen get out of this unlikely event?"

The Chief Commissioner, Hendrik Timmerman, who until now had remained silent, stepped in. "The Minister of Justice, the Chief Prosecutor and I have all agreed that if Janssen is willing to release this information as evidence, and it proves to be factual, then we shall reduce the charges to just the abduction and imprisonment of

315

Molly Baker, for which he must plead guilty, then he is probably looking at a maximum of twenty-five years in jail. And, as a further incentive for him to do this, he can serve out his sentence in Bastoy Prison, Norway, the nicest prison in the world."

The look of surprise stretched Luuk's face, "You can do that?"

"It can be arranged."

"There's one more thing," said Daniel. "Mr Woods' involvement in this case is the utmost top secret; Janssen is not to be privy to his existence under any circumstance, due to the nature of the man and the likelihood of dire repercussions. For now, the investigation has been purely police work, carried out in several countries. Is that clear?"

Snijder nodded solemnly. "What about when it comes to trial?"

"If he pleads guilty, there won't be a trial, just a sentencing hearing. By then, we want to be assured that this lunatic will not be in any position to cause harm to anyone in the world ever again."

We waited anxiously in the office for Snijder to return, going over the probabilities of Janssen agreeing to the deal and the lengthy process ahead if he did not.

I was betting on his ego being the deciding factor, not his loyalty to his troops. He couldn't give a toss about them. What he would be engineering right now was a strategy of damage limitation for himself, but also a way of inflicting pain on those who put him away.

If he does the full 25 years, he'll be 69 when he comes out, still able and willing to cause plenty of grief. Although I'll probably be long gone, my kids and grandchildren will still be endangered, and I'm not having that.

316

An hour later, Snijder returned. "He's thinking about it," he said.

My stomach was growling. I'd had nothing but tea and coffee all morning. "Lunch?" I suggested.

Daniel and Rhonda concurred, so we left the building and headed for a bar, relieved to be out of the strained atmosphere in the nick for a while, returning only after a phone call from Luuk.

Janssen had agreed to our terms if two conditions could be met. The maximum sentence he receives is 20 years, and his palace, and the art and classic car collections are to be sold as a job lot. They are not to be sold separately or individually; and he wanted that in a written binding agreement.

"Cheeky bastard," I blurted. "Who does he think he is?"

Daniel stretched his face. "Someone with bargaining chips, I'll think you'll find."

"Perhaps," I pondered. "Even if we can get the Council of Europe and the Chief Prosecutor to agree to his terms, then who in their right mind would buy an art and car collection that they couldn't sell on, a museum?"

"I was thinking the same thing, my friend; it's not a great prospect for a dealer, or for someone who wants the house and not the collections. It's baffling. Maybe there's a method in his madness," suggested Daniel.

"Maybe it's hope," proffered Rhonda. "He is very passionate about that car collection."

"Hmm," I pondered.

"Well," said Daniel. "None of this is our decision to make. I shall put forward Janssen's requests through the proper channels, and we will await the results."

And that was that, it would be a while before I heard anymore, so I decided to go back home and wait, thinking that this sly git had an ulterior motive with his property sale conditions. I couldn't see what it was yet, but time would tell.

Whilst in England, I had the pleasure of returning to Eastbourne, visiting the Whiteleafs once again, this time awarding them with a gift. The immaculate magnet, given to me by the retired ballet school principal in Leiden, complete with its box.

It was the just thing to do. The Whiteleafs help in identifying the fridge magnet was fundamental to the discovery of the Elusive's, and in cracking this case.

Their neighbour, Ted, amazingly, was still in his front garden, deadheading his Dahlias.

I nodded his way as I walked up to the front door of number 37. His eyes followed my every move.

Colin and Sheila were expecting me, they answered the door together.

It wasn't necessary, but I made double sure that Ted would hear a proclamation on the doorstep.

I held the little blue box out in front of me like I was offering an engagement ring.

"Colin, Sheila, a present for you, a token of thanks, for helping to solve one of the biggest cases in history, certainly in the last seventeen years. Your knowledge was pivotal."

"Oh!" said Colin.

Sheila was playful, "Could it be a magnet?" she grinned.

"Indeed it is my dear, a very rare and prestigious one."

"Well, you'd better come in then. I've just taken a Victoria sponge out of the oven. Cup of tea?"

"Don't mind if I do."

***

It was mid-August when I got the call; Interpol and Europol had both been busy in the shadows, working with airlines, putting hidden cameras in the holds of planes travelling the known routes of the cartels' system, and had captured plenty of incriminating evidence against ramp-men in several countries. This evidence could be used as a backup if Janssen changes his mind and we have to go through the whole shebang at trial, or it could be used in conjunction to support Janssen's testimony.

Interpol hadn't interviewed Janssen or Van Dijk at all since he agreed to turn informer. They were waiting to see how that pans out, but were growing impatient.

"And how is your charming guest these days," I asked, "behaving himself?"

"Yes, surprisingly. He reads a lot, newspapers, books, magazines. He loves his car magazines."

"No access to the internet?"

"Noooo, we may as well hand him the keys to the door if we did that. Listen," he said, "I'd like you back in Holland as soon as possible." His voice was hesitant.

"Why, what's happened?"

Daniel paused, exhaled and then said with some reluctance, "He knows about you."

In an instant, I left this world, suddenly floating in an opaque vacuum bubble, just above my blurred surroundings, my mind racing, my fears fully realised.

It took a couple of seconds to regain my senses, coming back to this plane with an air-sucking splat.

"What? How?" It seemed inconceivable.

"This devil's tentacles are very long, my friend. It seems he has somehow infiltrated the system, and somebody has been paid for information."

I blew through pursed lips. "How much does he know?"

"From what he is saying, he knows that a private investigator from the UK was the crux in bringing him down. He doesn't know your name, apparently, only that you had a team working on the Molly Baker case."

"Can't you just deny it?"

"I'm afraid not. He'll know we're lying and besides… He's brought in another stipulation."

"Which is?"

"The COE and the Chief Prosecutor have both agreed to his stipulated conditions and to his sentencing of only twenty years, but… He won't make any statements damning his henchmen and his cartel until… Until he meets you in person."

"Meet me! What for?"" The horrors of being in the same room as that scumbag hit me like a cricket bat full in the face.

"I don't know, pride maybe. Perhaps he can't believe that there is someone who outsmarted him. It's likely that he's enraged, insulted, and definitely intrigued. Anyway, he's not playing ball, and I know it completely goes against all the measures we have taken to protect your identity, and I am not insisting on this at all, far from it. I told my superiors no, but they obviously don't fully comprehend what Janssen is capable of, either from behind bars or in future retribution, but they've asked me to ask you. So here it is. It's totally up to you. I will understand if you say no. That piece of shit can stew in his own juices in a cell for all I care. Maybe he'll turn on his pals eventually, but if you came, it would accelerate the entire process. What do you think?"

I had no real concerns for my safety in going face to face with Janssen; the maniac was restrained after all. What could he do to me? My fears were entirely for the well-being of my family and my team, and as Daniel had said, we had spent months and an enormous amount of money keeping our presence a secret. That would all be in vain if I simply just went and met the bloke, even if I went in disguise with a false name. Once he got the use of a computer, it wouldn't take a genius to discover the real me. I'm all over social media, and my face is quite distinguishable.

I was going to have to think about this, and discuss it with my wife.

I told Daniel I'd call him tomorrow.

As it turned out, we ended up having a family meeting, the overwhelming consensus of which was that I shouldn't go; the biggest exponent of this conclusion was my daughter, Sam, who knew the criminal mind better than any of us.

She was adamant that this guy was a lunatic and purely out for revenge; she practically ordered me not to meet with him.

Under the current circumstances, she was right of course. I couldn't jeopardise the safety of my family just to save this thing from a lengthy trial, which of course I would be dragged into, but only after all the players had been caught, by which time Janssen wouldn't have any power, money or influence left to order a hit from inside a prison cell anyway.

It was final; I'd phone Daniel and tell him that the meeting was a no-go.

The despondency over the phone was palpable. Where Daniel was looking forward to getting this over and done with in a very short space of time it was now going to take months to gather all the evidence to destroy Janssen and his crew entirely. But he understood my reticence to put myself and my family in harm's way. Janssen of course was going to throw a hissy fit, but he was the Dutch police's problem now, and we could all walk away unscathed.

Two weeks later, I was on my stomach, peering with binoculars through a flap in a camouflaged tent, hidden on the edge of a wood, beside a field full of ewes in Dorset.

Paul had done the night shift. We had clandestinely exchanged places at 8 a.m., and now it was my turn until 4 p.m., when Olavo, who was still on the books until he sold his house and moved to Portugal, took over for the evening.

We had been tasked with sheep sitting, due to a large spate of wrangling in the county, where the farmers were losing money hand over hoof.

The owner of a large estate had employed my company in a surveillance capacity to try and capture evidence on the gang responsible. We were not to engage the culprits; just simply record their activities, identify the criminals if possible, and pass on the information to the police.

Day four and it was fruitless so far. The only thing I'd seen were aching bones, cramps, a lukewarm flask of tea and rain, oh and acres of sheep.

Around 10 a.m. my phone, on silent, buzzed in my pocket. It was Daniel.

"Hi, Dave. Are you free for a chat?"

"Yes, nothing much happening right now, just having a lie-down. How's it going with Janssen and Van Dijk?"

"Well, Ruby's her usual silent self. She's slipping into a deep depression and becoming unresponsive. It's a real struggle to get her to do anything. And as for Janssen, he went nuts after your refusal, smashed up his room and didn't speak to anyone for a week."

"Sounds about right. Is he talking now?"

"He's not only talking, he's given us everything we wanted, a full dossier on his entire operation, dating right back to its inception, up to the present day, in writing. Interpol has swooped and arrested all his henchmen apart from Miguel Garcia, who was apparently tipped off and has gone on the run, and dozens of lower-ranking hoods, including some ramp-men in several countries. It's been a total success, my friend. We have annihilated an entire drug cartel, all thanks to you, Dave. I'm surprised you haven't heard anything. The media are all over it."

"I'm out in the sticks, literally. Not much reception out here. And anyway, that's not all down to me, Dan. I had a whole team of players working on this, including you and your department, so I can hardly take the credit. It was an absolute joint effort, but that's marvellous. What a result! I feel like the weight of the world has been lifted from my shoulders. What made him do it?"

"Time. It's the logical choice. There's nothing more valuable than time. He knew we had him bang to rights, and he would die in a cell if he didn't spill the beans. To use a few clichés, it must have been a very bitter pill to swallow, but he was unequivocally caught between a rock and a hard place."

"So that's that, then. When is the hearing? I must let the Bakers know."

"It's set for a month's time. The courts are really busy, but that's not quite it…"

"What do you mean?"

"He still wants to meet you."

"Christ! I've really fucked with his psyche, haven't I?"

"He's obsessed with you."

The game had now changed considerably. Without Janssen's organisation behind him, he was powerless behind bars, and my family were at last safe from any callous retribution.

So I could see no harm in giving him five minutes of my time. Besides, I'd actually like to meet the piece of shit myself now. I had a few questions for him.

"I'll come," I said after a pause, "but only incognito. I'll keep the pseudonym of Mr Woods. It'll hold water for a while."

"Absolutely. I'll arrange it. When can you come?"

"I have to wrap up this case I'm working on in three days. I'll fly in after that."

***

Daniel met me at Schiphol. We drove into Amsterdam and went for a coffee on Prinsengracht, before going on to Police headquarters.

He updated me on events since we last spoke.

"He's expecting me today?"

"Yes, after lunch. He'll be cuffed to the table and there'll be the usual security guys in there with us also. You'll be quite safe."

"And he's buying it that my name is Mr Woods?"

"Who knows what he really thinks, but that's the story he is getting."

I bit my bottom lip whilst I thought about this possibly incendiary situation. He could go berserk and try to take a kick at me, or maybe he just wanted to measure me up for later reprisals. He definitely wasn't going to congratulate me.

This was a big deal, and many eyes were watching from behind the two-way mirror.

Crowding the small room were Rhonda, the Chief Commissioner, the Chief Prosecutor, Yara Tevling from Interpol, and a Dutch member of the European parliament, Filippus Hoek.

I followed Daniel into the interview room next door, anxious, slightly smug and determined to get this over with as soon as possible.

Janssen's icy blue eyes bore into me as I found my chair, calculating, assessing, until satisfied he had my mark, then a lopsided smirk Shar Pei'ed one half of his face.

They spoke in Dutch, but I understood enough to know that Daniel had just cautioned him, and then introduced me.

"You look familiar," he jabbed.

I made no reply. His aura was menacing.

"Huh! Gonna be like that is it, the strong, silent type?"

Janssen flicked his curly black hair out of his face with a single shake of his head.

"We're not here to play psychological games, Jaden," heeded Daniel. "Mr Woods has come all this way from the UK, against his own principles to appease your request and help accelerate this process. Now, unless you have any positive questions that will aid our agreement, then I will terminate this meeting immediately."

Janssen smiled, looking down at the table, shaking his head slowly from side to side.

"You're a very clever man, Mr Woods, if that's even your real name? Putting two and two together after all these years, where all others have failed. Bringing me down. What a great white hunter you are. Tell me, what did I ever do to you?"

This guy really was in denial.

"You insulted decency," I spat. "You broke the code of morality and you brought disgrace upon all humanity. You lower the tone, poison the water and stain the world with black oily sludge. But, most of all, you bring pain to all those around you and everything you touch, without conscience or remorse, or understanding. You're an odium, Janssen, a blemish on society and a menace to mankind, and for that, it was my duty to reel you in."

The criminal frowned. "You shouldn't take it personally, Mr Woods. I never do."

"How could you? You're not a person, Janssen. People have feelings and ardour. You're just an empty grabbing machine, biting the heads of those who get in your way. And look where that's got you, all that money you made, and you're contained in a brick box."

Janssen laughed and slow-clapped me.

"Bravo," he mocked, "great speech. Must have taken you all of what, ten minutes to write. Was it intended to hurt me?"

I sat back in my chair and folded my arms.

"You're forgetting one thing, Mr Woods. I have no heart, no feelings. You cannot hurt me."

This geezer had some front, but it was just that, a sham. He was hurting alright, but he was too vain to show it.

My eyes narrowed, sharpening a question. "Why Molly Baker?"

Janssen shrugged, as if my words unwarranted an answer. "She fitted the bill," he replied nonchalantly.

"And you didn't care that you were going to destroy an entire family by taking their child away?"

He threw his head back and spoke at the ceiling, "My God, you're so fucking melodramatic!"

His wild eyes came down to meet mine once more. "I couldn't give a shit," he slurred. "I needed a baby, and two came along at once, in their parents' arms, waiting at the back of the plane. They may as well have just said to me, 'Here you are Which one would you fucking like?' Idiots, should have taken better care of their children."

I really wanted to smack him now; I was erupting inside.

"You're one fucking deranged individual," I fumed.

"Tut… Flattery will get you nowhere," he sneered.

The vaguest smile entertained my lips as I exhaled a short snort through my nose. Rising to my feet I said, "I'm done here," and turned to walk out. Daniel got up too, but Janssen wasn't finished.

"How old are you, sixty-two, sixty-three?"

I turned back but didn't answer.

"When I get out of jail in twenty years, you'll probably still be around. I'll only be as old as you are now, fit and strong enough to come and visit you and your family for old time's sake. It'll be real nice… for me, anyway."

He was laughing again, the vile pig, thinking he still had a hand to play.

I didn't respond, just channelled all the vitriol I had for him in one focused death stare. His smile diminished, and I walked out of the door.

Daniel spoke as we marched along the corridor and up the stairs, "When he does eventually get let out of prison, he'll be tagged for five years while he lives in a halfway house and will have to report to a specified police station once a week. So I don't think you have any worries in your old age."

"It's not me I'm worried about, Dan. It's my kids."

We reconvened for a de-briefing up in the ops' room; there were so many people involved we needed the space.

The chief commissioner spoke first, "What do we have thus far on the valuation of Janssen's estate, Felix?"

Felix Andring, the Chief Prosecutor was a slight man in his late 50s, with a stoop, thinning brown hair and round lensed glasses. "So far, with the property, collections, artefacts, cars, land and bank accounts, we think it's in the region of one and a half billion Euro, but there's may still be more to come. He's bound to have hidden assets, foreign investments and off-shore accounts."

I was thinking to myself that I bet his palace and collections aren't worth half as much as they've been valued at separately.

And, they are going to be hard-pressed to find a buyer as the lot stands. Unless they sold the thing at a dramatically reduced price, they're gonna be left with a massive white elephant on their hands. Then I had an idea.

I voiced my opinion, followed by a possible solution. "What if the Council of Europe bought Janssen's estate with all its contents and outlying property for just one Euro…"

Incredulous looks stared at me from around the room.

"Hear me out. Then, open up the palace as a tourist attraction, charging say, ten Euros entrance fee and also collecting the rent from all the outlying cottages, etc. I reckon it'll earn its current market value in five years, and the COE will still have the whole thing as an asset, intact, and as Janssen wanted, therefore aiding to keep him subdued in prison."

Filippus Hoek, a man with expensive suits and elevated blood pressure, piped up. "This is a highly unusual course of action, Mr Skipper, one that will need very careful consideration by the Council, but I must say, quite brilliant." He bit his lower lip and nodded, deep in thought. "Yes, quite brilliant."

"Also, I've got a couple of requests," I added.

"Oh, yes?" Felix Andring stretched his neck out of his shirt like a tortoise craning from its shell.

"Sabrina Zegar, the nurse who Janssen had knee-capped a few years back, and her husband, Alex. They should be compensated from the proceeds of crime pot, for the suffering they had to endure, and their loss of earnings. After all, they did bravely come forward with a statement damming Janssen for his crimes."

"Yes, of course, it will be considered," said Hoek. "What sort of figure do you propose is fair?"

"A million euro."

"Oh, I see. Well, we'll take it on board."

Hoek's secretary was furiously taking down notes.

"And the other, err, request…" croaked Andring.

"The car from the collection that got Alex Zegar persecuted in the first place, the Ford Escort Mexico. He'd love a ride in that."

The whole room raised their eyebrows at me as if they expected some greater form of demand. They got one.

"I have a friend, Steve Murdoch. He's a champion rally driver, and he'd be more than happy to take Alex out for a spin around the estate in that car. It would make the two of them very happy indeed."

The commissioner's eyebrows met in the middle. "This is a very rare and cherished, vehicle I take it, Mr Skipper?"

"Oh yes."

"And it will be handled in an extremely professional manner?"

"You have my word on it, sir; Steve is one of the best drivers in England."

"Hmm, well then, if this all gets passed by the COE, maybe the Natuurmonumenten, our, err, National Trust, can make it a feature on the opening day of the exhibition."

"A very good idea, sir. Exactly the sort of thing I had in mind."

***

Almost eight months to the day, Steve Murdoch, suave, rugged and fully decked out in his white emblazoned race suit, posed for the media circus, with his arm over Alex

Zegar's shoulder, beside the 1978 Ford Escort MK II Mexico, Cosworth Rally special, a white car wrapped with a blue, yellow and red stripe around its body and two more over the bonnet and roof. She was a beauty, in pristine condition, glinting on the paved drive of Middelen Palace, in the April sunshine; a showpiece that had never before been tested.

I had brought the entire crew with me for the weekend, to enjoy the opening of the palace, along with my whole family and the Bakers'.

Simon and Marion Van Dijk didn't want to attend; they had no interest in viewing their ex-son-in-law's ill-gotten gains.

We had almost booked every room in a country hotel close to Groningen for my party, plus Daniel, Rhonda and Barbara, Julia and Fin Voss, Olga and Bernard Meijer, Colin and Sheila Whiteleaf, Jim Maxwell, Carlos and Ramona, and my mate Antonio and his wife, Caterina, all the people that had helped us along the way to put Janssen behind bars.

The open palace had attracted tens of thousands of people, not just to see the house and the collections but also to enjoy the rally race through the grounds, which the FIA (Federation Internationale de l'Automobile) had gladly added to its calendar.

I had neglected, though, to tell the Chief Commissioner and Filippus Hoek that my friend Steve Murdoch supplemented his rally driving career by also being a stunt driver on film sets, and that after he had taken Alex Zegar around the block in the Mexico, he was actually entered into the rally.

Another detail I'd purposefully excluded was that I'd paid Steve five grand to give the car a right hammering, bring it back rippled with dents and venting steam and oil. "Not a problem," he had assured me.

If I got into trouble with the National Trust and had to pay for repairs, it would be worth it. I knew how much it would piss off Janssen if we smashed up this particular unique toy. It would be an affront to his hubris and, excruciatingly rub things in, I had Paul install a couple onboard cameras to capture every crash, bang and wallop. Together with the TV camera footage here today, it'll make a wonderful montage to send to him in jail.

My plan worked beautifully. Steve even managed to roll the Escort over in a ditch, denting the roof as though it'd been sat on by an elephant. She limped home, hissing steam and trailing oil, much to the dismay of the judiciary that was here to witness the event.

Janssen caught the news report that evening on the TV in his room, but the clip only focused on the opening of his palace to the public, just briefly touching on the rally. So he never got to see the carnage inflicted on one of his prized possessions. Until, the next day, when he received an anonymous package containing a memory stick, which he swiftly took to the prison library and plugged into a computer.

Mary and Paul had spent most of the previous evening creating a comical little home movie about the demise of a once immaculate museum piece, in something akin to a demolition derby.

Janssen, however, didn't find it amusing at all. In fact, quite the opposite. He went mental, smashing up the library, beating up two other inmates, and putting three wardens in hospital.

When he was finally restrained, he was put in a padded cell for the night, and then spent a week in solitary confinement before being moved back to Holland and a much more conventional facility. During which time he was charged with GBH with intent and a judge extended his sentence by the maximum he could give for such an offence, a further 20 years in the slammer.

So, it was worth a paltry five grand for Steve to smash up the Mexico and a further seven grand to have it restored by Alex Zegar and his dad.

Finally, I got peace of mind; that article of filth would probably die in prison, or if not, he will be a very old man when he is released, and too frail to inflict any harm on anyone.

***

In August, team Skipper and our immediate families joined the Bakers on a four-day trip to the Van Dijks' palace. It was a splendid long weekend where we were made to feel quite at home, and this time got to see the entire house and its grounds.

I was particularly impressed with Simon's collection of military uniforms, weapons and suits of armour, some of them dating back to 1000 BC.

There were hundreds of mannequins behind glass, in specially converted long halls in the west wing, and apparently many more in storage or in the midst of repair.

"It's a lifelong passion of mine, Dave. I got the bug after my father and uncle gave me their old army uniforms. They hadn't seen any action, of course. Holland surrendered after just five days at war with Germany."

"Oh, is that all?"

"Yes, we are not very proud of the fact. We wanted to remain neutral, you see, but Hitler wasn't having any of that, He took Belgium and Luxemburg in the same swoop."

"Greedy bastard."

"Yes, indeed."

"I started buying them after that, at junk shops, second-hand clothing stores, and auction houses, anywhere I could. Away from work, it became quite an obsession."

"A man's got to have a hobby."

"Quite."

"I suppose they came in all manner of disrepair?"

"Absolutely. Marion and I used to patch a few pieces up, then Ruby used to help when she got a little older…"

Simon trailed off, lapsing into some fond nostalgia of his daughter in better times. Obviously, the pain of losing her was still raw. I broke his daydream somewhat insensitively. "Ah, so that's where Ruby inherited her sewing skills?"

"What? Ah yes, the Hi-Vis jackets. Yes, she was quite a seamstress by the end of it. There's a team of experts now who take care of all that of course."

"Of course," I said, wishing I had been more empathetic.

Throughout our stay, it was a joy to see the two families had bonded so well. The girls were almost inseparable, and so alike in their looks and mannerisms, it was uncanny. This was people-watching under a very unique circumstance, and I was so humbled to have helped bring this together.

Paul, probing a mystery as always, had been busy delving into both Jill's and Marion's ancestry. And, as unbelievable as it seems, they shared a common distant past. Both of their great, great-grandmothers shared the same surname and came from Comino, a tiny island north of Malta, so they were undoubtedly related, hence the likeness of Molly to Marion's great grandmother in the photo she keeps so dear.

Coincidence or fate, who can tell?

We made a pact to go to Malta the following year and a pilgrimage to Comino. The place looks entrancing.

Sophie caught me in a moment of quiet contemplation, out on the lawn, relaxed into a deeply-cushioned lawn chair, under the cool of a sprawling parasol, whilst many of the others were attempting croquet.

"Dave?"

I looked up, startled. "Mmm?"

"I feel like I've never really got to thank you properly for finding my sister. This past year has all been a bit of a blur, haven't really had the opportunity."

"It's been a long road, Sophie. Or are you Molly? It's hard to tell you two apart."

She laughed. "I'm most definitely Sophie." Her teeth were the most perfect I'd ever seen on a human being.

"Well, this is me formally saying from my entire family, thank you, Dave Skipper. You have given us our life back, and we are forever in your debt."

She leaned in, hugged me and gave me a kiss on the cheek. She smelled of Parma violets.

"In that case," I said, "could you pour me another cup of tea, my dear? I'm too immobilized to function."

Sophie smiled again and tinkered with the bone china.

Epilogue

Christmas day fell on a Monday this year, so, what with all the bank holidays involved and New-Years-Eve the following week, we decided to shut up shop at lunchtime on Friday 22nd for two weeks. It would give everyone a nice long rest.

I was alone, loitering in the office, twiddling my thumbs, waiting for our last client of the year, a certain Mr Michael Underwood.

There was nothing in the diary to suggest the nature of Mr Underwood's needs, just a time, 2 p.m. and a note from Mary saying that the client had paid for a two-hour session in advance. Which was a little unusual, because the first half-hour for all new customers is always free, just in case they are wasting their time hiring a private eye for something minor they can do themselves without too much trouble.

I'd always stop them mid-tracks within that half-an-hour if I thought their quest was too menial for a professional detective agency to take on. I'm not without scruples.

Around 1:30 p.m. our landline rattled into life.

I fully expected it to be Elizabeth; she was the only person who knew I was still here. But instead, I was surprised to find Antonio on the other end.

"Dave, hi. Are you expecting a client called Underwood around two o'clock?"

"Yes, why? How did you know?"

"I was expecting the same man, at the same time, but he has just called me and asked if I could pick you up and bring you to his house so we can all meet together."

"Really? That's a bit strange, isn't it?"

"Stranger still, he has requested that I take Jackie's car instead of my own."

"Hmm, interesting. Got issues, has he?"

"So it seems. I'm a bit wary. I don't know about you? This is not the way I usually conduct business."

"Well I'm used to the old cloak and dagger mate, but to have your solicitor arrive incognito as well is a bit unconventional. Is he insisting on false beards, sunglasses?"

Antonio laughed down the line. "No, I just think it's a very private matter. He seems quite compos mentis over the phone, and he's paid for the full two hours consultation up front."

"Same as, mate. Where does he live?"

"In Abbotts Lodge. It'll take us about thirty minutes to drive there."

"Okay, mate. I'll walk down. He's piqued my interest."

It was a monochrome day. The air was cold and still, and very little was moving in our little village High Street, apart from Sid the bookie, weaselling his way in my direction.

"Sid," I upward nodded as he approached.

"It's not gonna snow, Skipper." He grinned, exposing his missing rear teeth and hissing a wheezy laugh.

I guffawed. "Stranger things have happened at sea, Sid."

But he was probably right. I couldn't possibly hope to clean him out two years on the trot.

Jackie had been Antonio's secretary since time began; as soon as I entered the building, she dangled her key ring over the reception counter; it was loosely hanging from an outstretched finger of her upturned hand.

"Why you taking my car?" She looked like she really didn't want us to use it.

"Client's request. I know, it's an odd one."

"Well, you'll have to excuse the mess. The kids have absolutely zero respect for my things; it may as well be a dustbin."

I smiled, having less than fond memories of picking up the detritus discarded by my own little darlings.

"I won't think anything less of you, my dear; a dirty car is a dirty mind."

Jackie signalled be off with you with a forward swish of her hand.

Antonio bounded into reception like he had springs on his feet and his usual gleeful demeanour.

"Ready to go meet this mystery man then, David?"

"Raring to go; I've told Jackie that you'll clean her car for her when we get back."

His smile faded. "What?"

And to Jackie, I said, "Remember, it's double time this afternoon."

"What?" Antonio said again.

I chuckled as we left the building.

She wasn't kidding about the car; we would be required to wipe our feet on the way out.

I removed a sticky sweet from the passenger seat and covered the residue with a discarded McDonald's napkin. I didn't want that on my suit trousers. Then I cleared all the crap from the foot well, dumping it on the back seat, as we got on our way.

"Any ideas who this bloke is, or what he wants with the pair of us?"

"Not a clue, Dave. Thought he might be an old client who has previously used both our services, but nothing springs to mind."

We had a clear run to Abbotts Lodge. I knew the place from an adultery case I'd gathered evidence for some years ago. It hadn't changed a bit.

The cul-de-sac we pulled into consisted of around thirty ex-council properties in various conditions. Some had undergone extension, giving them porches, loft conversions, etc. Mr Underwood's property was in the rear, left-hand corner, a detached bungalow in good order, with a neat mature garden, sporting some hanging baskets containing winter-flowering plants and several tubs displaying the same.

The recently laid resin drive supported just one car, a very clean 16-year-old red Ford Fiesta. It appeared that we were dealing with a man who kept things very well maintained.

Antonio rang the bell, and it was soon answered by a fella in his late 60s, early 70s, wearing a heavy, hand-knitted, Native American cardigan with a very unique motif.

I knew this because Elizabeth bought one many years ago on a trip we took to the western states, but the name of the tribe who made them eluded me at that moment. All I could think of was how expensive it had been, £600 back in the day.

He welcomed us. "Mr Serrano, Mr Skipper, please, do come in."

I nodded silently and followed Antonio, who was being led into the living room.

Unable to switch off my detective instincts, I covertly scanned the immaculate parlour.

An oval-shaped silver platter sat on a doily on a walnut sideboard; it held three bottles of single malt whiskey, each worth a least a hundred quid, a bottle of brandy, a bottle of sherry and a bottle of Bailey's Irish cream.

338

On the dining table, two more expensive single malts were poking their necks out of a pair of gift bags.

A side table harboured a couple of the latest iPhones and a brand new Alexa Echo, which aren't cheap.

Something was not right here, an unbalance. Money was being splashed out frivolously on items that didn't suit their surroundings.

A lady of similar age to Mr Underwood, then walked into the living room carrying another silver tray, loaded with a designer porcelain coffee set, cream and sugar cubes and all.

"Hello." She smiled. "I've made coffee, but if you like, I can just pop back and make you some tea."

She shuffled in and placed the tray on the dining table.

"Coffee will be fine, thank you, um, Mrs Underwood?"

She eyed her husband. "Yes, that's right."

Mrs Underwood hadn't dressed down for the occasion. She had on a long, bright, floral-patterned dress of many hues, and was laden with an excessive amount of beaded necklaces, and gold and silver wrist bangles, which possibly weighed more than she did.

The Hippie look seemed juxtaposed to the décor of the house.

I was still trying to fathom what was happening here when Mr Underwood said, "This is Sally."

Who said, "How do you like your coffee?"

"Black, no sugar," I replied.

Antonio, whose bottom lip had dropped and who was staring at the woman like he was mesmerised, spoke as if he was running out of battery power, "Black, one sugar…" Finding more juice, he said, "You're Joe and Sally Forster!"

For a few seconds, the world stopped for all four of us.

Joe kick-started it spinning again. "Apologies, Mr Serrano. I'm embarrassed to have deceived you, but if I had given my real name over the phone, I don't think that you would have taken on the case."

It was Antonio's turn to look ashamed. "Well, I must admit that I have carried with me a great deal of guilt over not offering you pro bono work a few years ago. I'm convinced it would have saved Carol's and Beverley's lives."

"You have nothing to feel guilty about, Mr Serrano," said Joe. "You are a professional person and you charge your clients accordingly. It was the social system that let my daughter and granddaughter down. They are the guilty ones."

Sally interrupted, "Would anybody like anything stronger than coffee?"

Both Antonio and I declined.

"Maybe before you go," she suggested.

Joe turned to me and asked if I knew anything about their case.

I was just about to answer when Antonio jumped in.

"Dave and I have worked together for many years, on many cases; we have a confidentiality agreement which allows us to discuss case information that may assist with other, unrelated, inquiries. And, I have to admit, we did have a conversation about your case, which proved to be extremely helpful in another regard."

"That's quite alright," said Joe. "We have no issues with that. In fact, it might speed up things with our request."

I shifted in my seat, wondering what was coming.

He continued, "We'd like to employ both of your services in tackling a heinous crime…"

He then went to a drawer in the sideboard and extracted two folders and four envelopes. Handing us a folder each, he said, "You'll find copies of two letters inside. One from me to Children's Social Services, asking if we could have

340

some news or possible contact with our great-grandchildren; the other, their reply."

We both took time to read the letters there and then. I don't think I've ever seen a correspondence so blunt and cruel as the reply from social services; it read simply thus:

To Mr and Mrs Forster.

Both child A and child B have been legally adopted, and no further contact, either now or in the future, will be considered for their natural family.

The letter wasn't scribed or signed by any individual, just printed on social services letter-headed paper.

I raised my eyes toward Joe and Sally and felt their pain.

Also inside the folder was an A4 sheet containing a list of eleven male names, mostly foreign, all directors of Roebuck Children's Fostering and Adoption Agency.

The paper was headed with their address and a logo, an embossed motif of a Roebuck deer in full flight.

When we had finished reading, Joe elaborated on his intentions. "I have two jobs that I'd like both of you to undertake. One is to locate our two great-grandchildren and make sure they are safe and being well looked-after. The other is to investigate all the directors on that list, do background checks, and find out everything that you can on that agency. There's something dodgy going on there."

Antonio reacted first. "I'll do it, pro bono, of course."

Sally smiled at me when her husband said, "That won't be necessary."

I told the Forster's that we would spend a couple of weeks on it after Christmas, and see what we could establish.

They thanked us, and then Joe handed us each an unsealed vellum envelope with our names and the word

341

'expenses' on the front. Inside mine was a Coutts Bank cheque for the sum of one hundred thousand pounds. Antonio had the same.

"I can't possibly accept this," I said, handing the envelope back.

"No, no," he said, halting me with an outstretched palm. "It's what I expect to pay."

"But…"

Joe interrupted me, "Do either of you do the lottery?"

We both shook our heads, wondering where this was leading.

"Sally and I have been doing the EuroMillions religiously since it began. Haven't missed a draw, even when the bloody price went up to two quid a ticket. Costs a fortune every week. We do the same numbers each time, never stray, the kid's birthdays plus our house number, 34."

"Right," I empathized.

He carried on, "Three weeks ago, the biggest payout ever in the history of the EuroMillions, £197,757,302.20, was won by one lucky winning ticket here in the UK… ours!"

Joe's words hit me like a hex. I was stupefied, unable to move or process the information. The Forsters, who had suffered so much recent grief and tragedy, lottery jackpot winners? It was surreal.

"I don't understand," I said at length. "You've won nearly two hundred million pounds?"

"Yes."

"Then, why haven't you moved house, or bought a new car?"

"We don't know what to do with the money," admitted Sally. "I mean, we'd like to give away a load of it to our family, but we haven't told anybody yet, and we love our little house. We've got some great neighbours. Besides, we haven't a clue where we'd like to move to…" She paused, open-mouthed. "Would you like that drink now?"

"Um…" I stalled.

"Yes, please," replied Antonio. "I'll have a small sherry if that's okay."

"Y' Yeah, could I have a whiskey, please?" I stammered.

Joe smiled. "Why not, it's five o'clock somewhere in the world."

We sat around the dining table, discussing the Forster's intentions. I was still in shock mode. Jackpot lottery winners were never people you actually knew, just jubilant strangers on the TV holding a massive cheque.

"We haven't gone public yet, and may never do," explained Joe. "We don't want those bastards who stole our children to get wind of it; it will put them on guard."

I agreed. "Very wise."

Sally handed me a brand new, cut-crystal tumbler laced with a splash of one of the finest malts that money can buy. Joe had the same, Antonio and Sally their sherry, and together we clinked glasses as she made a toast, "To loved ones, on this side and the next."

It was a poignant moment.

Joe said that all he and Sally wanted was to see their great-grandchildren in this life, and that was why they put their trust in the both of us. He then handed us each the second envelope, saying, "Whatever the outcome, I want you both to have this."

Inside was another Coutts cheque to the sum of one million pounds. I almost asked for a second whisky.

"Eso es un montón de trabajo," Said Antonio. None of us understood.

I asked him to translate, and he said, "It looks like we have a job to do."

I got the feeling he had said something different.

On the drive outside their house, we received a handshake from Joe and a kiss on the cheek from Sally. "Do the best you can," were Joe's parting words.

The look of longing and hope said all the rest.

Antonio and I stayed silent for a good few minutes as we drove home, both of us absorbed, lost in a jungle of thoughts. Then Antonio asked if I had any sort of plan.

I blew through my lips. "Well, I've got the whole family over for the weekend, but I'll try and snatch a moment alone with Sam, and get her advice."

Antonio nodded.

"I won't mention it to Elizabeth just yet, not until all the kids have left on Christmas Eve."

My Spanish friend laughed and said, "As soon as Caterina finds out about the million-pound cheque, she'll be straight online and looking at villas on the Costa del Sol. She's been itching to get back to Spain for years now."

"We gotta earn it first, my friend."

"Hmm, too true."

"The Forsters seem like computer literate people, don't they?"

"I would say so, yes."

"Then how come they haven't bothered to find anything about the Roebuck agency yet? If I were them, I would have made at least a start."

"Hmm, that's not my field, my friend. That's, I suppose, why they have employed you."

It was my turn to say "Hmm."

Antonio dropped me off at home; my Range could stay at work until after the weekend. I invited him in, but he needed to get Jackie's car back. She had some last-minute shopping to do.

We wished each other a Merry Christmas, and I said I would phone him in a few days; we both needed some time to process today's events.

The weekend was splendid, two days with a house full of kids, me included. We'd been extravagant this year with the gifts, paying for all four of our offspring, their partners and children to go to Dubai for ten days in the spring. The Wild Wadi water parks look incredible.

To Jamie, my youngest, who is getting married next year, we gave a cheque of £50,000, so that he and his fiancé could get a start on the property ladder. We'd done the same for all of our children, only now, I could definitely afford it.

As always, the most exciting part of the Christmas present-giving ceremony was the big reveal of mum and dad's gift from the kids, and as usual they didn't disappoint. The whole tribe waited with excitement, for us to open the gold sealed envelopes containing tickets for a seven night, all inclusive, luxury cruise, through the Norwegian Fjords. Something we'd always talked about doing, but never got around to booking. It was a superb gift.

I'd had a hard time trying to corner Sam. There was always someone vying for attention and interrupting my efforts, but finally, I resorted to cutting in on a conversation she was having with her sister, Kathy.

"Samantha." She knew she was in trouble when I used her full name.

"Father?"

"Can I have a word please, dear?"

"Sounds serious."

"It may well be." I nodded towards my study.

"Hold that thought, I'll be back in a mo'," she said to Kathy and followed me down the hall.

I filled her in on Friday's events, showing her the letters and the cheques. Her eyes nearly bulged out of her head when she saw the million-pound disbursement.

She remembered the Forster family tragedy; I had told her two years ago, and found it incredible that they should now have this immense turnaround in fortune. The irony of it was stupefying.

She stared at the list of directors for some time.

"Why do I know that name?" she said.

"Which name? Who?"

"Gary Herbert-Cracking, an unusual name, I know, but it's come up somewhere before. I'll make some discreet inquiries in the New Year; see if there are any red flags."

I loved my daughter; she was more resourceful and definitely more suspicious than me.

"The last time you called me Samantha, Dad, you went on to solve one of the biggest mysteries the policing world has ever known, let alone bringing down the largest drug cartel in Europe. Is this going to be another protracted case like that?"

"Don't know, Sam, but it's unfairly occupying my mind."

"Well, let's not let it spoil Christmas eh? Come on, we'd better get back to the party."

The following day, after the traditional hearty breakfast at the Oak and coffee back at ours, we bade our children farewell, and then settled down to watch an afternoon film.

I was fully intending on telling Elizabeth about the Forsters after the movie, but I fell asleep and didn't wake until my wife shook me at 11 p.m. to ask me if I wanted a hot drink before bed.

Drowsily, I said I didn't, but I did have something rather important to tell her.

Pouring myself a small whisky, I began to roll out what had occurred on Friday.

She listened in that unique Elizabeth way, then she patted the sofa next to her, inviting me to sit down. As soon as I did, Chase jumped up between us and settled in, a warm hairy comfort cushion to indulge in.

We talked about what a wonderful weekend it had been, and then about the year ahead and how to tackle it. My head told me it wasn't fair on Elizabeth to take on another big case which might involve me being away for weeks on end again, but as always, my wife had the solution.

"Why don't I join you on this one?"

"Eh?"

"Why don't I join the team? That way we won't spend so much time apart."

"And who's gonna look after Chase?"

"He can come too; he has a great nose for unearthing buried things."

I had never worked with my wife before. It was uncharted territory. It could prove to be a disaster, but I was happy to give it a try.

As she went off to make her drink, I talked with Chase. He had no idea what I was saying, but he appreciated the attention.

When Elizabeth returned, she placed her Ovaltine on the coffee table and said, "You'll not going to believe this. Come with me and bring your drink with you."

I followed my wife dutifully out to the conservatory, where she flicked on the exterior lights.

Huge, inch-sized flakes of snow were falling silently to the ground, winter's parachutes, blanketing the garden with a pristine icy veil. Their descent was mesmerizing.

I kissed my wife on the cheek and wished her a Merry Christmas; she returned the gesture and then asked me what I was smiling at.

"I dunno, I guess it's because we are so lucky."

She squeezed my hand and said, "Yeah, I bet you'd like to be a fly on a certain bookmaker's wall."

If you enjoyed reading this book, would you be so kind as to write a short review and post it on either Amazon or Goodreads, or both if you are feeling frivolous. Reviews go a long way to provide some substance to the book's credibility. Thank you in advance,

Anthony and Doug

About the Authors

Anthony and Doug have been writing together since 2002. To date they have published three novels, the two previous, being, *The English Sombrero (Nothing to do but run)* and *The English Sombrero (The little white ball)*. Both books are comedies and 1 & 2 of a proposed series of 4.

They are currently working on three new titles, to be released in due course.

Anthony has released a novel of his own, *Tales of Tucson* volume 1, a sex & drugs & rock & roll extravaganza set in 80s America, and Doug has published a novel in his right called *What goes around comes around*, a story of kidnap and revenge.

Links

https://mybook.to/EnglishSombrero1

https://mybook.to/EnglishSombrero2

https://mybook.to/TalesOfTucson1

https://mybook.to/Whatgoesaround

You can contact Anthony here:

https://www.facebook.com/anthonyrandallauthor

Printed in Great Britain
by Amazon

20376070R00202